SHI

SOULS

Book 1 Ena

H.L Heidemann

SHIFTED SOULS BOOK 1 - ENA
Copyright © 2021 H.L Heidemann

First Edition

Cover design: Shower of Schmidt
Formatting: Irish Ink Publishing

Do you ever feel like you have a soundtrack to your life? That you'll go along with a song in your head for months then realise that it was actually how you were living all along? I'd never noticed.

Until I died.

Yes, this time last year, I died. When I did, many things changed. I found myself alone but not alone with a head full of lyrics that had never made more sense in my life than they did at that moment.

You might think my life changed the day I was meant to stay dead, but it wasn't then that it changed. It changed much earlier than that, and the events that led to my death were... unusual.

You might wonder, if I was dead, how did I know? Well, that's something you only find out after your physical body has gone, and it's just you, your soul, as you are in space, wherever that is. It's then that the feelings you felt when you heard those songs make you remember who you were.

Before I was me, as I am now, I had another life. A simpler life. I can share my story with you. Well, what I can remember of it.

I was once a normal single twenty-something with my whole life ahead of me. Looking back, I think how naïve I was. It was so very far from normal. It makes me laugh how unsure I was, how unsettled. Now, I'm far from settled, but I have learned to love myself as I truly am, and I know nothing defines you more than your experiences and how you react to them. I'll begin somewhere simple, somewhere my mind flits to when I think of the past. Somewhere when all I had to think about was my daughter and myself.

CHAPTER 1

Ena

Apple Shampoo by Blink 182 was on my playlist in the car as we drove back towards town. My best friend, Maisy, had dragged me out of the house for some girl bonding because, apparently, I didn't *do* anything or see anyone anymore. That suited me fine. I didn't need anyone but myself and Bea, and recently my mum, but that was a new development, and I was still getting used to living with her again.

Our shopping trip was coming to an end. My mum was at home looking after my eight-month-old baby, so I had to get back in time to feed her. Bea was the main reason for me moving back home from university, and the reason I was now happily skint and the proud owner of two huge bags of baby clothes. I loved dressing Bea. Myself, not so much, but Maisy had made sure I bought more than the lounge pants I had gone out for.

As I sang away, she playfully chided me for my toned figure. I pretended to be too engrossed in the music, but she knew I was really listening; my grin gave it away. True, it had only been eight short months since having my daughter, but I did spend a lot of time at the gym. In fact, it was probably the only place I ever went that wasn't home or the library where Maisy worked. I'd never really been comfortable anywhere else, which I suppose came from being moved around a lot as a child. My mum and I didn't settle anywhere for long, and just when I thought it was okay to feel comfortable, we upped and moved again. I soon learnt not to get attached to people or places.

My mum and I never had the traditional mother/daughter relationship, the kind where you're like best friends and share everything. She kept secrets and spent a lot of her time on her own. It was only obvious I would grow up to do the same, but I didn't want to do that with Bea. My heart ached for the kind of relationship Maisy had with her mum; a connection I had always been deeply jealous of. I refused to let Bea and I end up indifferent to each other.

As I drove and tapped my finger on the steering wheel to the lyrics, Maisy chatted on about my clothing choices. Apparently, without her guidance, I'd be so lost. I just laughed. There was something comfortable about listening to Maisy explain away my anxieties. I didn't even have to say them out loud. Somehow, she just seemed to say the right things at the time I needed to hear them. Always something simple, a positive outlook on everything I struggled to see the good in.

After dropping her at her place, I felt the familiar yet unwelcome hollow feeling I always did. I expected it but resented it at the same time. When I was growing up, there were times when I barely saw Maisy. A friend of Mum's would bring her to visit occasionally, but every visit was loaded with knowing she wasn't with me to stay. The hollow feeling had stayed with me ever since, so that even now, watching her grab her shopping from the boot and disappear into her front door, I felt it.

"Library tomorrow, and bring my baby," she called, sticking the keyring from her keys into her mouth so she could pull off her shoes. I nodded. "Pinky swear," she mumbled.

"Pinky swear," I called back with a grin.

I arrived home shortly after, and it had begun to rain. I parked on the drive and Mum opened the door for me. I launched myself into the house where Mum handed me a crying and snotty baby before I had time to clear the doormat. Bea, who was still flipping gorgeous despite the snot and tears, held me close and yawned the second she was in my arms. I dropped my car keys into my shoe that

I had just flicked off, then walked through the hall and kicked the door closed behind me. Mum disappeared into the kitchen as I sank onto the sofa to feed my daughter to sleep. I wiped her eyes and hummed softly as she drifted off. Mum passed through the lounge to grab my bags from the car, returning with wet hair and a dripping face but not saying a word about it. I thanked her and carefully lay Bea down in the Moses basket beside the sofa.

I showed everything to Mum over a cup of green tea, and although she loved Bea's clothes, as expected, she wasn't overly keen on mine. She frowned as she held up a pair of denim shorts and fishnet tights. Maisy and I had very different taste in clothes. She had thrown those onto the counter as I paid. Instead of making a scene, I rolled my eyes and paid for them too. Things like that would explain my lack of money. I didn't go out often, but when I did, I always went over budget.

I'm not going to lie, I was antisocial. I had always struggled with people. Mum and I were far from having a perfect relationship, especially as I had moved out and blamed her for pretty much everything that had gone wrong in my life only a few years back. I had always felt that, even though we were together, we were miles apart, the happy memories overshadowed by the lack of connection. Things were peaceful enough, but sometimes a little boring, and I was guilty as hell admitting that. It was complicated. To me, anyway.

I had gone to bed that night, exhausted, as soon as Bea had fallen asleep. My emotions had drained me, and I felt the only escape was to be unconscious. I carried Bea up to my room and put her in her Moses basket, knowing she might not sleep for long, then crawled into bed. It took a long time to drop off despite my tiredness, but when I did, I had my first surreal dream in a long time.

When I was a child, I was always dreaming. Sometimes in the middle of the day, and sometimes so vivid I could have sworn I was really there, or that the event had actually happened. I told my mum about it on a couple of occasions, but it was quickly brushed under the carpet, so I then kept all of my dreams to myself. Over time, I had forgotten all about it. It was as if they just stopped one day.

This time, I was small. Much smaller than in real life. From my eye-level in the dream, I must have just been about a foot off the ground, and it was very dark. I could only see a little light coming from a doorway ahead of me. My heart was pounding and my throat dry as I walked towards the door, the smell of wet dog hitting me full force. Outside was dark too. I couldn't see anything but a large grassy area, the dew reflecting the light from the moon. I put my head through the doorway a fraction and looked around. Apart from a deep, black fog, I saw nothing except the lawn ahead of me. Fear pulled me back into the safety of the place I had appeared from, but curiosity pushed me out and forwards. As I walked across the lawn, I realised I was barefoot, the coldness seeping in through my toes and causing them to tingle. It was at that point I became aware that I couldn't actually see my toes, yet I could feel them and my hands. It was as if I was crawling on all fours across the lawn, the pressure from doing so causing the mud to push up through my fingers. I looked down again in disgust but couldn't see my hands either. Panic swirled through my body and my heart began to pound. I looked up to the sky but couldn't see anything through the fog. Suddenly, I was running, the air rushing past my ears as I ran full pelt. I couldn't see where I was going nor where I had been; I kept my head down. A dark feeling pulsed through me, willing me forward, even though I had no idea what I was running from.

I woke covered in sweat, my hands stinging as if I had been slapping them against a brick wall. Confused, I pulled my phone towards me to check the time. Three a.m. As my heart slowed, I tried to time my breathing with Bea's soft snores and fell back to sleep.

CHAPTER 2

Ena

The following morning, I was up and dressed early with Bea. I wandered down to the lounge, made my breakfast, and breastfed Bea whilst I ate it in front of the TV. I knew Mum preferred me to eat at the table. She didn't say anything, although I could feel her watching me from across the room.

I wore my new skinny jeans, which Maisy had picked out, just to show her I did listen to her fashion advice sometimes. I matched it with a bright orange vest top and a black denim jacket. Bea wore a gorgeous little blue dress with tights that had rainbows on them.

Once Bea's belly was full, I covered her with a muslin cloth as I sat her up, putting my breakfast plate on the sofa seat beside me. Mum practically launched herself across the room to grab it and return it to the kitchen.

She clattered around in the kitchen as I prepared to leave, with Classical radio humming in the background. Vivaldi, I think. I pulled on my favourite black Converse pumps and tucked Bea into her pushchair. It was one of those that could be a pram lying flat or a pushchair sitting up. It was fab if she fell asleep as I could lie her flat again. She was so nosy though and loved shouting and squealing to anyone she saw, so sitting upright was where she wanted to be. She cooed and chatted away to me and kicked as I tried to tuck her feet into a blanket until I gave in and left her without. I tucked her changing bag in the space under the chair and we left the house for the library.

My house was only about a fifteen-minute walk from the library, so we made the most of the journey, stopping to look at the leaves in the hedges, birds, and the fire station. We must have greeted three or four people on the way, all older ladies, all friends of Mum's. I often wondered how she had so many friends. She never seemed to go anywhere other than the shops and to work. Mum worked as a teacher in the local school, so it was possible that many of them knew her from there, although she never mentioned any of them to me in conversation.

The singing session was at ten, so we were a little early, but that gave us time to have cuddles with Bea's favourite person who wasn't Mum or me: Maisy.

There weren't many at the session; only six children, including three who were much older at about three or four years old. They sang the nursery rhymes and joined in with the animal sounds in *Old McDonald*, and the story. Bea laughed at all the sounds and adored the songs. I tried to teach her how to clap, but she wasn't having it. Even though it was a nice group, I wasn't really friends with any of the mums there. After the session was over, they all left to go to coffee shops or home for play dates, and I stayed there with Bea. The only other person in the library by lunchtime was an older man on the corner sofa. Coincidentally, it was another friend of Mum's.

When we moved away, he was the only one of her friends who came to visit. Sometimes he'd bring Maisy with him as he was also friends with her parents, and sometimes he brought his wife. Mum and Mr E had been really close and thought of each other as family. From what I had been told, they spent a lot of time together before I was born, but something happened which meant they now kept their distance from each other. He was a strange man; I couldn't quite figure him out. I couldn't put my finger on what it was, but it wasn't sinister. He was friendly enough, just a bit odd. He had aged a lot since the last time I saw him. I frowned, trying not to stare. Maisy caught my eye, and I shrugged.

We sat beside the customer service desk with a

coffee and a packet of Custard Creams. I gave Bea half a baby biscuit to gum while we thumbed through magazines and chatted about Maisy's latest celebrity crushes. She knew all the gossip. I, on the other hand, was completely useless with men, but I did enjoy hearing all about Maisy's latest theories and fantasies. Well, some of the fantasies. Some she really should have kept to herself.

"I have no idea who that one is!" I said when she told me her new number one on her top ten list.

She laughed at me. "Ooh, he's gorgeous! You'll love him! I'll find us a film with him in it for tonight. Your mum okay with having Bea for a bit?" she asked, smiling at Bea. "If not, I'm sure we can find a nice family film for our little princess."

Bea held out her arms to be picked up, and Maisy responded by scooping her up and dancing around the library with her. She must have gone up and down every aisle before returning to me with not just a baby, but an armful of books.

Maisy read each one to Bea and did all the voices of the characters. Bea laughed and cooed. Guilt played on my mind thinking of Maisy doing the reading and not me. Perhaps even a bit jealous, but that was how it was supposed to be with awesome aunts. Maisy wasn't my sister, but she sure felt like one, and Bea loved her like an aunt.

I flicked through the magazine I had been given,

pausing on a recipe page about avocados. I tore out the page and put it into my jacket pocket. Once my coffee was finished, we checked out the books Maisy had collected around the library and headed home via the corner shop. That was as exciting as my life got. I was a walking meme for someone who got excited over dishcloths and vacuum cleaners.

Bea had fallen asleep on the walk home, so I enjoyed half an hour of yoga, followed by my avocado and eggs, which I shared with Mum. She was working on something on the computer, so I decided to unpack the books from the pushchair. There were several lift the flap board books for baby, a couple of awful romance stories Maisy had picked out for me, no doubt with explicitly described sex scenes. Flushing red, I shoved those back into my bag, hoping Mum hadn't seen them. The other two books were quite random. A guide to simple spells, and a dictionary of witchcraft.

Mum looked up from her computer as I snorted out loud. "What?" she asked, with both eyebrows raised.

"Just Maise," I said, smiling. "She's given me these." I held the books up.

Mum tutted and shook her head.

They looked quite interesting, but I dropped them onto the floor down the side of the sofa and curled up to play a game on my phone.

Later, noticing the clock on my phone screen, I

frowned. I had been playing the game for over half an hour. Throwing my phone onto the side of the coffee table, I yawned. I didn't know how I was tired because I hadn't really been anywhere or done anything.

I looked up at Mum every now and then. I needed to find a job soon. Even though she said she could cope fine, I didn't think this would work long term. The thought of going back to uni didn't make sense, although I knew some people were great at making it work. I was too anxious and stressy though. A job I could do. I thought guiltily about the clothes I had bought. Bea did need some new bits, but I could have done without. I made a mental note to ask Maisy if she'd heard anything about anyone needing workers and headed upstairs to change. The skinny jeans were digging into my sides.

That evening, as I arrived at Maisy's, I could smell the incense before she answered the door. This must have something to do with the books she had given me. I rolled my eyes as she answered.

"Quick, the pizza is getting cold," she said, pulling me in and slamming the door behind me. She had ordered a large pepperoni and potato wedges. I also spied a box of cookie dough on the coffee table. She really was the best at knowing how to cheer me up. Not that I was upset, but recently, I knew she'd got the vibe of self-doubt that seemed to be leaking from me on a daily basis. She could always see right through my attempts to be cheerful, or when I forced myself to be social. It comes with the territory of being my best friend. Plus, she was excellent at reading people's moods. A skill I often wished I had.

"Awesome," I said, stuffing a slice into my mouth and sitting cross-legged on her rug.

She noticed I had changed into my new lounge pants and threw a cushion at me. "Slob," she joked, so I threw it back at her, giggling. She poured us both a huge measure of wine, downing half of hers before she had even passed me mine.

"So, what the heck was with those books you gave me today?" I asked between bites.

She shrugged. "Mr Ealing was telling me all about them. He said he read them both and thought I might want a new hobby." She leaned over to grab more pizza. We had already eaten more than half of it in the first five minutes.

"Mr Ealing?" I asked, thinking about the old man from the library. "Curious."

"I know, isn't it just! We usually chat about whatever we're reading at the moment. For me, it's usually rom-com type books. He usually just reads the paper, or looks through the newspaper archives. Pretty boring really." She paused.

"So... he suddenly got interesting, just like that?" I quizzed, pouring a blob of ketchup onto a side plate, ready for some wedges. I couldn't remember a time when Mr Ealing did or said anything remotely interesting. Usually, he spoke with Mum in hushed tones. I had grown to ignore it.

"Yeah. It was so weird. We were sitting in silence having coffee, and he asked me if I had ever come across any good books on witchcraft. I thought about it and found him a few on the shelves, and a couple of days later, he asked me to read them. I had a look. Then he asked me if I had read them, and when I said yes, he said to pass them on to you." Maisy shrugged, and I raised an eyebrow.

"Me? That's odd."

"I know! Anyway, I do like the idea of incense, so I bought a box from the market on my way home today. Do you like it? Apparently, it's for cleansing."

I filled my lungs with the smell. It smelled familiar, like my childhood. It reminded me of a puzzle box I was given for my birthday once as a child. "Is it cedar?" I asked, and she nodded.

"A lot of it is a bit far-fetched though, and the only candles I have are Yankee, so I don't think they'd work unless my spell was to make the house smell nice." She held up a DVD box, and I gave her a thumbs up, even though I didn't have a clue what the film was. "Mr Ealing was going on about this space between the real world, the one we are living in, and another spirit world, where you can enter and be completely unseen aside from other souls in there with you. I was really interested in that part. He said there is a space between the two worlds which seems almost dreamy when he describes it. This afternoon, he gave me a book on shapeshifting folklore. Shapeshifting, seriously. I thought he was losing his marbles, but he seemed quite serious about it."

I stared at her, licking the ketchup from my fingers. I didn't know what to say. Maisy barely paused for breath.

"I asked him if he was thinking about trying to turn into a giant grizzly bear, but his son turned up and took him home, mumbling something about ignoring the old bugger. He could be kinda cute if he didn't act like he has a stick up his ass. The son, not Mr Ealing!" Maisy laughed. "Scruffy, but bloody hot, that one."

I laughed out loud and almost choked on my food. I tried to place his son in my mind's eye but failed. I recalled he had an unusual name too, but couldn't remember what it was. I almost asked Maisy but changed my mind. It was irrelevant now. You'd have thought Mr Ealing would have brought his son along when he came to visit us more often. Normal parents would have.

"So, you don't think he was researching something from the papers, or a book he was reading?" I asked. I was interested, but a bit confused.

"That's the thing. He hadn't checked out anything that would lead up to it, just those. He is getting on a bit now. In my experience, they all go a bit funny if they know they're on their way out. He has aged suddenly over the last few months."

She was quiet for a moment, fiddling with the DVD player with a slice of pizza sticking out of her mouth. She had a point. He *had* seemed to age suddenly. I wonder what he'd meant by the space between worlds. I opened my mouth to ask what happened next, but she'd already begun to reply.

"I had a look online after he'd gone. He'd been rabbiting on about it all afternoon, so I was curious."

"Nosy more like!" I chimed in.

"Shush you. I found a rough guide to shapeshifting that he'd been reading. It's quite amusing. Want to see?"

I nodded in reply, burning with curiosity. I could see she was too. The last few weeks had been pretty samey. Finally, something different.

We threw the pizza box aside, and I moved onto her sofa with her. She pulled out a Ziplock document folder and slid out the contents; a four-page document on shapeshifting. I wasn't sure whether to laugh or take it seriously, but I was suddenly a giddy teenager again, and it seemed quite fitting to pour us each another huge glass of wine.

Maisy read the title out loud and giggled. Hidden Falcon's Guide to Mental and Physical Shapeshifting sounded like something from a sci-fi TV series. She looked at me excitedly, though I think that was more to do with the wine than the guide. I picked up the first page and read it out loud. There was a bit about the guy who wrote the guide. Seemed like he was of Native American descent, and he referenced getting his energy from the rivers and forests where he had grown up on a reservation. He had written this guide for those who had left reservations and were looking to re-connect with the ways of their ancestors. It seemed pretty interesting, and as I would have expected from the title, Hidden Falcon preferred shifting into a falcon.

Maisy read the next bit about mental shapeshifting. If you needed to be brave, you imagined certain traits from that animal, and it helped you to deal with whatever you were facing. Sometimes, you could feel what the animal was feeling if it was close to you. Hidden Falcon mentioned it was a way to pay respects when hunting an animal, as you could connect with it and help to guide it to the other side.

"Ahh, here's the good bit." Maisy tapped the paper she was holding. "To physically take the form of an animal..." she winked at me, and I laughed. "...find somewhere completely safe and relaxing for your first time and for practicing. It can take a while to be comfortable shifting. Yep, we've done that." Maisy shuffled her back against the cushions and nudged a plate on the floor out of her way with her foot. "Become completely calm and focused. Deep breathing and meditating are the usual forms of calming yourself before a shift. I'm rubbish at meditating. Can you help me out, Ena?"

I nodded quickly and tapped the paper for her to continue. I was great at meditating. I did it daily.

Maisy carried on reading. "As you breathe, imagine your body going to sleep. Imagine your limbs becoming heavy, your brain slowing down, and your eyes getting tired. As you slow down, bring in parts of the animal you have decided to start with. For example, if you choose a mountain lion, imagine the shape of the animal enclosed around your shape. Feel your way into its skin. Imagine your hands feel like paws. Imagine your long legs and heavy head. Create the image of the animal around yourself and imagine your soul connecting with the animal. Only in a true relaxed state will you be able to feel as though the parts of the lion are parts of your body. It will feel like a sudden dream after falling asleep. It can be frightening when you realise it's working, but do not fear. The soul is a very vulnerable part of you. You must protect it at all times during the shift, as it is most vulnerable when it is halfway between human and animal forms." Maisy stopped reading and reached for her glass. I stared at her for a second and a chill swept over me. I shuddered and looked around for a draught. Thinking I was being silly, I took my glass too and emptied it. I took the next page of the guide and read it myself.

"It says at first you might not make a complete shift, and you will be in a shadow state between worlds. This is when your soul is in most danger. In order to move on quickly and protect your soul, you must practice and become confident in your new skin."

This all sounded very odd to me. Did people believe this stuff? I held my wine glass out to Maisy, who was already pouring herself another.

"Okay, let's try it." She giggled. "How do we meditate?"

I slid off the sofa and sat with my back against it. I waved my arm so she got the idea to copy me. I breathed in deeply, counted to four, then let my breath out again slowly. I closed my eyes, ready to take another breath, but before I could, Maisy burst out laughing. After a minute of giggling and attempting to try again, we decided to give up for a bit and finish the wine with a movie. The movie wasn't great, and we found ourselves talking over most of it. The hot guy she had taken a fancy too was in it, and yes, he was gorgeous, but there was no story line. Apart from staring at the screen every time he was topless or wet, we decided to leave it running in the background and try the shifting thing again.

This time, Maisy did okay at relaxing, and I deliberately avoided her gaze and forced myself to ignore her occasional snorts. My mouth twitched into a smile only once, and I was sure if she saw it that it would have set us both off giggling again. The amount of alcohol consumed and the thick smell of the incense which had filled the room certainly helped.

Once we had been deep breathing for a few minutes, I said, "Now, any thought that comes into your head, dismiss it and let it go. If you find yourself following any thought, you'll need to start all over again."

I didn't hear any sounds from Maisy, so I decided to try it myself. I wondered if her front door was locked properly, and I batted the thought away. Were we completely safe? Batted it away too. Of course we were. What if I fell asleep and was late for Bea? I was used to meditating. My body would respond to my phone ringing. I let go of thought after thought until I was almost in a state where I could have been asleep. Something in my brain sneered at the thought of the lion; too ambitious. *A cat might work.* I liked cats and used to have one when I was small, so I could probably imagine a few of its traits.

After what seemed like forever, nothing had happened. I had done everything I thought I could have done, right down to imagining the draught I could feel on my imaginary whiskers. I sighed and opened my eyes. They took a moment to adjust, and I cursed the wine. Maisy was fast asleep, and definitely not in the form of an animal. I put my hand on her knee and shook it.

"Well, at least I know how to meditate to sleep now,"

she said brightly, stretching her arms. "No damn wings though!"

I shook my head. "I was useless too," I picked up my phone and opened the Uber app. I didn't fancy walking home in the rain, plus, I didn't need to be under the influence to trip over myself. "Best head off though. That movie was crap, wasn't it?" A little deflated, I changed the subject.

She nodded and picked up the DVD box. "Ah, well. He was fit though." She eyed the box and then found the remote. "Might put that sex scene back on. He has amazing abs!"

Ahh, I loved Maisy.

CHAPTER 3

Mr Ealing

My wife was getting ready for bed when I came in. She'd gotten into her nightdress and perched on the edge of the bed with a book open, ready to read. She gave me a smile as I entered the room. She always had a smile for me, and I adored that about her. The wrinkles beside her eyes showed the deep creases, which proved the smiles were genuine. Even though the years hadn't been kind to our bodies or looks, we still felt like the age we were supposed to be, which was much younger than we looked. I sat down beside her, my knees sore from the arthritis setting in. My body was growing older a lot quicker in this lifetime. I wasn't sure whether to blame all my hard work, or just the fact that I wouldn't be needed here for much longer. I suspected the latter, and it troubled me. There was so much left undone, and I didn't know if I would have the time to tie up loose ends before my soul moved on. My brow furrowed.

Mally's hand on my back, spread warm energy across my weary muscles, instantly calming and soothing me. The pain in my knees eased a little, and I nodded gratefully.

"What's troubling you, my love?" she asked me, putting down her book.

I looked up at her. Her black hair framed her face perfectly. Her eyes shone lovingly as they always did for me, and for our children. She put her palm to my face, spreading the warmth there too. My body welcomed the gradual weightlessness that overcame it.

"I may have done something a bit rash this afternoon," I began, thinking back to talking to Maisy about shapeshifting. It had only been a brief conversation, but I knew that girl inside out. I had known her almost her whole life, and I was banking on the fact that she would pass it on to someone who would listen to her.

"What did you do?" she asked quietly, giving my cheek a squeeze. "I'm sure whatever it is will work out and not be worth the worry."

My brow creased into a frown again. "You know Ena?"

"Of course I know Ena, you silly man." Mally laughed. "Rachel was over the moon when she came home. She seems to be doing okay with the baby too. I told her there was nothing to worry about." She paused before remembering what I had said. "What about Ena?"

"She comes into the library now to see Maisy."

Mally's face was curious but impatient. "Spit it out then." She patted my cheek.

I smiled and closed my eyes, taking a deep breath in and out. "Well, I might have suggested she take home a couple of books on witchcraft." I waited to be scolded, but it never came. Instead, Mally nodded thoughtfully.

"Ahh, you're trying to form some sort of bond between her and Rachel. Well, I can see how that might help. She might begin to notice things."

"That's not the only thing. I might have mentioned shapeshifting. Maisy seemed quite excited about it. I almost printed off some guide I had found years ago, but I chickened out." I watched her face as she considered this.

"It might not be too bad. I'm sure Maisy will have her fun and then they'll forget about the whole thing. Don't beat yourself up about it. Everyone gets tempted to share something about themselves that no one knows about. You've been stuck in that damned library for too long. Find something else to talk about next time, then you might not be so tempted. Just out of interest, what made you chicken out?"

"Ivan," I replied, thinking of our son. A lump formed

in my throat whenever I mentioned him recently. I couldn't figure out if he was still on this planet. So aloof, so out of touch, and yet he had been such a happy boy. He still did as I asked, followed me round like a puppy, and followed every single instruction to the letter, but his heart just wasn't open anymore. He'd closed himself off. I suppose I had thought maybe someone like Maisy could reach him, but he and Maisy hadn't spoken properly for years. Then Ena came back. Ena gave off this energy that she was completely unaware of. It radiated from her; the same warmth Mally had. It was subtle, but it was there. I had watched her in the library the last few months. She was very similar to my Ivan. Quiet, alone. I wondered if perhaps the two of them could work something out, but recently his attitude was so awful. I didn't want to terrify the poor girl, so I hadn't mentioned it, not even to Mally.

"So, Ena then?" Mally asked, as if reading my thoughts. "What exactly were you thinking?"

"I wasn't thinking, like you said. I'm a lonely old bugger who pretty much lives in a library." I laughed, taking her hand and giving it a squeeze.

Mally shook her head. "Where is Ivan?" she asked before getting into bed.

I shrugged. "Out, I think. He wasn't downstairs before I came up."

A worried expression crossed her face, barely noticeable, and went as quickly as it came. Blinking, she pulled up the covers, and I knew that was all she was going to say for the rest of the evening.

–

Ena

After another non-eventful day, I headed to my bedroom for some alone time. It had rained all day, which made me feel a little depressed as the grey sky seemed to darken the house like a terrifying omen. It hadn't helped that Bea had also screamed the house down for most of the afternoon. Mum knew I was tired and anxious. She had suggested I go lie down for an hour until I felt better. I was probably more uneasy at knowing I was doing nothing with my life than being anxious about trying to do anything about it. That, and the fact that, even though Bea had been loud and exhausting that day, I loved her more than anything and refused to put her down. It had set my brain on high alert.

I sat on the bedroom floor and sighed. I had brought the shapeshifter guide home with me and skimmed over it again after coming home from Maisy's. I thought it might be a good way to de-stress. If I could summon something to help me with my anxiety or find a way to mask the self-doubt always hanging over me, that would be a great start to moving on. It might have seemed I had nothing to move on from, but when that doubt began to cast its shadows like that, things from all across my life were brought to the surface, and I found it hard to concentrate.

I breathed deeply and looked around my room, suddenly nervous, although I had meditated in there hundreds of times.

I could hear my mum downstairs, moving around. The TV was on, but I could only hear slight background noise from that. Maybe Bea had woken up and she was trying to soothe her back to sleep. Part of me wanted to go and check, but the other part of me wanted to stay and try to focus. Mum had given me the hour to meditate and relax, so I wanted to use the time given to me whilst I had it.

I leaned my back against my bed. I had a rectangular-shaped room with a window at each end. My bed was on the left next to the door, and on the right, was a dresser which held my candles and collection of gemstones. There was a mirror behind them, and a little tray full of sand, which I used to stand my candles in. When I was around twelve, Mum had given me a small ornamental dagger which I used to keep with them on display, but over the years, it had ended up in a box somewhere. Probably in the loft.

I also had a bookcase beside the dresser, and a wicker chair in the corner. A small chest of drawers stood at the other side of the bed, and the stand for the Moses basket, which was beside my bed at night, but now was behind the closed door. The basket was downstairs with Bea.

I wondered if Maisy had got this to work yet, or if she'd forgotten all about it already and moved onto the next crazy idea. My mind began to wander.

I took another deep breath and looked at my watch. It was 8.45p.m., so I had already wasted ten minutes. Mum wouldn't enforce the hour suggestion she'd made. She'd wait until I came down, but she knew how I worried about being selfish and would wonder what was going on if I did take longer. If someone said an hour, I tried to stick to an hour. She knew that more than anyone.

I set the guide down next to me and placed my palms on my knees. I sat cross-legged and closed my eyes. I concentrated on my breathing, slowing it as much as I could without being asleep. Usually, I would bring thoughts to the front of my mind and either work through them in my relaxed state or let them go. This time, I brought forward the idea of shapeshifting. I had already decided to stick with a cat as I had identified some of the qualities to focus on, so it seemed sensible. If any of this seemed sensible. I was about to think about shapeshifting, and I wasn't joking around this time. I just wanted to adopt some of the traits and make them work for me. Confidence, balance, elegance. All the things I associated with a cat, as well as being brave. I certainly didn't feel brave or confident. Normally, I'd have sneered at something like this, but for some reason, it kept flowing back into the forefront of my mind like it was being pushed there. I couldn't stop wondering.

I thought about the shape of the cat; the long, thin body and the slender limbs. The way it walked, the way it stood. I imagined the twitch of the ears and the soft movements of the head. I imagined the small paws and how I thought they felt, as if my palms were the pads and they could feel the ground beneath them. I imagined my tail bone extending, the long swish of my own tail, and how it was like a natural extension of myself. I then realised how easy it was to let go of myself to that form. I imagined my soul taking that form, seeping out from my relaxed, human body and slipping into the space Maisy said she believed existed between the world of the conscious and the unconscious. My mind wandered from thought to thought, no longer letting go but trying to put my thoughts into physical feelings.

For a moment, I didn't think it was working. I was about to pull myself out and imagine waking up, but as I turned my head, I caught the smell of the fresh air outside. It smelled different, thick, like wet leaves and soil. A bit like the usual smell after it has been raining, but deeper. There was a layer to the smell, almost like when you cook bread. I coughed to clear my throat.

I inhaled deeper, allowing the scent to wash over

me. I could smell the wet tarmac. It was different to the dirt, the leaves different again, and the air itself hung with a sweet scent I had never smelt before. I shook my head. This meditation was sending me off to sleep, and it was time to pull myself out of it to get ready for bed. When I opened my eyes, I found myself looking at myself. My body sat slumped against the bed, as if it was sleeping. I could see the soft rise and fall of my chest, and my fluttering eyelids. Was my neck really that saggy under my chin?

Yeah, that was the right thing to focus on.

Why could I see myself? In my moment of confusion, I let out a sound, a gasp, although it wasn't mine. It was a sound I'd never heard before, as if I was...? I looked down.

I had taken a spectral form. My form wasn't solid but was definitely there. The curves of the paws. I could see the end of my nose, and my field of vision was larger. I could see the sides of my body without turning my head. There were whiskers. I found myself going cross-eyed to stare at them. They wiggled as I made a disgusted face, and I started to panic.

This was a dream. It wasn't happening. There was no way I believed in this, was there? It couldn't be real. I backed up, finding my movements a lot clumsier than usual. My balance was completely off, and I fell on to my side with my paws flopping as I went down. I looked across my chocolate brown fur, but it was almost invisible in the soft light of my room.

My ears involuntarily twitched as I heard footsteps on the stairs. It must be Mum. *How do I get back into my own body? Will she see me?*

Looking at my body, I could almost see my heart pounding in my chest, a dead giveaway if she decided to enter the room. I had to try not to panic.

I struggled to my feet, but the balance was difficult, and I swayed, trying to feel the ground between four paws rather than two feet. I gripped the carpet with my claws.

I closed my eyes again and tried to slow down my breathing and my thoughts. The room was spinning.

In what appeared to be a long time but was actually only a few seconds, I snapped back into my body. As if a piece of elastic held me there, somehow connected to my soul and somewhere in my chest, it pinged back, pulling me back into my body. My eyes shot open, and I took a huge gulp of air.

Luckily, my Mum passed my door to the bathroom, and I sighed in relief. What had just happened? It had left me feeling more anxious and confused than before. It must have been a dream. I must have fallen asleep. My eyes fell on the guide next to me. I should read it again later, or do some internet research. *No. I don't Google dreams anymore.*

I made my way downstairs to find Bea awake in her

basket. She was sucking her hand, so I thought she was hungry. Settling down on the sofa to feed her, I changed the channel on the TV, hoping to distract myself from my dream. Mum returned, and we watched in silence for a while, although I was sure she kept looking at me from the corner of her eye. I pretended I didn't notice.

CHAPTER 4

Ena

I had pushed the experience to the back of my mind, giving it up as a strange dream. I'd had strange dreams before. Mostly the kind where you feel like you're falling and then suddenly wake when you hit the floor, only I didn't wake. I lay there, fully aware I had fallen but not being able to get back up. I had had a few really scary ones too, about being in some sort of wooden box with eyes staring at me. I had no idea what that was about, but I remember thinking I could smell the fear. I can still remember the rough sound of someone laughing in the background. I shuddered involuntarily every time I thought of it.

Bea was teething, so she was sleeping really badly, meaning I was sleeping badly too. I didn't really have the time nor the mindpower to sit down and concentrate on any one thing for long. I'd spent my days out job hunting like I had promised myself. I would have taken anything going. The longer I watched Mum working on the computer, picking up stacks of books and writing out lesson plans, the more I believed I could do more.

I knew looking after Bea was the most important thing I could do, and she needed me, but I also knew that feeling wouldn't go away until I found something to do to make a bit of extra money when my maternity pay stopped. To help ease the financial burden on Mum. Although she would never mention it, I knew it was there. I worried far too much. I pulled out my phone and opened Spotify. The Job Hunt playlist I'd created started with a track called *I'm a Fake* by The Used. Its lyrics seemed appropriate for my current feelings. I followed it with Jimmy Eat World's *The Middle*.

Mum was a teacher during term times, which worked out well, as over the summer and half terms, she helped me with Bea. During term time, I'd have to use a nursery, unless I could find somewhere with shifts, or just weekends and evenings. Surely there was somewhere that needed night staff. I could nap when Bea did during the day.

My mind wandered idly, thinking of how Mum had lived in that house for so long, alone. She'd not bothered with luxuries for herself, and had saved well. I remember we had moved there when I was around thirteen. It was the first home we had stayed in for longer than a year, and I had noticed over the years most of it had stayed the same. She'd never redecorated or had anything remodelled, but everything was still functional, even though it was now old-fashioned.

We moved around a lot, and because of that, she didn't really do much to the houses we were staying in in case we had to up and go. I never had a proper bedroom until we moved there, and then it was only decorated the once. Mum insisted she had enough money to cover us for a while. That didn't stop me from feeling bad though. Why should her hard work have to fund me as a grown adult? She said she'd fund me until the day I died if she had to because that's what mothers are for. If I tried to argue, she'd ask if I would do the same for Bea, and of course I would.

I didn't like the creeping feeling of living in her pocket, trapped, dependent on someone who wasn't there for me when I had needed her growing up. I had felt like I was spiralling out of control, struggling to fit in and know who I was and how I was meant to deal with things like hormones. She hadn't noticed, always too busy. Always distracted. Maybe she was making up for that now.

The only thing that did seem to change over the time I had lived there were the stones on the front and back of the house. Mum collected gemstones. Some of her specimens were huge, so big I couldn't pick them up. Some were tiny and could fit on my fingernail. She also loved candles. She had a whole cupboard full of the things. They weren't even scented ones. I made a point of not going near them. I hated the smell of the beeswax they were made with. I much preferred my Yankees. She had a shelf of those too that I had bought her and she hadn't used. Mum was quirky, and I tried to ignore that fact as I grew up. I didn't want to associate with things that might make me seem weirder than I already was. The kid who was always moving house, the girl who never talked to her Mum, the girl who didn't make friends. I never had anyone over. I always believed Mum might embarrass me, or the streams of questions might come about our unpainted woodchip wallpaper and a house full of old rocks.

I didn't really understand why we moved around so much. Mum said it was so my dad didn't find us. She said we were better off without him, but he would always be looking in case we crossed his path, or the path of one of his eyes. I always thought she was being selfish, that they'd had a fight and she'd run away. She didn't give me many details about him, and there were no photographs or anything. I had looked many times when we were packing and unpacking, but I had never found one, not even one of them together or with friends. The only picture that might have once held clues was one of Mum when she was younger. It was part of one which had been torn in half. I would have put money on my dad being on the other half.

When I had asked if I could visit him or write, she'd said no. Some of my friends got to see both parents after they'd split up, but I was never allowed. She told me that he knew I was born but was not the kind of man who could be a father, and that he was dangerous. She seemed to think he would steal me away. When I was really small, I often wished I was stolen away, but as I grew older, I just grew indifferent.

It took a long time for her to find somewhere she could relax without looking over her shoulder. After a time, she decided that the town where I was born was the best place, as he wouldn't have expected her to go back. That was where we lived now.

For a long time, she was on edge, checking the windows, sneaking her friends in, and even thought about security cameras. I wasn't sure she was okay, and at the time, I didn't understand her mental state, which was one of the reasons I left to live with Maisy and her family for a while before I went off to uni. The Ealings had looked after her, and eventually, I agreed to meeting with her again. Partly through guilt, but partly just to stop them from calling me.

I went to university and returned home just before I turned twenty, heavily pregnant with Bea. Mum took us in, asked no questions, and basically got on with it. She carried on as if I'd never left. Somehow, she knew I'd come back. Somehow, I did too.

Bea adored her grandma, and my mum had all the time in the world for Bea. I didn't want to destroy that. It was the connection I had always wanted for myself. I wanted Bea to have that.

Since Mr Ealing had started going on about the supernatural and shapeshifting, Maisy had been doing a lot of research on the side. She was constantly sending me photos of things she'd photocopied from books.

When I had gone to uni, she started working in the library as she wasn't sure what she wanted to do with her life. I always needed a goal, or to feel like I was achieving something. Maisy was very *go with the flow*. She didn't rush into anything if she didn't have to. She kept me grounded. She always had.

The library was mostly empty, except for her and Mr Ealing, who she often joked might never leave if a travel bed appeared one day in the corridor.

From what I had put together over the years, Mr Ealing had been Mum's best friend for a long time. He was, at one time, a best friend of my dad's too. As a child, I often wondered about asking him if he knew where my dad was, but never found myself alone with him. Mum was always within earshot.

I remember, for my birthday one year, he came to

visit us. I had hoped that he had brought me cake, but instead, his wife made me a huge braid of onions to hang over the front door and a dream catcher made from red and green embroidery thread. I had given my mum the onions but hung the dream catcher above my bedroom window. It was one of the only things I felt compelled to take from house to house. Although our location changed, it was comforting to keep some things inside the same.

Mr Ealing and his wife, Mally, had a shop in town. They had a grown-up son who I'd never met properly, but we had crossed paths when we were a lot younger. I remember he was always talking, not even about anything in particular. Maisy knew him a bit better than I did, but even then, they weren't friends. Just kids who had parents who were friends. Their son was a little older than me, but by how much I'd never asked. The odd occasion I had seen him tag along, I pretty much ignored him or stayed in another room of the house. After a while, he'd avoided me completely. We could be in the same house but not see each other for the whole visit sometimes. Maisy always said he was nice to look at but had the personality of a shoe brush after you've used it to clean horse crap off your boots. I think they'd had a daughter too, but they didn't mention her often. Mrs Ealing sold curiosities and candles, incense and gemstones, that sort of thing. That was probably why

Mum had so many candles.

Anyway, somehow, Maisy working at the library and retired and bored Mr Ealing spending all his time there had meant them having long conversations about pretty much everything, like the supernatural and witchcraft. Maisy thought it was lots of fun and loved the research. When I spoke with her on the phone, she said she had ordered a few extra books from the next town's library. She had also gone on about it every time I had seen her in the last week or so, more than anything else, even men, which was huge for her. It was because she was so set in her idea that this shifting thing could be true, and the amount of research she'd found suggesting it was was what started me thinking again about the whole incident when I was meditating.

I wondered if Mr Ealing had tried it himself. The idea made me laugh out loud, although stranger things had happened. I wondered what animal he would turn into if he could. I could imagine him as a badger, perhaps, or an old gopher.

Mr Ealing's first name was Devan, and even though he had barely seen Mum since I had come home, they had the kind of relationship most envied. That you could not speak for months and yet know they one hundred percent had your back if you needed them. I knew Mum would drop everything if there was a call with an emergency. That kind of friendship was golden, and the fact that I had witnessed it with them and then with Maisy myself, I knew how important it was, and how special.

CHAPTER 5

Ena

I'd gone to the library again that morning, and Mr Ealing was there when I arrived. He sat in the corner on one of the sofas with a mug of tea. There weren't usually coffee or tea-making facilities for customers, but Maisy said she couldn't go all day without a hot drink, and if she was making herself one, she wasn't going to make him sit there and watch her drink it. She automatically made him whatever she was having. She was hovering nearby, putting books back onto the shelves. I crept up behind her quietly, tapped her on the shoulder, and she jumped.

"Oh, you cow!" She swatted at me. I ducked back, laughing. "Where's my baby?" she demanded, with her hands on her hips.

"With Mum," I replied, feeling guilty for leaving her yet again, but they did seem to enjoy their time together.

"I don't have long. I have to feed her soon. So, how's things?" I shrugged.

"Pretty much the same. Hey, Mr E?" Maisy said loudly. Mr Ealing briefly looked up from his newspaper and raised his hand. "We have a ball." She laughed, and so did I at the simplicity yet closeness of it all. I wished I had something interesting to say.

"So, that shifter guide," I began, suddenly thinking about it. "Did you try it again?"

She shook her head. "I did, but nothing happened. I don't know. It seemed legit, but it didn't work." She continued to put books back as we walked. Her trolley was only half full, and I suspected most of the books were Maisy's, which made me smile. She didn't half fly through books.

"Ahh, same here," I lied, suddenly feeling self-conscious, I wanted to keep it to myself for now. "What do you mean a printed off the internet guide to turning into an animal seemed legit?"

Maisy elbowed me in the ribs. "Hey, just because you don't believe in it doesn't mean it's not true. Mr Ealing said Native Americans used to do it, and there were even groups of people in Europe who could do it. They used to form groups to protect each other because if they were found out, they'd be hanged, or dunked, or tortured."

I glanced at Mr Ealing. Perhaps he did know a bit

about this stuff.

"He gave me this book on shapeshifting folklore. It's pretty interesting. Apparently, some areas have lots of shifters because they're drawn to each other as if by magic. There are the odd lone shifters who think they're the only ones and too afraid to tell anyone, but Mr Ealing reckons there are small pockets of them all around the place living in secret." She paused.

Maybe I should read this book too. It sounded interesting.

"But no real turning into wolves and fighting off vampires for us, hey?" I pretended it was all a joke to me, but I burned for more information. There was something about the whole thing that sparked something in the back of my mind. Something I hadn't listened to since I was a child.

"Well, if I do manage it one day, I'll make sure I fly over to your house as an owl and keep you up all night for not believing me."

"Yeah. Just watch out for the flying pigs when you do."

It was wrong of me to lie to Maisy. She was my best friend, but how the heck do you tell someone you turned into a shadow cat for five seconds without them thinking you've gone completely crazy? She wouldn't have thought me crazy, but she would have quizzed me over and over, and I was too tired for that.

"Hey, don't mock what you don't understand, hater. This book says the Greek gods could do it too," she said lightly, flicking her hair at me and turning away.

So, now we were believing in Greek gods as well. I raised my eyebrow. There were lots of things the Greek gods claimed to do, but most of them were well off my bucket list.

"But have you found anything solid? You know, actual real research, or is it all *you have to take my word for it* kind of stuff? Has anyone actually studied it? Have you found anything scientific?" I asked, hoping she could give me a hint towards something to read, but also secretly hoping she hadn't so I didn't have to carry on the charade. I could feel Mr Ealing looking at me over the top of his newspaper. I glared at him until he popped it back over his face again. Nosey old man. No, not nosey. Interested. After all, he had started this whole thing. I bet he was getting a kick out of how we were discussing it.

"Well, not really," Maisy admitted. "There is some pretty interesting stuff though. We found something about entering the spirit world in your shifted form. It didn't say how to do it or anything, but it said you have to move your soul into the spirit plain and take up your animal form there. That way, if anything happens to your human body, your soul can slip away and survive until you can find a way back. If they can find a way to save your body, you can come back from the dead. Isn't that cool?"

I nodded and followed her down the aisle. "Sounds like you've been reading too many sci-fi novels." I picked up one of the books from the trolley. Another rom-com. I held it up. "Research?" I asked, and she blushed.

"Shh. Yes, it's research. When I meet the man of my dreams, I need to know how to bag him. Can't use candles for that shit now, can you?" She winked at me, and again, I laughed out loud.

-

Ivan

I sat at my desk, completely swamped with paperwork. It never seemed to end, and my email inbox was beeping at least once every minute because the incompetent buffoons in customer services wouldn't authorise anything without checking with me first. I ran my hands through my hair, feeling like ripping it out before glancing at my empty coffee mug. I'd had six cups and had only been at work a few hours, but there was no way I'd get through this mess before home time unless I was wide awake. Unfortunately, I had to help my dad out with a lot of things in the evenings, which meant going to bed ridiculously late. Even when I did go to bed, I couldn't sleep. I'd stare at the ceiling for hours, unaware how long it took me to pass out from exhaustion. The days just seemed to blur together.

I stretched my legs and prepared to stand, hitting print on a document I had been working on that needed to be signed and delivered to the boss. I wondered how the hell he ever made this business work. It was underfunded and understaffed, yet he paraded about all day so positive about it all. I ground my teeth together.

My tiny office had a window so I could see out onto the warehouse floor. I used to have an office on the main floor on the same corridor as accounting and purchasing, but it was too noisy, and I couldn't concentrate with people passing so often. Plus, when I mentioned to John that I didn't think the warehouse staff were working fast enough, he thought sticking me in a room I wouldn't even classify as a broom cupboard was the perfect solution. Yes, it was quieter because less people knocked on my door, but now all my computer did was ping with instant messages. Urgh. I wasn't a people person at all, and I sighed with annoyance when John appeared outside my door.

"Ivan? Ivan, can I come in?" he said brightly. I forced a smile and stood up to hold the door open for him as he entered the office. There was even less room in there now, which made me edgy.

"Of course, boss. Take a seat."

"No, I won't keep you. It's just, er... I was looking

through the figures for last month and it seems customers rated our delivery times as a lot slower than I'd like. I don't strive for less than five."

I nodded as he spoke. He meant five stars, and our ratings were hovering around three, which wasn't great. I had been telling him this for months. If he wanted faster delivery times, he needed more staff to handle the increase in business.

"What's the current situation?" John asked, glancing over at the document printing. I coughed so his eyes were drawn back to mine.

"We only have three members of staff during the day, and one who covers the orders made for next day delivery in the evening. I had two who covered weekends when next day isn't available, but you mentioned at the last meeting that you want me to let them go to save on the electric and security. To be honest, John, one person an evening cannot physically get the number of deliveries out on her own. We had over fifty yesterday afternoon. Over half of them selected next day delivery. There's no way she could handle it in the time she had. I had to let her go home and have the others pick up in the morning, which put them behind for the night time orders and everything else. I need more staff," I said hopefully. There really was no way one girl could get it done on her own without staying all night. A few more members of staff would make things run a lot smoother, and there was no way I was going to do all the excess orders when I had all my other work to do and needed to leave on time. I thought carefully about playing the safety card. A girl all alone on the warehouse floor at night... I blinked it away.

He'd think me a monster for suggesting it.

"Hmmm." John rubbed his chin. "Okay, let's start with one. We will see how much quicker things are, and if I have less complaints and therefore need to give away less things for free, we might be able to grab another. The big sale is coming up, after all."

Damn it. I'd forgotten about the sale. Looked like I had even more work now as I had to go through all the products that needed to be reduced and send the list up to the IT guys.

"Only one, John?" I said, my tone implying I needed a better offer.

He held up a finger and shook his head. "I can afford one. Pop a memo on the staff notice board. I see you're out of coffee. Perhaps do it on the way to the staff room." There was a coffee machine in my old office.

"Yes, boss," I said pleasantly. I sat back down at my computer and opened up the Word program, typing a brief job description out for the staff memo board. I'd do an official one for the temp agency after my trip to the staffroom. I'd rather not pay an agency to find someone for the job, but we didn't often get much of a return from putting things on the board. Still, it was worth a shot.

-

Ena

I headed home via the corner shop. I waited in line to buy some chocolate and enquire after a job advertisement I had seen on their notice board outside. The position in the shop had been taken, but the lady in the queue behind me had tapped me on the shoulder as I was about to leave. Her daughter was one of the buyers for a company who ran a warehouse on the other side of town. She said the company was expanding and taking on staff. Mostly pickers, but I'd take anything.

I left the shop with a phone number and the name of the lady's daughter. I ate my chocolate on my way home with every intention of spending a couple of hours playing with Bea, making my phone call, and then possibly heading to the gym for an hour after dinner. Instead, as I entered the kitchen, I was greeted by a huge note from Mum on the kitchen table. Why she hadn't text me instead I didn't know.

"Gone 2 feed the ducks and need to go 2 town. Ring if you need anything from Tesco. Bea had bottle at 11 so fine. Don't forget to express or ring if you need me 2 come home." I looked at my watch and saw it was only 11.32, so they hadn't been gone for too long. I'd probably only just missed them passing whilst I had been in the shop.

I made my phone call, and the lady I spoke to had passed me on to her boss. After a quick telephone interview, he explained that they needed a few extra hands to get orders out in the evenings. They had plenty of daytime workers, but often had orders come through late in the day who wanted next day delivery. All I'd have to do was read what was ordered from a printout, pick the items from the shelves, pack them into a box, drop in an invoice, and seal the box. I'd stick on a delivery label and leave the box on a unit to be posted. Seemed easy enough, and the fact that it was evening work meant it was perfect for Mum's work and me looking after Bea. He offered me a trial, which I gratefully accepted. In a couple of days' time, I would have my first shift, and I was a lot happier when I hung up the phone. Things were beginning to come together after months of trying to slot back into any kind of normal life.

Thinking of shifts, I had the house to myself for a couple of hours. I could head to the gym, or I could go up to my room and have another go at shapeshifting. The thought hadn't occurred to me until I realised I was at a loose end for a while. It crept up on me and caught me by surprise, making my heart flutter slightly. I was in two minds about it, but I was curious after hearing Maisy talk about it earlier. After sitting on my bed for a good ten minutes, listening to the silence of the house, I decided to go for it. I threw my half-full gym bag on the landing outside my bedroom door, so if for any reason Mum came home and I didn't hear her, she'd think I'd been to the gym and was getting changed. I felt a bit naughty, like I was about to do something forbidden. I couldn't help rechecking the front door was locked. I threw a Foo Fighters CD into my player on its lowest volume so I could still hear sounds from the rest of the house.

This time, it was easier than before. I settled my mind and tried to slowly ease out of my body and feel my way into the form of a cat. It didn't cross my mind to try any other sort of creature. It only took a minute, and I could see the ends of my whiskers flashing in the sunlight from my bedroom window, which I had left open.

My window opened sideways over a flat roof above my kitchen. There was a drop of about three feet on the other side of the window to the roof, but then there was the garden fence which came right up to the house on the kitchen side. I could go out if I was brave enough. With my ghost-like form, no one would notice me in the bright sunlight. If they did, they would think I was a shadow... if I kept to the walls and fences. It was reckless, but I needed the risk.

I stood up shakily and found my balance. This form was still new to me, and I needed to master standing, let alone jumping from windows onto fences only a couple of inches wide. I practiced by pacing around my room, feeling the sway of my tail and the swing of my hips. I shook my head, feeling my ears as longer extensions of my body for the first time, and my whiskers were the strangest yet. They tingled and buzzed whenever I came too close to something even as small as fluff on the edge of the bed. I brushed my head against my chest of drawers taking in the sensation. It didn't feel unpleasant, It was as if my whiskers were fingers. The soft pads on my paws squished gently into the rug, and I couldn't feel my claws at all.

I tried rocking back and forth on my front and back legs, gauging the power and pressure in my pads before attempting a jump onto my bed. The first time, I misjudged it completely, like a kitten climbing a curtain. My claws stuck into the duvet cover, and I hung awkwardly from the edge of the bed. Shaking my paws free, which wasn't as easy as it looked, I decided to try again. This time, I made it all the way up onto the bed. I was quite proud of myself, but still wasn't ready to head outside. From atop my bed, I could see the tops of my human shoulders rising and falling as I breathed, my hair sparkling in the sunlight, and I could hear the soft whoosh of my breath. It was fascinating watching myself from the outside. I usually hated looking at myself. I wondered if this was what it might feel like if the spirit world was real.

I practiced jumping on and off the bed several times before attempting the windowsill. The first time, I missed and slipped off the windowsill into the Moses basket, knocking it over and leaving me flat on my back, I surprised myself by making a hissing sound as I landed. I was grateful for thinking of leaving the music on as it made the noises from my falling and cursing not seem so loud. The second time didn't go too well either, but on the third attempt, I was perched on top of my windowsill, gazing out into the garden. I craned my neck.

What was amazing was how big and bright everything looked. The colours and shapes seen through new eyes knocked me back, and I couldn't focus on any one thing for more than a second as my eyes reacted to every tiny movement. A bird, dust, a leaf, the grass; it was beautiful. Everything looked as though it had its own harsh outline, a definition I hadn't noticed before with my human eyes. It made it a lot easier to see things farther away. Everything out there seemed to give off a soft glow as the light was reflected back.

The drop to the roof was more like a fall, but I shrugged it off. I was a cat now, and in my shadow form, didn't think it possible to get hurt.

I managed to get from the top of the wall onto the fence. All was going well, and I wobbled across the fence to where it met the house next door. I hadn't planned to go that far, so I didn't quite know which way to go. Back into the house to wait for Bea, into the garden to explore the smells and sights, or to head into the street. I chose the street. I put my newfound boldness down to being a cat, although thinking about it now, it was part of me becoming comfortable with myself.

In front of my house, we had a driveway. There was a brick wall between our driveway and next door's, which stopped when it met the public footpath at the end. Next door had a gate and a wall around their whole front garden; we had a wall but no gate. We didn't really do much gardening, so our front was mainly flagstones with a few potted plants for decoration. We always forgot to water them until Mum suddenly needed herbs for something.

"Hi." I heard a voice and looked down. There was a small white cat sitting on the path. "Are you new here?" She mewed up at me.

"Um, yes. Yes, I am," I replied, wide-eyed and confused before realising I too looked like a cat.

"What's wrong with you? You look sick. Come into the light." She craned her neck. She must have noticed I was quite transparent.

"I'm not feeling too well." I gulped, backing up. "See you later." I hurried back along the wall to the fence and hid in its shadow for a few minutes until I was sure she had gone. Luckily, she didn't follow me.

CHAPTER 6

Ena

Mum arrived back shortly after two with Bea fast asleep in her car seat. She showed me the photographs she had taken on her phone of Bea's face while she watched the ducks. I'd never seen Mum so happy, and it relaxed me. I let her tell me all about how Bea had loved her trip to Tesco's, smiling and cooing at anyone who stopped to talk to her. I told her about my job and lied about visiting the gym, which I instantly regretted as it meant I had no chance of asking to go later. I showered, cursed myself repeatedly, and put on my pyjamas.

We spent a lot of the weekend indoors as it was rainy. Bea wasn't too fussed, but Mum and I needed to get out of the house, so we went for a wander around our local garden centre for a browse and a coffee. Bea smiled at all the plants and tried to pull them from the shelves if we got too close. For a baby, her grip was vice-like. We ended up giving in and allowing her a handful of leaves, which she sat and picked into tiny pieces of leaf confetti across the floor.

That evening, Mum sat in the lounge, watching TV and knitting something. I have no idea what, and to be honest, I didn't think she knew either as she kept stopping, un-ravelling it, and starting over. I tried to concentrate on the show that was on, but my mind kept drifting off to shifting a couple of days ago. I found myself inhaling to see what I could smell around the room, staring at objects on the mantle to see if I could see them any differently, and twitching my ears back and forth. I'd catch myself doing it and flick my focus back to the TV.

"That was unexpected," Mum said from nowhere.

Crap, what had she been talking about?

"Mmmm?" I asked, looking at her.

She rolled her eyes and dropped her knitting on the floor. "Just checking you're still on this planet." She chuckled. "Something on your mind?" She looked me straight in the eye. I hated it when she did that. Suddenly I was five again, hiding cookies behind my back.

"No, just... migraine." I lied, although, if I carried on flitting my eyes back and forth, I was sure I'd get one. I put in a couple of sniffs for good measure, although I wasn't sure she bought it.

"Head on up for a lie down, darling. Bea is flat out,

and if she wakes, I'm here. I can bring her up if she needs you." I nodded robotically, trying to tone down the surge of excitement creeping through me. As I left the room, Mum shook her head and tutted. "Now, where was I with this flipping knotted mess?"

I pushed open my bedroom window and pulled a basket of laundry behind my bedroom door. Not that it would stop Mum, but it might slow her. I got comfy on my bedroom floor as quickly as I could whilst grinning like a lunatic. *Third time lucky.* I crossed my legs, closed my eyes, and took a deep breath. As soon as I made the shift, I took a step towards the door to listen out for Mum. All I heard was the TV and her tutting away at her knitting. I chuckled and surprised myself with the rumbling gurgle sound I made. Cats clearly weren't made to chuckle.

I lowered myself to the ground, ready to pounce up on the windowsill. I wiggled my back end as I did and gauged my balance with my tail. I made it up to the windowsill fine this time and slipped out into the night with my heart pounding.

I was still only just more than a shadow, more formed than I was before, but still had my body back in my bedroom to prove it wasn't a full shift. I screwed up my face in disappointment that I hadn't managed it yet. Sniffing the air, the breeze vibrated against my whiskers. They felt thicker than I expected and picked up vibrations

I wouldn't have otherwise noticed. Amazing.

I decided to stay close to home, just in case I was needed, but ventured a little bit farther into the street. The ground was damp under my paws, which wasn't pleasant, but also wasn't enough to keep me from exploring. I hoped most pets were still indoors with it being late and bad weather. I could smell next door's dinner; chicken and broccoli. Yum. I could also smell something smoky. Perhaps someone was trying to have a bonfire somewhere; the farm nearby was always burning things. My ears pricked up as I heard the roar of a car passing. I leapt back from the curb and gasped. There were so many new noises. I needed to focus, otherwise I would get hurt by ignoring one. The car had sounded deafening as it passed, but it faded to a groan as it moved away. I twitched my ears in every direction I could and pivoted to scan the street. It took me a second to get my bearings. Being so close to the ground and usually seeing everything from several feet higher was taking some getting used to. I couldn't see anything unusual. It all looked pretty much the same, except clearer somehow. I was becoming a little more confident. It was almost like a dream.

I caught movement from the left and turned my head so fast I swear I could have given myself whiplash. I tensed my shoulders and cowered lower to the pavement, reminded that it was still wet when my belly dropped and

I jumped up in disgust. I forgot that the more confidant I became, the more I could feel. The thing moving noticed.

Over a low wall, I saw two pointed ears and a furry face with a long snout and huge black eyes. It cocked its head and put up two paws, craning to get a better look. It was a fox. I could smell her. I don't know how I knew she was female, but instinct told me she was and not to be worried. I settled as she watched me. I nodded towards her, and she dropped down again. I could hear her claws clicking on the path as she rounded the corner to greet me.

"Evening," she said brightly. "Not seen you around here. Oh! You're one of those shifting folk, aren't you? I've seen some of you before." She gave me a sniff and my body shuddered.

"Um, yes. Yes, I am," I replied. I had never spoken to a fox before, so I had no idea what to expect. She seemed friendly enough, and no alarm bells were ringing in my brain, so I stayed for a few minutes.

"I haven't seen one half formed for a while," she continued in her soft voice. She had a slight accent; it was soothing. Her whiskers twitched and she cocked her head again, as if wondering what to do with me. I smiled to let her know I was friendly too, and she let out a sudden barking laugh.

"Ha. Cats don't grin. Not in real life, anyway. Maybe in that story about Alice. Have you heard that one? A dog at the farm was telling me all about it. Apparently, part of it disappears too, a bit like you guys. His human kids love it."

I frowned. "What do you mean, a bit like us guys?"

"There are quite a few round here. Shifters, I mean. More in the city. You'll come across them soon, I expect, unless you already know them. A few have territories in town, but they don't come by this street often, unless they're expecting trouble. Some stay in their chosen forms all the time, and some swap back. I've never seen it, but I know it happens. You can smell it. There's something not right about them." The fox must have sensed my terror. "Oh, not you, deary. I just meant... oh, never mind. A nice girl like you doesn't need to get mixed up in all of their hoo-ha. You look like you're not too sure if you believe it anyway, otherwise you'd be solid like them. It'll come with time if you choose it to, but you need to look after yourself, pet, otherwise you might not be a nice girl for long." She looked both ways down the street, and I opened my mouth to say something, but no words came out. She sniffed sympathetically. "It's a wonderful thing, sharing our world, it really is. I can't say I've ever wished to see your world, but there it is. I'd best be going. I don't have long. Cubs to feed." She winked at me and stood to leave.

"Thank you," I said warmly. "Thanks for the heads up."

She nodded and left me to it. I continued down to the end of the street alone. As she left, I cursed myself for not thinking to ask her questions. Others? Here? More in the city? What was that about not being a nice girl for long? I pushed the thought away. I was overwhelmed enough without adding the worry that there were people like me in that tiny town.

My intention was to go as far as the corner shop then turn back home in case Bea woke. I was losing myself in the sounds and smells of the street I hadn't noticed in my human form. Every time I thought I was getting used to something, I saw something in a different way, like the tiny woodlice at the base of the fence, or the smell of the moss growing along the wall. I could see the edges of things in slightly different shades of colour and wondered if cats were meant to even see in colour.

I must have been deep in thought not to notice it straight away, but when I did, it was too late. I had decided to cut across the driveways of some houses so I wasn't so obvious in the street, but I hadn't banked on being caught by one of the dogs who lived there. The people must have let it out for the toilet, as the first thing that hit me was the strong smell of fresh dog urine, followed by the sound of a low growl. I lifted my eyes slightly, too afraid to move my body. My hair stood on end. It fizzled like electricity. *Please don't see me. Please don't see me.* If I was sensible, I'd have bolted to the back of the house and over the back fence, which was much higher than the one I did choose to leap over. The German Shephard leapt with ease. He was fast too. I skittered under cars and almost ran straight into a lamppost in my desperation to get away. I didn't even know what would happen if he caught me. Could he grasp me with me only being half-formed? What was happening to my body back home?

I saw a conifer on the end of somebody's front garden and made straight for it. Something in my brain told me he couldn't climb; the same instinct that urged me to run faster, even though the rough tarmac was ripping chunks out of my sensitive pads. Out sprung my claws without me having to think about them. I launched myself into the tree and bounded up as high as I could go, then I pressed myself against its trunk and took a breath in. I could hear the dog's owner whistling for him from somewhere a couple of streets away. The dog gave up and trotted back down the road. Suddenly dizzy with relief, I almost fell from the tree. I was so terrified, I must have stayed up there at least half an hour, just watching the quiet road below.

After some time, I decided it was safe enough to come down. I lowered myself back down the tree very ungracefully, slipping and catching my claws. It was then I realised how much my muscles burned, which was surprising because of how much time I spent at the gym.

My paws stung and bled. Resisting the urge to lick them, I hoped my hands at home would be okay. Mum would be terrified; it must look like something straight from Freddy Krueger.

When I reached the bottom of the tree, I became aware of two eyes watching me from down the drive. I had had enough and was ready to walk home and have a hot shower. I didn't have the energy for anymore explanations or conversations. To let the eyes know I had seen them, I gave them a nod and pointedly turned the other way.

"Hey. Hey, wait," came an excited voice. The voice was male, but at that point, I didn't know exactly what this male was. Even though excited, it was also soothing, like the voice of an old friend. I rolled my eyes. I would have to stop and say something. My head told me to go home, but my heart pulled me back.

"Oh, hi. I didn't realise you wanted to talk. Sorry," I said in as tired a voice I could manage, trying to give them the impression I was in a hurry to get home.

"It's okay. I saw you falling from the tree. That was... er... amusing. I wondered if you were lost?" He chuckled as he said *falling*, and I flushed with the heat of anger and embarrassment.

"You did, did you?" I said hotly, and I began to walk. The magic of the connection zipped away quicker than it had appeared. He was making me look foolish. I wasn't lost.

Actually, I *was* struggling to get my bearings. I looked down the road, unsure of myself, but then shook it off and continued to walk anyway. He trotted along after me like a puppy.

"I'm Spider," he said brightly. He had shiny black fur and long, slim legs. I could see why he was named so. His ears also seemed a little too large for his head, and bits of his fur stuck out. I wasn't sure how old he was, but from his voice, I put him around my age.

"Ena," I said without thinking.

He nodded. We walked in silence for a minute.

"Ena," he repeated. I wondered what he had been thinking the whole time he was quiet.

"Yep," I said quickly.

"Nice name. Where's it from?"

"Thanks. I was named after my great grandmother."

He scowled at me. "Is that your real name?"

"No, I often go around giving fake names," I said sarcastically, then thought that might not be a bad idea when it came to this type of idiot.

"Oh," he said.

I stopped. "Okay, why is that such a bad thing? I didn't know we were giving fake names, although I should have guessed when you said your name was Spider."

He half smiled at me. There was something in that

smile that eased me a bit. I could feel he was genuine and friendly; it radiated from him like a warmth, but I was tired, hungry, and he was making me feel stupid, so I shook my head and sighed.

"Well, you're clearly a shifter. I assumed you knew the rules. We don't give out our real identities. It compromises the soul and body in the human world. If someone knows your true identity, they could kill you in both worlds if they wanted to, or hunt you, stalk you, expose you. Anything, really. You must be very new to this. Didn't your teacher tell you the rules before letting you off into the night? Not many witches or warlocks completely ignore the basics these days. Not with so many of us around."

"Teacher? No, I don't have one of those. I didn't know there were any rules. What the hell is a warlock?"

His eyes widened. "So, how did you get here? Did it just happen?" I could hear the excitement building in his voice. He must have noticed too because he coughed and turned away. I had the feeling he was impressed. The way he spoke made him sound a lot younger than I assumed him to be.

"I... um... I read a guide from the internet," I admitted.

He stood up tall. "Woah, really?" I nodded as he paused. "That's really cool. Also, really unheard of. Usually, we have to have a mentor, or at least a family member who shifts. Is there anyone in your family?"

"Just my mum. She doesn't do anything like this. She's pretty average." Understatement of the year. Mum was far from average, but I guessed, in a magical sense, apart from messing about with rocks and stuff, she *was* pretty average. I could see him looking me over and gave in to the urge to straighten up.

"Huh. So, you just came across this guide? What made you go looking?" he asked, pretending to be more interested in his paw. He must have noticed me noticing he was looking at me.

"Well," I began, "my friend found it. She has these chats with...."

"Shhhh," he interrupted.

"What?"

"Don't reveal your real-life stuff. You don't even know me and you're ready to tell me who you hang out with as a human?" He looked at me as if I was crazy. Maybe I was.

"Like I said, I don't know the rules! And how the hell are you going to figure out who I am? Are you going to stand and stare at my house all day like a crazy stalker?"

"People would," he said quietly. "Let's start again. Sorry if I upset you." He winked, and I melted. *How am I suddenly feeling friendly towards a cat?* I almost choked trying to hold back a laugh. Clearly, I needed human adult company of the male variety.

"Oh, gosh. Okay, sorry," I spluttered. "Let's start again."

"Hi. I'm Spider." He cocked his head towards me, and I giggled.

"Hi, I'm... erm..."

"How about Night Flower?" Spider suggested coolly.

"Hi. I'm Night Flower," I said, testing the name. I could go with that. Fake name for my fake body.

"Okay, Night Flower. Let's get you home." He nudged me with his shoulder as he passed me. The shock of electricity that hit me as he did made my breath hitch. I followed him, and the slight change in his swagger suggested he'd felt it too. "Tell me somewhere generic. Somewhere you can find your way to your safehouse without me having to take you to your door. Identity risk."

Safehouse?

"Um, okay. There's a corner shop..."

"Got it." He picked up the pace.

I managed to find my way home and back into the house. Something he said about keeping my identity safe made me feel I needed to be more careful about who saw me flitting in and out of the bedroom window. I sneaked back in and back to my body. Just in time too, as Mum opened the bedroom door.

"Ena," she said hurriedly, and I snapped my head up.

"Oh, what?" I almost shouted, still breathless from my trip.

"Sorry, darling. You fell asleep. I did shout, but you must have been well out of it. I didn't want to wake you, but Bea needs a Mummy cuddle." I nodded as she left the room.

How many times had she shouted? Had she come in before? I looked at the clock. I had been gone just over two hours. No wonder she was coming up to wake me. I stretched and yawned, suddenly feeling exhausted before looking down at my hands. There were no marks, but I would have sworn I had been rubbing them over a cheese grater. Balling my hands into fists to relieve the stinging sensation, I made my way back downstairs to Bea and fell asleep with her in my arms on the sofa. I dreamed of Spider.

CHAPTER 7

Spider

I'd left the girl at the shop as she'd requested but didn't follow her any farther as it was an invasion of her privacy. So far, she had seemed pretty clueless, so I was hoping she'd at least have a think about being more careful before coming back. I hoped she'd be back. She smelled really good for a cat. She'd almost kept her human scent, and it looked like she was finding becoming a solid form tricky. We all had that problem the first few tries though. She sounded like she was telling the truth, yet I couldn't understand how she'd have got so far on her own. Even partial shifts could take years with a good teacher.

I stared down the road into the night. I thought back to Night Flower mentioning her friend, how naïve she seemed telling me everything. Her trust was endearing, but also might cost her. I made a mental note to keep an eye out for her again. Her friend might have more information beyond a guide, and I hoped for her sake she did.

It wasn't really the best time for an unexperienced newbie to be hanging around. I had quite a bit to be doing with my time to be helping anyone else, but I felt compelled to help when I met someone who needed it. Plus, there were other shifters around who would take full advantage of a new girl like her. As much as I wished I was the only one nearby, I wasn't. It wasn't just that though. There was a new, nagging, selfish feeling I hadn't experienced before. One which compelled me to her side. My heart raced as she walked away. I had never met her, yet it was as though I'd known her my whole life. Though our words were few and it was clear our conscious selves didn't know one another, my soul recognised hers.

Things were getting more complicated in the area, meaning that the few of us in our group were expecting something bad to happen soon. At first, I had shrugged it off. I thought our leader was exaggerating. I didn't expect the other shifters would take much notice of us, but after we had offered help to some people from the city who had reached out to us, we had somehow gotten ourselves on some sort of hit list. I knew some of the shifters who didn't agree with how we ran things. I wouldn't have put it past them to enter our territory and cause trouble on a smaller scale, but a larger one, I had doubted until recently. I thought of Night Flower, how easily she had accepted the offer of her name. Although, in my excitement at meeting her, I had forgotten it. Emma? Ava? The thought she might have been recruited and sent in by our rivals crossed my mind. I wouldn't put it past them to send someone out to spy on us. There was something genuine about her though. I knew she was telling me the truth and didn't have anything to hide, apart from her real identity. Who else would she meet and give that information to? I made a mental note to have a chat with our leader about it. Perhaps he might allow me to keep an eye on her.

–

Ena

Mum dropped me at the warehouse reception desk at five-fifteen and waved me off. Bea had begun to cry, and for a second, I almost launched myself back into the car after her, but Mum assured me she'd be fine. I knew I had expressed enough milk for her to last until I came home, plus there was some in the freezer too for emergencies. I made a mental note to sit and do nothing but play with Bea in the morning.

I was greeted by the boss of the company. He was a middle-aged man named John, and he seemed very friendly, which put me at ease. We toured the offices where accounting and the buyers worked, the office where they dealt with the website, and his office in case I needed anything. We found the staffroom, which was tiny but tidy and had a small kitchen area, a couple of comfy sofas, and a coffee machine which I was sure I would make good use of. We then went onto the warehouse floor where I would be working. It was a tall building with a metal roof and sides. High shelving units stood in rows, the shelves in some areas reaching to the ceiling, and I could see small machines with ladders to reach the higher shelves, and a few standalone ladders. On the side of the room nearest the door was a row of printers, which was where we would collect our orders and address labels. To the right of that were stacks of flat-packed boxes and delivery bags, huge rolls of bubble wrap, and paper wrap for packaging. To the left was another office. Inside was a man yelling over the phone. He had his back to me, but I could see he was wearing an old-looking brown suit and ill-fitting trousers. I couldn't hear what he was saying, but the tone of his voice put me on edge.

"So, as soon as Ivan's finished on the phone, I'll hand you over to him. He will be your supervisor," John said brightly, not looking bothered about the man's shouting. "Oh, and don't use any of the ladders or machinery until you've read the Health and Safety booklet and signed the forms."

Unusual name, Ivan. I was sure I had heard it somewhere before, but my brain just wasn't making the connection.

"Are there any others starting tonight?" I asked nervously.

"No. There is another girl working tonight though. I'm sure Ivan will call her over and introduce you when he comes out. There was a young lad too, who sometimes overlapped shifts, but he quit, so I'll advertise his post this evening before I leave for the day. If you're okay waiting here, I've got a few things that need my attention." He turned to leave. "Good luck."

"Thank you again," I called after him, and the door slammed. The man in the office who had sat back at the desk looked up and locked eyes with me. They were so powerful I took a step back. After a few seconds, he looked back to whatever he was doing at his desk and didn't move for another five minutes. I got the impression he knew he'd intimidated me. The curl of his lips suggested he was fighting a smile. I was sure I recognised him from somewhere too. He certainly wasn't someone I knew in my adult life, but maybe someone I had known in school. I stood idling in the doorway thinking it over, until a short girl who must have been in her early twenties or late teens jogged past, did a double take, and jogged backwards back to me. I grinned. I liked her already.

"Hi," she said. "I'm Kym. You just starting?"

"Yep," I replied, trying to be as bright and energetic as she was. She was wearing black trousers, but they were stretchy fabric. *I can wear more comfy trousers tomorrow night.* She wore a smart blouse with a dark grey cardigan, her bright pink hair up in a bun, and in her arms, several packets she had obviously just collected for packing. My eyes wandered back to the office window.

"Ugh, Ivan." She groaned, rolling her eyes. "You may as well knock, or he'll leave you waiting all night. He's not really a people person." As if he heard her, he looked up. "Oops! Best get these packed. I've still got quite a few orders to get through. See you shortly. Honestly though, knock on. He won't actually bite. Trust me, I've baited him enough." She winked and ushered me to the office door before heading to the packaging area.

She was dancing to her own beat and loving it.

I knocked on the door and barely heard the grunt that followed. I pushed it open and coughed. His bright green eyes flashed, and I sensed something very dangerous about him, but I just couldn't get past the old-looking brown suit and the scruffy black hair. It looked like he'd never combed it. His shirt didn't fit well, and certainly wasn't ironed. I would never have put him as a supervisor had I seen him in a line-up of company staff. For someone who looked barely thirty, he could have been quite handsome if he tidied himself up. He seemed like he didn't care at all about how he looked. Still, I straightened up.

"Evening. John said for me to ask you to show me around, please," I said hopefully.

He rubbed his face with one hand like he couldn't be bothered. His eyes flitted to some papers on his desk then back to me. He looked me up and down before sighing. "Fine. It's not as if I have anything better to do, is it, Miss Bedford?" He got up and huffed.

I stiffened. It was going to be a long evening.

He showed me the same things in the warehouse that John had, only he spent a little more time showing me how the printers worked and nodding occasionally as Kym danced past, humming loudly. He gave me an order printout with three items on and sent me off to find them. Each item had two codes; one for the aisle and one for the shelf number. I had to read the item description to match the box on the shelf to the item on the order. It was pretty easy, although some orders had one item on one side of the warehouse and another on the opposite side. Apparently, I wasn't picking this up too quickly as he berated me about not being fast enough reading the orders. He laughed out loud when I mixed the shelves and aisles up on one order, and he took all the tape off another order because I had sealed the box lazily, he said. I swear, he just made things up for the sake of giving me a hard time. For someone who needed the staff, he was giving a very good impression of someone who wanted me to leave.

Every time he came too close, my skin grew hot and my hairs stood on end. There was something about him that made my body fizz and tingle, and I wasn't sure if I was afraid of it or curious. His eyes, even though young, had a depth to them that made me feel uneasy, and the creases on his forehead showed he'd had a frustrating past. No one that age usually had that many wrinkles on their brow, yet he wore them well. His brown suit have wouldn't have been out of place in a bag of rags headed for recycling, and it smelled like he hadn't ever washed it. Although, he did wear nice aftershave. I caught myself inhaling too deeply as he came up behind me, and he gave me a fright by booming, "If you need a tissue, you can have a five-minute toilet break, and I suggest you use it."

Ugh, he really wasn't a people person. Why were all the cute but scruffy ones always complete a-holes?

After about an hour of him timing me and commenting on how awful I was, he slid back inside the office like a snake and picked up the telephone. I didn't see him again until just before the end of my shift, when he came out to tell me the time and flicked off the lights. I hoped I was done. There were no more order printouts on the desk, and I didn't know how to check if there were more to be printed, so I grabbed my things and left, mumbling my goodbyes and thank yous.

-

Ivan

The evening dragged more than usual. I sat in my car, rubbing my temples, trying to relieve the migraine seemed to be brewing. I was mentally exhausted. Too much work, too many people, and not enough sleep. What I wouldn't give to leave everything and drive until I couldn't drive anymore. I could settle by the sea, alone.

People were so frustrating, especially the new girl. I'd wanted more help in the warehouse and had convinced John to look into hiring someone for James's position, as well as the extra night time help. James was one of my day workers who had quit recently, and I needed him. He had always been willing to help last minute, but the pay was crap so, of course, he'd gone. I had taken full advantage of his good nature, and I was just starting to get used to talking to the guy too. It was something I needed to work on. I didn't see people as potential relationships, I saw them for what I could get out of them. I was good at finding a trait I could exploit to make my life easier, and I did it without regrets, usually. If I'd gone a bit easier on him, he might not have quit, and I wouldn't have found myself with the prospect of having to get to know another completely new person. The new girl seemed fine. Nervous, shy, which was fine with me, but it grated on me when it lasted too long. I found myself getting impatient with her because she wasn't picking things up as quickly as I liked. For some reason, I had an unrealistically high expectation of her. Usually, I set my expectations low and had my standards high, but from the second I locked eyes with her, I felt something. A recognition. A feeling that she was there to cause trouble. It was unnerving, and I didn't like to be unnerved.

People were afraid of me. They wouldn't admit it, but they were. They thought I was unhinged, angry, aggressive, and they were right. It stemmed from frustration, mostly. Feeling like I was trapped, and this was all there was ever going to be. Mundane routine and people I didn't want to know, yet I did want to know about her. She put up with my rants quite well, but I half expected her to quit by the end of the week, if I didn't fire her. I sighed. I needed the help in the warehouse. I needed the ratings to go up. If it stopped John from coming into my office so often, that would make me feel better, at least.

I tapped my finger on the steering wheel, thinking back to my first encounter with Miss Bedford... I couldn't remember ever seeing her around town, but I sensed I knew her from somewhere which just made me more unsettled.

The pressure in my head eased, and I became ready

to drive home. I had to work that night for my dad. I couldn't work with a migraine, so I took two painkillers with half a bottle of Lucozade before starting the car.

There was also something else that crossed my mind as I drove, which meant I almost didn't stop at the red light. Something about the new girl had caused me to question how harshly I had treated her. Had I come on too aggressive for her first evening at work? What if she didn't come back? For a moment, I wondered how I felt about that, and not from a work point of view. I didn't know why it would bother me; it usually wouldn't. I decided I wasn't going to let her in, no matter how dazzling her eyes were. She'd quit, I could make sure of it. I didn't need distractions.

CHAPTER 8

Ena

I needed a cup of tea.

Mum hadn't picked me up because Bea was asleep, and she didn't want to take her back out in the car, so I walked home. It took ages. It wasn't that I was physically tired, but I was mentally drained after the constant criticism of everything I did, from not sticking the labels on the boxes correctly, to not being fast enough picking my items. Why was he timing me, anyway? Wasn't it supposed to be me having a trial and settling in? No wonder Kym kept out of the way. She barely had a chance to say goodbye before Ivan slammed the door after her.

The feeling I knew Ivan from somewhere had begun to creep up on me. Maybe I didn't know him from school. In my mind's eye, I pictured a little boy, no older than seven, sitting in the corner of one of our dining rooms. I had passed through the room to get to the kitchen, completely unaware he was there until I heard him talking to himself. He was playing some sort of game, his scruffy black hair all over the place, and he had the clearest eyes I had ever seen. I almost went over to ask him about it but heard my mum and Mr E coming in from outside, so I turned and went straight back upstairs out of the way. I bit my lip.

Could it be the same boy?

–

The plan the following evening had been to walk to work and take a taxi home. Mum and I thought perhaps if I went out as if going to the gym, Bea would be more comfortable about me leaving. Although, when the rain started, there was no way I was turning up for my second night completely soaked. I called an Uber.

I arrived at work with five minutes to spare. I left my coat and bag in the staff room and glugged a quick glass of water. As I did, Ivan swung open the door and strode in. He took one look at me and pulled a face as if to say, *urgh, not you again.* I coughed into my water and turned away, desperately embarrassed as I had sloshed water all down my chin. I faced the wall until he opened the door to leave, snapping, "Your shift starts in two minutes."

I took a deep breath. What a great start to my new job. I looked down at the water drops on my black top.

They were going to show up under the bright warehouse lights, but I had no choice but to head down.

Ivan stood outside his office door with his arms folded as I hurried into the warehouse. He took one look at my top and smirked before going into his office and slamming the door behind him. Why was he such an idiot? Was he trying to embarrass me into quitting? Kym saw me at the door and jogged over.

"He's an arse, isn't he?" She laughed. "Cute enough, but a total arse!" I laughed too and managed a nod.

"Come on, I'll give you a hand if you need it." Kym grabbed my arm and linked it with hers, then practically marched me over to the printer.

For the first couple of hours, I quite enjoyed myself. Kym helped me with a few things. I was happy filling boxes with items people had ordered and taping them up. She also taught me that the orders go a little quicker if you imagine the people ordering them, or what they're going to use them for. Although, her ideas for someone's uses of a ten pack of rubber ducks and a bathmat weren't exactly what I would have imagined. I was standing at the printer, reading an order for two floating shelves, when I turned around to find Ivan standing directly behind me. He hadn't said a word nor made a sound, so I walked into him as I went. His cup of coffee splashed onto the floor, just missing his shirt as he took a step back.

"Are you always this clumsy?" He chuckled, backing

up.

I clapped my hands to my mouth in horror. "I am so, so sorry. I had no idea you were there!"

"Are you always this unobservant, then?" He raised an eyebrow.

"Do you always creep up on people when they're concentrating?" I snapped, immediately regretting it.

His face changed from amusement to anger. "Do you always disrespect your superiors? It's an order form with two items on it. You really needed to concentrate on that?" Before I could answer, he put up his hand about two inches from my face. As I caught my breath, he left.

The ignorant pig. I held my tongue. I wanted to scream at him, but instead, all I could do was pull a face like a duck. How dare he talk to me like that? On the one hand, he was my supervisor, but on the other, he had been so horrible to me. My hand curled into a fist, screwing up the order form and reminding me with stabbing sensations of the pain in my paws the other night. I caught Kym's eye as she skipped past. She put her hand to her mouth in a shocked pose before glancing at Ivan's office window.

I stamped my foot. I had to release my anger somehow, but yet it was so childish. Kym laughed out loud before she disappeared. I wanted to go home. I was done with being brave. I needed my bed.

The rest of my shift dragged, and I didn't hang

around when it was over. Ivan didn't leave at the same time as me. He didn't even leave the office to say goodbye. I was thankful for that, at least.

Mum and Bea were fast asleep when I got home. I ran up the stairs and threw my things into my room before grabbing a towel off the banister for a shower. Shutting myself in the bathroom, I caught sight of myself in the mirror. I looked stressed. I *felt* stressed. Looking into my own eyes, I knew the only way I could escape this feeling was to go to the gym and run it off, only the gym was closed. Perhaps I could meditate. That had worked in the past.

I was already in the bathroom, and the window was open so there was fresh air when the rest of the house seemed stuffy, so it would probably be best to rest there for a minute. I sat on the bathroom floor with my back against the door and concentrated on my breathing.

Drifting off and not sure if I was still relaxing or if I had fallen asleep, I thought I'd open my eyes. When I did though, what I saw took me by surprise. I had shifted unintentionally, without even thinking about it. Whilst trying to meditate and de-stress I had shifted into a cat for the fourth time.

I still wasn't a solid form, but I was definitely less transparent than I had been. Did this mean I was starting to trust my form? Maybe I had been overthinking it.

Rather than switch back straight away, I decided to

go for another wander around. Everyone was asleep. If they woke up, Mum would think I was in the shower, but I wouldn't be too long. Just a quick wander outside to the corner shop and back.

Once outside, I stopped to sniff the air. I could smell the rain from earlier in the evening and feel the harsh push of the wind on my small frame as I left the protection of the wall on the front. I was wary after the incident with the dog, but also a lot more confident. I almost leapt out to cross the road. Perhaps I would meet Spider again. I wondered where I could find him. I had so many questions.

I went to the shop, where I paused to look around. The street was quiet at this time of night. I could see someone walking with their hood up on the other side of the road, and hear a few cars on the next street, but the shop had closed, so it wasn't likely that anyone would walk past. I looked up at the sky. Clouds moved quickly across it in the wind, but between the clouds, I could see the strong pinpoints of light from the stars. I gazed at them, wondering if I could see them better in my form as a cat, when I heard a sniff from behind me. I had to stop zoning out. First at work, and now in the street at my most vulnerable. I whipped around.

"Oh, it's you," I said, involuntarily grinning at Spider.

He winked and chuckled softly. It was so strange how I could be myself without even thinking about it, although I really should have had my guard up. It just felt like he had always been there, like we already knew each other.

"Sorry. I didn't mean to startle you." He purred, trying to cover the fact he had found it funny.

I cocked my head. "I didn't hear you."

"I've been here for ages. I thought you were ignoring me. Are you always so unobservant?" He laughed, staring into my eyes. I almost heard something in the tone of his voice I recognised, but I shook it away.

"How rude." I stuck my tongue out.

"Sorry," he said. "But you really do need to pay more attention if you're going to keep turning up around here. Good to see you attempting this again, by the way. It's fun, isn't it?" He sat down to lick his paw.

It really was fun. It was exciting, breath-taking. An escape from myself I had never allowed myself to experience before. It was as if I was meant to be there. I caught him looking at me, and he turned away. I also liked how this new form and confidence made me feel like I could reinvent myself and be someone totally new.

"Something like that." I found myself purring. "I had a bad day."

"Oh. Well, this is the best solution for bad days. I had one too. Absolute nightmare, so I just had to release."

I nodded. "Same here. Shall we walk?" I offered, although I had no idea where to go.

We wandered around for a while, him scent marking the occasional wall, which I never thought to ask about until I had got home that evening. I'd never seen a cat mark its territory before, let alone someone pretending to be one. I just took it all in, and even though before I had had so many questions, right then, I couldn't think of any. I was happy to walk around the streets, taking in all the smells and trying to remember the route back. After about half an hour, Spider returned me to the corner shop and began to clean his paws again. I wondered why a shifter might want to do this, but I supposed there were benefits to cats keeping themselves clean. I'd better act more like a cat in my shifted form, just in case I missed something important.

"Well, goodnight," Spider said after a few minutes. It was blunt and sudden, like I was being dismissed.

"Oh, okay," I said shortly, blinking at him.

I wanted to say more, but no words came out other than a muffled goodbye. As I walked away, I knew his eyes were boring into the back of my head and I smiled.

CHAPTER 9

Ena

The following day was my third shift at work. I spent the morning in the library with Maisy, where she had gone on for at least forty minutes about essential oils. Honestly, I had no idea where she came up with all of this. I took Bea and we went into the supermarket with Mum afterwards. Exciting times. We spent a lot of time playing and really not doing much else until time rolled around for me to be at work. Bea had napped, and I had made a new playlist called the *dealing with the boss* playlist. Paramore proudly took first spot with *Ignorance*. I really did not want to go to work. Ivan had completely ruined the new job buzz for me, and I was starting to wonder what the hell I was thinking in the first place, and whether I should quit and look for something else. However, I wasn't one to quit so soon, so I decided to give it another go and try to get along with him, even if it just meant smiling politely and avoiding him for the rest of the night. I couldn't have been more stupid for believing that would work.

It started as soon as I arrived. He was on the warehouse floor, giving Kym a dressing down for wearing her headphones whilst working. His eyes were dark and his tone harsh. Something kicked in in my brain which hovered between fight and flight, but I froze like a deer in the headlights, shocked by the snap of his words, not registering them, but feeling them vibrate through me. She stood looking at the floor as he shouted. I was sure there must be some sort of rule or law that prevented him from talking to staff like that. I just stood there and stared when I should have got on with my job. Kym caught my eye for a second before looking back at the floor, and Ivan noticed. He turned to me and scowled. My breathing stopped. I swear, for a moment, I could feel relief from them both at my interrupting. Relief, but for different reasons. It coursed through me like a hot knife through butter. I could almost taste it.

"You should be working. Unless you're enjoying the show, in which case, pull up a chair, grab some popcorn, and then I'll fire you." I must have looked terrified because he seemed to soften. "Get. Back. To. Work." He headed into his office and slammed the door.

Kym stayed looking at the floor until we were sure

he had sat down.

"Oh my God. Are you okay?" I asked, throwing my arms around her. She said nothing but melted into the hug like she needed it. "All that over bloody headphones?" She nodded at me, blinking. "Let's get through the next few hours, then we should go grab a drink or something." I patted her on the back. I could see tears in her eyes, but she didn't cry.

"Sure. Let's just get on with these orders," she said quietly.

I nodded, and for the next hour or so, we worked in silence. The only sound was our shoes tapping on the floor as we worked our way around the warehouse. John popped down at one point too and disappeared into Ivan's office.

"I hope he fires him!" Kym remarked as she passed me. I made a grunting sound in reply.

Kym left at nine, and I still had an hour left, so we didn't go for that drink. Kym promised me we would sometime over the next week if we both still had our jobs. She'd told me Ivan had never had a problem with her working in headphones before, but that day, he must have been in a foul mood already, because he collared her the second he saw her. It wasn't so much what she had done, but the intensity with which he'd dressed her down. Not the things he'd said, but the dark edge with which he'd said them. Kym didn't seem the type of girl who was usually bothered by a superior giving her a slap on the wrist, but there was something more to this I couldn't put my finger on.

The fact that Ivan hadn't left the office since John had been down couldn't have been a good thing. I picked up an order. I had three to go, then they were all done for the evening. I wondered if I could leave early if they didn't take an hour, but then realised there was no way I wanted to ask that question, so I headed off to the back of the warehouse to look for items 625, 783, and 114, which, of course, were on opposite ends of the warehouse. My footsteps echoed on the metal walls of the building and the heat it had held during the day was disappearing. A shiver washed over me in the cold, open space filled with shelves full of things I couldn't see through or past. It put me on edge, but there was nothing to be afraid of. If I was alone, there was no one to sneak up on me, and no one would get past the idiot in the office. I relaxed and continued with my order.

One of my items was on the fourth shelf. Those shelves were really tall, and there was no way I could reach them without using a ladder. I looked up at the boxes and wondered if I could manage one of them one-handed whilst up a ladder. I listened for sounds of Ivan, but I heard nothing but my own breathing.

The item wasn't heavy. It was a wall lamp. I jogged over to the side of the warehouse where I had seen a ladder and brought it back to the aisle. Leaning it against the shelves, I began to climb. As I reached the shelf, I pulled the box toward me, and it was then I lost my balance slightly and let go of the box to grab the shelf.

My foot slipped, and I knocked the box with my hand as I tried to grab the metal shelving unit. The box containing the lamp slid off the shelf and dropped. There was nothing I could do but let it fall. I gasped as I watched it hit the floor then screwed my eyes shut tight and listened to the sound I knew would follow. Ivan's office door.

I edged my way down the ladder slowly, feeling awful for breaking the lamp, but grateful I hadn't fallen with it. Maybe he'd take that approach.

He didn't.

He took one look at the lamp, and then at me with my hand on the ladder.

"You're fired, you silly girl," he said quietly through his teeth.

"I'm really, really sorry. I honestly am. It was an accident," I stammered, hoping he'd listen.

"Going up a ladder alone wasn't an accident. You signed the forms! Why didn't you come and get me? Oh, I know... because you couldn't be bothered." He raised his voice, and I found myself raising mine.

"I would have, but in your mood, you wouldn't have helped me anyway! I just want to finish my shift and get away from you," I told him, then thinking I was too harsh, I added, "I'll pay for it..."

I swear his face was purple. My eyes fell on his wrinkled forehead. If it furrowed any deeper, it would have looked like bark.

"You're damn right you'll pay for it. And another thing..." He was cut short by John, who had been standing behind us the whole time. My face reddened in embarrassment.

"And another thing?" John boomed, his expression stern. "Ivan, your office, now. Miss Bedford, I'm sure the last couple of orders can wait for our morning pickers. Please go on home."

I gulped and nodded, happy to get out of there. "Thank you, sir." I said quickly and turned to leave.

"Oh, and Miss Bedford. You're not fired."

I thanked him again and went to grab my things. On my way out, I heard him talking sternly whilst walking Ivan to the office.

"What the hell was she doing up a ladder on her own? You knew she was on the floor alone," he was saying as he shut the door behind him.

As I looked through his office window, he glared at me. His eyes burned into me like hot knives. There was no escaping this. He hated me. We both knew it.

–

Ivan

A warning. Thanks to that stupid new girl, I'd gotten a warning. To say I wasn't impressed was an understatement. I was fuming. Yes, it was my fault. I had completely forgotten she was out there alone because Kym had left early. I told John as much, which did help a little. At least he knew I hadn't left her alone on purpose. I suppose the fact that she was there in the first place was my fault too. I *had* insisted on more staff. I was relieved I hadn't tried to play the health and safety card to get more staff when I had asked for more help; that really would have made me look incompetent. Still, the girl didn't knock on the door. She knowingly signed the forms stating she wasn't meant to climb alone and still tried to do it herself. I'd have to watch her more closely.

That wasn't really what was bothering me though. My heart wasn't in the job, but I still wanted to do it to the best of my ability. I didn't want to slack off because I thought, without it, I might have fallen apart completely. It was the routine that kept me going, knowing what I needed to do from one minute to the next. I hated not expecting something. This new girl was unexpected.

She'd even had the audacity to argue back. Why couldn't she have just stared at the floor like Kym? Kym deserved it, however. I'd caught her snooping around my office earlier on but had no hard proof to go to John with, other than my word. Let's face it, after seeing how I spoke to the new girl before, why would he believe my word? I didn't know why, but she'd put me on edge. When I saw her dancing around with her stupid music on, I saw red.

I was working for my dad that evening, but I needed half an hour to sit and do nothing. I took off my suit and threw it onto the back of my desk chair, not even bothering to hang it up. I kicked my shoes off at the door and stood in my boxers for a few minutes, breathing deeply and calming my tense muscles. Catching sight of myself in the mirror, the pang of loneliness hit me like a train. I was fit. Some might say well-sculpted or toned, but I did spend a lot of my down time working out. I didn't have much down time though.

On the one hand, I was happy with how I looked. I was fit and could certainly pull off the look of wearing a better suit, but I didn't have the enthusiasm. I had no one to make me feel like it was worth it. I hadn't thought about being lonely before, not really. The last week or so, however, something had crept over me without me noticing. I found myself wondering idly if the new girl had a boyfriend. Or a girlfriend. Even if she didn't, she wouldn't be interested in someone who hated people. Thoughts like that had never crossed my mind when Kym had started working for me. I straightened up and ran my hands through my hair as I caught the sight of my shoulders slumping. I pulled on a pair of shorts and a loose t-shirt before lying face down on the bed, my face buried in my pillow, trying to clear my head.

I must have fallen asleep because a soft knock on my bedroom door made me jump. I looked at the clock. Eleven-twenty. I should have been out ages ago.

"Yeah, I'm up," I called back, and my mum opened the door a crack.

"Are you decent?" she asked.

"Uh-huh." I sat up and stretched as she entered the room.

"If you're that tired, love, get ready for bed. I'm sure your father can manage on his own this evening," she said softly. I could only just see her face behind her thick black hair. She usually had it tied back, but that evening, it was down. It made her look years younger. Her expression was soothing.

"Nah, I didn't ask anyone to cover for me. Plus, I promised Tiz I'd check a couple of things out with him," I said, still stretching.

She nodded but looked thoughtful.

"What?" I asked her as she watched me.

She hesitated but then said, "Why aren't you okay, Ivan?"

Well, that was a loaded question. Did I not look okay? I guessed the answer was that I was okay, but I wasn't feeling myself. I didn't really want to burden my mum with it. Whilst waiting for my answer, she tutted and came farther into the room, picking up my suit jacket and giving it a shake.

"What a bad mother I must be. You're a grown man and you still haven't learned to hang up your things nicely."

I gave her a lopsided grin. "Yeah, the worst." I laughed, taking the jacket from her and putting my arm around her shoulders. "I am okay, but I'm hungry. How about a snack before I head out?" I asked, trying to force a bit of energy into my tone.

At first, I thought she was going to push me to talk about it as she might have done when I was a teenager, but she didn't.

-

Ena

I shifted quickly and leapt out of the window. I was still so annoyed with my supervisor that the only way I could think of to clear my head was to shift. Bea and Mum were fast asleep in the lounge when I arrived home, so I grabbed a can of soda from the fridge, downed it quickly, then hurried upstairs. I had to get the anger out of my system.

Once I'd shifted, I made my way from the fence to the wall at the front of the house and paused before looking down into the street. Everything still and quiet. I needed to run and burn off some of this aggression. I jumped from the wall and ran full pelt along the street, my paws hardly hitting the ground before they lifted me, almost flying across the ground. The wind streaked past me. I didn't think I had ever run that fast as a human. I turned the corner and headed for the edge of the town where it met the fields. I didn't stop until my muscles burned, and I was well out of town. Panting heavily, I decided it was enough and stopped to rest beside a small bridge over the railway lines. There was no artificial light there apart from a couple of street lamps about a quarter of a mile back the way I had come, and one small light underneath the bridge itself, lighting up a section of the tracks. I tried to slow my breathing, suddenly aware it was all I could hear. I would need to listen for sounds of things that might be in the woods, not that I was afraid, but I didn't like being sneaked up on. I gave my legs a good stretch in front and behind me and sat looking back towards the town, the fields, and the bridge behind me. Now I had stopped, I could smell the coolness of the road after the rain, the damp grass, and the oil-soaked rocks between the railway lines. I could see quite well all around me; there was just enough light for me to reflect back, but I worried if I went on, I might lose it. I could hear my heart beating, the hiss of the tracks, the rustle of the leaves in the trees, and I swear a snore from one of the nearby farm houses carrying across the calm, quiet fields.

There, I could be completely alone with my thoughts. The guilt about running out on Mum and Bea started to creep in, so I tried to make sense of the fight at work and how I was going to get through my shifts, absentmindedly flicking my tail and twitching my whiskers. I was still only a little more than a shadow, not a full shift, so that would make it easier for me to be hidden, or so I thought. I caught the whiff of something coming up along the train lines, but I was too late to hide, so instead, I instinctively lowered my ears and head, crouching to the ground with a low growl forming in the back of my throat. After what seemed like forever, a large black and white cat appeared, climbing up the bank from the train lines. He didn't seem surprised to see me. In fact, by the smirk on his lips, he probably knew I had been there for a while.

"Don't worry about me." He purred softly, lowering his head too to show he wasn't going to be aggressive. I eased up a little but kept facing him as he circled me.

"You're only half shifted, aren't you?"

"How did you know?" I asked, glaring at him.

He chuckled, a beautiful low sound, cutting through the quiet of the night. "I'm not blind. I could smell you, so I thought I'd come up and have a look. We don't often get new females around here, so I was curious. I hope you don't mind." He purred, coming closer to me.

I gulped and took another step back. He was strangely alluring, and although part of me wanted to run, the other part of me wanted to stay with this smooth stranger. I was curious about other shifters, and I liked his confidence. His short coat looked shiny in the dim light. He was muscular too; black with white patches, but his face was mostly black. His ears twitched, listening to sounds from all around. He sat down, and I eased a little more.

"I was marking my territory," he continued. "I stick to this end of the town, mostly. I get the occasional male pass through, but rarely females. Especially shifters." He eyed me suspiciously.

"I'm just passing through too," I said, still captivated by his eyes. "Are you a shifter?" He chuckled again, this time sending a shiver right through me. I liked that sound.

I need to get out more.

"I am. I came here a few years back. My name is Eldar. What's yours?"

"Night Flower," I said confidently, pricking my ears back up and sitting down too. "I haven't been here long." He nodded, and I knew he could tell. "I really should get back though."

Something flashed across his eyes. Was it annoyance? Had I upset him? He hid it well with a smile, so I shook it off and tried to forget about it.

"I'll walk you back to town," he said, smiling.

One walk wouldn't do any harm, and it was easier to walk with him than risk offending him by going off by myself. Still, it was another new shifter, and I had completely let my guard down again. I had forgotten all about my supervisor and how angry I was. Now, I was curious and buzzing with anxiousness and excitement. As much as I hated to admit this world existed, I still needed to know more, to do more, to be more.

We didn't say much as we walked. He told me about how he lived as a cat and the territory he lived in. He seemed to like hunting and killing the mice and rats; seemed he had control and anger issues to work through. Mice sounded like a good way to deal with it. I could relate after my need to get away that evening. *Maybe I should consider hunting mice as a way to calm my aggression.* The thought made me laugh. I couldn't kill a fly without feeling guilty, let alone a mouse. Stalking them would probably be difficult for me too with my big clumsy paws. There was probably more grace in a teaspoon.

"Do you eat them?" I asked, fascinated by his way of life. He sounded a bit like Bear Grylls the way he was going on. He loved talking about himself.

"Sometimes." He smirked at me, watching for my reaction. "I mostly leave them for the barn owls, but sometimes instinct takes over and I eat them. That's how

I know it's time to shift back. Where did you say you came from again?"

Even though I was caught off guard by the question he slipped in, I was careful and explained I had come from the city and had travelled to learn how to shift away from my family and friends. He seemed satisfied with my answer and didn't push it further.

I should be more careful heading home tonight, in case I'm followed.

"Many seem to be attracted to this area when they learn to shift. No one knows why." He nudged me with his elbow.

"Magic."

He chuckled. "Yeah, it's probably magic." "Where exactly in the city did you say you were from?" He moved closer towards me.

I frowned and leaned away. "I'm not sure I'm ready to tell you that. We've only just met," I said as brightly as I could to hide the sudden feeling of nervousness.

He moved closer still. "Ah, of course. I mean not to worry you, only this sudden urge to protect you has kicked in, and I'm not sure whether to insist on taking you straight home or not." He gave me a quick wink.

This was new.

We came back to the edge of where I would usually turn down the road for my house, but I deliberately continued, not wanting to give away where I lived. I hoped my scent from my run earlier had carried off in the breeze by now. If he picked it up, he didn't say. I wondered where would be a good place to leave him. Should I head into town, or stop and wait for him to leave?

After a couple more minutes walking, he stopped beside the corner shop. I looked back at him, confused.

"I'm afraid this is as far as I can go," he said. "It is another's territory. I don't think he'd be happy about me entering, even if I am escorting a beautiful female." He winked at me a second time.

If cats could flush, I would have. It felt nice to have someone pay me some attention.

"I see." I glanced behind me towards the town and wondered who else might have claimed this part of it. Maybe it was Spider. I couldn't smell him anywhere. "In that case, thank you so much for walking me most of my way back."

He too looked beyond me into the night. "Your car parked nearby?"

I nodded. I told him I had driven there and parked at a pub in the middle of town. I shook my head after he asked if I had seen or smelled anyone else on my way out towards the country.

"Well, until next time." He purred softly, brushing his whole body against mine, sending little fizzes of heat into my sides. Although I was only part shifted, I could still feel, and he could certainly feel me as he laughed when I shivered involuntarily. My knees turned to jelly and threatened collapse until he broke away from me and turned to head back the way he came.

"Next time, park by the bridge. I'll meet you there."

I winked back at him, which he seemed to like; I could feel it. "I will," I said, watching him leave. He didn't run, just sauntered back down the road, not glancing back.

I sat down, lost in thought.

"He's bad news."

I heard a low rumble behind me and rolled my eyes. "Hello, Spider," I said without turning around. The last time I had seen him, I was buzzing. This time, I was annoyed he'd invaded my privacy, which was stupid with it being a public street.

"What are you doing over here, and with him?" he asked. His tone was a lot different than the last time we'd met.

"None of your business," I said sharply. "More to the point, why were you spying on me? I need to head home."

He dropped his gaze, and his ears seemed to droop slightly. I thought perhaps I had upset him, but I had already made my point. It was none of his business.

"Fine." He too turned to leave, his black tail swaying wildly as he marched off.

Great. Fine time to upset the locals.

I waited a while before attempting to head home. I wondered if I could find my way through gardens and decided that was a job for next time. I made a point of sniffing anything that could have been scent marked on my way back. At first I smelled nothing, but when I did, it was almost like musky aftershave. Very subtle, slightly sexy, but also with a hint of warning. My mind flashed with an image of Spider, although the more overprotective and irritated version rather than the playful one. A little farther along on the edge of my road, there was a stronger, more dominant scent. That of a much older male, laced with woody notes, but as an image of Eldar flashed through my mind, so did the same warning, although this time, the alluring, sexy after scent made my mind spin. My brain was getting all that from a smell? The warning must have been for the males, and the smell of single, confident male clearly for the girls. I laughed out loud and ran home before anyone woke up.

CHAPTER 10

Ena

I arrived home as irritated as when I'd left. The new buzz from meeting someone new had been ruined by the vibe given off by that nosey little Spider. I huffed my way down the stairs to grab another soda. Checking the time on the clock in the lounge, I saw it was gone midnight. I was lucky Bea had stayed asleep the whole time. I gave Mum a nudge to wake her and carried Bea back up with me.

I listened to her pottering about from my bed, trying to calm my breathing without thinking about meditating. I tried to match my breathing with Bea's.

After a few minutes, I heard a noise at the window, a sort of scratching sound, followed by sniffing. I slid out of bed, hardly daring to breathe. Glancing at Bea in her basket to make sure she was still sleeping, I shuffled over to the window. I held my breath as I reached forward to grab the curtain, hooking a finger around it and pulling it to the side. When I saw nothing, I pulled it back a little further, trying to position myself so I was partially hidden behind it while keeping Bea out of sight.

There was nothing there, just the darkness outside and my open window, which I reached up and pulled closed. Suddenly there was an ear-splitting screech, and a pair of huge, clawed feet crashed against the window, sharp talons scraping the glass. I screamed and leapt back. As I did, I woke up. Panting, sweating. It was only a dream.

The next morning, I sat in the kitchen with a cup of tea whilst Bea splatted yoghurt over the kitchen floor, occasionally stopping to dance to a song on the radio or aim some yoghurt at me. Mum had popped out but came back around lunchtime. She handed me something I half hoped would be food as my stomach was growling from not eating since yesterday. Instead, it was a smooth oval of haematite. I stared at the shiny black stone for a moment and looked Mum in the eyes. "What's this for?" I asked her, wondering if she'd noticed me slip out the night before and was trying to distract me into telling her where I had been.

"You know what it is," she said with a smile, busying herself putting her shopping away. "I picked it up whilst I was out. Mr Ealing brought it for me from the shop. I felt you were quite angry and upset when you came home last night, so I thought a nice piece of calming haematite could help."

I looked from the mineral to my mum. I had never really put much belief into energies or powers of rocks, even though I loved the look of them and had collected them over my life. I had always seen them as something beautiful but never practical. I was certainly more grounded now though.

"Um, thanks," I said, not knowing what else to say.

She pulled me into a hug. "Don't worry about a thing," she said simply. "Whatever it is, it'll pass." It was just like Mum thinking a rock could solve all my problems, and faking she was asleep? She must have thought I was in my room crying or something the whole time.

–

That night at work, I only saw Ivan briefly. He seemed so much more grumpy than usual. He spent most of his time in the office on the phone, only coming out occasionally to tell Kym and me to work faster as they were expecting a big week with a sale approaching. They were expecting a delivery the following morning, so they needed the warehouse clear of orders. He looked like he hadn't shaved in days, and the stubble was starting to show. The thought he might be attractive was dismissed as quickly as it came. There was no way he could be a nice person. I refused to allow myself to think on it, especially after having thoughts about two others I had literally just met.

Wow, it was true what they said. You go along not meeting anyone, then they all arrive at once. I understood what it was like to be living in one of Maisy's crappy romance novels. Kym and I worked mostly in silence; we both had our headphones in for most of the evening. Kym insisted John had said it was okay, and even though we didn't speak to each other, Kym danced and sang around the warehouse like she owned the place, which made me a lot more positive. That was until Ivan came out and made us put our headphones and phones away in a locker. I'd have argued, but I really didn't want to cross him again. According to Kym, he had received a warning for leaving me on the warehouse floor alone knowing I needed help with equipment, and for making me feel like I couldn't come to him when I needed it. I asked her how he got away without being in more trouble. A warning hardly seemed fair, but then, I guess I didn't exactly ask him to help me, and I had signed to say I understood the rules. Surely I should have gotten into trouble too, but Kym said John would have felt sorry for me if he caught Ivan having a go, and that Ivan had lied about knowing I was alone. I guessed John had also warned him about how he spoke to us on the warehouse floor, because that evening when he spoke directly to me, it was with forced pleasantness. It was quite entertaining seeing the look of frustration in his eyes, and his pursed lips and gritted teeth.

"Ten minutes to go!" Kym sang, with a quick glance at the office window before pulling me to the back of the warehouse by my elbow. I giggled. She'd stayed on a bit later to help clear orders. It had been a busy day on the website, but we had got it all done between us.

"There, the grumpy guts can't see us now."

"Isn't there a camera?" I asked, scanning the high ceilings.

"Not over here. Man, I need a gin. Tonight was long."

"I just want to curl up with Bea and sleep for a week." I yawned.

"Bea's your baby, right? Just you two and your mum at home?" she asked, peering around the corner of a unit.

"Yeah, she is, and yep, just us. So how about you? Who do you live with?" I asked, realising we'd not actually had this conversation yet.

Kym shrugged. "No one important. No one who cares, anyway. You know who does care though? This super hot guy I'm meeting after work. Honestly, the things he can do with his... Hey, why are you laughing?" She hit me playfully on the arm. Any sadness I had begun to feel over how quickly she brushed over her home life vanished the second she changed the subject.

"Sorry, you just become so excitable when you talk about men. I'm afraid I'm a bit of a prude."

"No way. You're gorgeous, you are. How many?" "How many what?" I was confused, but as she waggled her eyebrows, I got the point.

"Oh, geez. Not many. One or two."

She grinned at me. "Wow, you need help, missus. I swear I'll find you a man by the end of the year."

"What if I don't need one?"

"You really do. I can hook you up. Trust me, I know all the best ones. We'd best go now though, or psychopants in there will be wondering what we're up to."

We collected our belongings and left at the same time. I was lost in thought over whether she was right about me needing a partner? I didn't need a man. Not for any sort of status nor comfort, but a bit of fun.... I wasn't sure male cats counted, but I did enjoy their company. Following Kym to the door, I had to cover my mouth to stop me from laughing as she loudly announced, "Ivan, darling, shouldn't forget my overtime," before slamming the warehouse door. When outside, she jumped into a waiting taxi whilst I walked towards Mum's car, which I had driven to work.

I got in, started it up, and pulled out of the car park. I saw the police roadblock about a quarter of a mile down the road. Two police cars were parked with their lights on, and three policemen were standing by, letting cars through one at a time. They seemed to be checking inside the cars and boots too. It wasn't too dark yet with it still being summer, so I didn't feel as worried as I would if it had been dark. I saw Kym's taxi pass through, then it was my turn to pass the policemen.

I wound my window down ready, and he stooped down to look inside.

"Evening, Miss. Sorry to hold you up, but there has been an incident this evening and we're checking with the public in case they've heard anything unusual or seen anyone unusual."

I nodded. "Yes, I'll help any way I can."

"Thank you. Do you mind if I have a look in the back of your car? It would be helpful if you stepped out too."

"Of course. Take a look." I clicked the unlock button so he could open the boot. One of the other policemen smiled at me and shone a torch into the back of my car, pointing it down into the footwells. As always when something like this happens, my mind flicked to the worst-case scenario, and I imagined some burglar hidden in the boot of the car with a gun. My boot was empty, apart from a couple of bottles of water and a blanket.

"May I ask where you're coming from and where you're going?" the officer said, coming back to the front of the car. "Let's start with your name."

"Ena Bedford. I've been at work, on the business

park. I'm heading home," I told him, and he took my name and phone number on his note pad. I waited patiently for him to finish.

"Have you seen anyone acting suspiciously this evening? Or earlier on today if you've been out?" he asked, tapping his pencil on his notebook.

Unless he counted Ivan acting suspiciously pleasant...

"Nothing at all, sorry. The only people I've seen this evening were at work with me, and I saw nothing heading in." I pursed my lips and shook my head. One of the other officers shone their torch into my car one last time, checking the footwells.

"Okay. We have your details so we will ring if we need to ask you about anything else. Please call us if you remember anything, no matter how irrelevant it might seem." He wrote down a reference number on his notepad, tore off the page, and handed it to me.

"Quote this number if you do call." He gave me a smile and opened my car door for me to get back inside.

I nodded and thanked him, then I drove home.

I had no idea what or who he was looking for and had almost forgotten about it when I arrived home because I had been thinking about shifting.

Mum saw me pulling onto the drive and opened the door, holding up a piece of paper. "Police were putting these through letter boxes," she said, flustered. I took the leaflet and read it to myself. They were looking for a suspect and said not to be alarmed if we see the police in the street or checking gardens. The same reference was on the bottom.

"Yes, they checked my car. Roadblocks too. Must be serious," I said, handing back the paper. She didn't say anything, but I knew from her face she was worried. "Don't worry, Mum. They'll be long gone by now if they haven't got them yet." I smiled. Bea looked like she was asleep in her basket, so I said I was going up for a shower.

By the morning, I'd forgotten all about it, and Mum didn't mention it again. She was busy messing about with some herbs in the kitchen, and by the smells of it burning something she'd tried to cook. I didn't ask as she'd probably be embarrassed, but I cooked Bea and myself some eggs and settled in front of the TV for a bit. It was a lovely day out, so we managed to get over to the park. I dragged Mum out for a while too as she seemed a little off; maybe she was tired with being back to school soon. She needed to go into her classroom to move a few things around, so Bea and I had some time alone to wander over to the library before I had to be at work.

I told Maisy all about my supervisor over a coffee and Hobnobs. She seemed to be enjoying my descriptions of his many furious faces until something flashed across her eyes and she held her hand up to stop me mid-sentence.

"Wait, where are you working again?" she asked with a mouth full of biscuit.

"Over in the Gateway warehouses on the business park. Some online company. I've already told you what I...."

"No, not that... your supervisor. Is his name Ivan?"

I swallowed my coffee in a gulp and nodded. "Oh my God, yes. Yes it is!" I said.

I knew Maisy would know who it was. She glanced over at the opposite side of the library where Mr Ealing had settled into his favourite chair, reading a book about gardening. I gave Maisy a questioning look and she shrugged it off. Last week it was witchcraft, now it was gardening.

"So, where do we know him from? School?" I asked, returning to our conversation.

"It's Mr Ealing's son! Ivan Ealing. He's a right shit. Bad attitude, but bloody gorgeous. A bit scruffy though, but I only see him on occasion when he pops in to pick his dad up. I used to see him more often when visiting you, but he rarely came with us."

I wasn't sure what to say. I knew I'd recognised his name from somewhere, but it just hadn't clicked. Should I tell him? No, definitely not. I didn't want to give him any reason to be on a more personal level with me. I wondered if he knew. He'd read my CV. Surely he'd have remembered my name. He hadn't mentioned it though.

My mind flew in many different directions, until Maisy clicked her fingers in front of my face. I blinked at her and almost spilled my coffee.

"Earth to Ena." She laughed. "Does he recognise you?"

"I hope not," I said with a defensive tone, glancing again at Mr Ealing.

CHAPTER 11

Ena

I survived my first whole week at work, and as Mum was going back to work on Monday, we had a nice, quiet Saturday morning lazing about the house.

I thought about going into the gym that morning. I hadn't been in a while, although I pretended I had. I really should have gone as I missed the gym, so when Mum offered to take Bea out for the afternoon, I was pleased to have some me time. They left just after lunch, and I packed my bag ready to go. I'd had every intention of going. However, like an addict, the thought of shifting tugged at me from somewhere in my mind. No one was home. No one would be home for hours. No one would notice I hadn't been to the gym, so what was stopping me? I was a little nervous after meeting both Spider and Eldar over the last week, and I wondered who else was out there. Perhaps this new addiction would lead me down a path I couldn't return from, like the fox had hinted at. I should be more careful and put up some boundaries for when I met them again. Screw it. I had to have one more try, then I would leave it alone. I practically ran up to my room and dumped my gym bag outside the bathroom door.

I had a drink of water from my gym bottle and opened the window before shoving a stack of laundry behind the door and sitting cross-legged by my bed. Within minutes, I was outside in the sunlight, feeling its warmth on my back and taking in the new smells things gave off when they had been in the sun. Sniffing the leaves, I could almost smell them letting gases go. It was the freshest thing I had smelled in my life. It was so beautiful, I sat on the corner of the street with my eyes closed and my head back, nose to the sky, just feeling the world around me. Now I understood why cats laid around on the ground so much when the weather was nice. The cool ground below me balanced out the rays from the sun so my paws didn't feel hot. My fur fizzed though. It was strange to admit, but I was more myself than I had ever been. Like this was perfectly normal to me. Could I really give this up?

In the daytime, I had the confidence to go a little farther afield, so I passed the corner shop and headed down towards town. Before I reached the shops, I turned to the left and made my way toward the park, as if something was tugging me in that direction, like a piece of string had attached itself to my front and was pulling me along. I didn't think much of it and just followed my instincts. I trotted along the pavement, making sure I kept to one side, avoiding the feet of passers-by. No one seemed to notice me at all. It was also amusing to learn that from down there and with a much better sense of smell, people all smelled totally different from one another.

The park was busy, of course. It was Saturday lunchtime. Children ran around the playground, up and down the slides and on and off the swings. Mums, dads, and caregivers milled around on their phones or talking to each other, the occasional dog looking in my direction, but none were interested in me. I found a nice spot on the grass to watch, somewhere more shaded because I was starting to feel overwhelmed by all the brightness and noise. There must be a way to get used to it or filter some of it out.

I sensed another's presence and flicked my ears, my muscles tensed, ready to run. I think they wanted me to see them as they made a lot of noise in the hedgerow behind me. Maybe they knew I was new and didn't want to startle me. They smelled familiar but not someone I knew, so I sucked in a breath for confidence, then turned and smiled.

"Ahh, it's lovely watching families from this side of the hedge, isn't it?" The old cat purred. Her cracked voice seemed to speak in a way that made me feel instantly relaxed. Like a warm hand was patting me on the shoulder.

"It is," I said. "Do you sit here often?"

"I wouldn't say often, but often enough."

"I sense you're a shifter?" I offered, feeling bold. She smiled. When she did, her eyes glistened and danced, and her long eyelashes flitted as she blinked. I realised she seemed pleased with me saying that.

"I have been hearing things about you, so thought I would come and have a look for myself. Let me take a look at ye." I stood up straight, trying not to move, and allowed her to walk around me and give me a sniff. She laughed. "Sorry about the formalities, but sometimes a good sniff is the best way to find out about who a person is."

We watched the children play for a little longer. Her body was slightly larger than mine, her fur long and pale at the edges, but in the middle, a rich chocolate brown. One of her ears was torn, and her tail was short and stubby, but by the looks of it, it hadn't started out that way. One of her paws was white and another grey. She smelled like ginger biscuits and peppermint tea.

"I was told you have no teacher," she said. "No coven. No one to teach you the basics. Is there no one in your family you can think of?"

I shook my head. "What's a coven? And how did you know where I would be? Did you follow me?" I said, feeling comfortable enough to ask. I didn't notice anyone following me, but then I was too busy thinking about how passers-by smelt.

"A coven is a group of witches, sometimes friends and sometimes family. They can be men or women, but usually more than three of us."

My eyes widened. "So, you're a witch too? Do you need to be a witch to be a shifter?" I wasn't a witch, so that sounded silly when I said it out loud.

"No. Witches feel the energy in everything around them and have much respect for it. Sometimes through rituals you can help positive things happen and influence that which might not normally be influenced. Some witches found out they could take on the characteristics of an animal, and some found they could change into an animal completely. Although there are a few of us in this area, it isn't really a common trait in witches."

"So are there also shifters who aren't witches?" I asked. "Like warlocks?" I was sure Spider had asked me about those days before.

"Warlocks, eh? Well, they're witches who have been left behind by their coven for some reason. Either left or removed because of something they have done to hurt those closest to them. It isn't usually a word we use unless we have to. They don't tend to use the nicest kind of magic and have learnt to manipulate it in a way we choose not to."

"I'm sorry," I mumbled.

"It's okay. Everyone has to learn the basics first. Without dark, there would be no light. Unfortunately, opposites need something to be compared to. There are many shifters who only shift. Some don't believe in anything else. Some happened upon it by accident like you, however, everyone has the potential to become a witch." She was watching me as though waiting for something to register with me, but I wasn't sure what she was getting at.

"Oh, I thought it was like a family, generational thing."

"No. No one is born or forced into it. All we ask is that you choose it for yourself and are good to yourself and respect the energies of those around us."

"That sounds good."

"That's what I was hoping you'd say. Now, I can go through the basics if you like? It's fine to be on your own, but especially with you still being in partial shift, it's probably best if someone gives you a few ground rules for the area, especially as you might have been in contact with a few more unsavoury shifters recently."

I frowned as she finished. "So, it was Spider who told you about me. I thought he was following me around like a puppy." I almost growled in frustration.

"He does seem kind of fond of you." She chuckled, her voice soothing my growing anger. I couldn't talk to her without feeling secure and calm. I wanted to stay mad but found it impossible. Plus, when she said he seemed fond of me, my heart had skipped a beat.

Nope. I wasn't going there.

"Well, I guess he's not too bad. It has been nice to have a friend." That was true, at least.

"The problem with Spider is he prefers this world to the one he lives in. When he's human, he doesn't know how to connect with people, and the more he loses himself in this world, the more ties and friendships he has, the more time he spends here. It can be useful to my coven and my friends, but he becomes less human every time I see him. I fear one day he'll never come back."

"So, you know him as a human?" If she hadn't had my attention before, she had it then.

"I know a few of the shifters in human form, yes. Not many know me, but I know them. I suppose I have a gift for feeling and influencing energies. I can guess who a person might be if I have met them in both forms. It's a bit like matching pairs, but I need to have met them in both forms first usually. Sometimes I only have to pass them in the street to pick it up. Often though, it's a lot more subtle. Take you, for example, my dear. Even though your energy is subtle, it shows to those who know what to look for. I recognise you and your energy, child, and that is how I knew exactly where to find you. I'm sure I am not the only one to possess such a gift, so this emphasises the importance of keeping your identity secret and using the safehouses which are guarded either by spells or those who have left the human world completely to live in their shifted forms permanently. Oh, yes. There are some who you would never know once began as humans because they have been in their taken forms for so long. I am one of the original shifters in this area. I have been here for many, many years and because of this, many come to me for guidance. They call me The Wise One. Wise? I'm not too sure about that. Old, certainly, but not too old. Certain magics age people quicker than others, and I have certainly used a lifetime's worth of protective magic in my time here."

I lay in the sun and took it all in. I wondered why Spider being there forever was important to her. If she knew him in both forms and worried about him, would she be worried about me? That I might have done something to influence him? I dismissed the thought as I had only just met him, and the way she spoke, it seemed she was thinking maybe I was going to be around for quite a while. At least I knew how she found me. My face wrinkled involuntarily as I processed that she might have met me in real life. I strained to think of everyone I knew and drew a blank. I knew no one like her. I sighed as I realised I probably should head home. I thanked The

Wise One for her time and advice, and she insisted I come find her if there was anything I needed to know. I agreed I would and headed back home from the park.

The sunshine was beautiful, and I was enjoying the walk home until I got the feeling I was being followed. I should have been completely used to that feeling by then, and spun around, expecting to see Spider, but there was no one there. Shaking it off, I continued, but that something that told me something wasn't quite right gnawed at me, and I started to run. Not too fast at first as people would notice, but as I did, I heard the scrape of claws on the cobbles of something trying to keep up with me.

I cut down a narrow street, hoping I could speed up and disappear into one of the gardens, but whatever was following me was quicker, and it was on my heels sooner than I had expected. Sharp teeth nipped at my ankles, and instinctively, I spun around to claw whatever it was away. A thin, gangly creature snapped at me. Pulling my head back, I saw it looked a bit like a ferret; it smelled like one too. That suffocating, musky scent. Sharp, clicky teeth gnashed closer. I tried to bat it on the head with my paw. One blow landed, and it stopped for a second in disbelief before coming at me again. It grabbed my front paw and tugged me to the ground. My jaw connected with the pavement, but I pushed myself up and swiped again, missing. The ferret kept coming at me, hissing. I made a yowling noise as it grabbed my fur and pulled. I couldn't shake him off. The smell of blood filled my nostrils as he grabbed my paw again, this time breaking the skin. I screeched and swiped as hard as I could. The swipe made contact and knocked him back for a second, long enough for me to turn tail and speed down the street, my tail flat against my back. There was a man dragging a huge bag of leaves from his garden to his car. I leapt on top of the bag and up onto the roof of his car. The ferret was faster than me but couldn't leap as high. He hadn't expected me to head straight for the man, and I was so lucky to have gotten up high. The man saw me and then the ferret. He took one of the logs from the top of the bag and threw it. The ferret dodged it, then dodged another before giving up and pelting off back down the road. I collapsed in exhaustion on the car roof.

The man closed his boot and went back into the house, returning a few minutes later with a side dish of water. I lapped it up gratefully and even allowed him to stroke my fur. Against the roof of the car, he couldn't tell I wasn't fully formed. I thought it best to leave before he noticed.

CHAPTER 12

Ena

Every few steps, I stopped to check what was behind me. I sniffed everything along the way. I didn't think I'd feel relieved seeing Spider scent marking the sign and lamppost by the corner shop. He seemed to sense something was wrong because he dashed over to me like a protective big brother.

"What happened?" he asked.

I curled up with my head buried in his shoulder and cried. I couldn't hold it back. He just sat there and let me get on with it. Once I had embarrassed myself enough by crying all over him, I told him what happened.

"I know of him," he said. "You probably wouldn't believe me if I told you he was mates with your new friend. Perhaps you'd best head home and rest. You'll probably need to eat, and check if those cuts have affected your real body."

He was right, so I went home. He didn't attempt to follow me, just stared sadly after me as I left. Part of me thought it was strange he didn't want to follow me to make sure I was safe, but part of me was happy for the separation.

It was a good thing too. I was on my way home as Mum passed me in the car. If she checked my room and found I wasn't there but the door was locked and my keys inside, she would have a lot of questions. Luckily, I could go through a couple of gardens joining onto ours and arrived back into my room at the same time as she opened the front door.

Mum called me from the hall and I shouted back as breathlessly as I could manage.

I listened for her closing the front door, shoved the laundry out of the way of my bedroom door then slipped into the bathroom and turned on the shower. The hot water coursed over my aching muscles, and even though it stung like hell where I had been bitten, it hadn't broken the skin in my human form, although there were a couple of bruises I would have to blame on gym equipment.

I dressed and wrapped a towel around my hair then skipped into the kitchen as brightly as I could to hide the shock of how terrified I had been and how much I needed to cry into a pillow. I was about to ask Mum what we were having for dinner when I saw she wasn't alone. There were two police officers in the kitchen with her. Bea sat in her high chair and started to wave her arms and shout *mama* when she saw me. I grinned and scooped her up for a big cuddle.

"Sorry, I had to shower after the gym," I said politely. "Everything okay, Mum?" Mum looked at the officers and then back at me. "Oh, gosh! I'm so sorry. Were you waiting outside whilst I was in the bathroom? I had my music on loud."

The male officer said they hadn't and not to worry. Mum had no reason to believe I wasn't just in the shower whilst someone was at the door waiting.

"I'll have a chat with her now, fill her in on the details," Mum said to them, running a hand through her hair.

The female took her hand. "If you need us, you have our number," she said in a soft voice.

Giving me a nod, she and her colleague made for the door and Mum locked it behind them. I sat at the dining table, waiting to hear what had happened. My heart raced. Did they know about me shifting? Did they know I had been attacked? I was being selfish. What if something had happened to Mum? I opened my mouth to ask her, and she put up her hand.

I watched as Mum filled the kettle and put a spoon of tea leaves into the teapot. She wrung her hands together, and the look on her face I will never forget. It was the look I had seen many times before. Before we had had to move away.

"It's your father," she began. "He has been in the area looking for us. I don't know how he knew we were here after all this time, but I guess we've become too comfortable and that's that."

I wiped up the slobber on Bea's face with a cloth and pretended to be preoccupied. Bea was completely oblivious and continued to chew on her hands and slobber some more over my clean vest.

"The police say he was involved in an incident on Thursday. They didn't tell me what exactly except that there were three of them and he was one of them. The police dogs tracked him to the end of our road before they lost him, so the police wanted to check if he had tried to make contact." Her hands shook as she tried to pour the tea.

"I'm sure he won't bother with us. Maybe he just remembered the area and thought he could hide in one of the gardens?" I offered.

She shook her head. "If he's here he, must know. If he doesn't know, he will do soon. He has a sixth sense about these things." She almost dropped the teapot. I placed Bea back into her highchair and passed her a couple of soft raspberries to suck. I took the teapot and mugs from Mum, and after putting them on the table, I took her hand.

"I'm here now. I can understand how hard it must be after all this time," I said, suddenly thinking about how I'd pushed her away as a teen as she'd hidden from him. "I'm sorry how I reacted in the past, and..."

"Never apologise for how you felt. I never fully explained to you how dangerous he was, and how frightened I was that he might come back. He can be charming, and one meeting with you and he'd be off with you. I'd never find you."

I hugged her tightly. "He'd have a hard time doing that. I'm not a little girl anymore, Mum." I gave her a squeeze.

She glanced nervously toward the lounge window. "Can you nip through and close the blinds? Just in case?"

I nodded and then closed all of the blinds in the house. Just in case.

–

Spider

It was a beautiful day. The sun had been warm, and we were able to move around a lot easier when it was warm. Humans seem to be more complacent, more at ease. Distracted by the weather and focusing on playing with their families or enjoying the sun. People expect animals to keep to themselves when the weather is nice, so we get a lot less attention. If you're a shifter, this is perfect. Night time is also great for shifters. People expect some animals to be out and about in the evening and don't stop to give us any bother. It's on those days in between when it's cool or overcast that people tend to notice us more.

I'd had a lie in. Something I didn't normally do, but I was exhausted after all the running around I had been doing that week, especially the night before. Still, I had managed to visit a few of the safehouses that belonged to our small group. Usually, I had a lot to do with the magic on the houses which kept them hidden from sight. They were still there, but people didn't see them the same way they'd see another house. The night before, we'd had a security breach. It was common, and usually members from a rival group trying to mess us about and keep us on our toes. On occasion, it was just a random wandering around like Night Flower. She was on our radar now, and we needed to watch her. I was sure she wasn't a threat, but we had to watch her just in case, especially with her little wander over to meet with Eldar. Just the thought of him made my muscles stiffen and my teeth bite together. The thought of him with her did things to my insides I didn't know were possible. The more I thought, the more I was convinced her home must be in that little pocket on the edge of town where our territories blurred slightly. Eldar was allowed up to the crossing by the corner shop where I had left Night Flower on the night I had met her, so I couldn't access the housing estates from that side. I could from the back though. So, I assumed, if they wanted to follow her and she did live on one of those roads, they might be able to get to her house. I was secretly hoping it was at the back where our territory took over.

The thought had occurred to me the night before when checking the boundaries. I had been sent out with my friend Tiz to re-mark, check, and see if we could find anything out about the breach. We didn't usually spend any amount of time on that side of town because there was nothing to report most of the time, but there had been a criminal there, one which was known by my group from the city. The police had been out looking for him too. We thought they believed he was part of a robbery. I couldn't get much out of the dogs up at the police station, but they promised to try and find out for me. Why he had really come into town, we didn't know, but we guessed he knew we had only last week smuggled out a family from him and he was angry. The criminal ran a gang in the city, controlling shifters and those who couldn't shift at all. Drug dealers, thieves, those who owed him money. Some found they were in his debt and couldn't get free, this was the case for the family we helped to escape. As humans, the man in the family was a lawyer, and we didn't know exactly how he ended up in the clutches of the gang who lived in the city, but they were blackmailing him to pull strings for them. They were using his wife and small son to persuade him to lie and change evidence in some cases which were coming up. He told us he had also been asked to steal confidential files from his offices. He had come to Tiz one night in his shifted form, worried he'd be found out and jailed and then he couldn't help his family leave, or worse, fail and they would kill them all. Tiz and I had formed a plan. We had driven to the city. Tiz and I were very careful and there weren't many who knew us as humans and shifters. We posed as family friends taking them out for the day and managed to temporarily relocate them in town in one of our safehouses whilst another one of our friends worked on making fake documents for them and changing all their contact details. In the past, the boss of the gang of shifters in the city hadn't retaliated when we had freed someone of 'his', but he must have really needed this lawyer because, the night before, the town was crawling with shifters from the city. It took hours to find them all and fight them back, hence me feeling worse for wear.

We had picked up the gang bosses' scents all around this little dead-end road. I was following procedure and searching gardens for scents when I came across one which was frightfully familiar to me. It was a warm yet fresh scent, a bit like rose petals in the sun. It floated in layers on the footpath just outside one of the houses and got stronger as I approached.

One of the houses in the row we were checking was

the home of a lady who was a witch. I didn't know a lot about her, but I knew that our Leader and The Wise One did. She lived there with her family, and they didn't know about her being a witch. There were a few of them around, women or men who had once belonged to our coven but had left for some reason. They were still afforded the same protection as anyone else in our boundary. I could feel the magic coming from the house, see them almost like a haze of greens and blues. It made me smile at the subtleness of them. She'd used older magic to protect it, and even though it wouldn't stop someone like us who might try to get in, it would give her enough warning to get out and was useful at repelling normal burglars and opportunists.

Tiz sniffed at the gateposts and the walls before giving me a huge grin and winking at me. I laughed and swatted at him playfully. I had told him of Night Flower, and he was convinced I was becoming obsessed with finding her again, although he couldn't deny the scent on the walls was as beautiful as it was dangerous. He said it could possibly just be the lady who lived in the house if she still shifted from time to time. The lady who lived there, who was known by our witch, The Wise One, must have been in her late forties or even fifties. There was no way she could have been Flower, so I left the street feeling a little deflated and disappointed. The feeling quickly left me as, on my way back to town, I bumped into the girl herself. I wanted so much to be mad at her for how things were the other night, but the little bubble of something pushing its way to the surface told me now was not the time.

Tiz had gone back the way we had come to make sure we hadn't missed anything. He was hungry, so I guessed he wanted to head back, and I was about to make my way back home for a long afternoon sleep. I walked back along the garden walls, avoiding the main path, part of which wasn't on our territory anyway, and headed for the corner shop. After seeing Eldar there the night before, I marked the hell out of that to make my point. He'd probably cross one day anyway, and I'd be waiting when he did. The Leader had made all of us swear not to touch them if they were on their side, and we were to ignore anything they might try to get us to cross. I'd have loved to sink my teeth into his smug face.

My paws ached, so I stopped for a moment to stretch my long legs and give my claws a scrape on the fence. I loved the feeling of my sharp claws catching on the wood, the way they sank in with ease. As I pulled my paws down, they pulled the muscles connected to my claws and sent a shiver of pleasure through what would be my arms and into my shoulders. I did it twice before feeling better, then stretched my back legs and marked the lamppost. Almost as if summoned, she appeared. She looked terrified, and I could smell that she'd been running for her life.

She poured it all out whilst sobbing into my shoulders. At first, I didn't know what to do or say. I didn't make a habit of comforting people, and despite the way I'd come across as bouncy and playful, I really was far from it. Being a cat allowed me to feel like myself. Like I didn't have to explain myself or put up a front. I didn't feel alone, but I didn't make a habit out of seeking this sort of close attention from others. But the need to comfort her washed over me, to keep her safe and allow her to let it all out. At the same time, I sat rigid, not knowing exactly how to do that. Luckily, she took the lead, and I went with it. I was confused. She seemed so fragile, I could have held on to her and never let go, but as she explained what had happened, I grew angry. I knew exactly who she was describing, and I fought the urge to growl and head right over the boundary I had just marked to find him. I held on to her as long as I could until I had calmed down, not wanting to scare her if the look in my eyes was one of aggression and fury. I breathed in deeply, my head filling with ways I could make him pay for trying to hurt her. I wanted to make him hurt. As she leaned against me, her heart beating in sync with mine, my tense muscles eased. The fog in my mind cleared, and my eyes focused on the rise and fall of her shoulders rather than the red mist of anger which had filled them when she described the ferret. I wanted nothing more than to sit there with her for the rest of the day, warm in the sun, warm against her fur. Fur that smelled a little like roses, but also a bit like children. I took a deep breath in, trying to make it look like a sigh, but really, I was curious about the scent deep within her fur, a scent she hadn't picked up from the shifter plane but one that lingered from when she was a human. I pulled back suddenly, making her look at me with wide, surprised eyes. She was a mother. I could see it. As I gazed at her, I saw just how exhausted she was. She needed to go home, to rest, and to see her child. For someone who wasn't great at feeling things, it hurt like hell.

"Perhaps you'd best head home and rest," I began. My head lowered in a sadness I tried desperately to hide. I was just too tired to pull it off. This girl already belonged to someone and had a child. Whatever it was that had been brewing in my heart, something I had never known was there before, was shattered to pieces, ripped apart before it had begun. I had to keep away from her. I shouldn't have stayed.

I stared after her as she left, headed back over the boundary without a care. I turned away, not wanting to see where she went, especially knowing she was on their side of the lines, and that she was already taken and had at least one child. Damn.

CHAPTER 13

Ena

On Sunday morning, Mum looked tired, and I wondered if she had slept. To be honest, I hadn't slept much either and it left me feeling anti-social and grumpy. I made breakfast, which she hardly touched, and I watched as she flicked through the channels on the TV like a zombie. Bea cooed and banged two of her toys together, and I clapped my hands in approval. I was worried about Mum. She seemed really shaken up. Already that morning I had caught her peeping through the blinds into the garden, and she jumped a mile when I first came down the stairs. Her acting like that put me on edge. This wasn't how I imagined our time together. Hiding from something that might not even be there. I put one of my headphones in and selected my Linkin Park playlist. If I couldn't scream externally, at least I could in my mind.

"I need to see Mally," she announced a little later in the morning. I knew exactly what that meant. It meant she wanted something from Mally's shop. I had heard it all too many times growing up. Her body trembled as she looked toward the door. This wasn't my mum. She was my rock, my support system. She was the strong one.

"Shall I go?" I said, regretting it instantly. Usually, she would have refused, but she accepted and gave me a list scribbled down in pencil. I was in no mood for small talk. I made a mental note to get in and out and home as quickly as possible.

"Shall I leave you with Bea as a distraction? She needs to go down for a nap anyway," I said in a sing song voice in Bea's direction. She squealed back at me and pulled herself up onto her feet to cruise the sofa. My clever girl was growing up far too fast.

I went up to my room and pulled on a red cardigan over my tight black vest top and ran a comb through my hair. I pulled on my black skinny jeans and my Ugg boots. On the way out of my room, I saw the piece of haematite on the side of the cupboard and grabbed it without thinking. I handed it to Mum on my way out of the door. She looked at it then at me as if she was going to burst into tears.

I parked on the opposite side of the road to the shop, and for a moment, sat in the car and stared. It had been a while since I had been there, and every time I went, it made me feel like a small child, clinging to my mum as she hurriedly bought whatever she bought in there. I rolled my eyes and got out of the car. I could see Mally loitering in the shop doorway and thought I'd best go before she saw me. She waved me over like some old aunt who fusses, although Mum probably rang her and told her I was coming. I put on a smile.

"Ahh, Ena," she said, taking my hand in hers and kissing it. She looked up at my face, but we didn't make eye contact. I looked shyly at the shop behind her. *No small talk. In and out.* I should have been guilty that I was in such a bad mood. It wasn't her fault I didn't want to sit and socialise.

"Mum wanted a few things," I said, suddenly feeling really vulnerable. Being there usually coincided with us moving somewhere, and Mum going all batshit for weeks with candles and things.

"Of course, of course." Mally put up her hand to push a strand of hair from my eyes. I let her but still couldn't bring myself to look at her properly. I don't know why, and she must have sensed it because she turned and shuffled inside.

The shop smelled like nowhere else; a mix of cedar and sandalwood, roses and fresh herbs. There were layers to the smell like when you cook onions; the sweet and the sour at different times. There was also a smell that something had been burning, and something that smelled like warm salad dressing. My stomach growled.

Books on modern witchcraft and herbs sat on the shelves, mixed in with gemstones and candles and small paper bags of sand. There were house plants across one side of the counter, a few of which I could identify. I knew from being there as a child that somewhere in the shop was a huge piece of amethyst. Seeing some smaller specimens on the counter, a small stab of pain reminded me all those times the shop connected me with leaving. I wanted to leave and go home to Bea.

"Mum wanted these. I'm not sure what everything is though," I said, holding out the list. In honesty, I hadn't read it. Mally took it and looked down underneath the glasses she was wearing.

Whilst she pottered around the shop, picking up bits and bobs, I kept my gaze on the houseplants on the side. I did love house plants but could never keep them alive for long enough.

"I'll need to order one of these. I'll just make a note," she said cheerfully, tapping the list. "Looks like she's hoping to cast protection over something and cleanse a few things too."

"Probably," I said idly, flicking my gaze to her face. Her skin had aged a lot since I had last seen her. Her hair was still black but no longer smooth. It was rough and tied together in a ponytail by what looked like a piece of leather cord with two black feathers. "Sorry, I need to get back for Bea," I said, feeling rude for staring.

She made a sound that was a cross between a laugh and a grunt of approval. "Of course you do. We need to keep the little one safe too, don't we? I remember when you were that small. Oh, you were so full of life. Do you remember you used to hide behind the counter and not come out?"

I remembered, and my eyes almost looked straight at the little gap I used to hide in, but I shook my head. I knew if I looked, I would only see Bea hiding there; a small, frightened yet fascinated and curious child.

"You'd be under there for hours. My son used to hide in the exact same place. Remember, I always told you he'd never come into the shop when you were here. He worried you wouldn't like him." She held up my bag for me to take.

It was a good place to sit and think. I didn't blame him.

"Ah, well," I said simply.

"Just a moment. I wanted to give you this. I made it this morning when I knew you would be coming." She grabbed a glass jar from the shelf behind her and poured the hot liquid that looked like salad dressing into the jar, being careful not to pour in any of the bits of... they looked like sticks... into the jar, then attached a lid. I pulled a face, a mixture of curiosity and disgust.

"Just dab a little on yourself before you head out, and your little one too, if you like." I took the bottle and looked closer at the contents. It was a slightly brownish yellow oil, and I could smell it from the pan.

"Um, thanks. What is it?" I asked, annoyed at my curiosity as it meant I would be there longer.

"It's a very strong protection oil. It'll help to shield you. You seem to be in tune with the energy around you. If you are sensitive to it then you will notice dangers more often and have the courage to do something about them. If you choose to leave, it will protect and shield. If you choose to stand your ground, it will help you to draw on those energies."

I stared blankly. What was with everything recently? Had Maisy been telling Mr Ealing I was really into all this stuff? I knew they'd been discussing it, but I'd never really been part of it.

"Oh. So, it's witch stuff?" I asked. "Mr E giving me a book, you going on about oils and protection. Is this all the stuff Mum used to believe in?" Mally nodded.

Great. They were all batshit.

"Your Mum is a very gifted witch, did you know?" she asked.

"She's not a witch, she's just a bit odd sometimes. This is Maisy's fascination, not mine," I said, feeling a bit hot. "Please don't drag me into this nonsense. I really haven't got the time or patience." I grabbed my things, leaving the bottle on the counter, and stormed out. The words had tumbled out. I didn't even have chance to check them.

When I was back outside in the breeze, the guilt hit me for the tone of voice I'd used, but I wasn't going back in. She'd understand, put it down to hormones or something. I was going home to curl up in my PJs and eat doughnuts for the rest of the day.

Arriving home, I frowned in disgust at the mess Mum was making in the kitchen. By the looks of it, she was making her own odd salad dressing like concoction in one of the big pans. There must have been at least thirteen different oils in little jars strewn across the table, along with bits of fresh and dried herbs and a huge paper bag of salt. I picked up the nearest jar. Myrrh.

"Isn't this what they gave to Jesus?" I asked, holding it up to Mum.

"Yes, dear, and the frankincense." She pointed to another bottle.

Why did we have Jesus oil in the house?

"What's it for?"

"Er, I usually use that one for dandruff, actually. Works great with a little lemon," she said with a grin, and I laughed. She was starting to come round finally.

It was getting on in the day, around six p.m. I could smell the warm breeze coming in through the window.

"Am I okay to nip out for an hour when you're

finished?" I asked. "Bea is playing, but I'll bath her and get her ready for bed shortly, then I might go for a walk or to the gym."

Mum nodded but didn't look up, and I went to read to Bea.

After her bath and four stories, Bea had been fed, and she settled down for the evening. I had ordered her a cot bed online that afternoon so we could move her from the basket. It was okay whilst she was asleep, but if she tried to pull herself up on the sides, she'd be out and on the floor. For now though, I tucked her in into her basket and she stayed asleep. Mum settled in the lounge with a cup of coffee and her knitting, so I took that as a sign I could go out for a while.

Recently, my life had become very two-sided and routine. Aside from all the random things that happened in between, it was clear a pattern was emerging that I would be home, work, shift, then repeat. I didn't want to be living only to shift as I had so much going on in my life that I loved, but I couldn't give up the feeling I got when I was out in my new form. I wondered if that was how Spider had felt before slipping more and more into his shifted form. Deep down though, I knew it was literally only my daughter anchoring me to this world.

I did my usual route to the corner shop. Mum had thought I'd gone out, so I drove near Maisy's house and parked up on the car park for her building. No one would notice me in the car there. If they did, I would look like I was asleep. I parked at the back next to the wall and cracked the back window. I shifted quickly but stayed in the car for a while afterwards to make sure no one had noticed. No one had, so I left the car through the window.

The corner shop seemed like a good place for me to start, and to cover some more of the tracks I must have been laying around there with my scent. I didn't want anyone following me home. The thought of the ferret attack made me shudder. I trotted back towards my house from Maisy's. No one was there. I looked down the road towards where I had met Eldar and thought, why not? I started to pad out towards the farms. It might be worth getting some more intel about this sort of life from someone who seemed he had been around for a while.

I arrived at the bridge and inhaled deeply, trying to catch a fresh scent mark. It was a couple of hours old, but definitely the one my brain associated with Eldar. It was becoming normal to have a smell immediately attached to a being in my brain without me consciously having to think about it. I could now identify a few. Spider with his aftershave and coffee, warmth, and warnings. Eldar with his musky vanilla scent. It gave the illusion of his size and confidence. There was another there that evening though, which reminded me slightly of ferret. The warning Spider gave me of that thing being part of this group flushed through me, and I went cold. I was just thinking I should leave when I saw Eldar coming down the track from one of the farms. From the smell on the breeze, he'd just taken something's life. I could smell rodent blood. There was another smell in the air. He wasn't alone.

"Ahh, you're back." Eldar purred, curling his tail along my back as he came up beside me. A little over familiar, but certainly welcome. "I did wonder if I would see you again. I smell you around here and there, but I have been looking out for you."

I lowered my head. A train rumbled under the bridge and caused the ground to vibrate up through my paws. I lifted my front ones off the ground, not liking the way it tingled. Eldar held a curious smile.

"I have been around, but just half an hour here and there to practice," I said coolly, but I was distracted by the new cat. His friend came over to give me a sniff. He put me slightly on edge, and as if he knew, Eldar cut in and flicked his friend in the face with his tail.

"This is Cole. Don't worry about him. He can be a bit over familiar, but he's a good egg, aren't yeh?" Eldar nudged him with his head. Cole looked at me from the corner of his eye. He was shorter and stockier than Eldar and looked like he'd lost some fur on one side. He'd certainly lost parts of both ears, and he flicked them when he noticed me looking at them. If a cat could go red, I would have been crimson.

Colour-wise, he was a mix of blacks, greys, and whites, but mostly grey. His fur wasn't short nor long, but somewhere in between. I could see his strong muscles underneath his skin, but they weren't a patch on Eldar's, and instead of holding himself tall like Eldar did, he slouched a bit. I wasn't sure yet what to think. I didn't judge anyone on appearance, but there was something about him I didn't trust.

"Cole spends most of his time in this realm," Eldar said. "He does most of our patrols and helps with new recruits. He's our best fighter after me."

"I could take you," Cole answered smoothly to Eldar, then to me, he said, "Looks like you need some company, missy. What brought you over here? Some scary beings out there. You need to be more careful."

"She's from the city, mate. I'm sure she's seen worse over there. Am I right?" Eldar said. Almost like he was testing me.

"Nope. I've never shifted in the city except in my back garden. I see human crime though. There's too much of it. I usually drive down and park in town, although that's someone else's territory, right?"

Cole growled and was shushed by Eldar. I tried to read the hidden messages in their eyes but came up with nothing.

"Sorry," I backtracked. "I didn't know anyone. I

have met a few since I came here, but I take no sides. I am friendly to them purely so I can park and pass through."

Eldar raised his eyebrows. "I said you could park here. Carry on driving for a few minutes and you'll have no trouble from us."

"I could, but then I compromise my identity." I purred, trying to make light of it.

"You don't have to fear us, lil lady." Eldar head bumped me. "We can protect you." I was sure they could physically. They were both very well built for cats. I eased a little around Cole and relaxed my body.

For around an hour, we lay in the dirt against the wall by the bridge, chatting about things that weren't really important enough to remember. They chatted briefly about a football game Cole had missed. I mentioned I was working but didn't tell them where, but I did say it was at a warehouse and my supervisor was a complete nutcase. They seemed to like me opening up, although I was very careful not to mention Mum or Bea. As a human, I wouldn't have sat on the ground for so long. I'd have had to bring a blanket or something to sit on, but as a cat, the ground was no big deal. I just had to remind myself not to lick my fur later.

I should have been more wary of going out and meeting strangers. I was so anxious meeting people in my home town. I think it was the worry people might already know of me. When I was at uni, people just sort of merged. We met, exchanged a few bits about ourselves, and then went off on nights out and that was it. We could say what we liked, make up a whole new person and be it. No one would bat an eyelid unless you got too close. My flatmates knew me a lot better than friends from classes, but we were all thrown together and expected to get along. Heading out like this made me feel similar. They didn't know me. I could be the confident and strong person I yearned to be, and they wouldn't second guess me. It was exciting to get to know people, or cats, who had no knowledge of my past, my habits, what made me me. I could be whatever I wanted to be around them, and they had nothing to compare it to. Making friends as a human was harder because I was used to my human form, my flaws, my insecurities. Apart from being a completely different species, my insecurities there didn't have anything to do with my looks or personality, which should have been the first danger signs to myself.

Cole told me all about how he used to have a family. After a marriage breakdown, he had gone on a night out and met a bloke who tried to rob him. Apparently, he had shifted completely without any prior knowledge, and he wasn't robbed. I didn't ask for the details, and judging from the look on his face as he told me, I was glad he didn't.

Eldar told me he had a son. His wife was also a shifter, and they both had the same teacher long ago. They didn't see each other often as she lived her human life with their son, and he stayed with his clan. I felt bad for him. There was sadness in his voice as he spoke of them, but it was guarded. It was the done thing, he said, when one had children that they be taken away until they were old enough to understand and then brought into our world slowly if they chose to be. I could see why children shifting about all over the place would be problematic, plus, who'd be there to look after all those baby animals depending on what age they were when they changed? Cats age much quicker than humans, and different types of animals differently again. I shook my head just thinking about it. I couldn't cope with Bea becoming more mobile now, but Bea as a kitten? He told me they had a leader who watched over them, and I wondered if he was like The Wise One.

"So, are all shifters around here cats?" I asked.

"No. They can take any form, but some are harder than others. You must be in tune with the animal you want to take the form of. Once you can feel your way into another skin, you've already crossed a huge line. Some can only manage one form. The truly gifted can manage more than one, but it takes time and practice," Cole replied.

"Can you take another form?"

"Ha, I can take three or four. Eldar here is stuck with two, but he favours this one."

"I guess you're wondering why we all chose cats if we could be anything we wanted?" It had crossed my mind. "Well, how many lions do you see around the town? Any eagles? We tend to stick to things that blend in. Even rabbits and badgers are fine as they are local animals to this country. I suppose you could get away with more at night, but the more common the animal, the less likely anyone will look twice. A cat sauntering down the road, it's just another cat. A fox they'd notice because it's not usual. Even the type of cat is important. A huge white one would be noticed straight away, whereas a black one is most likely to be completely ignored. It's just how it is."

"What if you can't choose what colour you're meant to be? What if you just appear that way?"

"Usually those that are new or don't have the confidence turn out a darker colour anyway. It's like a protective mask that comes from your subconscious. A truly confident shifter could be bright orange if they wanted to be, but they would be seen by everyone. I suppose the reason you're brown is because you either have dark hair and it defaulted, or you weren't entirely sure what you believed when you tried it, and that you've not even thought to try and change it." In truth, it was a little of both. I hadn't thought much about changing my colour. I wouldn't know where to start.

He told me about their group, that there were quite a few of them all drawn to that area subconsciously, either for work, by chance, or noticed by another shifter and invited to visit. He said they were like a family and didn't turn anyone away as long as once they were there, they were respectful and loyal to the clan. I didn't ask about magic. This was a completely different side of the fence and from our interactions I gathered that these were shifters alone, separate from what The Wise One had been saying about witches. My mind wandered as I thought of what Mally and Mum were saying that afternoon about witches, and how much it was similar to the old cat in the park. I realised I hadn't been listening to Eldar and Cole because my mind was drifting, looking for things in my memory that might tie Mally to the shifter world. There wasn't any way I could ask her, and if I did and I was wrong, I would look ridiculous.

"So does that make more sense now, missy?" Cole eyed me suspiciously. With wide eyes, I shook my head.

"I'm sorry. I'm exhausted. It's been such a long day. I'd best be heading back home."

I put on a yawn, although I wasn't sure it was believed. "Thank you so much again for explaining everything to me. It sounds really exciting." Eldar purred in reply. I wish I had been listening. I had no idea why he was suddenly purring.

"Let us walk you back towards town," Cole offered with a stretch.

I nodded, the purr forgotten.

"Can't have you falling asleep out here now, can we, darling. Nasty things out here in the dark."

As we walked, Cole hummed a tune behind me, and Eldar walked slightly ahead, checking I was safe enough to pass without any trouble.

I crossed the road after the shop and looked back. The boys were waiting on their side of the scent markings, watching me leave. Eldar raised his eyebrow and nodded whilst Cole stared blankly. I strode off with my tail in the air and my head up high. *Confidence is everything.* As I rounded the corner, I spotted two green eyes watching me from the alley between two houses. I could smell the scent on the air. Spider knew I had seen him, but he made no motion to move, so I strode on and back to my car. Happy no one had followed, I leapt back in through the window and shifted back. It took me a few minutes to regain my human senses. Could I lose them completely? The thought worried me.

CHAPTER 14

Ena

As I drove home, I kept an eye out for the cats but didn't see any. This unnerved me, although I couldn't explain why. Mum opened the door as I got out of the car. She must have been looking out for me.

"Gym bag?" she asked, looking at my hands. For a moment, I was confused, but as the penny dropped, I gave a very exaggerated tut.

"No. I went to see Maisy instead. Last minute change of plans. Sorry. I never thought to say." I pulled out my phone, pretending to look at it.

**

I curled up on the sofa, eating a doughnut. Mum was concentrating hard on her knitting. The speed in which she knitted told me her mind was elsewhere, the motions repetitive, her eyes unmoving. That same feeling of worry trickled over me like rain. Instinctively, I listened for sounds of Bea's quiet but steady breathing before focusing on my own.

Mally had told me Mum was a gifted witch. I thought back through the last few weeks. The gemstones, the oils, the collections of bits from Mally's. It hadn't crossed my mind that Mum was a real witch. She'd never spoken about it out loud, nor said she was. Although, thinking about it, there was the obsession with candles and rocks; we did have a lot of them. Sometimes she did some strange things when she thought I wasn't looking, like touching certain objects and points in the house. The haematite in every room was likely to do with it. Nah, Mum was just a bit peculiar with these things. Possibly she meddled and took up a few of the bits that made more sense to me, like the energies of everything around us part, but not the whole casting spells bit. Right then, she was the most un-witch like person I could think of. It was easy to imagine Mally as a witch because she seemed to fit the old lady in a shop full of incense stereotype often given by movies, but Mum was a schoolteacher. She knitted and stayed home. She wore comfy PJs and ate doughnuts and watched crap TV. There was no way in hell you'd look at her and think any differently. It was possible, though, that she did things whilst I was out. Not in front of Bea, but maybe she used to before I came back. I wondered if that was why my dad had left.

"Something up, E?" Mum broke the silence. I realised I had been frowning at her.

"No, sorry. Just zoning out," I replied, with a real yawn this time. "Mum, do you know what happened to the library books I brought home? Not Bea's, but the other ones?" She pointed down the side of the sofa. I pulled them both out and yawned again. "I'll take Bea up now. Night night, Mum," I said, leaning to pick up Bea in my arms.

Mum carried up her basket on her way to the bathroom. I stood outside my bedroom door, waiting. When I heard the toilet seat being lifted, I said, "Oh, I forgot my phone," in a voice just loud enough for her to hear. I went back down and grabbed the books from the arm of the chair and quickly went back up to bed with them.

-

Spider

I watched her pass from the alleyway. Part of me urged my paws to move, like a magnet was pulling me toward her from somewhere deep within my soul. Somewhere where things didn't make sense, they just were. I ignored it and pressed my paws down hard into the ground, making sure I didn't move. I stood rigid, hoping she wouldn't notice me, but she did. For a moment, she paused, the breeze bringing her scent obediently to my waiting nostrils. I swallowed hard, fighting my will to go to her. I couldn't. I wouldn't. Especially not now I knew she was already taken. Glancing sideways down the street, I saw Cole and Eldar. That bastard Cole would be able to smell me, I was sure, with him being downwind. I bet that was why he stood so boldly. I wondered if she knew he was the ferret that attacked her. I hadn't been there, but I knew it was him. It was one of his favourite forms. *Step over the boundary,* my mind hissed. *Step over and let me get to you.* I knew I wouldn't have been able to stop myself once I had hold of him. My pulse throbbed in my ears, making it harder to focus.

Once she was out of sight, I saw them leave. I couldn't hear what they were saying, but they were laughing to themselves. Probably about her. I gritted my teeth. She wasn't my problem.

I wandered back, not really paying much attention to where I was going. It was going to rain again, so the air felt thick with moisture; my whiskers were heavy with it. I wanted to be indoors. As much as I liked the rain, I wanted to curl up and sulk. I hadn't wanted to see her again so soon, and yet I had. It seemed there was no escaping her.

I made my way to a place shifters used to meet up for training. It was a dusty old brick building on the edge of the railway line. It hadn't been used in years by anyone but us, and there were a couple of shifters who stayed there for longer periods of time. One even claimed to live there. I couldn't see how it could be comfortable. They'd brought blankets and food, but when I compared it to my lounge at home, I thought I was being selfish not inviting them all to stay with me. The Wise One had said they'd only refuse and then we'd all feel awkward about it, so I said nothing and pretended I didn't notice.

The Wise One must have noticed my expression, because when I arrived, she almost flew to my side with her questions. I shook my head.

"I don't really want to talk about it," I said, leaning against the old wooden doorway. It looked like they had been doing some sort of spell in there. I could see the pentacles drawn in the dust on the floor and evidence of sand and salt. The tell-tale smell from a candle that had been blown out still hung in the air. I looked around for The Leader, but he wasn't there. I wondered how much he knew about Night Flower. I had talked to The Wise One about her, but I wanted to run my confused feelings by The Leader. Perhaps she was a spy and I was trying to shake off some sort of spell. Could she know magic?

"I met her, you know?" The Wise One purred knowingly.

Of course she had. Yet another reminder she might be here to stay. Maybe I could leave instead. No. The

Leader would never allow it.

"Great." I huffed, looking away. I could feel her eyes still on me.

"You seemed so excited when telling me about her before, child. Why so sad now? Has she done something? I heard about the ferret... Tiz..."

"Tiz can shut the hell up." I growled, turning to leave. I didn't want to talk about her or that bloody ferret.

"I see." She raised her head. Something in her voice made me stop to listen.

"What?" I asked, annoyed.

"I see you like her. I knew you would." I could feel her warm smile without looking at her. I gave in and sighed. I was tired of holding back all the emotions I was building up. I winced as they washed freely over me.

"Why does that matter?" I drew a circle in the dust with a claw before sitting down, my shoulders sagging.

"Why would it not matter?"

"She's taken." It hurt even more to admit it out loud. What the hell was wrong with me? Of all the things running through my head.

"Is that all?"

"I'm sorry, but what the hell...?"

"She's not taken in the way you're thinking. Did you even ask? Probably not. Anyway, it doesn't matter. I know her, and I know you, my dear. I think you should have more respect when I'm talking to you. Remember, I *am* the one who is meant to be wise." She winked at me, and I couldn't help but laugh.

"What do you mean, you know her?" I asked, her statement distracting me. This must have been her intention.

"I just know, and because I know, I know that whatever you think you know, you are mistaken. You should ask her. I feel she might be important to us all. She hasn't shown up by accident." The Wise One put her paw on my shoulder.

Her words gave me comfort. Optimistic lifted my spirits again. She was rarely wrong about these things, and it gave me hope I didn't know I needed.

"She seems to be friendly with Eldar," I said.

The old cat beside me frowned and licked her dry lips. "I know. This could be a problem. We just have to hope she comes to trust you and us more than them. If you're not up to persuading her over to our side of things then I could ask Tiz or one of the others. Shed, perhaps." She paused as I let out a low growl I didn't mean to release. "In the meantime, you have a job to do. If you hear about her from the other side then by all means dig for information on her, but don't make it obvious."

She was referring to one of my newer roles. The Leader wanted someone to try to get on the inside of one of the rival groups to find out information. I put myself forward for the job, and I had to find a way to make friends over there without being detected by the ones who knew me by sight or scent. I did have contacts I knew in human form. Those we were working on helping escape, so I had a rough idea which groups to approach, which to avoid, and which crossed paths with Eldar and Cole. They'd recognise me without a doubt.

"I'll get to know her," I said finally, and her eyes lit up. "If it's important to you."

"It's important to you too, child, and you know it. Don't fight it." She walked, leaving me looking up at the sky. Spots of rain began to spit. I knew it was going to throw it down, so I mumbled something about heading home before I left. On my way back to my safehouse to shift, I thought about what The Wise One had said. She said Night Flower wasn't taken in the way I thought. I wondered what that could mean. Why hadn't I asked her? I assumed she meant Night Flower wasn't paired up with anyone, but that didn't explain the smell of child that clung to her fur. Maybe she cared for another's child. A close relative, perhaps. No, she was definitely a mother. Separated? As I arrived back, my heart and head were lighter, and I slept well for the first time in years.

–

Ena

"I got a warning because of you." The tone was

rough, but not as rough as it could have been. I almost dropped my coffee down my front.

"Yeah, I heard. I'm really sorry."

Ivan stood in front of me and said nothing. The rapid rise and fall of his chest told me he was feeling something; I assumed anger and frustration. Clearly, he blamed me, and who wouldn't? "I know to ask if I need help now. It won't happen again."

Still, he said nothing. Feeling the urge to lower my head and submit, I took a step backwards, biting my lip. Unnerved, I put down my half-drunk cup of coffee and headed onto the warehouse floor fifteen minutes early. I began work straight away and didn't even notice when he came down from the staff room. I hadn't seen Kym yet, but I assumed she was around somewhere. It was a big warehouse. I didn't think she was on the floor, but probably in the building. Every now and then, I caught Ivan watching me from the office window. The third time, I gave him a wave. He flushed scarlet, and I didn't see him looking again. *Ha, that'll teach him. Trying to intimidate me whilst I'm working.* I smirked and put in my headphones. Rival Schools, *Used for Glue.* Perfect.

With an hour to go, I had almost finished my stack of orders, but when I came back to the packing table with my two litre container of PVA glue, I saw that all but a couple of my packages had been reopened. Why on Earth would someone reopen all my orders? I knew it must have been Ivan. Kym wouldn't do that. He must have wanted revenge for his warning. I wasn't going to take this without an explanation.

I rapped my knuckles on his door and entered without waiting for him to respond. He had his ankles crossed on his desk and was leaning back in his chair. He would have been kind of cute if I didn't want to smack him in the face. His smug look infuriated me.

"Can I help you?" he said smoothly

"My orders. Someone has sabotaged them," I began.

He held up his hand. I hated it when he did that. "Ah, yes. That was me. I had a complaint about a wrong item delivered last week. One of your orders, so naturally, I had to double check tonight's. Congratulations, they're all correct."

Utter disbelief didn't cut it. With nothing to say, I left the room and slammed the door behind me. I took a deep breath and began resealing and triple checking all my orders. I wouldn't have put it past him to add something dodgy to one of my boxes.

Five to ten rolled around, and Ivan turned off the lights to his office and made a point of making eye contact with me. "I see you're almost done. Well done. Good job," he said in the most patronising voice I had ever heard.

Fighting the urge to snap back at him, I took a deep breath, which hitched as he took that moment to run his hand through his hair. "I've just finished," I said brightly, hoping he hadn't noticed my sudden breathlessness.

"What about those last couple of orders. With all your efforts resealing those boxes—they look perfect by the way—you must have forgotten all about those. See you tomorrow."

Again, I was speechless. All I could do was watch as he walked through the door. I was alone on the warehouse floor. Certain one of the rules was that no one was meant to be alone on the warehouse floor, I decided to wing it and leave too. If I passed the boss on the way, I would explain. If not, I was sure the morning packers would grab the last few. I hadn't seen Kym all night. The temperature had dropped and there was a cold silence around the warehouse. Even if there were people still in the building, I was very alone down there.

I jumped into the car and turned on the radio. Muse's *Supermassive Black Hole* played. How ironic as I was just thinking about shifting to blow off some steam after such a pointless evening. I must have seen the *Twilight* movies about ten times each. I wondered if one day I could turn into a wolf like Jacob. No, I was getting distracted.

Mum was still worried that Dad might be in the area, even though the police had insisted he would have left knowing they were actively looking for him. I wondered what he had been involved in. There had been nothing in the paper except that they were looking for someone extremely dangerous and to call the police if sighted. I still couldn't attach much emotion to the whole situation. Yes, it was unnerving, and I was worried for Mum, but I hadn't been upset hearing he was around. There was just a big gap where my emotions should have been. Maybe I was broken. Maybe that was why this shifting thing made me feel whole. The realisation flowed through me. It did make me feel whole. It made me feel like I could explore every aspect of myself. Even though the guilt that plagued me for leaving Bea was immense, I was still pulled too strongly the other way to give it up completely, despite recent disasters. I was determined to make it work. Instead of heading straight home, I text Mum and asked if I could go to Maisy's for an hour. I knew Maisy was out with her parents for someone's birthday dinner so she wouldn't actually be home, but I could use her car park. My phone beeped. *Yep, Bea asleep still.*

Bring on the shifting.

CHAPTER 15

Ena

Instead of heading to the corner shop, I skirted around the back near the park. It was September, and it was starting to get darker earlier. The thicker, humid air told me it was likely to rain, so I didn't want to be out for too long. Just long enough to get a little more practice. I still couldn't transform my whole body, which I hated. The fact that I just left it there slumped against things like I'd died filled me with disgust, perhaps it was the lack of being comfortable that was my problem. I hoped that the more time I was out, I might be able to finally complete a full shift. Not this time though. I still had my body lying in the car, even though I was sure it was slightly less solid and I was slightly more, but it could have been the light. Jumping out of the back window wasn't too bad, but I dreaded getting back in. Last time, I hit my back paws on the window. Plus, if it rained, the seat would get wet, and I didn't fancy having a soggy car seat.

I picked up a few scent markings. My nose was becoming really efficient at telling who was a cat, dog, fox, and which were shifters, although some I had to smell for a little longer for the human layers to filter through. As I trotted, I hummed to myself, pushing away any anxieties. I picked up Spider's markings more than once along the route and guessed the park was shared territory. I padded along the cobbled path, taking in the details on the wall, the deepness of the sky, the darkness caused by the clouds, and the sound of the vibrations on the road made by cars passing by. I slipped by like a shadow, flat against the wall, but careful enough not to touch it. I passed a hedgehog snuffling about in the moss. She looked at me but didn't speak, her wet nose wiggling at my scent. I could see the tiny fleas hopping around in her spines and hurried on, hoping none would leap my way.

This time, I wasn't nervous or surprised when I heard the light tapping of paws on the wall above me. I didn't need to look up to know it was him. I could smell him before I heard him. Spider dropped off the wall right in front of me with a huge grin on his face. I almost laughed out loud.

"Evening," he said in a high tone. "Where you headed?"

"Just exploring." I pretended I was more interested in the moss on the wall behind him. The fact he'd decided to come over and not hide in the corner took me by surprise, as did the tone of his voice. His mood swings were worse than mine.

"Ah, okay. Well, this is the park."

I raised an eyebrow, and he laughed. It sounded pleasant against the background noise of the town.

"Sorry. I still don't know where you're from. I assume you know the park though. You just sort of appear, although I can smell you around sometimes. It's really weird. Sorry, too much info?" He mewed. I shook my head, and this time I laughed, although it was a bit forced.

"No, you carry on," I replied lightly.

He must have detected the slight stress in my voice. Could cats smell hormones? "Ah, more work stuff? I had an annoying day too. There is the most infuriating dependant in my office. She always seems to be right in the way."

She? Why did this make me jealous?

"How annoying. Someone I work with deliberately sabotages my work. I mean, who does that? He's got a screw loose, I swear."

"Want me to find him for you? I could bite him."

"Spider!"

"Sorry, just trying to lighten the mood."

"No. you're right. I should bite him myself next time, but I'd probably get fired. So, you been up to much?"

His whiskers twitched under the streetlight, and I watched them, mesmerized by how they glistened.

"This and that. Checking out the territories, running errands for The Leader. Oh, I heard you met The Wise One. She's not bad for an old one, ya know? She was the one who taught me about, well, everything!"

"That sounds pretty cool. She was nice. I wouldn't mind seeing her again on one of my wanders." She made me feel calm.

His eyes lit up and he practically jumped to his feet. "Oh, well, in that case, I can take you over to her. I know where she is." He pricked up his ears and looked around. "Just gotta make sure there's no one else here." He bounced back up onto the top of the wall and I held back a laugh when he almost slipped on the damp moss. After a few minutes of checking the immediate area, he returned and waved his paw, which meant for me to follow him.

We walked right back past the park as if we were going out of town, past the town hall and Mally's shop, which seemed intimidating in the darkness. I was certain the barn owl perched upon the gutter of the roof of the house next door was watching us, but it didn't bother me. Walking alongside him, I could feel the warmth of his body, smell the coffee and aftershave. We had only met recently, but something inside me was already far too invested. I found myself leaning in to breathe in his scent. I wasn't sure if he noticed, but he didn't look at me as we walked. I swear he walked a little taller and straighter than he would usually though. Turning right, we were almost at the train station when he put his paw up to stop me, wriggled through some broken fencing, and disappeared. I looked up at the sky. It was getting thick with clouds and was certainly going to rain. I was just considering heading back to the car when his head popped back through the hole in the fence. "Follow me."

I did, although not as gracefully as him. I caught my back legs on the fencing and tripped, face planting the dirt on the other side. He laughed out loud, which made me scowl at him.

"Not fair," I said, getting up and giving myself a shake. I stuck my tail in the air stubbornly. "Go on then."

Spider winked at me, and my heart fluttered like a butterfly in a box. We walked into a clearing where there was an old outhouse, something to do with the railway by the looks of it, but not a signal box. More like storage that hadn't been used in years. As we approached, I noticed pairs of eyes surrounding the clearing. One in the trees which belonged to an owl, and in the corner, perhaps a fox. I strained my eyes to see, but whoever it was backed away into the darkness of the bushes.

"This is one of our safehouses," Spider began. "We have a few. One nearer to where I live where I shift, this one, and a couple more in town."

Fascinating. I really hadn't given much thought to why these things were needed, but I guessed with a group that big, they needed somewhere safe to hide.

"Ah, my Flower." I heard the soothing, cracked voice of The Wise One. She appeared from behind the door of the outbuilding. I could see glowing lights inside and suspected candles or a gas lamp. There couldn't be any electricity here, surely.

"Hello again." I purred, not wanting to seem too familiar, but it was hard not to when she made me feel so connected. So grounded. So myself.

"I see Spider has been showing you around."

I nodded and looked around for him, but he had gone. I felt a little deflated and hoped it didn't show.

"Come inside and get warm." She placed her paw on my shoulder. I did as I was bid and followed her inside.

Inside was very basic. The walls were bare exposed brick, and the ceiling was high with wooden beams. The glass in the window was broken and boarded up, but it was still draughty, the floor just dust and bits of broken rock. Empty crates were lined up and stacked by the walls, and in the corner was what looked like a desk and a couple of old wooden chairs. Someone had laid a pile of blankets on one of them.

"Does everyone here know each other?" I asked before I could stop myself.

The Wise One sat down closer to the fire. It was only a small fire in a metal box, but it gave off plenty of heat. Several candles were also lit and arranged in a shape on the floor. I craned my neck but couldn't quite make it out.

"In a way, we do. We all trust each other and know we will not harm one another. However, we don't all know each other's identities. There are few of us who do. I know everyone, but not everyone knows me. The Leader knows, but only one or two know him as he really is."

"The Leader? I thought you were the..."

"Oh, no. Not me. I just assist with the things that need assistance." The Wise One purred, drawing circles in the dust on the floor with her claw. "Spells and things. Banishing. They come to me if they need something. I help where I can, but mostly, we protect."

There was that protecting again.

"Protect from what?"

It took her a while to answer. I thought perhaps she hadn't heard and was about to repeat the question when she did.

"There are those out there, some not far from here, who are harming others. Through whatever channels they can, they will hurt one another and those we love too. I have seen it, and I have those who come to me to ask for ways they can go from here and not have to worry as much as they have."

"Are there other shifters who might attack?" I thought back to the ferret the other day and almost retched. The Wise One's fur waved with the warmth from the flames; it was hypnotic.

"There are. There are humans in particular in the city who cause many problems for loved ones in human form, and there are shifters who target us in our shifted form. It can be very dangerous sometimes. There is a group in the city. Most are gamblers, thieves, those who buy and sell women. I fear their leader is a powerful shifter, but in either form, we cannot get to him. He causes quite a few problems for us."

"If I knew someone who might need to be protected, could you show me how? Could I learn, or could you do something to protect her?"

A look of knowing passed in her eyes before she looked into the fire. "I know of who you wish to protect. It is possible for you or me to do this. However, you might be surprised that she is doing a great job on her own and always has. Perhaps, though, you should take a break from our world, just to make sure."

My heart leapt into my throat. How could she possibly know I wanted to protect my mum or what my situation was? Perhaps they really had been following me. I chose not to reply, and she didn't push me to. I was deep in thought when Spider returned.

"Shall we go for a walk?" I heard the hope in his voice and stood to leave.

"Thank you again. I will return."

The Wise One put her paw on my shoulder and bowed her head. My instincts told me she had more to say. Instead, she held out her paw to the door. I caught the exchange of glances between her and Spider as we left.

Back out in the night air, I could tell straight away it had been raining. The ground was only slightly damp, but I could sense it with my whiskers and feel it on my fur.

"Feels good, doesn't it?" Spider asked, guessing my thoughts.

"Does it always feel this... thick?"

"Yeah, mostly. It's worse when there's a storm coming. Wait until you feel the snow. It's amazing on your paws." Spider threw himself on to the ground and rolled on his back. He rubbed the back of his head against the ground then paused to look at me. "Sometimes when your fur gets all watery in the air like this, it's nice to roll about a bit and scratch it off. It's like a massage. Try it."

There was no way I was throwing myself onto the path to roll around, and I made that clear by stepping over him and carrying on back toward the park. Rather than look for the way home, I navigated my way back using my instincts.

"You're getting good at this. I wish I could have taught myself," Spider said with amazement, and I flushed. I didn't know I was doing something special.

"It's nothing really." I tried to deflect his pride, although I did feel a little prouder of myself.

"It really is. Usually, you have someone to teach you, tell you how to look for things, and what needs to be seen, but you, you're winging it and getting it spot on." He nudged me, and as we connected, a fizz like an electrical current shot across my body. I pulled myself back, unsure whether to mention it.

"I still can't become one hundred percent solid though. I still have to leave my body somewhere and hope for the best. I can't seem to do whatever it is I need to do to become here properly." My heart ached. Why couldn't I achieve it?

"It'll come. It'll be something really simple. You'll figure it out."

"You think so?" I asked quietly.

"Yeah, I really do. Honestly, you're fine." He mewed then looked at me for a little longer than he usually did. The moment was awkward. Like we both thought the other was going to say something, but then didn't, so we ended up passing the moment in silence before I looked nervously at the ground and cleared my throat.

"I should start heading back." The roads were busier

nearer to town, and I was starting to feel self-conscious, although there was good coverage from the hedges and small shrubs which grew outside the shops and gardens. A thick laurel hedge ran along one side of the path, and every few feet there was a planter put in by the council with various shrubbery and flowering plants. I could smell the petrichor as small dots of rain fell around us, like touches from feathers on my back.

"Are you sure? You haven't been out long, and I was... well, I was kinda hoping we could spend some more time together tonight."

"Sure, I guess. What did you have in mind?"

"Er, well, I have no idea, but just walking and talking is nice. I'd like to hear more about you. Only what you feel comfortable telling me, and I can tell you anything you'd like to know about me."

Why was it that I had thousands of questions, but when someone offered me the chance to ask them, I drew a blank?

"That sounds really nice. Thanks again, Spider. You've been so helpful so far." I thought of the little wobbles we'd had and wondered if it was jealousy that made him ignore me the other night.

"Okay, I'll start. Are you seeing anyone?"

"Seriously, Spider?" I laughed out loud, but from somewhere within, the excitement of being asked and wondering where it was leading flowed through me like

I'd taken a drug.

He hung back. "You don't have to answer that. Sorry, it just came out."

I forced away a smile and tried to keep my voice plain. "No, it's okay. I'm not seeing anyone at the moment. It's been a while, actually. Erm, how about you?" It seemed polite to return the question, but now I didn't know if I wanted him to answer.

"No, me neither. I'm not really a people person in the human world, and down here, you don't get to really meet anyone new."

"Phew. No Mrs Spider attacking me in a jealous rage! One less thing to worry about!" I giggled, and his eyes brightened.

"I can't imagine why it's been a while... for you, I mean."

"Do you mean as a cat, or a human? I'm pretty sure I'm not up for any animal-based relationships." The thought was suddenly creepy to me. "I'm too antisocial. I find it hard to talk to people. I think I live in a bubble sometimes."

"Easily done. I'm very much the same. Usually. With you though, I don't know. I feel like I can be myself."

"That's really sweet, thanks."

He was being so nice, and I really didn't want to leave. He seemed to have a genuine interest in me, and I was interested in him. Sure, when we first met, he was really annoying, but he grew on me. He was still annoying, but now I craved his contact. When he was walking with me, I could almost feel the energy between us. A bit like when you stand too close to the fire and it heats up your skin, but it feels so good you don't want to take a step back. Then, when you do step back and the heat subsides, you feel the cold and the doubt trickles back in. I realised I was frowning.

"What are you thinking?" Spider asked softly, looking up at me with his huge emerald eyes.

"Nothing. I just feel like you were always there. Like we're connected somehow. That sounds really stupid, I know. Maybe we knew each other as kids or something."

Why was I being so honest? The occasional hum of a passing car was all I could hear over the fluid rushing through my ears.

"Wow." I could feel his eyes boring into me and had to look up. "It's like you're saying exactly what I'm feeling right now."

I couldn't breathe for a second or two. We sat inches from each other and neither of us moved. We were so close that when I forced myself to breathe, I was taking in the air he was breathing out. In his eyes, I could see right into his soul. Held captive by them, ambushed, carried away to somewhere I couldn't return from. I'd never had that feeling before, this shutting down of things. My brain didn't seem to be able to cope with the closeness.

Our moment was broken by a shout from across the road. I had forgotten we were so exposed still, despite the hedges. Two cats on the end of the street wouldn't be of much interest to humans, but to other shifters, we were very interesting. I knew the voice. It was Eldar.

CHAPTER 16

Ena

"Hey, Flower. You coming over tonight?" he sang across the road. Spider stiffened beside me, and a wave of guilt crashed over me.

"You still hanging out with that guy." It wasn't a question, but a statement. I shuffled my paws.

"A little. Our paths have crossed."

"I see."

Eldar called me again. A knot formed in the pit of my stomach. *Oh, to be invisible right now.*

"I guess you'd better go," Spider said flatly.

"Come with me?" I asked hopefully, already knowing it was a no go.

"I can't cross to his territory," Spider said, looking at me through pained eyes. I could see the hurt and wished Eldar had shown up later on or not at all. Still, if

I ignored Eldar, I was making enemies, and I got the feeling Spider was a lot more forgiving than he was.

"What happens if you cross?"

"I die. If I cross over there, they are allowed to kill me. Same over here. If he crossed to our side of the markings, I would be allowed to rip his throat out." A growl grew in his voice. Eldar must have heard too, as he coughed a very obvious 'chicken'.

"Okay, well, there's going to be no throat ripping, especially not over me. I don't want to upset either of you, so I'll be back later, okay?" I offered, but Spider was already turning away from me. Eldar whooped, and I rolled my eyes.

"Whatever," Spider whispered, skulking off the way we had come. I bounded across the road, shaking off the negativity.

"I thought you weren't coming," Eldar said in a high tone. "I've been looking for you."

I grinned. "Me? Why?"

"Don't like to think about you out here all alone, getting wound up with oddballs like that one over there." I heard a low hiss from nearby and knew Spider hadn't left.

"Hey, he's a good guy," I protested to Eldar's roar of laughter.

"Come on, it's too crowded here. Let's walk."

More walking. I was lucky I hadn't been out too

long. I could still pass for being at Maisy's but had no idea what the time actually was. I looked around for anything that had a clock face on it. There was one in town, but it was in Spider's territory, so I couldn't look for it now. We walked around the back end of the park, not far from where I had been attacked. Adrenaline surged as we walked past the bit of the wall where the ferret had appeared, and Eldar suddenly leaned his whole body against my side. His warmth calmed me immediately, but no sparks like with Spider.

"Why so tense?" He purred, rolling his shoulder into mine.

I sighed. "I've just had an odd couple of days." I avoided eye contact, and he picked up that I didn't want to push the matter.

"Well, I've been out tonight hunting rats. Nasty buggers! There are a few huge ones down by one of our safehouses, but I got 'em. Now I'm wired and can't seem to come back down. You're soothing to me. You make me feel relaxed." I blushed. "So, that Spider... he seemed pretty jealous when I showed up. Are you and he...?"

"Oh. No, not at all. We're just friends," I lied. There was definitely a hint of more than friends unless I had imagined it.

"Good. I feel a bit better now. You're too good for him, anyway. I can see how he looks at you. How he looked at you when you crossed over to me."

I didn't see that look. I was glad I hadn't.

"Like I said, we're friends, and if you guys hate each other then that's probably all it was."

"Nah, there's more to it. I know because, well, I'm into you too."

That was a bold statement and completely unexpected. I mean, I thought he might have liked me a little, but to come out and say it mid conversation... This night was getting stranger by the minute. I'd gone from having no one to having two guys into me. However, I was a cat. There was no way I could pursue either of them in real life, nor could I stay there to see where anything went. I was a half-formed spirit, for goodness sake. I choked back a laugh.

"Something funny? I open up to you and you laugh at me?" He tried to sound light and amused, but there was a hint of hurt or embarrassment too.

"I'm a cat." I giggled. "I'm not really here. I have a human body. It's so bizarre."

"You have a body. A beautiful one, might I add. Your eyes are always the same. Did you know that? They are called the window to your soul for good reason, and when I see your eyes, it wouldn't matter which form you have. I'd remember those eyes."

I considered this for a moment.

"How old are you?" Not what I was thinking, but that was what came out.

"What?"

I tried to cover for myself. "How old are you? I mean, you have a kid. What if you're, like, fifty?"

"How would that matter? What are you, twenty? Twenty-one?" I nodded. "I'm thirty-six," he said proudly.

"There you go. Old enough to be my grandad!" I laughed, nudging him back and leaping off ahead of him. Energy finally started to fizz. It had taken a while, but still, it was a different kind of energy. More flirty and fun than anything serious, and possibly fuelled by my encounter earlier in the night.

"Oh, that was below the belt!" Eldar snickered. "Plus, you have a kid too."

I froze. "How did you know that?" I asked, barely daring to.

"I can smell her. You carry her scent when you move. It lessens over the time you're here, but it's there."

I took this in. "Yes, I have a child. I like to keep her out of this." Surely, he'd understand. With a kid of his own, how could he not?

"So, you going to keep driving me crazy?" he asked.

"Sorry, I'm not..." Caught off guard again, I wasn't sure what he wanted me to say.

"Are we a thing, or just friends like you and the loser on the other side?"

"I think I need more time. I've only met you twice," I said hurriedly. "You are amazing, but I've not been here long. It's hard to know what I want." After a few seconds, I added with a light giggle, "Plus, there's the whole age thing. That'd be gross."

"What you want and what you need are two very different things," Eldar began suggestively, trying to hide his glance at my hips. I subconsciously dropped my tail and shifted my body slightly. By this time, we had skirted around the park and almost come back to the middle, but on the other side. I didn't go there as a human. We stayed near the ducks and the play park. I could hear a stream swishing in a ditch from the quiet of the park.

"What I need is to head home." I had to put it to an end before it started. I had a feeling he wasn't impressed.

"Ah, well. Until next time." He groaned, shaking his tail and scent spraying the wall. I supposed this mark of dominance was trying to cement him as the best candidate in my mind. I could smell the power and ferocity in his marking. I almost melted and gave in. I was curious, *No, not tonight. Not with someone else I barely know.* I thought of Bea and the feeling subsided.

"Until next time," I agreed, closing my eyes as he kissed me on the forehead.

"Come on. I'll walk you back."

We cut straight through the middle of the park. It was empty, apart from some sleeping ducks. Eldar eyed them greedily until he saw my scowl, and he pulled a shocked face before sticking his tongue out. I wondered if he would eat them. The grass was wet and felt horrible to my paws. It was sticky and dotted with slugs and worms. I refused to retch, even though I couldn't get past the grossness. In boots, it's fine, but on my bare paws, it was horrific. Eldar seemed to find enjoyment in this, and he distracted himself, watching me trying to carefully place my paws and jumping into the air when I saw something slimy. I shrieked my way across the lawns like a child, with at least two legs in the air at a time. Suddenly there was slug on the edge of my paw, and I flicked it so high I probably killed it. I screamed too, which was not the best thing to do when out with a guy who was into you and walking you home. Oh, well. It couldn't get worse now he knew I was a complete wuss.

"Well, that was different," Eldar said, raising an eyebrow. "You're very entertaining, Flower."

I glanced over onto the other side of the road. I knew I had to cross back to the other side for my car but didn't want to run into Spider again. I knew I'd hurt him by coming over here, but I had to keep all my options open, or I'd be restricted to where I could go. I supposed that wouldn't be such a bad thing, but if Eldar really could smell Bea on my fur, he could just as easily pick up the same scent whilst we were out. He'd guess who I was straight away. I didn't want to add in enemies where I didn't need them, and after all, Eldar was very alluring. His size, his muscular form, the smell of him, and I could almost feel the power of his embrace. I warmed as I imagined what he might be like as a human. As if hearing my thoughts, he leaned against me and nuzzled my neck, filling my lungs with the smell of him. I inhaled deeply, feeling dizzy. I rubbed the back of my head along his cheek, leaning back into him. For a second, I thought I might fall, but he supported me. He rubbed his chin against my collarbone and lightly nipped my shoulder. I let out a squeak, which he seemed to like. He let out a sound that was almost like a groan. With him, it was purely physical attraction. More like an urge to get what I needed and go. We didn't have the bond I was forming with Spider; that was different. The feeling of betrayal gnawed at me, but it was hard to stop, especially when it had been so damn long since anyone had paid me this kind of attention.

"Until next time," he said, bumping me with his head one more time. I took that as sign to go before he became too invested in what he was working up to.

"Of course," I replied shakily, stepping out into the road. "Oh, and watch those ducks. Leave some for the kids."

He grinned.

There was no sign of Spider as I crossed, but I guessed he must he there somewhere, watching. My stomach lurched when I realised my interactions with Eldar had been completely out in the open and couldn't have been missed if I was being followed. Goodness knows what he must think happened in the park. I scanned the laurels in front of the houses as I backtracked in my mind to check if there was anything else that might make him think more happened than it did. Did Eldar say I was entertaining? That could be so misinterpreted.

I was almost back at Maisy's when I came across Spider's scent. I had hoped I would make it without running into him again, but I guess it was inevitable. I knew he was there but hoped he wouldn't approach. I was filled with the dilemma of whether to run to the car and risk being seen as a human. Who else would be pulling out of a car park at that time of night? I could have hidden somewhere until he'd gone, but then Mum would be worried, and my phone was in the car. I made the decision to stop just short of the car park and wait to see if he made himself known. After a few minutes of waiting, he did.

As he approached, I could see the look of disgust on his face and cowed away from him. This wasn't just jealousy. This was him being angry with me for going over, and for whatever he thought had happened when I did. Why should I be ashamed though? We really weren't together, and I wasn't really there either.

"You're back," Spider noted, coming to a halt. He was two feet away from me and didn't come any closer. His black tail twitched, and his voice was low. His eyes darkened through his thick eyelashes, and his ears were back slightly in distrust. I scraped my claws in the dust on the pavement, shifting my weight from paw to paw as guilt threatened to pull me under. For what though, I wasn't sure.

"I am. I have to get to my car."

He nodded once. "At least I'm useful for something, even if it is only car sitting." He raised an eyebrow and nodded in the direction of the car park. Damn, he must have followed my scent right back to where I'd shifted. The sneak. I'd have to find somewhere else to hide next time.

I tried to keep it light, but I was going to struggle. "I appreciate it, but I don't want to pick sides, Spider." He didn't reply. "Do you want to talk about it?" I hoped he didn't but thought it was the right thing to say.

He leaned forward slightly then pulled a face and shook his head. "You smell too much like him," he said, breathing deeply. "His scent is all over you."

Suddenly, I was so angry my fur was burning. I didn't know why this was so important, or why my thudding heart might leap from my chest. All I had done was have a cuddle. Yes, Spider and I had some sort of connection, but that was it. I had to remind myself he was a cat, and so was I. This was ridiculous.

"I don't belong to anybody," I said hotly. He hung his head. "None of this is real," I added quietly.

"Whatever you think, this is very real," Spider muttered. When I looked up, he had gone. I could have cried. Instead, I bit my lip and sat in silence, listening for any sounds before heading back to my car, absolutely exhausted from it all.

CHAPTER 17

Ena

In the car, I had three texts. One from Mum saying Bea hadn't woken up yet, but she was going to bed. The other two were from Maisy.

One said she was bored stiff out with her family, and the second asking why I hadn't replied. I typed a quick reply that I had gone for a drink with a friend from work. I hadn't had a chance to put the phone down before the reply flashed across the screen asking if it was a guy. I grinned and replied, *maybe*. I half expected her to phone me, but it was almost midnight, so I text her back quickly, saying, *I'll pop in to library 2moro*.

Driving home, I thought about how quickly I had replied to Maisy when she had asked about a guy. Which guy was I thinking of? Spider or Eldar? The warm, fuzzy feeling you get when you first realise you've met someone you like was tingling in my veins, although, as a human, I couldn't quite process exactly what I was feeling. The Eldar thing I guessed was more attention and lust. He made me feel special when I saw myself as unimportant, yet Spider? Spider was very confusing. Then there was that feeling it could be neither. Ivan, as infuriating as he was, did things to my insides I had never experienced before. Plus, he was actually human, which was a huge bonus. I couldn't exactly bring a cat home to meet my mum, could I?

Pulling up at a junction, I looked to the right before I turned and saw Eldar trotting back along one of the paths with a huge duck in his mouth. I made a point of turning to go the longer way home in case he caught a whiff of me on the outside of my car. He didn't stop, so I thought I had gotten away with it this time. I would have to be a lot more careful. Perhaps I should start looking into a safehouse, somewhere safe to shift between worlds. But who to trust with my identity? Less than an hour ago, I was running through the same park with the same soul, yet feeling as though I could flirt away without a care. Now, I didn't want him smelling me here. I had to decide to put my complete trust in one side or the other.

–

Spider

None of this was real? Who the hell did she think she was? I stalked along the street, absolutely fuming. I was mostly angry with myself because I thought perhaps we had something. Perhaps I could actually be a nice guy, someone who had friends, maybe a girlfriend. It wasn't meant to be, and I was infuriated that I allowed myself to believe there might have been something there. Sure, we were both in shifted forms and didn't know each other really. Could that have been what she meant? I didn't think so. I thought she believed that, for some reason, her shifted form didn't matter. Like it was a dream being in that plane.

I'd had it all planned out. I wanted to get to know her. I wanted to spend some time with her and test out the strange connection between us. I couldn't begin to understand why I felt like I did, yet she walked away so easily. What a fool I had been. Just thinking of the look on Eldar's smug face made bile rise in my chest, and I growled out loud. I should never have listened to The Wise One. I made myself look bloody desperate. *It must be so easy for her, swanning in and playing with people's feelings.* I was stuck here. Stuck shifting between worlds. For life. If she wanted to, she could stop and move on. I didn't have that luxury. For once, I had hoped I had found something, someone, who could make that a whole lot easier.

I hadn't followed her. It had been really hard not to,

and I desperately wanted to. My possessive instincts had kicked in, and I spent the whole time she was over on the other side of the border pacing up and down, shaking my head and growling before following her scent back to where it began. I had found her car quite easily, and then headed back toward the border to check if she had returned. It was only later on I realised I could have checked inside and found out who she really was. No, I wasn't that sneaky although I couldn't shift the feeling that was tugging me toward her, and I hated it. I didn't want it, but it was there.

I made up my mind that she wasn't what I needed. I needed to be alone, especially for my job. I needed to be in many places and meet with many people, and she would only slow me down. I needed to be rid of her. All of this back and forth, wanting and not wanting. It was changing me, and I didn't want to be changed. I had just started to feel better when I could smell her coming back, thick with the scent of Eldar. There was no time to get out of the way. I would have to see her, and as much as it pained me to see the hurt in her eyes, I couldn't hide my disgust. What the hell did she see in him? She stank of him. Bile rose in my chest, my whole body tensed.

I decided to go for a run before heading home. I ran until my muscles ached and my paws burned. I ran straight to the other side of town and halfway back to my safehouse before I started to think more clearly. This girl had to go. I had to remove myself from the equation, but I wasn't sure how I was going to do it. The Wise One was clearly enamoured by her, which should have been a good thing, but now it hung over me like a thick fog. She could send Tiz in to make friends with her for all I cared. As a human, I didn't need anyone. I wanted to be left alone. Everything was too much. A haze that hung around me like a bad smell. I could see it in people's faces when they tried to speak with me. I just didn't have time for talking. I knew I should have felt something, even for my family, but really, they might as well have been talking to a brick wall I was that stony. As a cat though, or a bird, or whatever I chose to be, I became freer than I ever had as a human. It was me, and I was seriously considering staying on that plane, if it were possible.

There were a couple I knew of who had transitioned permanently and been okay. They set everything up before making the change and hadn't gone back. There wasn't anything really keeping me in the human world except maybe my parents, who needed my help from time to time, but they'd be okay. I could be of more use and help here, enchanting safehouses, chasing off enemies. There was the small issue of eating. Pizza was way better in human form. Cats can't even taste sweet things, so there goes ice cream. Overall though, the life here was much better. Even more so now Flower had joined us, but to be together, it could only be in this plane. I could never be the human she needed, which was why it would be much easier to cut her off now. Her leaving with Eldar made it clearer that we were incompatible. She had no sense of danger, and although she was smart figuring all this out herself, she was crazy flaunting herself about like that. I thought of how vulnerable she had looked crossing over and wondered how she saw herself. None of this was real? I sighed. I hoped for her sake it didn't get as real as I knew it could be, especially on their side.

-

Ena

Have you heard the My Chemical Romance song, *It's Not a Fashion Statement, It's a Deathwish?* Well, that was exactly how I felt that morning. Knowing things were already getting harder. I couldn't stop thinking about the world of shifting that I had opened up for myself, full of beautiful new experiences, but also, there was an edge to it. Raw, ready to destroy me. Feeling I had an emotional connection to a soul, yet feeling I couldn't trust that. Somehow, deep down, I thought I was going to get hurt, or maybe I was going to be the one hurting someone else. My head thumped with a migraine, but the lyrics still spun around my head. Would Spider really have it in him to kill Eldar? Could I imagine him as a killer?

The phone rang, interrupting my thoughts.

"Morning, Ena. It's nothing to worry about, but Ivan said you didn't finish your orders last night before leaving. I would like you to come in half an hour early and get them sorted today, please. The pickers this morning have their own separate set of orders to work on, and yours really should have been out by today. I can't be doing with angry customers, Miss Bedford."

Of course he reported me. I looked at the time. 9.15 a.m. It must have been the first thing he did. What the hell was his problem?

"Of course, John. I'm sorry. I had a problem with some of the packing last night, so I must have missed a couple. I'll sort it this evening, I promise." I should have mentioned it was Ivan's fault, but instead, I reached for the Nutella and a spoon and sat frowning at the kitchen table.

"E, honey?" Mum called from the garden.

After my dad almost showing up the week before, she had called in sick for the first few days of term to get over it. Her school was very understanding and said to take a few days before coming back in. Unfortunate timing, but luckily, they had a good staff base and she'd catch up with her class quickly. She seemed a lot more settled, but I knew if the police showed up again, she would lose it. Bea sat on her playmat in the garden with some giant Duplo bricks whilst Mum re-potted various things.

"Yeah."

"Can you nip across to Mally's? She's just text and my order is in. Please? I've got to finish something before cracking on with some schoolwork." Text? Mally? Couldn't witches just telepathically beam across their messages? I smirked.

"But it'll only take you five minutes in the car. I really should stay in with Bea," I protested, looking longingly at my Nutella.

"Yes, and it'll only take you five minutes. I'd have to wash and change and..."

"Okay, okay." I stuck the spoon in my mouth. "I'll go now whilst she's happy." I gave Bea a big smile and a wave wave in my silly voice that she loved. She waved back at me, clearly used to my comings and goings. It pained me a little that she didn't seem to miss me, but I was happy she was happy.

Ten minutes later, I stepped into the shop, annoyed that Mum had sent me to collect her package. I had thought about the thing with Ivan at work and the phone call with John all the way there and was in such a bad mood. I pushed aside the string of onions hanging in the shop doorway and swatted away the dust that fell as I did. It was only Mally's shop, so I wouldn't have to make small talk. She'd know I had to get home to Bea.

With a pre-planned idea to do what I did before—get in and get out—I was surprised when I automatically stood at the counter and looked straight into her eyes. They locked with mine for a second, and the tension in my body dropped. I knew those eyes. Why hadn't I noticed it before?

Something Eldar said the night before about your eyes staying the same hit home suddenly. This look was personal; I *knew* her. I flushed with embarrassment and stumbled sideways over my own feet.

She smiled and winked at me. This new guilt was sharp, cutting through me like butter. Great. She must have known all along. What a cow I must have seemed last time I was in, when I'd refused to look directly at her.

When she smiled, her whole face lit up. Her spirit seemed young, despite her wrinkles and aging skin. Her long black hair was in a braid over one shoulder, with a couple of blue feathers tied into the end. She wore a long necklace with thick wooden beads, and huge wooden earrings. I don't know why I didn't pay attention to her before. I was a bad human. Clearly she wasn't bothered. Her smile was welcoming, calming, just like her presence at the outhouse and the park. Her happiness was genuine and fuelled by the fact that I had put two and two together, connecting with her on a more personal level. No, it wasn't personal. It was spiritual. Like when a vine wraps itself around another, and within each other they find support and comfort. My morning frustrations slipped away, and I felt lighter for it.

"I..." I started. I had meant to apologize, but she held up her hand.

"I know," she said softly in her cracked voice. "It's okay."

She bent down to fumble underneath the counter and brought up a small wooden box. "Your mother's," she said.

I looked around the shop to escape her gaze. There were different coloured boxes on the shelves, packs of incense, candles, gemstones in all shapes and colours. I used to love coming into this shop as a child. I couldn't remember when the magic had been lost. Yes, I could. It was when I started associating it with having to leave, or with Mum being stressed and having panic attacks. Before the darkness, I had loved it in there and played with the candles and gems, making potions from herbs and oils and proudly decorating the shop in them.

I had come into the shop last week but didn't really think about it. When I was there the time before, it was when we were leaving again. I had sat on the floor in the corner next to the huge amethyst geode, which then was taller than I was, and I gazed into the centre of it as if I was lost in another world. Mum popped in and out of the shop in various stages of stress and anxiety, and after what seemed like forever, we got into Mr Ealing's car and drove away. I dreamt of that geode for weeks after, often imagining I was in a cave on another planet. If I could have curled up and slept inside it, I would have. When I was curled up under the counter, that was exactly what I pretended I was doing. My experiences had darkened how I had originally seen things, and it had taken the last few weeks to work my way through it and process something I didn't even know needed to be processed.

I looked at the geode, still in the same corner and now covered in a fine layer of dust. It didn't sparkle but still I sensed it's magic. I fought the urge to go over and touch it.

I was torn from my thoughts by the slam of a door. My eyes whipped up to see a man who had just walked in. He had a hand over his face as he rubbed his temples, but in my gut, I knew straight away who it was and let out a groan. It was the man I had argued with at work. Ivan. I'd know the smell of that aftershave anywhere, and the ugly, creased brown suit. Although I had made the connection that he was the son of family friends, and that he must live there or at least visit, I hadn't been mentally prepared for him to walk through the door.

When he noticed me, the face of tiredness turned to one of disgust, and he shook his head and swore under his breath.

"Following me?" he snapped as he stormed forwards. Even with that look on his face, he was striking.

With a little more sleep and some sun, he could have passed for a model.

"Why the hell would I want to do that?" He walked behind the counter and to the door behind, not registering Mally was there. "Oh, and thank you for the phone call this morning. I bet John was very interested in my incompetence."

Before leaving, he turned back to look at me one last time, as if he was going to say something clever in return. In his eyes, I swear I saw something else. Something I didn't see at the warehouse. It was him. Not just my supervisor.

It was Spider

My hand shot to my mouth in shock. He shook his head again, clearly changing his mind about speaking, and he made a snorting sound before he slammed the door. My eyes then met Mally's.

"He doesn't know. He doesn't know it's you," she said in a hurried tone. "He can't know. Our worlds shouldn't cross." She held out the package, came around to my side of the counter, and ushered me to the door.

"Why? What'll happen?" I asked, suddenly afraid for making the connection. All that tranquillity gone in another turn of events.

"Nothing. Nothing at all. It's just..." she paused as we reached the door. "It's so, so complicated. Do you remember me telling you he immerses himself in that world to escape this one? I'm worried one day he'll never come back. Meeting you there, he feels the pull to be away more than he did."

I could feel the hurt in her words and nodded. Suddenly, his importance to Mally became very clear. He might be the arse Maisy had told me about, the impossibly grumpy supervisor at the warehouse, but on the other side, there was something else there. Another side to him that shone when he was Spider. This was not the time to push this, but at the same time, I knew there was more to it. Surely, knowing who I really was could pull him back to this world?

CHAPTER 18

Ena

On the way home, I remembered I said I'd go into the library to see Maisy, so I took a detour there. She was sitting at the customer service desk with a cup of tea. Mr Ealing was over by the computers with his head behind a newspaper. The only other people in there were a mother and son in the children's section, and an elderly lady over by adult fiction. I was getting better at taking in what was around me; a trait I had picked up from shifting.

"Hey, Little Miss Stop Out! I want to hear everything!" Maisy said excitedly, jumping up and pulling me in for a hug. I slid over another chair and sat next to her behind the desk.

"I'm not sure what's included in *everything*," I joked. "I don't know where to begin."

That was completely true. The night before, when I

had sent her that text, I wasn't sure which of the three possible men had caught my attention. Now, there was only one on my mind. Weirdly, one man was actually two of them.

"Begin from the beginning!" she urged. "Name, eye colour, height, where's he from? Does he have an accent?"

"Woah, slow down! Erm..." I glanced over at Mr E hiding behind his paper, and my cheeks flushed. Damn it, I just had to go for it. If I made it up, she would know. She was the master at those sorts of things.

"Well, it's kind of a secret because he's my supervisor, so you really can't say anything to anyone. You have to pinky swear." Nothing beats a pinky swear. She held her little finger to mine and pretended to button her lips with her fingers. "Well, you know that guy you said had a stick up his arse..." I watched her face as she realised who I was talking about. She looked quickly at Mr E then back at me with her hand clamped over her mouth.

"Oh my God. No," she mouthed. I must have gone through several shades of red and purple before she stopped inwardly screaming at me.

"Shh. Seriously, keep it to yourself," I urged, feeling a little less like I wanted to tell her.

"So, yeah, that's about it. He's horrible at work. I'm not sure if I hate him or not. Outside of work, he's completely different. He's sweet and thoughtful and..." Maisy looked as though she wanted to roll on the floor laughing.

"Fine. Now you know we don't need to discuss it any further," I said hotly, slamming my hands on the counter. "I've got to get home."

"Oh, no. E, I'm sorry. I'm just really shocked. He doesn't seem your type. He doesn't seem anybody's type... No, that came out wrong." With a sigh, I stood up. "Have you... you know... seen his *stick*?" I could tell she was trying to be serious, but she couldn't contain her excitement. She was my best friend, so why did I find this so difficult?

"No, nothing on the *stick* front." It was meant to be a completely innocent statement, but the way it came out took the whole thing to another level. I started to laugh with her; laughing felt so good. I'd had such an intense few days that laughing with my friend over something like this was exactly what I needed, and what I had missed being so involved in my shifting. I had needed this to remind me what was at stake.

"It doesn't matter, anyway. We had a bit of a falling out, so I don't think I'll see him again outside of work. At first I thought he was just a mean person, but then I thought perhaps it was a front to keep people away. Now, he swings from one mood to another between work and out. I haven't got a clue where I stand." I shrugged, feeling a slight empty space in my chest. Thinking about Ivan and Spider, the thought of being with Eldar disgusted me.

"Sorry to hear that. You can't have been seeing him for long." Her mood changed. I knew she could feel I was getting upset. *Why* was I getting so upset though?

I shrugged. "Not long really. We only saw each other out of work a couple of times. A week maybe." Wow, only a week? It really had seemed much longer than that, especially if you included the times I saw him in shifted form too.

"And you never said! Damn it, E! Seriously though, sounds like you really did see another side to him briefly. I hope it works out."

Man, I loved Maisy.

I shrugged again. I had nothing to say, so instead, I picked up my bag and pouted. She took this as my cue for leaving.

"Next time you come in, bring my baby!" She gave me a wink before turning to help a lady waiting in line by the desk.

Mr Ealing caught my eye as I was heading toward the door, and he beckoned me over. Just one more minute wouldn't hurt. I hoped it wasn't about Ivan, and I hoped Maisy wasn't listening. She was busy with the mother and boy, showing them how to use the self-checkout system.

"Hello, Ena," he said slowly. "I was wondering if you read those books Maisy passed on to you. She told me you tried the guide too. Interesting stuff, isn't it?"

I glanced back to where Maisy was. As I looked back, I caught a brief feeling of pride, which faded as soon as it arrived. I frowned. This was getting overwhelming. I didn't want to be in too deep. I'd had enough of the sneaking around and the witch stuff. I'd had enough of choosing sides. I'd just had enough. My head fogged.

"I don't know what you mean," I stammered, unsure of myself. "The books were interesting, yes. I did give them a read." I'd jotted down a couple of the things I wanted to remember, but I wasn't going to tell him that. I'd already given too much of myself away recently.

"And the guide? It's one of the better ones." He laid the newspaper in his lap as if to tell me I had his full attention. There was that glimmer of pride again. I couldn't make out why my mouth was suddenly as dry as the Sahara. I looked him dead in the eye. He was balding, and the hair he did have was grey and mostly around his ears. Like Mally, he looked a lot older than he was, but he had young eyes. Eyes that were very similar to Ivan's.

"I think perhaps the problem you've been having stems from your inability to trust yourself. You want both worlds, but when you start to feel secure, you doubt what you're feeling and miss what you're giving up. You need to trust what you feel. There can be a balance..."

I stopped listening. Of course Mally would have told him of my problems. The problem, I assumed, was my solid form, and he was spot on about the doubts. I couldn't control the fact that I thought I was about to burst into tears, and I couldn't fight the heat that was creeping through me whilst he spoke. I couldn't concentrate on his words with the thudding in my ears and the pounding of my heart. I had to get out of there.

"You assume it worked at all," I snapped. "I haven't time for this rubbish. I'm sorry I'm not who you thought I was." I regretted my tone, but I couldn't help that now.

Without waiting for his reply, I stormed out, ignoring Maisy calling my name.

We both knew I had lied. It seemed so ridiculous of me, and by the time I got back into my car, I couldn't hold back my tears.

-

Spider

My breathing was ragged, and my chest heaved as I caught my breath. The rain had stopped, but it had left the ground wet and slippery, especially down here by the park where the moss and algae had grown thick over the cobbles during the long, wet summer. I had been out on patrol and picked up the scent of two unknown shifters who had chanced crossing into our territory. A few of us had been out together and had followed them as they made their way along the boundary line across the park. Probably trying to pick up scents of individuals and attempting to identify them. I didn't know these scents; they were new. Our rivals had been sending out so many newbies recently. I could have sworn they were trying to confuse us or seeing how far they could get with those who were expendable, or both. This was the third group of idiots to cross that night. We'd already lost two groups back over the borders. It was becoming tiring.

We'd had to run to catch up with this pair until we caught sight of two rats scampering along, using the planters and bollards along the road as cover whilst they paused and sniffed. We had been lucky enough to be downwind as we watched, but after some time, they realised we knew they were there and had run. We chased them about half a mile, and now we had them cornered where the wall was a little too high for them to climb and there were a few too many of us for them to pass us and escape. There was my friend Tiz and a female who had taken the form of a stoat along with me on this patrol. Us and these two rats.

"What's the plan?" Skeet breathed. She had already regained her breath but was poised to strike the second one of the rats made a run for it. From the sounds of it, she was relieved we'd not lost these two like we'd lost the others. The rats had their backs against the wall, the larger one slightly in front of a smaller, skinny one.

"Why are you here?" I asked loudly, and one of the rats snickered.

"Enjoying a stroll. What's it to you?" He sneered, his beady black eyes shining with the tiny bit of light. He stood boldly on his hind legs and gnashed his sharp teeth.

"I'll ask you again. Why are you here?" My voice became a growl. I wasn't in the mood for playing games. I was fuelled with pent-up frustration. I needed to bite, to fight. I needed a release, and I dared them to dare me.

One of the rats hid behind the other. From the scent of it, it was afraid. There would be no fun in killing that one. It had already given in, but the one at the front, challenging me, wouldn't last five minutes. Still, I denied myself the sensation. I tried to remind myself he wasn't really a rat, but a man, and we could use what he knew. On the other hand, he wasn't going to give anything up easily. Tiz's paw landed on my shoulder. Tiz was a good friend. I relaxed a little. If I hadn't been running in circles all night, I might have been more patient.

"Mate, shall we take them back?" he said, eyes never leaving the pair. I nodded and gave in.

"Yeah, we should." I raised my head to talk. "Come with us. We can talk. Whatever he has over you, we can work through. We just want to know why you're here, what you're looking for, and then you can go." The rat at the back nodded quickly. It knew it wasn't getting out of there without telling us anything unless it was dead. The one at the front, however, lowered itself back onto four paws.

"No way. How about you just walk away, and we leave," it said with a snarl. It advanced towards us, and my patience was wearing thin. The smaller rat squeaked and covered its face with its paws.

"You're the one they call Spider, right?" The rat sneered, coming closer. Tiz's energy changed, his body responding with hostility like mine. Skeet kept her cool, but I knew if one of us was attacked, she wouldn't falter. She was damn fast.

"And?" I growled, claws out, head down, ears back. Saliva rushed to my mouth in preparation to bite.

"You can't hold us all back. There aren't enough of you. We've proven that theory tonight. You can't catch us all."

"Our strength isn't in our numbers," Skeet hissed from my heel, her teeth bared. He winked at her, her disgust hung in the air.

"She's a feisty one, isn't she? Whatever he does to keep you here, love, you're not loyal to him. Come back with me and we'll make sure you're treated like a queen."

Skeet laughed. True, she was feisty, but I knew she had my back.

"I'm tired now," I said, pretending to yawn. "This isn't going anywhere."

"It's only a matter of time," the rat said. "And we know where your Flower is."

My ears pricked up, but the sudden heat from Tiz's body leaning against mine grounded me. I didn't need to listen. There was nothing this rat could tell me; he was baiting me, and I really did just want to head home. I could hold out a little longer and not give in to my urge to kill it. He had known to mention Night Flower though. Her absence had been noted by us all. The way he stood there with his open-mouthed grin told me he knew he had said something to unnerve me. I had looked for her, despite how empty she had made me feel, but hadn't found any trace of her for a while.

Filled with the sudden need to sink my teeth into his neck, I pounced. The rat skittered to the side and leapt up against the wall, its paws pushing itself back with enough force to hit me in the side. The rat wasn't very strong, but as it started to shift into something bigger before our eyes, adrenaline and animal instinct kicked in. I was no longer thinking like myself. There were no thoughts, only instincts. I grabbed it by the throat and hung on to the thick windpipe as it grew, using all my weight to pull it down. I had no idea what it was becoming, but it had chosen the wrong time to shift. I bit down hard on its neck, feeling the crunch and crush between my sharp canines. I tasted the blood spurt into my mouth with such heat and force I almost let go.

My heart raced, and I swung my body up and over onto its back, using my weight to push it to the ground. The windpipe ripped away before I let go with my teeth, but I held on with my claws. Its once snapping jaws dropped feebly as its head hit the cobbles. I jumped off it, seeing that it had attempted some form of dog. The thick stench of blood filled the small corner, and it glistened on the moss. Skeet and Tiz hadn't aided me. They knew I didn't need them to. Instead, they had stood by, making sure the second rat didn't escape. It cowed in the corner with its paws over its eyes.

"I'll take this one back," Skeet said without even an eyebrow raise at what had just happened. Snaking her way behind its back, she nudged it forward.

I licked the blood from my paw and faced Tiz with a raised eyebrow. He looked thoughtful.

"He's right though, mate," he said, staring at the body behind me. "There aren't enough of us."

I nodded slowly and padded back the way we had come, not bothering to check if I had killed the thing. I could tell by the way it smelled that I had killed at least its shifted form, so I didn't look back. By the way it had shifted, I was sure I had gotten him completely. He wouldn't be able to save himself now, even if he did know the right spells.

"He is, but what can we do?" I said.

221

"What if they send in humans next?" Tiz asked. "You know there's nothing we can do about humans."

I sighed. "No. Humans can move freely. We can't attack humans as humans without them seeing our faces. We can't risk that."

"So, what can we do? Stay on this plane and keep doing what we're doing? What if we come across gang members as humans now? There is no truce. Could shifters take them down?"

I considered this but shook my head. It would take quite a few shifters to take down a human, which was why we had always been purely on the protective front. Now they were testing us, sending in human criminals and shifters into our territories. I would have to consult with The Leader and see what he thought. I wasn't happy about it though. Humans we didn't know were harder to detect, especially if they came in during the day when our bodies were more spread out over the town.

We were on our way towards the police station, passing a large junction with many sets of traffic lights, when we came across yet another set of scent markings that had been clearly sprayed so we would cross their path and know they were on our territory. We looked at each other and sighed. This was going to be a long night.

Killing shifters in animal form was one thing, but killing humans? I wasn't sure I could do it.

CHAPTER 19

Ena

Just over two weeks passed, and I hadn't shifted. I spent more time with Bea on my days off and worked at the warehouse in the evenings when Mum came home from work. She had started the Autumn term now it was September. I was painfully aware I wasn't starting back at university as was originally planned. I deferred at first, but I decided to quit for now and start again in a few years' time. I was sure I could make it work with studies and Bea, but I didn't want to go through all of that right then.

Mum usually arrived around four, and every other day, I hit the gym for an hour. I made sure I showered and dressed for work while I was there, and the routine seemed to work for me.

John had brought in a couple of students to help

with the workload, which was an interesting move, as Kym described John as a Scrooge. Some nights they were needed and welcome. Some nights I wondered why he bothered paying us all. I did my 6-10 shift and came home to dinner made by Mum. Usually Bea was asleep. She still woke around 1a.m. for her night feeds, but that was okay because I didn't have to be up early. Things were settling down nicely, and my brain fog was finally lifting.

I went to the library less too. I was ashamed I hadn't told Maisy about the shifting, and that I had made a mockery of it in front of Mr Ealing, who by now would have told Mally all about it. I was embarrassed. I still took Bea to the Rhyme Time though. She had a cuddle with her favourite aunt, and luckily, neither Maisy nor Mr E had mentioned Ivan.

I had a couple of recurring dream themes. I'd dreamt everything from Spider and Eldar fighting, to them both dying. Many times, my dreams were of Ivan and I getting a little too involved, which was really odd because I hadn't had a good interaction with him as a human. My brain seemed to attach Spider's playfulness and Ivan's face and body. Still that horrid brown suit though, but dream me didn't seem to notice. In fact, dream me didn't leave it on him for very long.

Bea and I went to a couple of new children's groups I had found on Facebook. A singing and baby signing class which was lots of fun. I had learnt the signs to foods and animals, and she had learned to smack me on the nose because it made the teacher laugh. I had also started a baby swimming class with her, which she loved. I wasn't much of a swimmer, and the pool was so damn cold sometimes, but it was worth it to see her splashing about in her teeny arm bands with her new baby friends. I tried hard to put the same enthusiasm into making friends there as I did when I had been on the other side but found it more difficult and more forced. Whenever I approached the other mums there, I could almost feel them tensing. They must have noticed I was being fake. I didn't belong there, not with them.

Work was about the same. I turned up on time, and I had managed to avoid my supervisor most of the time, often picking orders that took me to the other side of the warehouse when he was on the floor and doing the others whilst he was out. I had become quite good at knowing where things were, and my spatial awareness had really improved. The times we did have to work together, I kept talking to a minimum and avoided eye contact. He seemed more stressed and rude as time went on. I wondered if it was anything to do with me disappearing from the other world. I decided I was being ridiculous. How could anyone so self-centred and rude be bothered about me disappearing? How could he be so horrible to people he worked with and then be the opposite an hour later? I thought about when he said I was always in the way; he was probably right. Maybe he thought I had chosen sides and was off with Eldar or Cole. The thought made part of me want to shift and tell him that wasn't so, but I wasn't going to. That part of my life had come to an end as quickly as it had started. I was finding I could live my life just as fully without it. The addiction was being handled, although I had been tempted on a couple of occasions. Especially after dreams about Ivan or Spider, or when Ivan had humiliated me at work.

For two whole weeks, I had tried to avoid everything that reminded me of that glimpse into another life, and everything that reminded me of Spider and Eldar and Ivan. At work, it was easier to think of Ivan and Spider as separate beings because, at least once, I had come close to chatting to him in the same way I would have Spider. In the end, I stopped talking to anyone at all.

Finally, Friday rolled around. I was looking forward to the weekend and having Mum at home. I loved that she was back at work, but I missed her in the day time. It wouldn't be long before it was half term, and we could plan some proper days out together.

Mum arrived home just after four. I had made dinner early for us as I wanted to hit the gym before work. Running on the treadmill with my headphones on and the music up as loud as it could go was the best way to drown my thoughts as meditating was completely out of the question, just in case. I put Mum's and Bea's food on the table; cottage pie with lots of broccoli for Bea, then grabbed my gym bag and left. I'd eat when I got home.

After throwing my things into a locker, I pulled on my gym trousers and a tight black vest. I pulled my hair back into a bun and took my sweat towel and water bottle. I went to my favourite treadmill in the corner by the window, overlooking the car park where I could watch people come and go. I put on my headphones and turned up the music. System of a Down blared through my brain, my feet making contact with the machine as if to the beat.

I was halfway through *Toxicity* and my five-minute sprint when I realised the guy running two treadmills down was the one man I had been trying so hard to forget. I don't think he had noticed me. He also had his headphones in and was staring blankly out of the window. I pretended I hadn't seen him and kept running, sneaking sly glances to my right every now and again. My pre-programmed time was coming to an end, and I jogged my cool down before stopping, getting off the machine, and stretching my legs and back out. I would usually wander over to the weights and spend twenty minutes toning up, but that night, I was going to get out of there as quickly as I could.

Picking up my phone, I turned the volume down. The track *Spiders* came on; of course it did. In my head, I'd grab my things and sneak out like a ninja. But no. I stumbled over my own feet as I reached for my water bottle. My arm shot into the air to grab the side of the treadmill. As I stood back up, I whacked my head on the side of it. I bit down on my lip hard in an attempt not to make a fuss, but damn, that had hurt. He saw the movement from the corner of his eye and glanced toward me. I cursed myself, out loud too, damn it. At first, he looked away and pretended he hadn't seen me. That was good. I could slip out and head home without ever having to make contact, but for some reason, he paused his machine and stopped. My heart sank. I could see the curl of amusement on his lips. Ivan picked up his towel and dabbed the sweat from his brow then pulled out his headphones. His black t-shirt stuck to his abs with sweat, but I refused to let myself look down at them. I stubbornly stared at his gorgeous face. My insides twisted and ached. I wished I could slap him and leave.

"You sure you're not following me?" he said evenly, turning to face me. My heart fluttered like a tiny bird.

"I was just leaving, actually," I said, flustered and edging toward the exit. He stood in front of me and very obviously gave me a look up and down. I blushed and realised I was covered in sweat and still breathing a little heavily from my run. He seemed to have regained his breath already. I regretted wearing a top that showed off my middle and wanted to pull it down to cover myself. My self-consciousness hissed at me, I'd exposed myself, even though the important parts were covered up.

"I won't hold you up," he said. "You at work tonight?"

I found this an odd question seeing as he created the rota. Maybe he thought I was sacking off work for my workout.

"Of course." I tried to keep my voice even, though I was filling with some unknown emotion, and it took everything in me not to bolt.

"What you listening to?" He nodded toward my phone.

"System of a Down. You?"

"Ahh, cool. Placebo."

I raised my eyebrows. "Nice." Feeling we had both run out of things to say, I put my thumb over my shoulder toward the door. "I have to go."

He didn't answer, just put his headphones back in, turned around and continued his workout.

I was confused as I left for the changing rooms. Had he just been sort of nice to me in the real world? Was that a show for those at the gym who might notice if he was an arse? It couldn't have been, because he could have ignored me, but he stopped and said something that wasn't an insult. I over-analysed the whole thirty second conversation again and again on my car ride home, then again in the shower.

After my shower, I looked through my wardrobe for

not only something comfortable, but something that made me look nice. I had loads of leggings. I chose a stretchy pair that clung to my curves but were still great for jogging up and down a warehouse all evening. I found a nice grey blouse style top that worked, and a cardigan to match. I paid close attention to my mascara and lipstick too. I didn't wear them often, but that evening, making an effort to look nice seemed like a good idea. It was only when I began to tie up my hair that I realised what I had been doing. Furious with myself for bothering, I threw down my hairbrush and stomped downstairs.

I walked into work that evening and had booked my taxi ride home for ten past ten. After visiting the staffroom and meeting Kym in there, we walked to the floor together, chatting about our days. I didn't mention I had seen Ivan at the gym. I didn't want to talk about him to anyone else.

The evening flowed as usual for the first two hours. One of the new guys dropped his package at the packaging station and was completely chewed out by Ivan. The way he laid into him, I thought the guy was going to either thump him or quit. He stood his ground well and glared at Ivan with eyes that said *this is the only time you will talk to me like this*. Even Ivan seemed to sense it because he hid in his office for the next forty minutes. Go, new guy.

Later that evening, most of my orders had been completed and left in the packaging bay. So far, I hadn't had any run-ins with the supervisor or made any mistakes. I was hopeful I could make it to the end of my shift and go home after a nice, non-stressful night. The time came though that I needed a ladder for one of those dreaded lamps on the higher shelf. I would need to ask for help.

I skipped along the back of the warehouse, cheerfully looking for Kym, then realised as it was gone nine, she had probably already left. One of the new lads should have been around somewhere, but when I reached the end of the next aisle, it wasn't one of them in front of me but Ivan himself. He was checking codes from a clipboard with those on the shelf and sticking little stickers on. Oh, God. I had literally been skipping too. If I could have slapped myself in the face, I would have.

"Stock take," he said, holding up his clipboard.

"Oh."

"Were you looking for something or just making up for your lost workout time?"

His tone wasn't aggressive, however, he did fold his arms and his face was stony. I couldn't make out what he was trying to convey.

I gulped. "I, er, I need someone to help me with the ladder," I said, feeling hot and red as a beetroot.

He nodded once and dropped his clipboard onto the

shelf. "Don't want a repeat of last time, do we?" He winked at me.

Wow. I was half expecting him to say no. Perhaps he had softened a little. That, or John had threatened him with more than a warning. Probably the latter.

Ivan insisted on heading up the ladder for the lamps while I held the bottom. He then insisted on carrying it all the way to the packing area for me. He didn't mention the incident I had with the ladders; not even one joke about it. I was impressed and confused at the same time. In fact, he was silent the whole time.

"Thank you," I said with genuine warmth, forgetting he didn't know me like I knew him. He didn't smile, but behind his eyes there was something highly guarded, like he wanted to smile but couldn't. With me, smiling was involuntary most of the time. I was such a bad actor, I couldn't hide anything, but the more I had practiced sneaking out, the more I had learned. Maybe he had gone too far after all.

"No problem," he said flatly. Our conversation ended, and he walked back to the aisle he had left. I noticed myself hovering to watch him but forced my body to move and act like I didn't care. Part of me did care. Part of me seemed to care a lot. Anxiety rose in my chest like bile, and I forced it back down with everything I had. I would not fall for Ivan Ealing. It was not going to happen. I feared it already had, but the problem was, Ivan Ealing wasn't interested in Ena Bedford in the slightest.

He only had eyes for Night Flower.

-

Ivan

I hid in my office for the next half an hour. I actually hid. Like a child in a closet. It was laughable.

I had made my mind up to just get on with things, to let them go. Night Flower seemed to have dropped off the face of the Earth, and who could blame her after hanging around with those gits from the city? I couldn't compete with that no matter how hard I tried. I'd asked Tiz to keep an eye out for her, but he hadn't seen her either. Part of me was glad it might be over, but the other part of me felt like I needed to know where she was. I needed to know she was safe.

Over the last week, I'd been irritable and sulky. Funny, because I always came off as irritable and sulky to others, but that week, I really felt it, and for the first time, I didn't like it. I didn't want to feel that way. I tried to persuade myself it was just a phase, over-tiredness, and I wasn't bothered I came across that way, but somehow, I was. It was best I kept out of the way, but there seemed to be people everywhere. People like Ena Bedford.

I had caught myself idly thinking about her from time to time and had even dreamed about her after seeing her talking to my mum. Her huge, dark eyes and long eyelashes hovering just centimetres away from my face, her lips touching mine. Before bumping into her at the gym, I'd forced the thoughts away and brought Night Flower to the forefront of my mind. Yes, she was a cat, but she had a glow about her. If only I could find out who she was in real life. I knew better than to ask her, but I had hoped she might tell me. It was a fantasy, a fairy tale. Apart from knowing the shifter world existed, I didn't really put much stock in fantasy. The reality of it was a lot more gritty and mundane than the expectation. Nothing was coated in fairy dust. There were no magic wands or levitating wizards, just those who could do it and those who couldn't. The pain, the deaths, and the effort we had to put in was real. I think that was what played on my mind when she had refused to be part of it anymore. She had picked her side and I had to get over it. I told myself over and over that I didn't need her, and I should start looking into finding a human connection somewhere. But if I did meet someone, how the hell could I explain that in my time away from work, I was mostly running around on four paws? There was no explaining something like that.

Thinking of the girl at work was hard at first. A strange guilt had settled within me for letting her in, especially when I was growing fond of Flower, but what if she didn't want me? Ena Bedford wasn't too bad. Usually people were people. I kept those who weren't already close at arm's length, with the thought of ever letting them in never crossing my mind. And she hated me. On some level, I hated her too. I hated that she was beautiful. I hated that she had swept in and made me feel things I didn't know existed. I hated that she made me want to be a better person, but at the same time want to be a horrible one. Life recently hadn't been great, but it had been easier before she had thrown herself into the mix. Even when she was pleasant, I could tell it was forced. She wasn't terrified of me like most of the workers, but I had caught her glaring at me on more than one occasion, so maybe she was just irritated by me being there. It infuriated me because I had no idea what she was thinking, and there was no way I was going to ask.

That evening, she had caught me off guard. I'd been working on the stock take and my mind was elsewhere when, all of a sudden, there she was, right in my face. Looking into her surprised eyes, it was as if my whole world shifted. Everything stopped, even my heart. She seemed timid and unpleased to see me, but instead of feeling glad she was unnerved, I was a little sad about it. Usually I wouldn't care what someone thought of me, but her? In that moment, I got the impression she wasn't hoping to see me around the corner, but someone else. I didn't like the thought that she might have been actively trying to avoid me. I had caused that uncertainty. I didn't want to hurt her, not that I'd cared in the past. I'd wanted her to quit at the start, but now, for some reason, I didn't want her to hate me as much as I needed her to. I was confused, so the best course of action was to act as if I were helping my boss. Get the job done, be civil, keep my mouth shut, and get out of there. Sweat threatened to betray how uncomfortable I was. Thank God for the warehouse being so cold.

I resolved to pretend she was just another manager I needed to ignore and get away from her as soon as possible, so I took charge and did most of the job myself. In a way, I was showing off, showing her I could be a decent human being if I wanted to. Something about her made me want to. Damn, I was a crappy human.

The worst part was that after the job was done, she had had something to say to me. I desperately wanted to know what it was, but the trouser traitor downstairs who made decisions based on more primal urges had other plans. I had to leave. I went to my office and stayed there until she had gone. She probably thought I couldn't get away from her quick enough because I didn't like her, but in fact, it was becoming the opposite.

CHAPTER 20

Ena

I approached the house in the taxi after work. I was mentally drained from overthinking every tiny thing. The gym, the way he looked at me, the way he looked right through me as if I wasn't even there. I'd come to realise he had gone too far. It wasn't my job to bring him back, and as hard as it was to move on and forget about it all, I had to. I had to for Bea, for Mum, and especially for me. I couldn't afford to be distracted like this. I needed to look for a new job. I wasn't committed to this one yet. I still had time to leave without getting a bad reference.

Getting out of the cab, I noticed Mum peeping through the upstairs blinds. When she saw me, she let them drop and hurried down to answer the door. She threw herself into my arms when I'd barely crossed the doorway.

"Wow, Mum. You okay?" I asked, kicking the door shut behind me and wrapping my arms around her. Her body shook with sobs. I held her tightly, feeling stupid stroking her hair. It was usually me doing the crying into shoulders.

I let her cry for a minute then pulled her head upwards, held her face, and wiped her tears with my thumbs. "I'll put the kettle on."

I led her to the sofa to sit down. I knew by instinct Bea was okay and in bed because Mum would have reacted differently. This was to do with something else, and my instincts were telling me it was Dad.

After poking my head round the door to my sleeping baby, I made some camomile and thyme tea, poured Mum and me a cup each, and sat on the sofa with mine. Mum paced the room and peeped between the gaps in the blinds. I hadn't asked her what had happened yet because she was too on edge to have a conversation, but now I needed to know.

"Mum. Sit down." I added a sternness to my voice to focus her, not sure she'd listen to me, but she did. She sat opposite me on the armchair, but her eyes kept twitching back to the blinds. I pulled the curtains across them and tucked them into the radiator. "So...what do I need to know?"

Mum closed her eyes and shook her head. Her eyes were puffy and her lips dry. I handed her a tissue, and she blew her nose. "There's nothing to know," she said with her eyes closed and her hands over her ears.

I shuffled over to her and put my hands over hers. I could feel the softness of her skin, something I hadn't paid much attention to before.

"What do I need to know?" I repeated, moving her hands from around her ears and holding them in mine.

She took them and gave them a squeeze. "You're going to think I'm being really silly now. But I thought I saw someone on the front drive before, not long before you came home." She glanced at the window again, now hidden behind the blinds and the curtains.

"And?" I gave her hands a squeeze to encourage her to continue.

"It was a man, I think. He was only there for a second, then he was gone, only..."

"Only?"

She looked at me and smiled widely, catching me off guard. "How the roles have changed. You shouldn't be looking after me, I should be looking after you."

"We look after each other." I smiled back, handing her her tea. I supposed we did now.

"I looked out of the window and saw him there, but a second later, he was gone. Only, there was a cat sitting on the wall at the end of the drive. It looked as though it was staring right back at me. I shut the blinds and went straight up to Bea." Her hands began to shake, but I steadied them with mine and she calmed.

"A man and a cat," I said slowly, taking it in. A couple of months ago, I would have agreed that sounded ridiculous, but knowing what I knew now, I wondered who it could have been. Was Eldar looking for me? Could he have followed my scent? Or was it something else entirely?

My voice couldn't hide my nervousness as I continued with the only logical question I could think to ask. "Did you recognise them? What colour was the cat?"

She gave me a curious glance as if to question whether I believed her or not. She leaned back into the cushions and rested her elbow on the arm of the chair. Her fist balled up under her chin, and she nodded to herself slightly then shook her head.

"No, I don't think so, and it was dark. Black, I think. Ahh, let's leave it at that. I'm tired. Let's go to bed." Mum finished her tea, and I sat holding mine, listening to her go up the stairs to the bathroom.

It was nice to sit in the quiet and warmth of the lounge, alone with my thoughts. I didn't like the idea of someone looking straight into the house, especially with Bea being here alone with Mum. It made me queasy. I hoped it was only Eldar following my scent. If it was, he surely wouldn't think my mum was me. Maybe he followed Bea's scent. Either way, it was worrying, and I was too troubled to sleep when I climbed into bed that night. When I did finally fall asleep, I dreamt Eldar had come into the house in his cat form and transformed into a man. In the dream, he wasn't charming and attractive at all. I knew from the second he showed up I should fear him. He attacked my mum and took Bea from me by force, but Ivan arrived and fought him to save Bea. It ended with Ivan and me and the sofa, and I rather enjoyed that part of the dream and woke up feeling refreshed.

The next day was a Saturday. I'd been loving our family weekends together and didn't want to waste this one, so by the time Mum had come downstairs, I had Bea and me washed and dressed, ready to head out when she was. I'd put Bea in the cutest corduroy pinafore dress with her rainbow tights and bunny slippers. I finished it off with a mustard-coloured cardigan.

I fed Bea and convinced Mum it was a good idea to get some fresh air to clear her head. It was a nice day so far. The sun was bright, but there was a chill in the air with the year drawing on toward winter. I promised Mum that if she still didn't feel comfortable, we'd head straight back home. She wasn't one hundred percent sure, but agreed.

Something Mally had said to me jumped into my mind, and I leapt off the sofa and into the kitchen to find the box Mally had asked me to bring home for Mum a few weeks ago. Mum had left it in the back of the kitchen in the window and filled it with pieces of string, offcuts of paper, pieces of burnt down candle or wick, and lots of bits of wax she'd obviously picked off whatever she'd had the candle burning on. There it was. In the box amongst all the other oils and essences Mum had opened and thrown in there was the little box of oil Mally said she had made for me.

"Here," I said, holding it up to Mum. "Mally reckons this will help."

Mum crossed the room and took the bottle from me, opened the lid, and sniffed it. She then nodded and dabbed a bit on her finger. "You're a funny one, Ena," she told me with an expression of bewilderment.

I shrugged. "Well, if you do believe this stuff, then let's run with it."

It wasn't the oils and apparent hidden witchyness of my Mum that had bothered me but the secrecy. I had always imagined Mum to be a bit different in the things she did. Now, it seemed there was more to it, but still not as complicated as I had always believed witchcraft to be. I thought witches, shifters, everything I had learned over the last couple of months would be as they were on TV and in books. Supernatural theory, things normal people didn't believe and frowned upon. If someone said they were practicing witchcraft, they were either avoided or going through a phase. I had never considered it to be a part of our lives. Perhaps it wasn't hidden after all, I had just never seen it for what it was. That was what unnerved me. That my whole life, I had never seen what there was there right in front of me. I had blamed and shamed Mum for all our moves, for my anger, and ignored the fact she was holding it all together for me, to keep me safe. It was difficult for me, although I had accepted that it was creeping in. From all the shifting and the things I'd learned about Mum, it was apparent it was a part of my life now, as it had always been. I was finding it hard to say, *yes, this is me.* I didn't have the confidence or the mental strength to get myself to openly agree that I was starting to believe. It was easier for me to brush it under the carpet and say it was someone else's calling, not mine. But it was mine too, and I had to take responsibility for it. I had to choose it. At that moment, I wasn't prepared to.

"You've gone quiet," Mum said, while I just stood there. She was already putting Bea into her car seat.

"Hmm. Sorry. Just tired, I guess." I grabbed the car keys and pulled on my plimsoles whilst she wrestled the heavy car seat into the car.

A few hours later, Mum and I left the café and walked down the town's main street, looking in the shop windows and pointing out things we liked while Bea slept in her pushchair. I was tired and full of brunch and too much Earl Grey. I was looking forward to an evening on the sofa instead of being at work. The sun was out, but there was still a chill, so I wore my cardigan. Now we had come back outside, I pulled a thin blanket over Bea. I wished I had put on longer trousers as my ankles were chilly in my cropped jeggings.

Town was busy enough, people passing us by without a second glance, children skipping along holding on to the hands of their carers, the occasional policeman nodding their greetings as people passed. Part of the town was cobbled and uneven, and it was the older shops which had been in the town a lot longer that ran along the cobbles. The street we were on had an old pub on either end, and in the middle, there was a bakery, and an old grocers, which was becoming more popular now with loose fruit and veg after having a rough few years. There was a butcher's shop before the last pub, but I noted that the fishmonger had gone as the old shop was empty as we passed. As a child, when I lived there, I used to look through the window every time we were in town, trying to see the crabs and find the biggest fish I could. My favourite florist was on this street too, and I paused briefly as we passed to smell the flowers in the buckets on the shop front. They had yellow freesias in bunches, so I went in and bought a couple to cheer Mum up. As we reached the end of the street, we turned left for the car park. We had to walk down a small alleyway from the street to the car park. It was pedestrian only, so it wasn't very wide. As we neared the end of the alley, I saw something move from the corner of my eye, and I suddenly the hair on my arms was standing on end. Instinctively, I leaned forward to smell the air, but then remembered I wasn't a cat, but I did see something I wouldn't normally have seen. Was I starting to lose myself too? Impossible. It had been weeks. I hadn't been part of that world for long.

"What is it?" Mum asked, stopping short of the end of the alley. She put her hand on my shoulder, which made me jump and snapped me from my thoughts.

"I thought I saw something."

As if she could detect the anxiousness in my voice, she stood between the end of the alley and Bea's pram. Crap, I hadn't even thought to do that. I had a lot to learn.

She tilted her head slightly as if trying to listen, which I had seen her do in the past, but seeing her do it now filled me with curiosity. Was it a bit like me leaning forward to smell?

From around the corner of the alley came a man. He wasn't particularly tall, but he was well-built, and in a t-shirt that was a size too small. He stopped and stood at the end of the alley right in front of us and tried to stare us down. Mum stood her ground, and so did I, her strength giving me strength.

He had scruffy brown hair and a moustache and

beard, which were also unkept. His neck and cheeks were flushed, and his hands curled into fists so tight the knuckles were turning white. It was then I noticed the smell, like wet dogs and stale alcohol. I wanted to run so badly, but with a pushchair, I'd never get far, and neither would Mum.

Tattoos wove up his arms like vines creeping up from his wrists. I could see the ends of them meeting where his t-shirt ended at his neck. He had a slight smile on his lips, and he winked at us. The cheeky shit.

As he advanced towards us, we slowly backed away down the alley and became aware that there were others behind us on the other side of the wall. Probably casually leaning on the wall so they didn't look suspicious, but ready to grab us if we made a run for it. I looked over my shoulder and couldn't see them, but somehow, I knew they were there. Mum and I stopped moving back and stood our ground. The tension grew as no one moved or spoke.

Suddenly, he put his hand forward to grab the chair.

I rolled my shoulders back and they cracked so loudly that even Mum whipped her head around. I shook my head until my eyesight was clear, my hearing sharpened so I could hear the swish of my hair as it whipped past my ears. My ears which were now half the height they had been but so much more focused. I felt the power in my legs and arms as they formed the muscular legs of a panther, and my snarl ripped through the alley. My front paws slammed against the cobbles, and I stretched my back ones out behind me, ready to leap. Mum grabbed the pushchair as I pounced on the man. I didn't think, just followed my instinct as I pulled at his clothes, shredding his top and jeans until they were nothing, and the man beneath me struggling was almost naked. I could see the sharp grazes caused by my teeth on his chest when grabbing the fabric. My teeth sank into his tattooed arm, and I've never heard a sound like the one he made before he was my prey. As soon as I smelled the blood, I feared I wouldn't be able to stop. He pushed my face from him, but it wasn't enough to hold me. There were tears in his eyes as he clung to my skin and pushed me back. I knew I was stronger than him, so I forced his hands back until my nose was an inch from him. I could smell the fear in his tears and breath. I could see in his eyes that he thought I was going to kill him. I wasn't a killer. So, as quickly as I had advanced, I leapt back and let him go. My eyes narrowed to slits and the growls still came from between my bared teeth, but I stood between Mum, Bea, and him, ready to attack again should he not run. He lay on the floor, bleeding and panting. I could literally smell the relief leaving his body.

In that second, I had seen myself ripping him apart. I was prepared for the heat, the blood, and the fact that he would die at my hands, but as I stood over him, looking into his eyes, I saw my reflection. I knew I was more than that. I didn't have to give in, but I didn't have to cause harm. It wasn't self-defence if they had given up but revenge, and that was different.

The other men had heard the commotion and hovered between us and the street. They had seen what had happened and hadn't moved in fear and uncertainty. I turned to face them and paced slowly forward, head and shoulders low, growling. One of them shook his head and ran. The other shrank against the wall to get past me to his friend. I let him, keeping my body between Bea and Mum and the man. He pulled his friend to his feet, ignoring that he was dripping with blood and barely clothed, and they shuffled off around the corner. I knew they weren't moving fast by the sound of their feet, but I didn't shift back until I heard the click of the car door and smelled the car leaving the car park. I knew there was no one else nearby to disturb us as I could hear only them.

Sighing, I let my body snap back. This time, I had made a full change. I hadn't left my body behind; I had changed my body too. Spider had said I could do it if I focused, even without proper training. I just had to believe it without thinking about it. I must have been more powerful than I thought. Maybe this was the push I needed. For a second, I thought of Ivan, his sharp green eyes, and his scruffy, black hair. I imagined him running his hands through it like he did at work and shivered. Not the time nor the place.

"Ena?" Mum asked quietly. I had forgotten she was there for a second.

Damn Ivan. Damn the attacker. Damn everything.

"Um, yes?" I said, not sure what to say. She nodded and looked me up and down. My shoulders were tense and my back dripping with sweat, more than if I had done a session at the gym with weights. I was still breathing heavily as I recovered from the adrenaline and shock. She put an arm around my shoulder, which made my whole body twitch.

"We need to talk," she said. "Not here. At home."

We walked to the car in silence, and I seethed. I'd just saved us from a thug who could have done anything to us, and all she had to say was that we had to talk? Ugh, I was so over this whole thing. I'd felt powerful, felt it running through my veins. The heat of it was amazing. I'd never experienced anything like that in my life. Perhaps I wasn't over it after all. It was only on the way home, watching the world as we passed in the car that I regained more rational thought. Mum couldn't possibly have had that conversation with me in a car park, and there was that relentless, nagging guilt again. I wished to be free of it. Luckily for me though, she let my brief surge of frustration go.

CHAPTER 21

Ena

When we arrived home, Bea needed feeding, so I curled up on the sofa with a mug of tea and fed her whilst Mum busied herself in the kitchen. This seemed to be normal for us when anything happened. We didn't talk about it until we had made a hot drink and sat with a few minutes to think about what we wanted to say. The act of making the tea was in itself methodical and therapeutic and part of the routine Mum and I needed before opening up. I knew if we got straight in and talked, it wouldn't have been the same.

Bea fed on one side for a while then swapped before falling asleep again. I was sleepy myself after my transformation. Dropping off into my own thoughts, I imagined and planned another shift. A mild one only, to see if I could do a full body change. I didn't think Mum would be too pleased though, and I wouldn't be able to leave Bea unattended. I was nodding off when Mum came in and sat down on the chair opposite me.

"Ena." I looked up at her sleepily. "So, you don't seem to have too many questions about what happened this afternoon. So, I assume you've done that before."

My eyelids snapped open, and I stared at her, thinking how best to answer without upsetting her.

"I have."

She took a deep breath in. "How long?"

"Not long." I sat up straighter. "Just before my new job. Maisy found a book in the library and printed off a guide. She thought it was a bit of fun, but she couldn't do it. I tried, and I could. She doesn't know though. I could never do it fully until today. I had a few practice sessions, but then I decided I didn't want to become addicted to it and stopped. I haven't thought about it in weeks." A slight lie, but I didn't want her to think I'd been thinking about it too often, especially with me keeping it from her. I should have mentioned it from the start.

"You were more like a ghost?" she mused, nodding. I took a quick gulp of tea and wriggled out from under Bea. I lay her on the sofa next to me, hoping she'd stay asleep a little longer. My arm was numb, so I shook it until the familiar tingle of pins and needles swam towards my fingers. "When did you find the time...? Ahh, meditation, and possibly the gym."

I smiled at her as she put two and two together. Seemed like we were both completely unobservant when it came to things like each other shifting and messing with witchcraft.

"I'm sorry. I didn't know what was going on, and before I knew it, I couldn't stop. I did stop for a while though because Spider said you can lose yourself in it and not come back. The more people I met, the more complicated it was to know what I was doing."

Damn. I had wanted to get away with this without mentioning the others, let alone Spider. Why did I mention Spider? Every time I opened my mouth, more came out than I had intended, and I spoke quickly, like a child trying to explain themselves. She had a new interest now, and looked concerned more than curious.

"So, you're keeping your identity a secret, I assume? This Spider, he told you all about that, did he? Or the *people* you've met... do you know much about them? Where they're from?"

"Yes, my identity is a secret. Spider was the first shifter I met that wasn't an actual animal, although the fox I met seemed to know all about shifters too. Spider saw me and knew what I was. Don't worry though. I don't think I'll see him again."

I must have looked disappointed because Mum said, "It's not that I don't trust you, Ena. It's just that I know this world. I was in this world. So was your father."

That surprised me. I sucked in a breath and stared into my teacup, feeling the warm steam flow over my mouth and nose. I might have guessed at Mum, being a witch, and with Mally and Devan. I should have figured it out and mentioned it to be sure, but my dad? I thought of Eldar, and him leaving his child so they could grow up away from all of this. I wondered if that was what happened with my dad.

For half an hour or so, Mum pottered around the room tidying, and I sat in silence watching Bea sleep. Nursing my tea and my thoughts.

"Those nights you left with the car. Was that really the gym and Maisy's?" Mum asked as she took my cup from me and disappeared into the kitchen. I followed her as we talked, her doing bits of housework and me wandering behind answering her questions. I had a few of my own.

"I left my car at Maisy's." I admitted, embarrassed I had just left my car and my body in a car park. It seemed reckless now I explained it to her, although I was relieved to finally feel comfortable having this conversation out loud instead of in my head. "I shifted and left the window open. I think it was safe enough, but I know better now. They might be able to follow my scent back." I didn't mention that Spider already had.

"Who is they?" Mum asked, raising an eyebrow. She didn't seem surprised that I'd met others, but curious.

"I met some other shifters. Don't worry, they don't know a lot about me really, except maybe one who did seem to know me." My cheeks flushed but Mum didn't push me to say more.

"There are different groups of shifters around here, Ena. Some are peaceful, on their own and just doing their own thing. We rarely hear from them. Then there is a group which came together to help to protect each other when they needed to. They became a family group and trust each other, or a coven if you will, as some of them are also witches. There is another group I know of, in the city." She paused and turned away from me. It was a few more minutes before she continued. From the kitchen doorway, I could see Bea stir on the sofa, and a lump rose in my throat fearing that if she woke our conversation would be over, for now.

"This other group in the city is the one your father left to join. They aren't the nicest of people and even worse as shifters. Sneaky, cunning, but only one or two actually know about witchcraft which makes them even more powerful. Your father used what he knew to get in to this gang. Because he had powers they did not, he rose very quickly in the ranks and was rewarded by their leader at the time. They steal, gamble, traffic women, and if you owe them a debt, there isn't any getting out from under them until it has been repaid with interest. Some people and some shifters go to them for help. Some are blackmailed into it and find they can never leave without paying a higher price than they'd imagined. The local coven of shifters, the one I am desperately hoping are the other shifters you mentioned meeting, sometimes help to hide those hunted by the gang. They help relocate their families and offer them protection, which is why the city gang is targeting them. You must be very careful, Ena, with who you trust. Not everyone will be looking to help you."

"So, Dad left to be with them?" I was disgusted, and Mum nodded slowly.

"At first it was just a few of us. Your dad, me, and a few of our closer friends. I favoured the form of a barn owl, flying softly over the rooftops and trees. The wind beneath my body, lifting me up. I felt weightless and powerful. It was a great way to escape the real world in a time where there really wasn't anything in the human world for me. I almost lost myself to that world. Your father actually did for a long time."

"So, what happened?" I asked, not daring to take my eyes from her. She looked like a rabbit in the headlights. I thought if I broke eye contact, she would bolt, and I would still need answers.

"We were a small coven, hurting no one as our oath, but he learned some darker magic. At first he perceived he could better our lives as humans, bring us money and have people treat us with more respect. I didn't agree with him, and so he'd practice these magics in secret. Darker magics."

"Sorry, what do you mean by coven?"

"It is loosely another word for a family you have made for yourself. Not necessarily blood ties but tied by magic and common knowledge. We protected each other's secrets and took an oath to never harm anyone nor each other. Your father broke that oath, and as hard as it was, we had to cast him out."

"Cast him out?"

"He made some very bad decisions, got into trouble with the wrong people in the city. When they came for him, he killed them. He endured no remorse, said he was protecting the coven, but it was he who put it in danger in the first place. We had to leave him, break our magical bonds, cloak ourselves from his sight. He was angry, found his own followers, and left with the gang in the city. We didn't see him for a long time, until..."

"Until?" I was on the edge of the dining table seat.

"Until he found out I was expecting you. We tried to keep it a secret, but he somehow found out and came to claim me, to take me back to his new group. I refused, and he tried to kill me. We lived by a code Ena. Harm none unless in protection of someone who cannot save themselves. He broke the code and didn't care. He saw me as his property, and you, my unborn daughter, as his property. He wanted to raise you in his world as a powerful leader by his side. A mix of magic and shifting. You'd be rich and everyone would fear you. This is a life you must choose for yourself, so I hid you away. Moving every time he tracked us down, with the help of my friends in the shifter world and in the human one. We were protected, but he was too powerful. If he actually got to us, I'm not sure we'd be able to stop him from taking us."

I was so absorbed in her story I hadn't noticed that we'd both started to cry. I bit my lip, wanting to hold her tightly but unable to move my muscles. Instead, I hugged myself and sucked in my breath through my teeth.

"I'd imagined some broken man deprived of his child. Instead, he was hunting us down to steal me from you," I said in a voice I wasn't sure she had heard. Hearing this stabbed into me like blades.

It would seem I had inherited her power to change forms, which was proven by my panther. Although still the form of a cat, it was certainly different and had come to me when I hadn't even called it. Mum said my gift had come to me when I wasn't overthinking it, a bit like Mr E had said in the library. I made a mental note to apologise next time I saw him. He must have known what was going on. I was sure he and Mum still talked occasionally; they were the kind of friends who were always there for you even though you didn't see them as often.

"Your father was able to form the biggest of

predators and brought down anyone in his way. He was brutal, and valuable to his leader. The dark magic changed him, made him insecure and greedy. At first I was sure he thought he was actually doing something good for us, but luckily, I saw what was really happening and never let him have you. They've never stopped looking for us, him and his followers."

Somehow, it would seem my shifting must have led them to her. Guilt caused me to physically ache, but I also needed more answers. Mum told me it was inevitable he would catch up to us one day, and it was probably more coincidence that I would figure out how to do it now, especially as I had Bea to protect too. We couldn't hide forever.

I told her Mr E had given me the guide to shifting via Maisy, and this amused her. She said he did try to help in a roundabout kind of way. Perhaps he'd sensed my dad and his gang in the area.

"He's a funny old man, that Devan," she said with a small smile. "You never know why he does the things he does. He might have been trying to prepare you or he might just have been bored." I snorted. I could imagine both being right, the old badger.

Before all of this, I would never have thought to watch for animals watching me, never have thought to feel with my instincts if there was something following me, but now I did.

"I think you need to go back in," Mum said eventually. "I think, after today, you need to go and see if it feels different. To try a full shift, alone, without the threat."

I turned it over in my mind, anxiety gnawing at me. "But what if something happens whilst I'm there? What if I can't get back to you, or ..." I looked at Bea, welling up with emotion. I had turned my back on shifting to spend more time with her and end the complications, but it looked like I had just added more. I had every reason not to return to shifting, but the pull back in was growing stronger with every minute I allowed myself to feel it.

"Bea will be okay," Mum insisted. "You'll never know if you don't try, but please, let me know when you go so I know you're on the other side and I know where to look for you."

She'd never tell me to stay away completely because she knew first-hand how hard it was once you'd started, but I was to be very careful and never shift back directly at the house. She had said pretty much what Spider had said. I needed a safehouse to shift, somewhere protected so the eyes who saw me going in and out were those of good friends, and that those in the human world could cloak the entrances and exits briefly whilst I left. It seemed far too complicated to me.

Mum gave me a cluster of amethyst and told me

that if I decided to go back and couldn't bring myself to tell her, or if she wasn't home, I was to leave it outside my bedroom door so she knew when she came home. She had Bea in the evenings anyway whilst I was working, so it would just be keeping an eye on her for an extra hour or so after work. I could live with that. For now.

On the Sunday after the incident, Mum and I only spoke of it a bit, and I was grateful for it. In the evening, however, she brought me into the kitchen to tell me she intended to cast another protection spell over the house and the immediate surrounding area. She admitted to casting them in the past whilst I had been out, but with this one being a little bigger, she didn't want to exclude me anymore now I was involved.

"I would never ask you to believe, nor would I do anything if you refused. I would never ask you to perform a spell or even be in the same room if you decided not to. All I ask is that you accept it is what I believe and respect that all I want to do is protect the ones I love. If you refuse the spell, I will not cast it." Spell casting was a lot about consent. With me now knowing why she had done things the way she had, she was trusting me to make the right call.

I assumed that now I could refuse to have the house protected, which meant Bea would be exposed to anyone who might come prowling, Mum was asking me to trust her judgement. I told her I did, and if she thought it was the right thing to do, she should do it.

Mum laid all of her essences and oils out on the kitchen table. "It's important you understand where I'm coming from. Each essence and oil has different properties which make it useful for different spells."

"Are you going to make a potion?" I asked, feeling silly saying the sentence out loud. Mum laughed a little.

"Remember when you used to make stick potions in the garden when you were little? There really isn't a special word for it. Spell casting, incantations, potions, brews... you can call them many things. Much of it is about feeling what you need. It becomes an instinct. However, it still needs to be taught. You can't just throw some things in as a child might. Saying that, you did seem to have an extra sense about you when you made them. It was very interesting to watch."

I blushed as she said it. She took a couple of candles from the windowsill.

"We'll start with a basic protection spell as a base, one you can remember if you ever need to. You don't have to do anything, just listen and watch." She did something she called casting a field, with salt around the dining table where she had laid out her candles and oils.

She told me it was very important that I either stay inside or outside of the field, because if I broke it, she would have to start over. I decided to stay on the outside, fearing it a little. The look on her face was intense, concentrating as she laid out her candles and dotted oil over them from her little bottles before lighting them.

"The field around me protects me whilst I work, and it focuses the energy," she said with a furrowed brow. "But don't worry, when the spell is complete, it will extend to you and Bea, and the house as I close the field."

I nodded and hardly dared to breathe.

Bea was asleep in the lounge on some cushions on the floor. I was going to take her up to bed, but for some reason, that night I wanted to keep her downstairs with me where I could see her.

"The field will also protect me from anyone I don't want to see what I'm doing. These sorts of things can be detected by those who know what to look out for and can work against my spell to make it negative. If my field is strong, they won't be able to see or feel exactly what I'm doing unless, like you, I have allowed them to."

A chill filled my bones as I watched. It was suddenly as cold as winter, and I rubbed my arms, trying to get warm. Touching my fingers to my face, they were like ice, but I didn't dare move, apart from to put my head back round the door to check on my sleeping angel.

When Mum had finished and told me it was safe to wander around, I stayed in the doorway until she had cleaned up all the salt and put it into a small box. Then I left the room, and without thinking about it, curled up on the floor next to Bea, my head on the cushions, watching the rise and fall of her little chest. My whole world had flipped right over. One day, I was quiet, fed up, just going with the flow and not really wanting anything, but everything had changed that day when Maisy had given me those books. Mr E must have known it would have some sort of effect on me, and now I didn't know what to expect, or what was expected from me. I hoped they didn't expect much. My brain wasn't ready to fit in anything more than coming to terms with the things I was experiencing already, yet my heart secretly yearned for more.

We're not done yet. We have more to learn.

"Mum?" I called.

"Yes, E?"

"If you die in your shifted form, what happens to your body?"

Mum peered around the doorway and looked at me lying on the floor with Bea. "What makes you ask that?"

"I was just wondering. Do you just disappear?"

"Well, it's a little more complicated than that. If you're still connected somehow to this world, then your soul will be snapped back, ripped from your shifted form into human form. It will be incomplete, but you will be alive."

I nodded. "So, you can live but never shift again?"

"Something like that. Your shifted form, if solid, will

die. It will be as any other dead thing, and you will no longer have any connection to that world. You will be blocked out. The part of your soul that gives itself to the shift will be gone. If they kill you in your human form too, you will be gone."

"So, if someone killed me as a cat, I would snap back to being human, but there would be a dead cat there?" Mum nodded. "Does that work the other way round too?" I asked before I could stop myself.

"It does. If your human form is killed, then you will remain in the shifter world. Again, incomplete, but alive. There are very powerful witches who can sometimes reconnect you with your soul if they act very quickly, usually as soon as you have died but before your soul has had time to fade away. It can be reattached, and you can recover."

This was too heavy for me, and the wave of sleep drifted over me. I yawned. "What happens if you've already been in the shifter world too long? If you, you know, don't ever go back."

"Ah, I see what you're getting at. If one has chosen to give up their human form in this world completely and gives in to the shifted form, then when they die, they die. That's it. Just like any human who has never shifted or refuses to try. They just fade on."

Time moved on, and Mum was still nervous about the incident in the town. Who could blame her? I was still unsettled about it but tried to act as though it hadn't bothered me. So far, I hadn't allowed myself to shift. I had refused to go back in. Mum respected my decision, although I was sure she watched me more closely over the days that followed.

CHAPTER 22

Spider

I'd already been out most of the night and was on my way back to the safehouse when I sensed something wasn't quite right. The street was quiet apart from the hum of cars close by and the familiar drone of buildings. The sound was a combination of electrical items and humans inside moving around or sleeping, pets scraping, televisions on low, fridge freezers buzzing. Something stopped me dead in my tracks, something I hadn't actually heard. It called to my subconscious. My soul knew something had happened to cause it pain, and I paused to listen, scraping the tarmac with anxious claws. Something terrible had happened, and I had missed it. What was it? My blood ran cold. I knew it was nothing to do with Night Flower, but the sudden terror that gripped me had come from someone I had known. Someone my soul knew. I turned back down the dark street, the streetlamps reflecting in puddles on the road. From the town, I could have sworn I heard a woman scream, one that sent a bolt of lightning through my bones.

I could hear paws coming from around the corner, thudding against the ground. The being was much bigger than me, and I prepared my body and mind to face it or flee, change forms, or stay as a cat. I wasn't sure until I saw what the paws belonged to, but I knew they were coming for me. I was the only one there and I had just scent marked that corner.

I pressed my back into the shadows by the wall. My heart hushed to a whisper and my paws stilled. I listened.

Relief crashed over me as the being rounded the corner and pelted down the street toward me. It was Harry. I stepped out of the shadows onto the pavement in front of him, and he slowed to a stop, panting heavily with his huge tongue lolling out. His head was almost as big as my entire body, but I wasn't afraid of him.

Harry was a huge, long-haired German Shepherd. His fur was dark and looked even darker in the night. His eyes weren't as accustomed to the low light as mine, so he squinted down at me, giving me a good sniff before trying to slow his breathing. I waited patiently. Trying to keep my breathing regular was difficult seeing his so ragged. He must have run all the way from the station. Harry was a police dog.

"What the hell happened?" I asked, stepping toward him.

"It's Sam," he panted, sitting down on the ground and scratching his ear with his back paw then biting his foot as if the itch had transferred. I'd always liked dogs, but some of their habits were a little strange. My eyes grew wide.

"Sam Mathis?" I asked more urgently.

Harry nodded, his long open snout making the movement more exaggerated. "He's been shot. You have to hurry! The ambulance is on its way."

As soon as he said it, I heard the blaring of sirens only a few streets away. If he'd come to tell me about this himself, it must have been significant. There must have been something I needed to know before he was taken away. I took control.

"Get Gray," I ordered. Harry nodded again in acceptance. He didn't mind taking orders; he was made for them. "Get The Leader. Then meet me at the Mathis' place." I was already running back towards town. I didn't need to look back to know he was already heading into the yard of the safehouse to check for Gray. If it wasn't so urgent, I'd have got him myself.

It wasn't far to my friend Sam's shop. It was a popular betting shop he ran with his dad. Sam wasn't a shifter, but his dad was. He was friends with my dad. Sam knew about our world but was never able to fully join it.

Still, he kept our secret and knew quite a few shifters in his human form. It made it easier knowing that if I really wanted to, I could bring up my Night Flower dilemma with him and he'd totally get it. Maybe I'd never have the chance if he died. We didn't really hang around much anymore. We both had commitments. He to the young family he was starting, and me with my... whatever I had. Still, we were always there for each other. Even after not speaking for months, he had agreed to help me with the idea to get in and spy on some of those who opposed us. For him to send Harry to me must have meant he really needed me, otherwise he'd have waited until I could see him in hospital. I was fast on my four paws. I could have shifted into something faster but didn't want to waste a second. I already knew I wouldn't make it because no matter how much I put into my run, I still couldn't match the speed of the ambulance and its head start.

As I reached the betting shop, there were already several police cars there with their blue lights flashing and one officer putting up tape to keep onlookers at bay. Not that there were many. It was really late. I had no idea how late, but it was well past midnight. I paused, surveying the scene. Police cars, officers, a couple of dogs, which was why Harry must have been there. They were searching for someone. There were two ambulances, both with doors open. Into the back of one, the paramedics were taking a covered stretcher. Whoever was under there must have passed on. My soul told me Sam was still alive, and I didn't have to ask who might be under there. Dad was going to be heartbroken.

There was no way of getting to him as they took him to the ambulance. He too was on a stretcher, but I could see he was awake but covered with blood. Who knew if it was his own? I could smell it over the diesel fumes and sweat, thick, rusty, and a bit like cold baked beans. I slipped like a shadow past the officers and neighbours. They couldn't see me. I had cast a spell over my being so they wouldn't notice I was there unless I wanted them to. Not unless they were looking specifically for me, and why would they? Why would anyone be looking for a cat right now, especially one with my face? *Fools*, I thought as I passed and slid sneakily through the door. Two officers stood in the doorway. Their boots reeked of leather and bleach, but that was nothing compared to the smell from the shop. The smell of death. I recoiled, retched, and gagged as the smell filled my lungs. It was a sour smell, not unlike rancid pork. I looked around, my eyes adjusting to the light before padding in further, not sure exactly what I was looking for until it was staring me in the face. The body of a cat lay stretched out across the lino flooring, its back twisted unnaturally back on itself, and its paws splayed, eyes staring at me. I knew that face. It was the face of Sam's father. This time, instead of retching, I was sick. A fire burned within my chest. I knew it wasn't the bile, although that burned too. It was a rage. This was a targeted killing. A shifter killing.

-

Ena

On Monday, Mum was working, so I took Bea to the library. I just had to get out of the house, and seeing Maisy was the first thing I thought of. I knew it would be quiet, so I packed a few snacks and Bea's changing bag and walked to the library. The sun was out and there was barely a cloud in the sky. It wasn't warm, but I didn't need my coat either. Bea was happily babbling away in her pushchair and waving at anyone we passed. I was happy she was so happy. I loved watching her interact with the world and wondered what it must be like to see things the way she did.

As we arrived, Maisy's face lit up. She had clearly been missing us as she rushed over and unclipped Bea from the pushchair. Bea held out her squishy little arms for her favourite friend and made a high-pitched cooing sound, which made Mr E look up over his newspaper. Of course he was there. I nodded a greeting to him, my face growing warm, and he smiled in return before popping the paper back over his face. He knew, I knew, we all knew and didn't need to talk about it. Except Maisy. How could I possibly put this into words? I had found them for

Mum, but she already had some idea of what was going on. I didn't know where I could start with Maise, and the fact I had hidden it for so long just made it harder to say out loud.

Maisy danced around the library with Bea, singing, whilst I put the kettle on and settled into her chair behind the customer service desk. There was no one else there, so I didn't see why it would be a problem. On her desk were copies of today's newspaper, and by the way they were open and scattered, she must have been reading them before I arrived.

I poured us both a coffee and one for Mr E before joining them in the children's area. Maisy was sitting cross-legged on the floor, holding up a picture book, whilst Bea crawled around on her mat, picking up books and patting them. Bea loved the library, and why wouldn't she? She had had some great experiences there with Maisy, reading and singing, and the groups we visited. Even when it was quiet, it was colourful and smelled like books. It was peaceful.

"Did you see in the paper what happened last night?" Maisy asked, lifting Bea onto her knee.

I pulled a face to express I didn't know. "I saw the papers on the desk but didn't read them. Why? What happened?" I stood up to grab one of the newspapers and joined Maisy and Bea on the playmat.

On the front there was a headline.

One dead. Two critically injured in suspected robbery. My eyes flickered down to the text. It happened in our town last night? I read the article as quickly as I could, and Maisy watched my face for my reaction. A couple of sentences from the end of the article was something that made my blood run cold. *The body of a cat was also found at the scene, shot dead.* I held my breath, looking to see if anyone had been named.

"A shooting?" I said out loud, finally allowing myself to breathe. I exhaled in slight relief as the men's names were ones I didn't recognise.

"I know. Shocking, isn't it?" I stared at the paper. Nothing like that ever happened around here. "They think its linked with that incident a few weeks ago, when the police were looking for people. Remember, you said they stopped you? They think one of the men shot was involved then too. They have police in with him, so when he comes round, I'm sure they'll question him."

"That's not in this paper," I said, scanning the article again.

"No, it's in one of the others. I had a quick search online. It was at the betting shop on the high street. Probably some customer who didn't like not winning, I guess, but so odd. And who would shoot the cat too? That's taking it way too far." She sighed.

We watched Bea crawl around the book boxes, pulling out picture books and dropping them in a pile before pulling herself up on one of the boxes to get a better look inside.

"Yeah, you're right. To shoot someone. To kill someone. Then the bloody cat?" I said, unsure whether to chalk it up to another coincidence or to accept the gnawing feeling it was linked. Why would someone kill a cat too, unless the man was a shifter, and they were after both forms? Or maybe they were just sick.

Unable to ignore the urge any longer, I glanced over at Mr Ealing, who had put down his paper. Maisy read my mind.

"What do you think, Mr E?" she called. She stood up to grab her coffee from the side, and I copied her. After taking a swig, she called to him again. "What do you make of it all? Shootings only round the corner?" When her questions were met with silence, she shook her head and turned back to me. "I did see the police on the high street when I went into Tesco this morning on the way here but thought nothing of it. I didn't think until I saw the headlines on the pile of papers when I got here. I looked online, and apparently there was another man, but he ran off. They don't know who he is. There's a reference for Crime Stoppers." She collected all the papers together and put them into a rough pile.

Maisy had a pile of papers delivered to the library daily; the paper boy left them outside the door for when she opened up. I don't think anyone but Mr Ealing read them though.

"It is a very sad day," Mr Ealing said after a while. I'd almost forgotten he was there as my mind wandered. He stood shakily and reached for a walking stick he'd propped against the computer desk next to the sofa he'd been sitting on. With a look at the newspaper in Maisy's hand and then a glance at me, I knew straight away there was more to it.

"I'll pour you a tea this time, yes?" I said nervously, suddenly feeling the need for the routine of making a brew. I was fumbling for the tea bags in the draw, my mind racing, when the weight of his hand warmed my shoulder.

He gave me a squeeze and took a seat at the customer service desk. I put his tea on the desk and scooped up Bea, needing the comfort of holding her.

"Now, this man who was shot. I knew him back in the seventies. We worked together for a while." He tapped the headline on the front of the paper.

Maisy's expression changed to one of curiosity, and she pulled up another chair. "You knew him, Mr E? I'm sorry for your loss," she said in a tone that was neither empathetic nor interested. I suspected she was trying to cover for how nosey she was feeling.

"Aye. Now, Mr Mathis, he owned the betting shop on High Street. He also had that one on the corner of Brierton, do you know it?" We both shook our heads.

"Well, one of the men shot was his son, but he's still with us, thank goodness. I can't be sure who the other one is. I expect his son's wife will sort the funeral." Mr E sadly sipped his tea.

Maisy put her arm around his shoulder. "I really am sorry," she said, with honest sympathy this time.

Bea squirmed in my arms, so I put her back onto her playmat. "Did you know him well?" I asked.

Mr Ealing nodded. I was hoping he wouldn't. "I did, yes. Martin was a good friend to me. He was the one who introduced me to Mally all those years ago. Ivan and his son used to have play dates. I expect Ivan will be a little worried about his friend." His voice trailed off, and I thought that last part had been aimed at me, although I didn't know why. Maybe he wanted me to try and talk to Ivan about it, to comfort him.

We talked about Mr Ealing's friend and finished our teas. The library had stayed quiet for the rest of the day, so I had stayed a bit longer before heading home to meet Mum.

CHAPTER 23

Ena

If Mum was bothered by the news, she didn't say anything. I went off to work as usual. I took the car though and parked as close to the door into work as I could.

Kym was in the staffroom when I arrived, her hair blue and pink and braided tightly from the top. She wore baggy black trousers and had her phone and headphones clipped to her belt.

"Hey." She danced over to me. "Hear about that shooting? Oh my God, it's not safe anywhere, is it? You know, they don't know who shot who, apart from the dead guy. Obviously, he wasn't the shooter, but there could have been another one who got away that they don't know about. I wonder if they got CCTV in there. Oh, and

I'd avoid Ivan if I were you. I've never seen him in such a bad mood. Honestly, I was two minutes late for my shift and he hit the roof. It's been so busy. I had to go out for a loo break, but now I'm back to it. I'll follow you down."

I'd barely had time to hang up my bag on a peg and put my phone into my back pocket before she took me by the arm, guiding me back out.

"I hope he's in his office when we get there." I glanced behind me to make sure he wasn't behind us to hear me.

"Probably will be." Kim held a door open for me. "You know, I know the guy who was shot."

"You do? The younger one or the older one who died?"

"The younger one, of course. Well, I kinda knew him. I met him in a nightclub."

"Sounds like you meet everyone in nightclubs," I joked, and she grinned at me.

"Actually... you're right about that. I do. He was friends with my ex, druggie friend. I'd just dumped said ex, we'd had an argument about something, I can't remember what but it's irrelevant. This guy who'd been selling stuff to him came over and asked me to dance. He seemed nice, and after all, I was out for a good time, so we had a bit of a dance, a bit of a kiss, a bit of a feel." Kym elbowed me in the side, and I tried to dodge, giggling. She didn't stop talking. As soon as I opened my mouth to ask her what happened, she carried on.

"Well, we went into the toilets, and I waited in one of the cubicles whilst he shot up by the sinks. There I was pants off, ready to get it on, but he changed his mind, came over all teary and blabbed about being married. Honestly, I was fuming. I slapped him across the face and went back out to the dance floor, the idiot. Forgot my bloody pants too. He could have come home with me, but I left alone. It's not often I leave alone."

I nodded with wide eyes. Who in the world forgets their pants?

"It sounds like you don't. You really eat your way through men, don't you?"

I wondered if that was too bold a statement, but luckily, she found it funny. By this time, we'd hit the warehouse floor and we both peeped though the door, checking for Ivan. As she sorted through a list of orders, I couldn't help glancing towards the office window. Mr E had said Ivan was close with the man who'd been shot, just like Mr E had known his father. I wondered if that was why he was in such a foul mood. As my mind wandered, the idea that Ivan might be on Kym's list of exes popped into my head. I shook the thought away, the pang of jealous startling me.

The first few hours floated by as I busied myself with picking and packing. Kym danced around the warehouse as usual with her headphone volume up so loud even I could hear the music. When it was time for her to head off, she gave me a huge open-mouthed grin and two thumbs up as she left the warehouse backwards, with her headphones still on full volume. I laughed at her and shook my head. Kym was brilliant. She just didn't give a crap about anything. I wished I could be more like that.

Another hour passed, and I was just finished packing some stationary when I realised I needed the toilet. I wasn't meant to have breaks with it only being a four-hour shift. Still, I needed the toilet badly, and it wasn't going to wait until I got home. I looked around the shop floor. Ben, one of the temps, was there somewhere. I'd seen him arrive, but I couldn't see him now. I looked through the office window for Ivan on my way to the door, but he wasn't there.

I slipped through the door in to the corridor on my way to the toilets. As I walked, I noticed two people in a side corridor leading to the accounting offices. I knew straight off one of them was Kym, but as I turned to give her a wave, I saw the other person standing with her and paused. He had his back to me, leaning almost casually against the wall, his arm above his head, hand in his hair. I'd recognise that awful suit anywhere. The way he leaned forward towards Kym was almost too close for me to be comfortable with. Clearly, they had been having a very intense conversation about something. Kym clocked me passing and gave me a big wave with both hands. I responded in the same way, but as Ivan turned to me and our eyes met, a sudden surge of jealousy wriggled through my veins that made me want to throw something at him. The body language, the way he'd been leaning. I didn't like it. What had they been talking about? I checked my watch. Hadn't she left an hour ago? Had they been standing in a side corridor talking for an hour? He'd been close enough he could have kissed her. I frowned at myself in the mirror in the women's loos. Was I bothered by this? I thought they hated each other. Yet didn't Ivan and I also hate each other? What if they were having the same crazy hot and cold relationship we were?

There's no 'we'. Not in this world, anyway.

I had been back on the warehouse floor for around forty minutes before Ivan finally returned to his office. I had walked quickly past the corridor I had seen them in and not looking at them, although I could see from the blur in the corner of my eye as I passed that they hadn't moved. I found myself in a bad mood, even ignoring Ben when he came over for a chat about something. I hadn't found out what because I had walked off, pretending I hadn't heard him. I hated myself for it afterwards and made a point of smiling at him when we passed on an aisle.

I pressed my lips together and did the same with my teeth. Ivan passed me without looking at me, and I could smell coffee and his aftershave waft over as he slammed the office door. I grabbed an order and moved away without looking back. For some reason, I was absolutely fuming with him and he hadn't even done anything. He seemed to know it too because when he did finally come out at the end of the evening, he snarled, "What's with you?"

I didn't reply. I headed down the nearest aisle, and when out of sight, gave in to a jog to the farthest corner of the warehouse. I thought I would cry, but I didn't. I stubbornly decided to get on with my shift and go home. I was being silly. There was nothing between Ivan and me, there never had been. So why was this feeling so overwhelming? It was like I was being physically crushed. Maybe he had had a thing with Kym. Maybe they were talking about Ivan's friend. It would be just like her to stick her nose in and make the same comments about drugs and their hook up to him too. Why would he be horrible to her at the start of her shift then spend almost two hours having a chat? Why couldn't they chat in the office? I had to stop thinking like that. I needed to clear my head, finish my work, and get out of there before I exploded.

I had my iPod in my back pocket. I pressed play, and Korn blared into my ears. It soothed me temporarily as I focused on the items I had to pick.

After picking, I returned to the packing station, surprised to see Ivan still standing outside his office door.

He tapped his ear and pointed at me. I assumed he wanted me to remove my headphones.

"Yes?" I asked, pretending not to be bothered.

"What are you listening to?"

What was I listening to? I was so confused. This man was infuriating.

"Korn."

"Oh, okay." He nodded like it didn't matter. "See you around. I'm done for the night. Ben is here somewhere. You both finish at ten. Security is locking up."

I looked at my watch. I still had a while yet before I finished. I wondered why he had made a point of telling me he was leaving. I tried not to show I cared. Instead, I nodded and turned away to pack my box. I didn't look back until I was sure he had left the warehouse floor. Perhaps he was meeting Kym. Would knowing either way make me feel better? Probably not, but I wanted to know anyway.

–

Ivan

I drove home with my music on so loud there was no way I could hear the road, even if I wanted to. It didn't drown out my thoughts though. They plagued me relentlessly.

Somehow, I got home on autopilot. I sat in the car

with my fists tightly grasping the steering wheel until I became aware of pins and needles in the ends of my fingers. I breathed in and stepped out of the car, grabbing my rucksack from the passenger seat and kicking the door shut. I wasn't precious about my car. I had the money to buy a really cool one if I wanted to. My parents were really well off, despite how frugally they lived. They had passed on an allowance to me over the years. Money every birthday and Christmas, and it had all added up. I rarely spent anything either, so if I wanted to, I could go out and buy a nice house on the beach. One with a huge glass wall so I could watch the sea crashing against the sand and see the rain running down the glass whilst I relaxed in an expensive suit with expensive whiskey. I could have a top of the range car and drive it wherever I wanted, if I wanted. I didn't though. I wanted the freedom those things seemed to scream. To be free enough to head off on my own and start my own life would be amazing. I could start my own business, and maybe find a nice girlfriend, one without complications. In reality though, the way I had been brought up was not to head out on my own and make something of myself, but to protect and help my parents when they needed me. Don't get me wrong, I loved and respected my parents, and they gave me everything they had, but it was expected of me to follow in my dad's line of work and, one day, take over. He was very secretive about his work, but also let me in just enough so I knew what was going on. I was thinking it was about time he retired and let me carry on the work he was doing. I was brought up to copy the way he did things, to learn the things he knew, and to work where he no longer could. I enjoyed it, and to be honest, it was the only real life I had. Working at the warehouse and coming home alone wasn't anything I really cared about. I didn't need the job, but I took it just to be doing something. I rarely slept, but then again, I never *had* slept much. If I was home during the day, I'd only drive myself crazy with not being able to settle. I needed the distractions a day job gave me. I had liked it once. Now it was more like I was keeping up the routine before what was left of me fell away.

I was angry I couldn't just leave, and I was angry I believed I needed to. Why spend money on things if they meant nothing in the life that had been planned out for me? No wonder my sister left and had nothing to do with any of us. She had been the lucky one. If I left too, there would be no one to look after my parents. They raised me to take care of them, of others, and because of how generous and caring they were, it seemed selfish to me to want or need anything for myself. I think they just expected me to be as generous as they were to others, but that left very little time for me to be me.

The door to the kitchen was unlocked. Mum was in the kitchen, making something on the hob. I snuck past her and was almost at the door when she called me, turning to me whilst wiping her hands on a tea towel.

"Nice day at work, love?" she asked. She sounded tired. She looked tired.

I forced a smile, but she would see straight through it. "The usual, " I replied, scratching my neck. "I'm tired. I'd best shower."

Mum watched my face whilst I spoke. Her face fell slightly, and guilt washed over me. She wanted so desperately for me to admit I was going through something, anything, but the words wouldn't leave my lips. I'd already talked about my friend being shot more than I'd have liked to with Kym. She'd seen me standing in the corridor with my head resting against the wall and paused to see if I was okay. Even after me having a go at her. She was a strange one. Nosey, but her heart was in the right place.

"Your father was looking for you. He was expecting you home hours ago." She turned back to her pan.

I had promised him I'd finish early, but I'd forgotten. Mum sniffed, and I got the impression she'd turned away because she had tears in her eyes. If I were a nice person, I'd have put my hand on her shoulder, comforted her, and asked her about her day. I wasn't a nice person though, so I said nothing and walked away.

I stripped off my suit, not bothering to hang it again. I off kicked my shoes into the corner and stopped to look at myself in the mirror. My recent obsession with the gym was paying off. I made a mental note to add in a few more sessions to work on my already solid abs, but then a thought from the back of my mind crept forward. *Why bother? Who are you doing it for?*

After taking a shower, I headed back out of the house to my night job. I made sure I said goodbye to Mum on the way out.

"You not hungry, Ivan? I've made you some soup. Honestly, you must be starving." She put the bowl of soup onto the table, her eyes pleading with me. I ignored them.

"Sorry, Mum. I've already eaten," I lied, but upon seeing the look in her eyes and knowing she would be expecting me to be upset about my friend, I added, "Save it for later. I'll have it when I get home."

-

Ena

"Do you mind if I go out for an hour?" I said, after returning home. It came out as almost a whisper, as if I didn't feel I deserved to go out at all. In fact, I was half hoping Mum hadn't heard me.

She looked up from her computer. "I have the baby monitor on, but don't be long. Bea might wake. Plus, I don't like the idea that there are murderers hanging around, even if it was in town," she said tiredly. "Oh Ena," she added. "Number four are away for the week. I have their house key to feed the fish."

"Okay," I said slowly, not understanding the connection. I pulled on my shoes.

"Pop over and feed them for me. Shift from their house tonight before you come home, then if there is anyone around, they'll think you've been there the whole time. You must find a safehouse or I can't possibly let you go out again after this. I can find one for you."

I considered it for a moment, then replied, "No, it's okay. I'll see if I can find Spider."

As I left, Mum picked up her phone. I wondered who she'd be messaging at that time of night.

CHAPTER 24

Ena

"Night Flower!" I heard him call my name across the breeze, and a smile curled on my lips before I had a chance to stop it.

I sat atop the brick wall at the end of my street, not far from where the boundary between the two territories was. It was Spider. His long legs carried him in an effortless bound toward me, his long, scruffy fur blowing in the breeze. Even though he infuriated me at work to the point that I wanted to throttle him most of the time, here, he was different. He was more playful, like an old friend, even though we hadn't known each other long. I enjoyed his company. He was silly but safe, yet at the same time, there ran a small twang of pain in my heart when I thought of his mother and what she had said. He must have been really depressed in the real world, and I wanted to help. I wanted to scream at him that I was there, but I couldn't. I wanted to be mad at him for how he had made me feel that evening at work, and I wanted to ask him what Kym had to say that was so important. I couldn't, of course. I could have pretended to be mad after how he behaved when I saw him last though.

No. All I could do was carry on like normal, avoid him like the plague in the town, and here we could just be Spider and Night Flower. If that was what was keeping him afloat, I was going to run with it, even if it meant he'd be there forever. I couldn't commit to forever, but I could commit to part time. I also knew part time would never be enough for this to work between us.

"Yes," I said simply as he leapt up beside me onto the wall. I heard a low rumble in his throat and was suddenly wary. My ears flattened until I realised what it was. "Are you... purring?" I almost laughed out loud at him. He looked away, clearly embarrassed.

"Sorry." He coughed and licked his paw to hide the hurt in his voice. "I thought you'd left us for good. I haven't caught your scent for a while now."

"I had. But I came back," I said with a grin.

"What for?"

"Oh, you know, this and that," I said playfully, not wanting to ruin the atmosphere. I watched the moonlight dance across his fur as it ruffled in the breeze. Damn my short hair. Why couldn't I have long, silky fur that flowed in the wind? Perhaps I should imagine that when I next shifted.

Mum had said if I wanted to try shifting, I needed a proper place to shift, where I couldn't be followed back home easily.

"Remember when I was here before, you told me about safehouses. That one we visited, am I okay to use it?" I asked. "Except I'm not sure how that would work. It's quite far to walk and someone could see me leaving my car."

"I have one or two. The Wise One said you could use them before you disappeared. Of the few, the one I use is probably the safest, and it's closer to here. It's well protected. You could leave your car there too if you needed to." He looked at the floor below the wall like he was preparing to jump down. He'd let me off lightly, not asking for more information about why I hadn't been around. Knowing Spider though, that would come later.

"Your own safehouse?" I asked. "Aren't you worried I'd be like some crazy stalker and try to figure out who you are? Wouldn't it be pretty obvious?"

He paused for a moment, then said. "Well, yes. There is always that possibility, I guess. There are a few of us who use it, but even I don't know everyone. There are ways to cloak yourself as you approach and you can be hidden until you emerge too. It's really complicated magic and I haven't got the hang of all of it yet. There are a few who help me with the trickier bits. We're peaceful, like we said before when you met The Wise One, but we do have our enemies. If they knew where the safehouses were, they would definitely try to figure out who we are. They're always looking out for them, as are we. The other gang would like nothing more than for us to be gone so they can have our territories in both worlds. We can't let them have them." He stopped talking and looked as though he was annoyed at saying too much.

"Why not? How can you spot a safehouse? Do people just disappear?"

He grinned at me. "Well, we kinda protect people from the gang members. The ones who come over from the city. They aren't nice people. They'd kill you before asking questions. You know, a bit like gangsters, only less Hollywood. We have scouts out looking for their safehouses all the time. Occasionally, we can find a new one and reverse the enchantments before they're made solid, but once they're solid, they're really hard to see, even if you know what you're looking for. A good safehouse won't stand out. You can stare at it all day and see nothing. The strongest ones will cloak someone who doesn't want to be seen for a good hundred metres. You could be staring at it all day and anyone who knew it was there and wanted to be hidden could walk right under your nose and you wouldn't know they were there." He puffed himself up a little. "They are good though. The others, I mean, at finding them. They know what they're looking for, and somehow, every now and then, they get in. I can't figure out why. I trust everyone in here, but someone must have let someone else in who passed on information. We have to be careful."

"And you're suddenly so ready to let me in? What if I was the one who blabbed?" I said, instantly regretting the words tumbling from my mouth. Of course I wouldn't betray the safehouse, but how did he know I wouldn't? How was he so sure when he was so blind to how close to all this in the real world I was.

"I trust you," he said simply. "So does The Wise One, and our Leader. If they trust you then I can't argue without saying I don't trust them." He shrugged and paced around me in thought, almost knocking me off the wall. I concentrated on my breathing, trying not to look at him directly, focusing instead on a piece of moss growing through a gap in the pavement. He paused to look at me with a puzzled look on his face, and even though I didn't return his gaze, I grew hot and hoped my suddenly rigid stance didn't betray my subconscious secrets. He must have decided not to say what he was about to because the mood shifted, and he became his bouncy self again.

"Hey, guess what?"

Now I returned his gaze, relieved the moment was over and had come to nothing. "What?"

"I heard their boss can turn into a dragon."

"Dragons don't exist!" I scoffed.

He looked hurt and thoughtful again. Man, I was really pushing my luck. I needed to change my tone. I remembered the last time we'd seen each other I stank of Eldar, and we had left each other on a low. He must have still been wary about me because, let's face it, he couldn't prove I hadn't gone to both of them. As far as he was concerned, I was still seeing Eldar and had been the whole time I'd been away. I decided to just roll with it if I needed this safehouse.

"They do," he said, raising an eyebrow and studying my face carefully. I let him without looking away.

"I'm sorry. I clearly have a lot to learn. Start again."

"Well, they used to exist a long time ago. They're just a myth now, but experienced shifters can take any form, apparently."

"Can I turn into a dragon?"

This time it was his turn to laugh. "Um, no. No way. Don't get me wrong, tonight you look more... solid.." *Nice save,* I thought as I caught him looking me over. "But you have to be really powerful to change into other things. Plus, The Wise One told me that to turn into a dragon, you need to have been broken. Completely broken in spirit and brought back from the edge by love. Only then can you become a dragon. Shifters usually stick to what they're comfortable with. Something they can relate to and visualise. No one who exists today has ever seen a dragon, so they can't truly imagine them. No one of clear mind would attempt it. They need to be in a dark place and then have it all changed by hope. Their leader is capable of anything, so I wouldn't put it past him to try. I don't know him as a human, but I know whereabouts he lives and see how heavily guarded he is. In this world, he's mostly a cat, but I've seen him as a ferret and a bear. To try to be something you've never even seen in real life, you must have some balls. I mean, what if it went horribly wrong?"

I shuddered at the word *ferret*. He noticed and leaned up against me. He wrapped his tail around mine. The warmth that radiated from his fur was like nothing I had ever known. My insides began to tingle as I allowed the feeling to pulse through me in waves. I almost forgot to breathe.

"Sorry, I'd forgotten about that," he said, trying to make eye contact, which I avoided. "I don't think it was him that attacked you though. He doesn't come anywhere near here and we'd know if he did." Something flashed across his eyes so quickly I felt for a second he was lying, but I didn't push it. I might have been imagining things.

"Look," I began, still avoiding his gaze. With him being so genuinely nice, explaining myself became important. With Eldar, it was easy. It was like having a friend at uni. A laugh, something I had fallen into, but dangerously like what had happened the night I had conceived Bea. I'd never change that night because of my beautiful baby, but the sudden and intense whatever it was that began and fizzled out just as quickly was probably the best way to describe the thing with Eldar. "Last time I was here..."

"Forget it," he said sharply, pulling away from me. Clearly he hadn't forgotten but wanted to let it go. I was relieved he didn't want me to continue, but perhaps I should have anyway. I took advantage of him being next to me and leaned back against him, tall and slim, yet strong. I thought about seeing him at the gym last week and almost forgot myself.

There was that sound again. The unmistakable sound of purring. I hip bumped him off the wall with a giggle. Of course, he landed on his feet; I wished he hadn't. Stupid Spider. Stupid Ivan.

"That's enough," I said rudely. "It's odd enough we're not really cats, but when you start purring too, urgh."

He grinned even wider than before, and I thought I might melt. "Yeah, I remember. It's not real and all that." Spider shuddered as though someone had walked over his grave.

"I wanted to feel it was real," I murmured. If he heard, he didn't acknowledge it. The rain began to patter on the path around us, getting heavier until I hunched my shoulders and pulled my head in, like that was going to help.

"Come on. Let's find my safehouse. It'll be dryer in there."

"Are you sure I won't stalk you?" I said as playfully as I could.

He raised an eyebrow. "I think I'll be okay."

I decided not to tell him I'd turned into a huge panther-type cat. Did that count as other animals, or just a cat? I decided it didn't matter either way, although, maybe other animals might be an option for me too. That was exciting. Our journey was a short one as it was mostly a run from the rain before we get soaked, but I did ask him if he could change into anything else. He had replied with a no, but he had never tried so couldn't be sure.

Our journey had taken us across town to Mally's shop. I could smell it before I could see it and wondered exactly what made the layers of scent that clung to the street around the shop. I wondered if Spider actually knew who I was and was just pretending, but then, I had never seen that flash of recognition in his eyes. Not even a glimmer of something that would give away that he knew.

I was deep in thought, trying to figure out if he could know, when he stopped by a gate to the small parking area at the back of the shop. There was a tall brick wall to one side, and the end of the house/shop on the other. I could see space for parking, and to the left of me, the back door to Mally's shop. There was a light on inside, but the blinds were down and I couldn't see anyone inside. As I stepped onto the tarmac in the yard, it pulsed with tiny sparks of electricity. This must be part of the magic. Spider watched me carefully, like he was waiting for my reaction. I looked up at him, asking him with my eyes what it was.

"You feel that?" he asked, puffing himself up proudly. "That's a good sign. It means you're in. No one out there can see you unless you want them to."

My eyes widened in surprise, and I looked behind me down the street, watching the cars passing. It was strange knowing that even if they were to notice two cats on the side of the road, once we'd passed into the protected area, they wouldn't see us at all.

"Sometimes it doesn't work. I have to trust you enough to let you into the spell. Seems I do," he said, not trying to hide his excitement.

I blushed at his boldness. "Er, thanks." I looked warily at the shop and wondered if I should tell him I knew what it was and who owned it.

"Don't worry about that place." He nudged my shoulder. "They're cool with us being here." He was trying to cover the fact he was involved with the shop too, and he would have succeeded had I not known otherwise.

"This one over here." He tilted his head to the right, where there was a house I hadn't known was there. It was strange how I hadn't noticed it before when I must have passed it so many times in my car and walking around. Even now, as we entered the car park, something about it made me want to turn the other way and forget all about it. The magic it was giving off was trying to repel me, for some reason. I couldn't look directly at it. Spider noticed me trying.

"That will pass." His amusement was clear in his purr. "It always starts like that." I was going to be sick. Bile rose in my chest, and I retched suddenly.

"Yeah, I forgot about that part. Sorry." He quickly darted back to my side. "It will pass."

I managed a nod and followed him across to the gate, which was open a few inches, enough for us to slip through. Once inside the gate, I could feel the presence of others but couldn't see anybody.

"Where are they?" I whispered, keeping my head low and my ears back. I became aware I was flattening myself to the ground as we walked. Spider stayed walking tall with his tail in the air.

"They will show themselves when they're ready. Right now, they will stay where you cannot see them. It's right to be wary. I could be leading you into a trap, or you could have me as your hostage."

I let out a laugh. "Does that actually happen?"

"It has been known to happen."

We only walked a little way down the path, just enough for me to be completely inside all of the various spells and enchantments placed on the house and the surrounding area. Now I was inside, I could look up at the old house. It was a two-storey house, end of the row, beside the road. The garden was a good size; I wasn't sure I could see all of it from where I was. The flagstone path ran up to the back door, which was closed, but there was an open window I assumed would lead into a kitchen. Under the window was a small wall, which looked like it had been put there just for access to the window. Looking up at the two windows on the second floor, I noticed there was a light on upstairs. I could smell toilet cleaner and bleach. Somebody must have maintained the house during the day.

As if reading my mind, Spider said, "Nobody lives here. Not permanently, anyway. There are a couple of shifters who stick around in their chosen forms who don't shift back anymore. We have a couple of shifters who look after the house just in case anyone decides to suddenly visit."

I nodded, taking it all in.

I could still smell Mally's shop, but also, on the breeze, I could smell the rain, which had slowed to the occasional drop. I could smell at least two male animal forms, but had no idea what forms they were, only that they were larger than me. I could smell Spider's wet fur as he shook himself and flicked his paws before licking the rain from his legs on the path ahead. Accepting the urge to do the same and copied absently.

My ears pricked up hearing a sound approach from the gate. Spider looked up and groaned. I turned to see The Wise One padding through the gate towards us.

"Ah, my beautiful Flower. I see Spider has finally brought you to see another one of our safehouses. Interesting choice using this one though." She shot a glance at him, and he cowered slightly then narrowed his eyes.

"What's wrong with this one?" he asked sharply. Suspicion bubbled within; this was more to do with me being too close to the situation.

"I'm very grateful to be here." I began to try and smooth things over. "But I don't have to be. I can leave. I won't come back." Spider gave a low hiss, and I rolled my eyes.

The Wise One chuckled. "No, stay." She purred. "I did tell him to offer you use of the safehouses. I was just surprised he brought you to one he uses himself."

"Yeah, she's already stalking me," Spider said flatly. The Wise One wasn't amused.

"But you could be stalking her. So trusting. Too trusting." I believed this comment was directed more at me than at him.

"Well, now you're here, my Flower, keep an eye on this one. Remember what I told you." She turned her back to Spider and raised an eyebrow at me. He didn't see the look on her face, but I did. It was a warning to me not to tell him anything.

I forced a laugh, playing along. "Don't worry. I can handle Mr Hissy Pants."

Spider glared at me, clearly annoyed at my exchange with his mother, even though he didn't know I knew who she was.

"I have to go somewhere tonight with The Leader," The Wise One said as she left. "You're in charge, Spider, until we return." In a heartbeat, he was back to his proud self.

"I must get home anyway," I said slowly, thinking about how I would get away now and shift back to myself. Spider nodded but seemed distracted. I didn't say anything as we headed back the way we had come. After a while, we arrived at the corner shop. We both stopped and sat down. Even though he was too distracted to talk to me, he was alert, sniffing, his eyes darting from one side of the street to the other, and his ears constantly twitching.

"What is it?" I finally asked. The urge to run home tugged at me, but so did curiosity. He flicked his eyes in my direction then back at the street behind me, watching the road to the farms. I assumed he was looking out for

Eldar.

"I shouldn't talk of it here," he said quietly, letting out his breath. He moved his head closer to me so I could hear his whispers. My head swam as I could smell his warm fur only millimetres from me. "If Wise One and Leader have gone out, they must be looking for something or someone. They rarely leave together at the moment."

"Why?" I whispered.

He checked the street again. "We've heard someone is trying to find out who our Leader is. You know, in his human form."

"Oh," I said dumbly. "Will he try to kill him?"

"Of course. If he kills him as a human and as a shifter, it won't be good for anyone. We must find out who it is and why. I just hate them both going out together." The realisation ran through me that perhaps the Leader was someone close to him too. If Mally was his mother then the Leader could be a family member. Perhaps Mr Ealing. No, he didn't seem the type. Full of knowledge and loyalty, yes. Gifted with magic, very possibly, but The Leader? Nah. I just didn't see it.

"Anyway, I'd best be off. I need to run a check on our boundaries. Should probably find a few extras to help me." He half looked as though he expected me to offer to come with him, but I had to go. I couldn't leave Bea or Mum any longer. I had already been out too long. I wanted to ask if the shooting in town was linked, if he knew whether Mr Mathis was a shifter, and if he had been the cat, but for some reason, I didn't. If Mr Mathis was the cat? Then who did they find dead in human form? The numbers didn't add up.

"I would, but I can't," I said, looking down the dark street too. "I really must go."

Spider acted as though he didn't care, but I could feel I had hurt his feelings again. I wondered at his expectations of me.

"Another time then," he said, turning away. Without waiting for me to reply, he started to run and was gone.

I padded home the long way, through as many gardens as I could manage before settling on shifting in my neighbour's garden. When I knocked on the front door, Mum opened it and pulled me in for a hug. I loved her. She always knew what I needed, even when I didn't know myself. It was in that moment that I fully let go of all those years of resenting her.

CHAPTER 25

Ena

My work shift was almost over. I looked at my watch. Five to ten. Soon I could sign myself out, drive home, and see Bea before getting into my PJs and curling up with a mug of hot chocolate. It was Friday again, and that week, work had been hectic. The company had had a big warehouse clearance sale on, so we had to run around, trying to get our orders picked and packed before our shifts ended. There were orders left over, and I knew they'd ask the few of us left in to stay until they were packed and left in the shipping area. There were only five or six left; I could do them in half an hour. I shuffled through them, distracted, until I heard a cough from behind me. I groaned out loud. I had managed to avoid Ivan all night so far. I was too drained to have a conversation, let alone one that took so much effort.

"Hi," I said brightly, trying to be positive. I had to remind myself Ivan was a completely different person to Spider.

"Staying late?" he asked. I shrugged. What a stupid question. Maybe he wanted to help. Perhaps hell had frozen over.

"We need to get these done. There are only these left now though." I held out the orders for him to take, only he didn't. He just looked at the orders in my hand.

"Get on with it then," he said, taking off his suit jacket. As he took it off, his crisp blue shirt came untucked, and I got a glimpse of a smooth, muscular frame underneath. He wasn't weedy at all. In that suit, he looked like he could have anything under there, but firm abs were probably the last thing you'd expect. My thoughts drifted to his wet t-shirt at the gym. I flushed and turned away.

"Great. Okay. I'd love to do them myself anyway," I said sarcastically, marching off.

When all the orders were done, I double checked the addresses and left them on the shelves in the packing area, ready for the postage guys to collect first thing. I was relieved it was all done, and it was only twenty to eleven.

As I was about to clock out, Ivan slid out of his office right in front of me, still jacketless and smelling of coffee. He put up his hand to wave at me, and I paused instinctively to wait and see what he was about to say.

"All done?" he asked.

Totally not what I was expecting him to say, but at least it wasn't sarcastic.

"Yep. I'm headed home now. You?"

"Yeah, well. Not exactly. How well do you know Kym?"

"Kym? Not really well. I only see her here, although she's invited me out a few times." He nodded but didn't say anything, so I added, "How come?"

He looked at his watch and his mouth twitched. "She's invited me out too," he said, running a hand through his hair and looking down at me through his long eyelashes. Just seeing him do that made me want to tangle my hands in his hair too. I bit my lip.

So, he and Kym were going out. Well, that was that then.

"Oh, that's nice." *That's nice? Where did that come from?*

He chuckled. "Yeah, so I might go meet her," he said as he locked the office door. "You should come too. It's Friday."

"Nah, I really can't. Not tonight," I answered without even thinking about it. Why was I turning him down? Why was he inviting me out with him *and* Kym? "You and Kym have fun," I said, a little harsher than I intended. His expression changed from neutral to stony.

"Whatever." He pushed past me, walking through

the door and not even holding it open for me. I stomped up to the staff room to grab my coat and my bag. He followed me in. He must have been waiting in the corridor. *Ugh.*

"What's your problem?" he asked whilst I had my back to him. The staffroom was empty, but I was one hundred percent sure he'd still have exploded. I didn't like his tone. It was darker, daring me to argue back. "You've always had a problem with me. Come out and say it."

"What the hell, Ivan?" I turned round. "One minute you hate me, the next minute you're trying to be nice. Is this some sort of joke to you? Does treating people like crap get you off or something?"

My thoughts poured out and there was no way to check them. My face was hot, and the whole time, he stood there expressionless, not saying a word. I was furious with him and his stupid non-reacting face.

"In case you've forgotten, you treated me like crap the moment I arrived here. You had the problem with me. I tried to be nice. I tried to get over it, but you were such an ignorant arsehole I decided you weren't worth it. Until I saw you at the gym. You can be nice when you want to be, so why not all the time? Why so hot and cold? Why the nastiness and the sabotage? What the hell did I do to make you hate me so much? Now you ask me to go out with you and Kym? No fucking way would I want to be anywhere near you, you antisocial, backwards moron!" I couldn't stop the tears in my eyes, incensed by the fact he stood there and said nothing.

When I was done yelling at him, he walked away, leaving me angry and sobbing in the staff room. I stomped my foot like a toddler. Why was he so much effort, and why couldn't I just walk away?

I can't remember how I got home that evening, but I did. It was gone eleven when I arrived, and Mum had left a note on the table saying she had gone up to bed and Bea hadn't woken since she put her to bed at eight. I stared blankly at the note, reading it several times before it made any sense to me. I needed to get some fresh air; meditation wouldn't cut it.

With the note in my hand, I ran up to my room to check Bea. She was fast asleep in her cot in her little grey Eeyore sleeping bag. For a few minutes, I stood and watched her sleep. The blush on her cheeks and the flutter of her eyelashes. I loved her so much I could have burst. Guilt swept me away as I knew staying there with her wasn't enough to calm me down. I checked the baby monitor was switched on and poked my head around Mum's bedroom door to see if it was still on in her room. I could see the little green light on the nightstand by her bed and heard the muffled sounds made by me on the landing. Satisfied all was well, I considered a shift. I grabbed the amethyst Mum had given me and left it on the floor outside her bedroom door. On the back of the note she had left me, I scribbled *gone out 11.15* in a red crayon and put it under the gemstone. I headed downstairs, grabbed my keys, thrust my feet into my Converse, and left.

I walked around for a while in my human form before shifting, unsure whether to attempt the safehouse or not. In the end, I settled for shifting in the car park by Maisy's home. I still hadn't told her about all this. The thought flashed across my mind, but then I thought she was safer not knowing.

I sprang out onto the street, stretching my legs out one by one. The air was sharp. The temperature had dropped with the sky being so clear. I could smell the coolness on the breeze. I didn't know what I was looking for, nor what I was trying to achieve, but I needed to release some of the stress.

I needed to make sense of the events of the last couple of weeks. Why was I so drawn to Ivan? Why Spider? Why did I scream my feelings at him? Was I jealous of him meeting Kym? I think I was mad because I wanted him to notice me for me. I wanted so badly for him to make the connection, but then, why was I so bothered? He was horrible as a human being. He might have been struggling as his mum suggested. I got that, but the venom and the spite in him that was so unprovoked I didn't understand. Where did that come from, and how could he project it at someone he barely knew? I must have been walking around for about an hour before I started to smell the scent markings had changed. I had wandered out of Spider's territory. I hadn't expected to see him anyway, not if Ivan was out with Kym, but deep down, I was hopeful. I needed to tell him who I was. I couldn't see any other way.

I was about to turn around and walk back to the car when a voice shouted, "Wait up!" I recognised the voice but wasn't sure whose it was. Turning, I could see it was Cole. I sighed. I couldn't just run off, he'd be offended, so I waited for him to catch up.

"Bad day?" he asked, looking me up and down.

I shrugged. It must have been more obvious than I thought. "You could say that."

"Sometimes I find a good mouse hunt helps clear the mind. Fancy joining me?"

I hesitated, but still in need of a stress release, I agreed. He raised his tail and puffed out his chest. I assumed me sticking around a while pleased him.

"Where's Eldar?" I asked as we padded towards the farm by the bridge. I sniffed the wall as we passed. The scent wasn't fresh, maybe a day old.

"He's around here somewhere," Cole replied gruffly. "Probably hunting."

The farm had a long, gravel driveway leading up between two metal barns. One of the barns was full of hay, and the other had some young cows which I could smell a mile off as a cat but usually ignored. Right then, I wondered how many were in there, and if cows could understand us. We followed the gravel path up towards the house and turned left at the end of the hay barn.

"Stop. What can you hear?" Cole whispered, leaning his well-built body against mine. I leaned slightly away instinctively.

"Um... your breathing?" I offered.

"No. In there." He gestured toward the field beside the hay barn. I listened again and heard scratching and scraping noises, little squeaks, and tiny heartbeats.

"Can you smell them?" he asked, staring into the field.

I sniffed. I could smell their warmth. I could smell their breath. I could almost smell their blood.

"You need to be still. Always listening. Always smelling." He pressed his body against the floor. I copied and he watched. His eyes flashed and he looked impressed with something.

"Nice." I could hear his heart racing and put it down to the mice.

"Now what?" I asked.

"You need to feel where they are. Make a map in your head. Imagine you can see them. A bit like when someone throws a tennis ball at you. You grab where you think the ball will be, not where it was when it was thrown, right? Imagine you're pouncing on the mouse. Imagine where it will be, not where it is."

I nodded. That didn't sound too difficult.

I watched Cole hunt for a while; he was really good at it. I forgot all about being uncomfortable around him and just watched him hunt, although I did get the impression he was showing off a bit. He was quick despite his frame, and light on his paws despite his stockiness. He knew exactly where to pounce and didn't miss, swiftly killing the mouse each time with a quick nip. Time flew by, and he must have caught four or five before he suggested I have a go. I wasn't sure I actually wanted to kill them, but pouncing on them seemed like something I should probably learn if I was going to be spending more time as a cat.

I settled down behind a hay bale on the edge of the barn and followed his instructions. I missed the first two times, but on the third, I caught a mouse. Not knowing what to do with it after catching it, I lifted my paws and let it scurry away. Cole looked at me warily as he crunched through the spine of a dead mouse.

"Just kill the damn thing," he said gruffly, licking the mouse blood from his whiskers.

"I'm not really in the mood for that, although the pouncing is fun."

"Yes. Pouncing is fun." He raised an eyebrow. There was that uncomfortable feeling again.

"Perhaps I should go now. It's late, and I have places I need to be tomorrow," I suggested with a real yawn. Cole's eyes flicked to mine, then to my paws, then back to my eyes.

"Stay a little longer," he said, his voice slightly higher than before.

"I really appreciate you distracting me this evening. I definitely needed it. You were great company, Cole. Thank you." I stood to leave, and with the speed he stood up too, I thought he was going to shout *stop* at the same time. It threw me back a bit, but also made me more certain it was time to leave.

"Please tell Eldar I was here," I said with a smile. "I will have to come back soon."

"I'll walk you back, but before you go, do you fancy getting a drink with me?" Cole mewed hopefully, and I rolled my eyes. Trust him to try it on. That was all I needed. His green eyes looked me up and down, and he made a low purring sound in his throat.

I smiled politely. "But that would mean you knowing who I am on the other side," I said playfully, with no intention of telling him who I was. I had to get somewhere safe to shift and hope he didn't follow me.

"I'll show you mine if you show me yours." He padded round me. I was sure he could feel my unease.

I forced myself to relax in the same way I would meditate. "Maybe one day, however, I do have to get home now." I tried to shut him down by turning to leave. As I did, I caught the eyes of another cat watching from the shadows on the bridge. My heart pounded until I realised it was Eldar. I gave a sigh of relief. With him there, Cole surely wouldn't try anything.

Cole chuckled. "Ah, Eldar." He sounded amused. "You just interrupted something special."

Eldar raised an eyebrow at me. A smirk played on his lips. Now, I wouldn't have minded a drink with him as a human to see if he was as smooth in real life as he was in this one. I couldn't imagine what he would look like, only that he'd be dark and muscular... I didn't want to start down that road. We were friends only. I shook my head.

"I was just leaving," I said confidently. "We were saying our goodbyes." I shot a glance at Cole, who held up his paw in the direction of the bridge.

"She was just leaving," he said, nodding. "Shame we couldn't get her to stay."

"We?" Eldar asked, sitting next to me but facing Cole.

"Yes. Weren't we going somewhere this evening?" he said slyly.

Suddenly, I felt a lot less safe. There was something going on. Something had changed without me noticing. I needed to get out now.

"Have fun," I said brightly, heading in the direction

of the road back. I held my tail high to keep up the charade of confidence.

Eldar inhaled deeply and rose. He was at my side before I could blink. "We will escort you. I'm sure Cole was about to. As gentlemen, it's what we do." He winked at Cole.

"It's really not far," I insisted, but he wasn't to be thrown off.

"We know a shortcut back to the town. Keeps us off the streets. There's trouble brewing in the territories. We don't want you getting mixed up in it, do we, Eldar?" Cole hissed quietly.

I nodded. It didn't look like I had much choice in the matter. Cole made it clear with his tone he intended to walk me wherever we were going, and by the change in Eldar's body language, there was definitely something not right. With one of them on either side of me, how could I get away?

-

Spider

That night, I was out with Leroy. He was my contact and gateway into the gang from the city.

At first, this new job had been about getting into the heart of the rival gang, trying to figure out how many of them there were, and how serious they were about our territory. They seemed to be quite a large organisation, much larger than we'd thought, but because of its size, it was easier for me to sneak in and meet with shifters who might not know who I was. I needed to find out why they kept pushing us so hard. Was it that they wanted more ground? Was there something in the town? Or was it simply because we were there and had claimed it as ours that was the problem? By the way those guys operated, I suspected it was the latter. The bosses were very territorial and if they could take it, then it should be theirs. Any form of pushing back was met with a childish aggression and violence on their end. Sure, we could have sent in shifters who were less well known than I was, but I needed to see it all for myself.

I hadn't been with them very long. Weeks only. I had made the decision to cross the boundary and look for Leroy. I had been told he was always looking out for shifters or those who might possess the ability to shift but had never tried. Sam, my friend who had been shot, seemed to be recovering well. He knew a couple of the shifters as humans, the ones who bragged about their strength and abilities whilst high on God knows what. He would dip in and out of their gang from time to time whilst dealing. I pretended it didn't bother me, but it did. Had he not been shot, I might have brought it up, but now, he'd learnt the hard way not to mess with them.

I visited him and convinced him I was unhappy with

my lot over there and the way things were handled, so I was on the way to find somewhere I could live in peace. Played the rich boy feeling trapped and needing freedom card. He believed it easily. I let him convince me to try their gang. It was all part of the plan, and so far, it was working. They had only given me small jobs though. They didn't fully trust me, and I hadn't met any of the leaders properly yet. I had only seen the big boss from a distance; I'd never gotten close. He had three leaders under him. I had met Tray briefly, and of course, I knew Eldar and Cole from our territorial scraps. I had met Eldar once on this side, but as far as I knew, he hadn't challenged the fact I was spying. As much as he hated me, I doubted he'd rock the boat until my time came to be initiated into their gang properly. Once you had been accepted, you were theirs for life.

Leroy had told me about an initiation that was going to happen that evening, so we were looking out for females to invite along with us. We skirted around the edges of the farmland, following a dirt track before it joined a towpath by the canal. We were about ten or fifteen minutes' walk from the town, so I knew Leroy wouldn't pick up my scent markings out here, warning shifters to keep out. If he had, he might have been more curious about why I would mark a boundary and then leave to join the opposition. I think he really did believe my story about wanting to join them and spy on my coven, so if he did pick up anything closer to town, hopefully he'd overlook it. My scent screamed dominant male, and although I wasn't the biggest nor the strongest, being the son of The Leader meant I had an automatic status, and living in a family sort of way as we did, no one had thought to challenge it.

Apparently, under their boss, Cole, Eldar, and Tray looked after their own sub groups and brought their new recruits to initiations to fight against each other. The winning fighters took the prize. Not only were they accepted as full members of the gang, but they used females who were on heat as part of the prize, to do with whatever they wanted. It seemed barbaric to me, but I had to go along with their ways or I wouldn't last very long. I needed information, so I had to lower myself in order to try to get it. Plus, the scent of a female ready to mate was probably the strongest and most alluring scent I had ever picked up. Even though I wasn't a real cat, I couldn't deny it was powerful. It could turn the strongest of us to jelly.

We had already met a few females that evening, a shifter or two, and some house pets. We had taken some back to a holding pen at a bungalow in some old man's garden closer to town. I didn't spend much time over there as it wasn't on our turf, but I recognised it from my travels as a human. They were holding the females in some sort of disused dog kennel. From the smell of it, it hadn't had a dog living in there for a long time, but it was perfect to keep them all in one place. Damn, I was starting to think like them.

The initiation would allow some of the newbies to move across into a more full-time situation within the gang. This meant they would have to give up their identity in both forms and be posted where needed as bouncers in the clubs in the city, bodyguards, drug dealers and the like. Until they showed their dedication through the initiation fights, they wouldn't be trusted to be told anything. I still wasn't ready. Leroy had told me I needed to wait a little longer to prove myself before he took me to his boss, Tray. I had told him my name was Claws, which was a stupid name, but he seemed to accept it. I had been totally unprepared on the name front that when he asked me, I just said the first thing that came to my mind in a panic. Again, Eldar hadn't challenged the new name when we had seen each other, which was unnerving.

For me though, the job had shifted slightly. When I had arrived, I was angry. I never felt like I could let go. I was a tightly wound spring, but no matter what I tried, I could never find a way to release. For some reason, over the couple of weeks before that, with every new morning, a little of the tension had subsided. I didn't notice right away, but after a couple of days it became clear, although the reason for my newfound mental relaxation was not. I idly wondered if it was some sort of reaction to meeting Night Flower. I had been attracted to females in this form in the past but rarely acted upon it because, in the back of my mind, there was still the strange guilt that reminded me I was a liar. The only times I had acted on it had been due to that amazing, intoxicating scent they gave off. I hadn't been short of offers, and then there were females like Lila in our coven, who wouldn't take no for an answer.

There was something about Night Flower that I couldn't quite put my finger on. Yes, she was gorgeous. Well, as gorgeous as a cat could be, but there was something else that made me want to protect her. It was almost as if I knew her. The Wise One was always saying that souls moved on and often met the same souls in other lives, but I had never believed in the whole soulmate thing. What if my soul *did* actually know hers? The jealousy and aggression flared when I saw her with those idiots who tried to con her over to this side of the fence, but then, who was I to her but another con artist trying to tempt her in the opposite direction? No wonder she was confused and kept leaving. Still, I couldn't get her out of my head, even in my human form. It had become impossible to not feel like I needed to head out onto the streets and track her down. I didn't feel myself unless I knew she was around, which was strange because I hadn't been myself for a very long time. I didn't even know what

I was supposed to feel like. All I knew was, worrying about what I was supposed to feel like disappeared when she was around.

"What's up with you?" Leroy asked, giving me a nudge in the side as we walked. We were almost back to the bungalows and hadn't come across anyone new to bring with us. I shrugged.

"Thinking about the initiation, I guess," I lied, sniffing a fence post on the edge of the path. It had been freshly marked from the smell of it, within the last ten or fifteen minutes. The scent was a warning to stay away, which gave me the impression that the initiation was about to begin. I raised an eyebrow to Leroy, who nodded in return.

"Ah, your turn will come, kiddo. Don't you fret." He mewed, rubbing the top of my head with his paw.

We both jogged the rest of the way back. Leroy went over to bump heads with Tray, whilst I took a seat to the right of the garden, right at the back where hopefully Eldar and Cole wouldn't pick up my scent. Cole was a randy bastard. There weren't many females given the choice if he decided he wanted them, and from what I had heard, he wasn't the gentlest. I shuddered as I thought of him speaking so smoothly with Night Flower, and how she was completely oblivious to it. If only she knew. I imagined what I'd like to do to that sweet-talking ferret, but I couldn't let myself be caught out. If I stayed enough out of their way, the scent of the females, and the blood, it would distract them enough and they wouldn't think to look out for anyone who shouldn't be there. I could smell the females from where I was sat, the smell of fear, and bile rose in my throat, but I ignored it. I couldn't break my cover, and this was their ceremony. I had to just grit my teeth and accept it, for now.

CHAPTER 26

Ena

I followed Eldar and Cole down the dirt track that led below the bridge to the railway lines. It was poorly lit, but my cat eyes adjusted well though to the low light. I could smell rats down there, and the scent of oil was thick in the air. I could also smell the scent markings of Eldar; rich, and almost like whiskey. It smelled warming and alluring. I could almost roll around in it. It was the strangest sensation, pulling me in like a magnet. Then I could smell Cole's scent on the edges of the tracks themselves. He smelled sharp and choking, like sniffing straight vodka. There was a danger to the smell, but also the snap of strong, single male that sent a shot of electricity straight through me. I tried to keep my head up to the fresher air above. It was strange how the markers in the scents from the males sent images and signals to my brain, each one giving me a picture of who left it. I had a male either side of me as we padded down the lines towards another field on the edge of town. I knew our housing estates and our road would be somewhere to the left of the fields. I hoped they didn't pick up any scents of me in the breeze from the window I'd left open.

We skirted around the back of the town for about twenty minutes in complete silence. It was very uncomfortable for a while. I planned my escape, but there was no way I'd get across the fields and into the town before they caught me; I wasn't that fast.

Every five minutes or so, I picked up the scent markings of either Cole or Eldar. They seemed to alternate along the track and the fence surrounding it. We walked up a bank to a small hole in the hedge where we squeezed through onto a narrow public footpath which followed the tracks through the field. We picked up the path and turned left, back towards the town centre. Just before we reached the houses, they edged me back towards the right and out of town. I had absolutely no idea where we were going.

"Are you sure this is the right way?" I asked, leaning to the left towards the houses. Eldar leaned on my side heavily and pushed me back to the right. Cole narrowed the gap between us. It became very clear they were leading me somewhere and didn't want me to leave, but where was I going and why? Fear snaked through my body until a lump formed in my throat. I needed to bolt, and I needed to do it now while I still had surprise on my side. I leapt in the air and twisted my body to the left. After a deep breath, I pelted towards the town as fast as I could go. I could hear Eldar's roar behind me as I ran, and then seconds later, Cole's sharp claws in my shoulder blades.

I hadn't reached the town, not even close. In those few seconds, I had managed to exhaust myself and was now pinned to the tarmac path, Cole's body weight pushing me flatter as he climbed on top of me. I could feel all four of his paws forcing me down, claws out and digging into my skin. I could smell blood. My blood. I opened my mouth to speak, but he shoved his paw onto the back of my head, pushing my face into the floor. Stones scratched my nose, and my nostrils filled with dust. At first, I could feel the rage and the heat coming from him, his powerful body forcing me to submit after he caught me.

"You little minx," he hissed into my ear. I whimpered. He licked the top of my head roughly. "I could take you right here." I didn't like the evil edge to his voice and let out a squeak. "That's it. I like that sound." He chuckled. I struggled underneath him as he dug in his claws.

"Cole!" came a shout from behind. Cole's weight

shifted, and he sighed. I was terrified, and he knew it. He was playing with me like he'd caught a mouse.

"Oh, come on." Cole laughed. "You can't blame me for trying."

"You know the rules. The winner gets the chance tonight, no one else. You'll just have to beat me in the ring." Eldar mewed.

What ring?

"Damn it." Cole growled and retracted his claws. They slid out of my skin roughly, and the wounds prickled.

"Save it for the ring," Eldar said patiently. "Let her up. No one will want her if she's covered in blood and dirt." Eldar used his paws to help me to my feet and his body to steady mine.

"She still looks good."

My legs shook like jelly. Although there was no way I wanted to go with them, there was no way to escape now. I had no choice but to walk with them. We walked with one either side as before, but both pressed tightly against me, holding me in the centre.

With my ears back and eyes narrowed, I put my head down low, seething with anger but absolutely terrified at the same time. Mostly angry at myself for trusting them, and for ignoring Spider. Thinking of Spider, I was sure I caught his scent before. The warm smell of aftershave and coffee mixed with confident single male. It smelled powerful, but not close. I thought of Ivan as we walked. I winced with every step as my sore shoulders stung where Cole had cut them. My heart sank as I wondered what Ivan and Kym were up to. Why hadn't I just sucked it up and gone out with them? I could have been having fun, instead of here, like this.

We came to a small bungalow in a row of four. It was the end one, and this end of the road was a dead end. I didn't know where the other led. I wasn't familiar with the road at all.

Each bungalow had a hedge around it on the front. There were two street lamps which provided light. Neat rows of flowers lined the beds under the front windows, and well-maintained lawns and weeded driveways lay before each one. From the smell of older people and various medicines, I guessed these were retirement bungalows.

As we approached the one at the end of the road, I picked up many more scents, many warm bodies from the back garden. We slipped through the hedge by a gate that reeked of multiple scent marks from different males. Some of them I was sure weren't even cats, but I couldn't place the animal until the garden opened up and I saw not just cats but a couple of dogs, a fox, two ferrets, and a magpie, all chatting loudly with each other. They made such a racket I was sure they'd wake up the residents, but glancing at the window assured me the owners were fast asleep or too deaf to hear them. All the lights in the house were off. I curiously glanced at the next house to see their lights were off too. I wondered what time it was. I could almost feel the eyes of the animals watching me as Cole and Eldar guided me across the lawn, tails held high in triumph of offering me to whatever game this was. I tried not to be sick. The stench of them all and the staring; dirty air filled my lungs. I retched. Cole nudged me into Eldar with amusement, and Eldar hip bumped me back to him. I couldn't concentrate, my vision blurred with tears.

At the end of the lawn there was a small, raised flower bed, and behind that, a wooden outdoor dog kennel. There were no dogs in there now, but from the sounds and smells of it, several female cats were. I heard the pounding of their hearts and their mews. Some were shifters, but not all were.

With a wink, Eldar shuffled me toward the kennel. "Inside now, there's a good girl."

I did as I was told and slunk inside the door.

Inside, there were five females. From a quick sniff and a look around, I guessed two were shifters and two were not. The two which were not were a small tabby who lay in the back corner with her paws over her face, and a white cat who must have been a little older as I could see the weariness in her. With them at the back huddled another cat, but I couldn't quite tell from her scent if she was a shifter or not. She watched me closely, so I leaned more toward shifter than curious house pet. The dark kennel hid the true colour of her coat, but it looked grey in the dim light. The two I knew straight away were shifters stared right back at me in knowing. One was a tortoiseshell with blue eyes, the other a jet-black female with long fur and green eyes. She smiled and held out her paw to me. I went straight to her and collapsed into sobs.

"Yes, I know, I know." She purred, stroking the back of my head. The other female began to lick my ears. It was strangely comforting.

"Where are we?" I asked, blinking at the entrance to the kennel. Outside, I could see Eldar and Cole standing guard whilst the two dogs scuffled on the grass.

"I believe we're at some sort of initiation," the female with the black fur said slowly. "I'm Nita. I was out in the city when one of the old boys I know asked me to join him for a walk. Before I knew it, I woke up here. I don't know how I got here."

"I was forced here too," I said, hating myself and hating Eldar for doing this to me. I was so stupid for trusting him and Cole.

"Try to stop crying though. They love it when you cry. Be strong. It won't last long."

"What won't?" I asked.

The tortoiseshell answered. "They'll get the new recruits to fight. Then the leaders of each group will choose who they want to be part of their select group. Each group deals with all the drugs and keeping the city folk in check." I couldn't believe what I was hearing. "Then the leaders will fight. The winning leader gets his pick of a female, or all of them, if he wants. Then who's left will be up for grabs by those he's chosen for his team. The leaders usually pick shifters. Sometimes they can force them to shift so they can pleasure themselves both ways. The new recruits are usually left with the clueless house pets."

She nodded in the direction of the other two. The tabby let out a sob, whilst the white cat hissed loudly at us.

"Not my rules, love," the tortoiseshell said. "They decide it, not us!"

"What do you mean, they pick the shifters?" I began, already knowing I didn't want to hear the answer. My back legs trembled.

"The leaders of each gang are usually quite skilled. There is an enchantment that can bring you back to your usual form. Not all can do it, so it depends on who wins."

I buried my nose in Nita's fur.

So that was it then? I was to be awarded as a prize to some foul, aggressive fight winner? One who would probably have experience in this sort of thing and know how to change me? My identity would be out there for all to know, and what they would do with me I dreaded to think. I wrapped my tail around my legs protectively and wished my mum was here. Mum and Bea. I hoped they were okay. Would I ever get back to them? If they knew my identity, goodness knows what they could hold over me. They'd know everything about me. I didn't have time to think on that because, outside, a shout had quieted everyone. It was a voice I didn't recognise, but it must have been one of the leaders because the silence was instant.

The tortoiseshell bristled and made her way to the front of the kennel. The door was wide enough for the three of us to stick our heads out slightly to see what was going on. I retched again, and a frown from Nita told me not to be sick on her. The house cats and the other possible shifter stayed huddled at the back of the kennel, but I knew they were listening.

The one who had spoken was in the form of a huge black cat. He had a couple of patches of fur missing on one side of his body and on his face. From what I could see in the limited light of the night, there was a scar across the left side of his face. He had a piece missing from his left ear too. He looked around the garden before taking a seat on the side opposite the kennel. Three skinny females draped themselves around him. The way they moved made me think they were drunk or drugged.

"Cole," he said, sounding almost fed up. Heaven forbid he be entertained by his own games, however insane they were. Cole stepped forward and cleared his throat.

"This year, we have seven new recruits. Each one will be announced and then take their chosen forms, if not in that form already. Fights are until one of you doesn't get back up, or if one of you cannot go on. In that case, shout, 'I'm out.' If we do not hear that, then we will assume you can go on. Remember, if you do opt out, then you've opted out for life, and you'd best get out of here before we catch up with you."

One of the cats closest to us twitched his tail; I bet he was new.

"Each of you will fight, then the winners will move to the left and the losers to the right. If you lose, you will heal and fight again at the next initiation. Winners will be chosen by the team leaders. There are three of us present this evening. The leaders will then fight, but because there are only three of us here, we will all fight each other. Winners get the females and choice of patch in the city. Losers... well, you get nothing but pain." Cole sniggered as whoops and cries went up from the crowd. It seemed there were quite a few spectators.

"No female leaders?" I asked, looking around. I barely saw any females at all.

Nita shook her head. "They don't operate like that, girl. They're sexist, violent pigs," she spat in a tone so aggressive I didn't dare ask anything else.

CHAPTER 27

Ena

The new recruits moved forward and took their places on the edge of the lawn, which was to be the 'ring'. Of the seven, four were cats, one a dog, another a fox, and another a magpie. Although sickened, I was curious how they would be matched.

"First up, Mole, recruited by Eldar, against Badass, recruited by... wait, Badass? Tray, did you name this guy?" One of the cats sitting closest to the cat I assumed to be the overall leader laughed out loud. He was huge. If he'd been a house cat, I would have put him on a diet. His whole body shook as he laughed.

"Of course! What's the point of a secret identity if you don't get a cool name!"

Cole gritted his teeth. "Fine, Badass recruited by Tray. Whenever you're ready, boys." Cole retreated from the lawn and sat beside Tray, shaking his head. Tray laughed harder.

I needed to cower in the back of the kennel, but I also needed to watch. I was compelled to see who was going to be the one to win us and see just how much trouble we were in.

Mole was a slender grey cat. His fur was smooth and dense, which was probably why he took the name Mole. I wondered if he had chosen the name, or if he was named, like Badass. Mole's rival was a thick set, stocky ginger Tom. His huge muscles certainly cried out *Badass*. I learned quickly that he wasn't as fast as Mole, who struck first, leaping at Badass who wasn't ready and still looking toward his recruiter.

Mole sank his teeth into Badass's shoulder blade, making him cry out with shock. He shook himself until Mole slid off his back and turned to face him, Mole's claws raking his face. Badass didn't seem to be bothered about that as he snapped forward, his teeth trying to latch onto whatever they could before finding Mole's ear with such force he ripped it right off. Blood splattered across the lawn and Mole howled so loudly I craned my neck towards the house to see if any lights went on, but they didn't.

With Mole temporarily distracted, Badass tried to jump onto his back, but he wasn't as quick as Mole. Even in pain, with blood pouring over his eye from his ear, he still slithered out from under him every time. Badass grabbed him by the leg and pulled Mole under him. Jumping onto his back, he sank his teeth into the back of Mole's neck. Mole howled again and flipped himself over to rake at Badass's belly. I was sure it hurt like hell, but Badass didn't let it show, even though his fur was coming off in clumps with every kick. Badass leant forward and clamped his jaws over Mole's mouth, stifling anymore noise, but also cutting off his air supply. Mole thrashed in panic, trying to throw him off, but Badass clung on until Mole collapsed onto the lawn. After Mole stopped moving, Badass looked toward Tray, asking with his expression if he should let go. Tray waved a paw in reply, and the huge ginger male let the smaller grey go.

Cole rushed forward and gave Mole a kick. "He'll live," he announced, with a look of disgust. Mole was dragged from the lawn, and Badass waddled over to sit on the left. He looked forlornly at the wounds on his belly and began to lick them clean.

"Are they all shifters?" I asked Nita with a shiver. She nodded once and put up her paw to shush me.

From the second group to fight, River, recruited by Cole, went up against an unnamed Tom who had found the group himself by chance. Tray immediately nicknamed him Death Stare because of how he glared at his opponent, waiting for the introductions to be finished. River won this round, but Death Stare wasn't as injured as Mole. He didn't take it well and lay on the right side of the lawn, growling to himself, whilst River looked as pleased as a teenager after his first time.

"This next round is a bit different," Cole began. "We have Fleet, who has chosen magpie form, although I'm not sure how that will help him, recruited by me. And Gruff, recruited by Eldar." Gruff looked like a white and ginger Jack Russell terrier. I bet he had some speed in him. "Then finally, the fox recruited by Tray. What bloody stupid name have you given this one? He's a fox called Fox. You wouldn't have stopped at that."

Tray gave a belly laugh and elbowed Eldar in the ribs. "Fox is for short. He's called Fux You Up."

"I am not saying that," Cole hissed as the crowd roared with laughter. "Where the hell..."

"Cool names, mate. Cool names."

Cole rolled his eyes. "Just fight each other. We will pick one overall winner from this round, but as you are at a disadvantage with there being three of you, if we think you have earned it, we will choose two." Cole left the lawn.

Gruff was a blur of white and ginger as he streaked across the lawn after Fox, who was just as fast and managed to gain some space to spin round and leap right over the back of the Jack Russell, landing behind him before spinning round again. Gruff spun to face him and snapped his jaws. Fox lowered his belly and head to the ground so his jaws were underneath Gruff, and he snapped at his chin as the dog thrust forward. Within seconds, the two were on their hind legs, pushing each other with their front ones and snapping at each other's faces with their teeth. Fleet flew down and repeatedly pecked them on the head or back wherever he saw a chance, but there wasn't really any way into this fight. He swooped low again, grabbing the fur off their backs with his claws as they snarled and slashed, completely oblivious to the bird's advances. I wondered what the point of his form was, unless it was his only confident form. It was useless in this fight.

Fox managed to kick Gruff off and leapt up high to try and grab the bird, but missed, hitting the ground, ready to face the dog. However, the dog seemed annoyed with the bird even having a chance to dodge and escape. He leapt onto the back of the fox and up into the air, grabbing the magpie by the feet and pulling him down. The dog and fox were on the magpie within a second, pulling out feather after feather and not stopping to check if he was still alive with their rage. It was only after Tray boomed, "Enough!" that they put him down and turned on each other again.

I couldn't see from where I was, but the pile of blood and feathers being dragged off the lawn couldn't possibly still be breathing. I was going to be sick. Nita kicked me in the side as I retched again.

Gruff and Fox were as one, growling and yowling, blood and fur flying through the air, neither one letting the other go, but neither faltering. The boss seemed impressed for the first time during the whole thing. Fox let out a growl and grabbed Gruff by the throat. Gruff yelped but didn't give in. He twisted his face around and grabbed Fox by the side of his throat. The noise was horrendous, almost deafening, with growls and pants filling the space between howls and yaps. Fox's face was covered in saliva, and it dripped from him as he shook his head. Gruff's eye was pasted together with blood. I could smell the thickness of it mixed with dirt and wet grass.

A light went on in the house. Everyone froze because the light fell across the lawn. Gruff and Fox relaxed and let each other go, and the animals on the grass began to slowly back up into the hedge or against the wall to hide in the shadows. All was still. No one dared breathe. If the light stayed on the lawn, they wouldn't notice us. I was almost tempted to dart out of the kennel and make my escape, but Nita held me back. It was too dangerous. After a few minutes, the light went off again, the owner satisfied the fighting animals had moved on.

My heart pounded in my chest. Promising to burst out, and I placed my paws over it to quiet it. Trying to remember my meditation, I breathed deeply in and out until I had calmed. I wondered what Mum was doing and whether my phone was repeatedly ringing in my bag where I left it. Did I leave enough milk for Bea if she woke?

When I looked up, Cole, Eldar, and Tray stood in the middle of the grass, talking quickly and quietly. "It is agreed," Cole said loudly enough for everyone to hear. "Four have made it through, one lost a life, and two will heal and retry." He glanced slyly toward Mole and Death Stare, who lay by the wall. "Eldar wants Gruff. I'll have Badass, and Tray wants Fux You Up." There were some chuckles from the observers at the sound of the latter. "The winner of the next round takes River and the contents of that kennel. Trust me, I will be winning this one." He grinned, looking straight at me. I couldn't hide my anxiety and let out a small yelp.

The three cats paced the lawn in circles, all facing each other. They had done this so many times before that they knew each other's secrets and flaws. They knew each other's moves and weaknesses; it was going to be a hard fight.

The anger inside Cole couldn't wait as he threw himself at Tray. Tray dodged Cole but didn't dodge Eldar, who slashed him across the face with a claw before turning to slash at Cole. Cole had a hold of his tail and yanked him backwards with such force he was thrown off balance and the skin on his tail split. The fur and skin tore with a sickening sound. He screamed and launched himself on top of Cole, digging his claws into the muscle above his eyes until he let go. Tray took this opportunity to grab Cole by the back end and dig his claws into his thighs. Cole flipped onto his back and kicked his back legs up at the soft underbelly of Tray so he bounced up and off him. The three cats flew at each other at the same time, in very much the same way Gruff and Fox had, but there were three of them clawing at each other's chests, each one in obvious pain. I squeezed my eyes shut, trying to ignore the grunts and sounds of skin and fur being ripped off. I could smell hot blood. No, I could taste it. The crowd roared as someone had been kicked out of the fight. When I opened my eyes, I saw Eldar had bowed out of this one, his left eye closed and swollen, and his lip ripped down the edge, dripping with blood.

"I'm out," he called, limping to the side. The boss nodded his approval and patted the ground beside him for Eldar to go and sit out.

The fight continued for what seemed like forever, although it could only have been minutes. For such an overweight cat, Tray certainly knew how to move. I cursed myself for misjudging him and hoped it would be enough to pummel Cole. The thought of rooting for one of these thugs sickened me, but at least I might have it easier with Tray. There was no way Cole would let me go. As if hearing my prayers, Tray pinned Cole to the ground with all four sets of claws digging into his back. Cole was exhausted and couldn't seem to muster the power to throw him off. Tray put his full weight into the pin until Cole's face was flat into the muddy grass. Tray pushed it down further with a heavy paw, the same way Cole had done to me earlier. I flinched thinking about it.

"I win then." Tray sounded more amused than exhausted.

Cole shrieked, a high-pitched noise that echoed across the fields beyond the bungalows. "No!" he roared, wriggling beneath Tray, spots of blood collecting where the sharp claws pinned him through the skin. I wondered if they reached the bone. As much as I didn't want either to win because I knew what came next, I hated Cole so much after how he treated me, he deserved everything he got from Tray. I willed Tray to hurt him more. I glared at him through narrowed eyes and his met mine. He struggled further, trying to free himself from Tray's clutches, but Tray dug deeper. He was heavier set than Cole, and his hearty laugh matched his larger form.

The boss held up a paw. "Enough," he said, and the two cats stopped struggling. Tray stepped gently off Cole and leapt away, expecting him to strike the second he was free, but he didn't. He got up slowly and spat out a tooth.

"Good," the boss said. "Tray wins." With that, he stood up and left the garden, his females following closely at his rear.

"You heard him. I win." Tray beamed, showing he too was now missing a tooth. "Well, since Fox is a damn fox, and the ladies in there are all cats..." he began with a low rumble in his throat. Fox tightened his jaw. "I guess they're all mine then." Tray made a move toward the kennel, and I was aware it wasn't only my heart pounding as I backed up to the back of the box.

"That one is mine," Cole seethed, looking straight toward me.

Tray scoffed. "Maybe when I've had my turn, you can track her down again tomorrow. If I've let her go by then." He looked toward some shifters in the crowd. "I want them moved to my safehouse, now."

"I fought well. I deserve at least one," Cole said. I wasn't surprised he looked as though he was ready to fight again. Tray, however, seemed bored of it all and stuck his tail in the air.

I caught the scent of two males I didn't recognise outside the doorway. One of them ran a claw over the wood above the door.

"Time to come out, ladies," he said in a voice that made me sick to my stomach. "We won't bite."

CHAPTER 28

Ena

Nita nudged me forward. "If we don't go out, they'll come in. It'll be okay."

With her head high, she marched out of the box, her dark fur shining in the moonlight. The tortoiseshell followed, and I followed her too, afraid to be left alone inside for them to come in and get me. The female I couldn't quite see nor smell followed me as closely with her ears back and head low. It was like having a shadow. I saw in this light her coat was grey after all. One of the shifters in ferret form slipped by me into the box, and the other two females shot out, shrieking as he bit their ankles as he chased them.

"Walk like you own the place," the tortoiseshell whispered, straightening her posture.

"You done this before?" I whispered back.

She nodded once but kept her eyes forward. "Show weakness and they'll play on it. If you're strong, they'll treat you differently."

I nodded and tried to copy her. It was difficult to feign confidence in this horrific situation, but if it would help, then I had to try.

Now out of the kennel, defenceless, vulnerable. I looked around the garden at all the leering eyes; some staring at us, others at the blood and fur on the lawn. I searched the faces of the shifters, hoping for something I could hold on to, but I found nothing. I tried to hold my head high like Nita and the tortoiseshell. I tried to ignore the smell of the fight.

I couldn't do this. My head was telling me to cower, to run back to Mum and Bea. I looked straight ahead. Then suddenly, I saw them. Two huge green eyes watching my every movement. When I first locked eyes with him, I saw the expression in them change from curiosity to panic. I knew those eyes. It was Spider.

He stood up and his jaw dropped. I flushed with anger for a moment, forgetting where I was. Why was he there? Had he watched all of that? Did he know I was in there? It was sick enough having to watch when forced to, but to volunteer to be there? I didn't know the full story, but I knew he hated Eldar and Cole. I knew they were from opposite gangs. I thought Spider was either a huge liar and a hypocrite, or he was there for another reason I couldn't possibly know. Wait, hadn't he been trying to convince me to go out with him that evening? Was this where he would have brought me? I began to veer toward him slightly as our eyes didn't break contact, but one of the males nipped at my ankles, snapping me back to the reality of where I was. I had to move. Tray was back on the road in front of the bungalows, his minions delivering his prize to his safehouse where he could do what he liked with it. As I passed Cole, a surge of lust and anger filled him, and he grabbed me by the scruff of the neck, pulling me from the procession like a doll. I squeaked, but nobody stopped him from pulling me back toward the lawn. The males herding us just stood there and let him take me. Clearly, it wasn't anything they were prepared to deal with now the other leaders had gone. Cole dragged me to the side. One of Tray's higher up lackeys had turned to see what the hold up was. He hissed and growled at Cole, but Cole stood his ground, his teeth tight around the scruff of my neck. I was paralysed. My feet didn't feel my own as they curled up involuntarily. I was like a helpless kitten. Nita and the tortoiseshell stood back against the hedge with the house cats. Two more males flanked them in case they tried to run. I couldn't run if I tried, and Cole knew it. He bit down on my neck and growled back. I could feel the sweat and blood on his fur, the reek of his stale breath.

Panic raced through me. What if I never saw Bea

again? I was convinced Cole would kill me. The strength in his jaws proved how powerful he was, and I could smell the scent he was giving off; masculine and dominant. Tray's lackey began to back off before running back to the road, I assumed to get help. Spider held my eyes, but from the corners of them, I could see most of those left there were completely oblivious to what was going on. Most had already gone. I couldn't see Eldar anywhere. I stopped fighting it and let my eyes close. I couldn't do it anymore. The look on Spider's face, in his eyes. He didn't know what to do any more than I did, and the fact he hadn't moved to stop this showed me he wasn't prepared to intervene. In that moment, I gave up. I was lost. I was injured. I wanted to go home. I squeezed my eyes shut. I wanted to cry, but no tears came. I let my body hang limply. Cole must have registered the shift in my weight because he dug his teeth in harder and put his paw around my waist, his claws out, ready.

After a moment, I did open my eyes. I couldn't see Spider anymore; he must have left me. Cole began to drag me to the left towards the small patio area by the house.

Many things happened at once.

I was being dragged on my bum across the wet grass, Cole grunting, his teeth still embedded in my skin. Suddenly though, he stopped. His body went rigid and a low growl rumbled in his belly. This wasn't over. I took a deep breath in and that warm coffee and aftershave scent that made my head swim filled my lungs. My eyes snapped open. Spider was at my side and my body went from limp and giving in to tense and having hope. Just the feeling of him there filled me with strength. Maybe he was going to fight for me after all.

Spider was a lot smaller than Cole, and not as muscular, but he was fast, and he wasn't injured. He gave Cole a sharp nip on the rump, and Cole let me go in surprise. I lay there, not daring to move, assessing the situation.

"That was a mistake," Cole breathed. I cowered to the ground, not taking my eyes from Spider.

"She's mine," he said confidently.

Cole spat out a laugh, his blood-stained teeth showing as he grinned widely. "Come and get her." Cole glared at me and began to shudder. His whole body shook violently, and his slender cat form seemed to shrink away. His flat cat face elongated and sharpened, and his teeth and nose narrowed. His pointed ears became small and round, and instead of a long cat tail, he now had a shorter, more rounded tail. His legs shortened and his body lengthened. I couldn't hold it in anymore. I turned my head and was sick on the floor. The snapping and slapping of his body changing, writhing, and growing and shrinking all at the same time was too much for me to take in. He didn't stop looking at me. Even when I was sick, his eyes bored into me like a drill. When his body was done, I could see he had shifted into something that looked like a muscular ferret; his bloody teeth in their new form of pointed needles caught the light of the moon. I could smell the scent he marked the tracks with. That scent would be with me for the rest of my life.

I gasped as Spider glanced from me to Cole then back to me. "Run," he mouthed before looking back to Cole and pouncing. The lithe ferret snuck past him, heading for me, but Spider managed to grab him by the tail and pull him back. I heard him cursing. One of the house cats made a run for it, distracting Tray's shifters. I saw Nita dart across the lawn behind Cole and Spider, who were now circling each other, hissing and spitting.

I didn't stay to watch the fight; I turned, and I bolted. Nothing had ever surged through me like the desperation to be as far away from there as possible.

I flew through the hedges of all four bungalow gardens toward the main road, guided by fear alone. I had no idea where I was going but pelted on anyway. I ran down the road and followed it to where I thought the town should be, adrenaline fuelling my flight. I tore across the tarmac before a car in the road made me stop dead. For a second, I stopped, listening to the sounds of the night over my thundering heart. I heard paws coming up behind me.

"Go!" shouted Spider, racing past me. Without a second thought, I ran after him, following every turn and twist, expecting any second for our legs to be taken out from under us, but no one followed. My muscles were burning. This was more intense than any gym session I'd had recently, and I had the sudden urge to go to the bathroom too, which didn't help. I gasped for air and slowed to a jog as a stitch sneaked through my side. Spider skidded to a halt just ahead of me, sensing my pain, and watched my back as I caught up. I lay on the pavement, trying desperately to get my breath back. I stretched my back and sides to rid myself of the stitch. Spider sat watching the street we had just run down. I could see his ears twitching, but otherwise, everything was still.

When he was convinced we weren't being followed, he helped me to stand. After all that running and adrenaline, my body was in some sort of shock. It didn't want to respond to my brain telling it to get up, but I somehow made myself anyway. We padded down a street I knew. I was only minutes from home, but as much as I wanted to run there and be safe with Bea, if we were being followed, they would know where I lived, so I followed Spider back to one of his safehouses. There were two that I knew about. One beside Mally's shop, and the one near the train lines, but we didn't head for those. We headed for a place in town, not far from Maisy's. Spider insisted it was much safer in this situation, and I wished I had brought the car and parked it nearby. There was no way

Mum was going to let me walk around alone after this.

The flat was ground floor and had glass patio doors at the back. There was a cat flap installed in the glass, which filled me with relief as I didn't have to climb up any windows to get home.

Before we went in, Spider stood on the edge of the tiny concrete yard to check again for sounds. We would now be protected by the safehouse, but if anyone had seen us disappear as we approached, they would now know to wait for us as we left as humans.

"Let's get our breath back first and make sure they're gone," Spider said quietly, his green eyes flashing. I agreed and sat down on the path close to him. We barely knew each other, but after the night I'd had, I wanted someone to hold me whilst I cried. I wanted the warmth of another person telling me it would be okay. I craved attention, although not the kind I would have been given by those evil bastards back by the bungalows. I began to cry silently. Spider must have sensed it because he turned from the path and looked at me. He used his paw to tilt my head upwards.

"Don't cry," he said softly. "It's over now." I let out a very unattractive snort, which made him smile.

"I'm sorry. I..." I started, but he shushed me with his paw.

"Don't. It was my fault. I knew you were hanging around with those bastards, and I didn't warn you enough."

"You tried." I sniffed. I wanted to ask if he was injured, but the words didn't come.

"I didn't know he would shift into something else," I said, thinking of Cole. I wondered what had happened to Tray and Eldar, whether they were now searching for them too.

"I expected it," Spider said, looking at the floor. He sighed. "I should have protected you. I should have made you believe me when I said they were bad news." He looked broken, his posture submissive, tail low. He couldn't look at me.

"Speaking of protecting me, why were *you* there, Spider?" I said in a tone I wasn't sure was mine.

"I didn't know about you. I knew they had initiations, but I'd never seen one before. When I arrived, they told me I wasn't ready and to watch. They didn't trust me yet. I was to enter the next one. Enter, ha! You're forced into it, you don't enter."

I looked at him in surprise. "You want to be one of them?" Of all the things I had thought of Spider or of Ivan, him being just like them had never crossed my mind.

"No. I don't. You don't understand."

As I let out my breath, I realised he was looking at me in a different way again. Not in pity, but in attraction. I didn't want any of this. After what I had been through, this was absolutely not the time or the place. I bristled.

"What?" I demanded, getting flustered.

"It's nothing except.... Sorry, it was just.... your eyes," he said softly. I took a step back.

"Of all the fu..."

"Shhh!" He cut me off sharply and jumped to his feet. I shook away the feeling of frustration and listened, panic creeping back in like it did before. I had heard the sound that time too. The sound of paws drumming on the pavement. Getting closer.

"Inside, quickly," Spider said, nudging me toward the door. "Change, then leave. Leave quickly and run. I'll draw them away, so they don't see you leave. They can't see who you are as a human." I opened my mouth to answer, but he slammed his paws into my side. "Now." I pushed my way through the cat flap and into the house. I needed to get out, and fast, I needed to shift, but how, with my mind so fogged? I had come into a kitchen. I wouldn't shift in front of the patio doors, even though I knew no one would be able to see through the spells. I headed into the dark lounge area. There was a huge armchair and a two-seater sofa. Over the sofa was a chequered throw, and some cushions in the same fabric. The TV in the corner was dusty and unused, and there was a dead potted plant on the windowsill. Although the place smelled like Dettol, it was tidy enough.

I shuffled into the gap between the sofa and the wall

and closed my eyes. I imagined myself in human form, crouched in the corner. I forced my way back into my body. Using everything that I had left to give. I made a complete shift. I was getting much better at this. The only problem now was that I hurt. Everywhere. My legs ached, my shoulders were sore, I was bruised, and I had sharp pins and needles shooting through my sides. My head swam, and I almost collapsed with the dizziness. I leaned over and was sick again. I couldn't just leave that on someone else's floor. I realised I wasn't wearing my shoes. Where were my shoes? I had no time. I crept over to the window and looked out into the darkness.

There was no one on the street, and I couldn't see any movement between the cars. A cat's screech pierced the silence, and my heart leapt, hoping it wasn't Spider. What would happen if I just went into the bedroom and hid under the bed until the morning? My gut told me they'd be waiting outside, knowing I was here somewhere. They'd smell me. I had to leave now before they came for me.

Opening the front door a crack, I peeped outside. I listened for any sounds or movements but heard nothing. I knew even with the door open, the protective spells on the flat would keep me hidden until I stepped over the front step and onto the street. I just had to take the risk. I slipped out of the door and closed it slowly, trying not to make a sound, then I glanced down the street. It was clear, so I picked a direction I thought was towards my house and started to walk. As my muscles warmed and the pain ceased slightly, I started to jog. After a minute, I was running. Thank goodness I trained regularly and often pushed through my barriers, otherwise I'd have been crawling home. My bare feet scraped the pavement, my skin torn from the rough ground, the numbness from them aiding me until I stopped on my doorstep.

CHAPTER 29

Ena

Mum knew something was up the second I got home. She met me at the door and pulled me into a hug. I hugged her tightly and couldn't hold back the tears anymore. My shoulders shook as I sobbed into her hair, and after a few minutes, I sniffed and straightened up.

"I had a bad feeling. I've been on edge all night. It's gone one in the morning. What happened? Where were you?" she asked softly.

I couldn't find the right words, so I slipped past her and winced as I padded up the stairs to check on Bea. She didn't need anything as she was fast asleep, but I had to hold her. I picked up her tiny, warm body and held her close, breathing in her smell. Mum appeared a few minutes later with a mug of camomile tea and a hand on my shoulder.

That night, I didn't say anything about what had happened. I had gone for a shower and cried. I must have cried in the shower for a good thirty minutes, washing away the blood and the smells. I scrubbed my skin with an oat and honey pumice just to feel the scratching, to remind me that I was still here. I picked the bits of dirt out from the cuts in my hands and feet, and took off my torn toe nails, the hot water washing away as much as it could, but not the feeling of betrayal and fear. I was sick again in the shower. It made me think of who would be cleaning the safehouse. Mum would have heard me and would most likely be worried, but I wasn't ready to say these things out loud, not yet. I scrubbed my scalp with shampoo until it stung with rawness. I could still imagine Cole's claws in my shoulders but didn't dare touch the skin where they had been. One of the hardest parts was that even with seeing the others with different forms and shapes, and seeing Cole transform in front of me, it still didn't cross my mind at the time that I could have changed form too. Why hadn't I thought of that? I cursed myself as I scrubbed at my skin, angry at myself for letting me down. It might have meant things ended a lot better than they had.

In the morning whilst Bea sat playing with a shape sorter and watching TV, I told Mum everything, right down to Spider helping me escape. A lump formed in my throat as I talked about him, and how I didn't know if he would be tracked down for this.

Mum suggested I lie low and stay home for a few days, but just to make sure I was protected as a human, she wanted me to go and see Mally first.

"Mally is a truly gifted witch," Mum told me in the car on the way over there, echoing exactly what Mally had said about her. "Hopefully she'll be able to help us out with some extra protection."

"What about you, Mum? You were a witch, right? Could you not do something?"

She was quiet for a while. "I probably could, but I don't have the supplies for this. I stepped away from that life when I had you. I'm about twenty years out of practice. I have done those couple of basic protection spells for the house, but that's all. If someone comes by who knows what they're doing, they won't hold."

Mum drove the car round to the back of the shop. She paused just outside the entrance to the yard with the parking spaces, checking if there was anyone around to see us go in. The road was quiet, so she pulled into the yard.

Mally opened the back door and met us with a smile. Mum went straight over for a hug whilst I pulled out the car seat and clipped it onto the pushchair. Bea was fast asleep.

"It's been too long since we had a proper catch up," Mum said.

"It has, it has." Mally laughed in her cracked voice. She sounded tired. "Let us get inside. Ivan has just made some peppermint tea."

She made eye contact with me over Mum's shoulder. Ivan was home. This had turned my curiosity about the house into anxiousness. Actually, my subconscious mind betrayed nothing about my feelings for him. Not now. Not after what we had just been through. I was frustrated by how he treated me at work, but then as Spider, he had risked his life to save mine.

I couldn't fall for a cat, especially after the night before and me being treated like property. What was all that *she's mine* business? I didn't belong to anybody. I had had a lot of time to think overnight as I hadn't slept well. The more I thought about it, the more confused I was. Of course, I had been terrified. Spider could have been killed. I could have turned up to a very different Mally. She could have been riddled with grief. Instead, she was chirpy and friendly. Shame writhed through my blood. I should have been more careful. Spider wouldn't have been hurt then, but no, he was there too, and not by force. He must have had his own agenda. As for Ivan... I could fall for him, even though he was a complete dick to me. I couldn't stop thinking about the way he flicked his hair, or the abs under his shirt, or the way he seemed distracted as he paced the office. All that frustration and no release other than to snap at us. Was he thinking of

Night Flower? Suddenly, I was aware of my heart pounding in my chest. Anyone with heightened senses would know.

I looked down at myself. I didn't usually care what I wore, so why care now? I was wearing a pair of denim shorts, not too short, but short enough to be sexy if I wanted them to be. Underneath, I wore the black fishnet tights Maisy had told me to pair with them. Perfect. They covered the broken and bruised skin underneath well enough, but with a kick of *who cares*. I wore a black tank top with a bright pink vest top underneath. The tank top hugged my figure, showing off my curves. Still, why did I suddenly care how I looked? I parked the pushchair in the corner of the kitchen next to Mum and kicked off my black Converse into the space by the back door, trying to hide my wincing as my socks stuck to where my toenails had been. I made a mental note to find some plasters when I got home.

Mum and Mally sat at a huge wooden dining table, laid out with small cloth placemats. In the middle was a huge teapot with knitted cosy, and four blue and white striped mugs. A plate with homemade biscuits was on one side. It looked like a normal country kitchen, all wooden worktops and stone floor, except the huge wooden cabinet at the end whose shelves were full of various jars of herbs, candles, incense in all colours, various gemstones, and wooden objects like a carved wolf and a carved cat. I found myself staring at it for some time, until my soul sensed his presence. The hair on the back of my neck prickled, and I suddenly tensed. Mally must have sensed it too because she looked straight at me. In my mind, I heard a soothing *shhh* sound and calmed.

I made a point of leaning against the wall by the back door. I didn't look up until he was fully in the room because I knew I would go bright red.

"What's she doing here?" I heard his voice, loud and clear. Relief flushed through my veins. I knew he was there, but hearing his voice cemented it in my mind. I could relax a little.

It took everything I had not to leap from the table and wrap my arms around him, or leap up and punch him in the face. Either way, I was so elated he was alive and there in the kitchen. I couldn't hold it any longer. My eyes snapped up and locked with his. I would not blush. Instead, I forced any negative feelings to the surface in an attempt to look like I was still seething with him after the night before. The night we had last seen each other as humans. He had no idea I was part of last night. He had a black eye, his right eyebrow was swollen, and his arms were covered in small scratches. He scowled when he caught me looking. Mum looked from him to me but said nothing. I pouted, fighting the feeling of calm trying to push back against my frustrations.

"Shush, Ivan," Mally said, flapping him aside. She turned back to me. "Dear, why not follow Ivan into the front room so your mum and I can talk? Don't worry about the little one. She will be fine for a while."

My eyes widened. I didn't want to follow him anywhere. I couldn't feel confident following him as Ivan, not with how things ended with Spider. I planted my feet to the floor and tensed my muscles. I was staying in the kitchen, where it was at least emotionally bearable.

"Of course Rachel's your mum. Now the fact you're around all the time makes sense," he spat, picking up a mug and looking into it then placing it down again.

"Go on, E, for goodness' sake," Mum said, completely ignoring his tone. "Ivan, lovely to see you. You've grown." Mum beamed at him, and I was seething with him when he didn't smile back at her. I wanted to scream at him to use his manners. The funny thing was, all of us seemed to know what was happening, who we all were across shifting planes... except him. Why the hell hadn't he figured it out yet? Was he just stupid or keeping the two so separate he just couldn't see it? I shrugged and shook my head, exasperated.

"Thanks," he said quietly, glaring at me, then he gave in and sighed. "Fine. Come on."

I followed him through the door, but not without shooting a scornful look at Mum, who shrugged. Urgh, how embarrassing.

I pushed up my boobs and flicked back my hair. I had left it down so it fell around my shoulders, leaving the faint scent of shampoo in the air. Before coming out today, I had made sure I scrubbed my sore body raw in the shower for a second time. It didn't wash away the fear I had felt though. Plus, my hair helped me subconsciously hide the horrendous claw marks on the backs of my shoulders.

The front room was huge. Opposite the door we had entered from was the door to the shop. There was a key in the door, so it must have been locked when the shop was closed. There were two huge leather sofas in the middle of the room, and a coffee table which looked like it had a marble top. On the far side of the room was a handmade wooden desk with a computer and a printer, and next to that, another large wooden table. Upon that table, I recognised the metal dish full of sand, glass jars full of what looked like herbs, and one was definitely salt. There were also a few old-looking books, and a dagger in a leather sheath.

"Nosy much?" he said, sinking into the sofa.

Oh my God. I could have melted. He was wearing tight black jeans, the kind that clung to him in all the right places as he stretched out his legs. I eyed the ripped knees and wondered if it was fashion or wear. There was no scummy brown suit here. What was he thinking dressing like that at work? His loose white t-shirt didn't give away much, but I already had an idea.

"Rude much?" I snapped in return, sitting on the sofa directly opposite him. "What's your problem?" I looked him up and down, pausing occasionally on a bruise or a scratch. His nostrils flared.

"My problem? You've been a pain in the ass since the second you walked in, thinking you ran the place!"

"That's bullshit. I wouldn't have been trying to own the place if you could do your job properly." Arguing with my supervisor, risky? Yes. Fun? Yes. Dangerous? Probably.

"Brave." He leaned back on his elbows, his body open and vulnerable, and laughed. I loved that sound.

No. I was angry.

"Certainly." I raised an eyebrow.

"You almost cost me my job with your ignorance more than once. I haven't got time for that. I haven't got time for you and your whining. You're lucky our mums are friends, otherwise I'd have gone out." He smirked. He was enjoying this.

"My ignorance?" I fumed. "You infuriating piece of... urgh."

Fine, he'd won that one.

"Told you you whined."

"Well, you flounce around like an idiot half the time, not actually doing any work, just moping about like a lost puppy! The rest of the time you're having a go at everyone."

I swear he winced, but it was only for a split second.

"Crap night with Kym?" I shot at him.

If he was taken aback by it, he didn't show it. Instead, he grinned. Maybe he thought I was jealous. Maybe I was, even though I knew he'd spent most of the evening somewhere completely different.

"That's your mum then. Not seen her in years!" he asked, glancing at the kitchen doorway.

I nodded. Nice subject change.

"Don't remember you though." He raised an eyebrow.

"That's because you were always an antisocial, backwards moron. You'd have remembered me if you stayed in the room long enough to actually talk to me." My neck became warm as I grew angry again.

"I don't care." He stood up. "I don't give a shit anymore."

The already strained atmosphere took a nosedive. I prickled with electricity, and I had to act on it. I stood up at the same time he did. The power between us hummed so loudly I couldn't just feel it, I heard it.

We stood just inches apart, avoiding eye contact. I could feel his warmth, hear his breathing, and I was sure he was registering the same things. He thought he hated me. Maybe he didn't? There was a strength to the warmth. Not just heat, but like we were connected.

Maybe he did feel something after all. I took the risk. I leaned forward and kissed him.

I expected him to pull away, but he kissed me back. His hands were suddenly around my waist, pulling me closer, and mine were on his chest. For what seemed like forever, we let ourselves go to the energy that flowed between us. My hand ran up his chest to his hair. Then, just as quickly as it started, it stopped. He let go and shoved me backwards roughly. I lost my balance and fell back onto the sofa.

"Hey!" I shouted. He killed my buzz, and possibly bruised my coccyx.

"What the hell?" He threw his arms in the air and turned to leave the room.

I had to save this.

"Sorry, it was just... your eyes," I said. That had gotten his attention because he stopped. The muscles in his back tensed.

Slowly, Ivan turned around and our eyes met. This time, he knew. I could see the recognition in them. I could see the very faint blush in his cheeks. He scanned my body, his eyes resting on any bruises or marks. He was holding his breath. *Finally*, I wanted to scream. *What the hell took you so long?*

In that moment, I felt something soften, in both of us. I tried to keep the stern look on my face but couldn't. There was something between us, and this time we were human.

"I'm sorry I kissed you. Is there someone else?" I asked, barely able to speak. Why this question, of all the questions in my head?

His eyes didn't leave mine. "There was," he said. "Now though..." He shrugged. "So, your name's E for Ena, right? I should have known. I am clearly so unobservant."

Just as I was about to answer, Mr Ealing shuffled through from the hall, blissfully unaware of our awkward situation. However, I was more relaxed with another adult in the room. Mr Ealing always had a calming presence.

"Ena, my dear," Mr Ealing said, taking my hand. "May I trouble you for a mug of peppermint tea?" He winked at me, which made me grin.

"Of course, Mr Ealing. Anything for you." I shot an annoyed glance at Ivan then slipped into the kitchen, back to Mum and Mally.

At least now I knew he was okay, and I didn't have to worry about the gang members ripping him to pieces. Although desperate to go and ask him what happened, I didn't. After passing Mr Ealing his tea, I sat still and half listened to what Mum and Mally discussed, which was mostly about me and my panther, escape, and general mess. They made me describe the boss again, and each of the three leaders. I don't know how I wasn't sick thinking about it; it was still too fresh in my mind. I saw Ivan hovering in the doorway. I don't know how long he'd been there listening, but I hoped he hadn't heard all the stuff about me being a panther. Recalling Cole, I retched. Ivan caught my eye; he was staring at me. My cheeks flushed. He smirked as he noticed how I'd reacted to him. I almost threw my tea cup at him. Yet how Mally beamed when I told her how Spider had come to my rescue. I knew she had realised Ivan had finally figured out who I was by the way she jumped up to hug him. I did wonder, if he hadn't made the connection in the lounge before, what conclusions would he have jumped to by listening to our conversation. He slipped through the kitchen to get out into the yard. I wished I could follow him to ask what he was thinking, but then Mally began to talk about Mum and her being a witch. It would seem that somewhere, deep down, I had accepted I was a witch too. Great.

CHAPTER 30

Ena

The next few days were uneventful. I went back to work on Monday to find out Ivan had quit. I guess that had taken away the need for more arguing or clumsy conversations. John, who ran the company, had come over and asked me if there had been any trouble, and I had said no. He said Ivan had been distracted for a while now but never expected him to quit, and that he must have been planning it for a while because all of the paperwork was up to date, including jobs he hadn't had to start until the following month.

I worked my shift and left as I usually did for the first part of the week. Went home and fed Bea and stayed in. Anything to give Mum the illusion of safety.

The day John had come in to ask about Ivan, I had started thinking about him and wondered what he was up to. I hadn't seen him in shifter form since he saved me the week before. Was he waiting for me? I had fought the urge to visit him at Mally's when I first found out he hadn't turned up for work.

I left the warehouse at 10.01 as there were no extra orders to pack, and John had already left for the evening hours before. A couple of the older guys who worked in the office, in accounting and security, were going to lock up.

I had decided to walk to work that evening. It had rained from Monday to Wednesday, but was clear and warm now, so I took advantage of the nice weather and carried my work hoody over one arm and my bag over my shoulder. I wore a black t-shirt and black leggings with my comfy black converse, my hair pulled back into a bun. I toyed with the idea of putting in my headphones and drowning out the noise of the street and my thoughts about Ivan, but something told me to be more aware of my surroundings. There was an edge to the night, an edge I could usually only detect when in cat form. There was a stillness to the air as it hung with humidity, and with it, a musky scent, laced with an aftershave and the bare trace of coffee that I recognised.

I glanced around, trying not to make it obvious that I was checking for anything in particular and was preparing to cross the street. I couldn't see him, but I knew he was there. My heart pounded, and heat ran through my veins. I needed to shift but had to make it to the safehouse. I tried to keep it casual. Usually I would have been terrified at the idea of being followed, but now I knew I could turn into a huge panther and take them out in one swipe, and I knew exactly who was following me. I hadn't realised how badly I needed to see him. The fact that I couldn't see him made it even more exciting. The streets were quiet except for a few cars, and it was getting dark with autumn creeping in, yet I still couldn't let myself go. The safehouse wasn't far, perhaps five minutes. Those five minutes lasted a lifetime, and by then I knew he knew exactly where I was going and why. He knew I didn't live in the direction I was heading.

I played out all the scenarios and conversations in my head, from giving him a telling off for ditching work, to falling into his arms whether he liked it or not, although, in my private thoughts, he liked it as much as I did.

I crossed the street to the yard behind the shop. The kitchen lights were on, but I prayed no one was looking out of the window to see me enter. Mally would call Mum, and she'd panic. Maybe I should tell Mally first. I stuck to the shadows to the right of the wall and slipped by the gate. I held my head high as my entering the garden was registered by Gray, the huge, scarred cat with the swollen face, and then by Thomas, the small, gangly runt over by the far wall. We hadn't officially met, but Mally had explained who they were. Even though I hadn't shifted, I could smell the damp grass and the cats' scent markings.

Gray's eyes flicked from me back to the gate, and I knew Spider must have followed me into the garden. Shit, he had never seen me shift before. What if I pulled a strange face, or if I couldn't do it due to feeling so anxious? What if I looked ridiculous?

I turned and put up my hand to stop whoever was behind me. Two sets of green eyes watched me from the darkness. I went inside.

I went straight up and through to the bedroom at the back of the house and flung my bag and hoody onto the bed. I pulled my mobile phone from my back pocket and keyed in a quick message to Mum.

At Maisy's, having a last minute film night. Back soon. How is Bea?

Then I typed one to Maisy. *If Mum asks I'm at urs. I met that bloke I was telling u about. Going for a drink. Mum will freak out. Call tomorrow. I owe u 1.*

I threw my phone onto the bed next to my hoody and stepped into the en-suite.

The white tiles shone with the bright bathroom light as I went to the toilet and then washed my hands and face. I had become very nervous. I could feel the tightening in my chest, and in the mirror, could see the red flush across my cheeks and neck. Five minutes ago, I was desperate to shift, desperate to see him, but now I seemed to be fighting the urge to leave the safety of the bathroom. My phone beeped.

It was Mum. Ok but more notice next time. Have fun. B OK she had all her milk, down 4 night now.

Ok love you. Won't be too late, I'll wake you when home.

I opened a second text, this one from Maisy.

OMG you madam! Ivan right? Call first thing. I need details.

I laughed out loud and sat on the bed, running my hands through my hair.

Okay, let's do this.

I inhaled deeply and cleared my mind, imagining myself changing, feeling my way into my new body and letting go of myself. This time, it took no time at all, and I opened my eyes to see every detail in the room. It wasn't a big bedroom, and there wasn't much in the way of furniture. I stood up, still getting used to my surroundings. The rough carpet underneath me brushed my sore feet, and I stretched my long, muscular legs, feeling the power and heat flood every inch of me. I was still a little achy from Friday, but a lot better than I thought I'd be. Mum made me take a couple of baths in lavender and salt, which had helped. Across the hall, I heard hushed voices. It was time to head out and greet the other shifters.

I padded into the kitchen. The moonlight shone on the kitchen floor from the open window. With the door now closed, I leapt up onto the worktop quite gracefully compared to last time and craned my neck to see outside. Gray and Spider stood by the gate, talking, but both stopped when they caught sight of me in the window. Gray nodded and stepped back into the shadows, and Spider slipped back through the gap in the gate into the yard.

When I reached the yard, I couldn't see him anywhere. Before I had time to be frustrated, I took in a huge waft of his scent leading to the left and out of the yard into the street. Now he was making me follow him. With a glance at Mally's kitchen window to make sure there was no one there, I bounded after him into the dark street.

I followed my nose around corners and across gardens for a good mile or so, sometimes sure I would catch him around the next corner then being upset or alarmed when I didn't. Part of the time, I allowed my intuition to drive me forward when I lost the scent. Luckily, I had good instincts. This boy was fast though. How quickly was he going? This chase was half thrilling, half annoying, and by the time I did catch up with him, I wasn't sure if I wanted to claw him to death or talk to him.

Spider had his tail in the air, scent marking a fence post by the post office on the edge of the town. Beyond the post office were a few small bungalows, then fields. I could smell the water from the nearby lake on the air. I had no idea water could smell so fresh. After marking the post and giving his tail a shake, he flopped down onto the path on his side and stretched out his legs. He lay there twitching his tail, watching me watching him. I padded towards him, and I swear he was fighting off a grin.

Not wanting to look intimidated, I flopped down onto the path beside him and gave my own legs a stretch, my tail twitching too.

"So, you lied to me," he began, concentrating on my expression. His voice had a playfulness that unsettled me.

"No." I mewed. "I never lied to you at all."

"You didn't tell me you knew me. You knew me and didn't say a thing."

"I thought we had to keep our identity secret. I guess I thought if I figured it out, you would too. I hoped you would, only you were distracted." I flicked my tail faster.

"Distracted, yes. By you." He sighed. "It didn't click that I knew you in real life."

"I knew you by your eyes," I said shyly.

"I wasn't looking at you that closely."

"Well, neither was I! You were a complete dickhead! Why would I look twice at you?"

He sighed again and rolled onto his back.

"You did look at me. We made eye contact loads of times. I thought after you were nice at the gym you had figured it out," I said quietly.

"I looked at you, yes. You're pretty, but, I wasn't looking at you, more like through you. I guess I thought if you were interested in me, even though I was a bastard to you, I should try to be a different person than I am."

"But you saw Kym? Is that it?" I sighed.

"Ah, this is a mess, isn't it?"

We both chuckled.

For a while, we said nothing, but lay on the path, occasionally giving each other a look. He was right, this was a mess. I had been out too long. I needed to head home.

I made a move to get up, but his paw shot out and tapped mine.

"Not yet. I'm just happy you made it home the other night, not that you didn't come back for me until now."

"Oh." So, he was expecting me to come back for him. I could barely think straight that night, let alone go looking for him. Plus, I did go looking for him. Sort of. With Mum, the next day, in human form. And I found him. My mind raced.

"What was the point of this? I mean, you following me, me following you, lying here for hours for nothing? Just for you to ask why I lied to you? Well, now you know, that's the end of it. I'm going home."

Perhaps I should have stretched before leaping up; I was going to feel that tomorrow.

Spider flattened his ears and hissed. "What do you want from me? Want me to mount you? Like those thugs last week?"

"Urgh, no. Where the hell did that come from? I found you the next day. I worried like hell all night. If you were expecting me to come back the next night, you clearly didn't care at all." Suddenly realising how hurtful I had sounded, I looked at him and lowered my head in an attempt at peace.

"I cared. I looked for you all night to make sure you had got home. When I couldn't find you, I assumed you had made it out. I went home and didn't sleep. When you turned up and told me who you were, I was relieved. I really was."

"Sorry," I said. "I'm so confused. I don't know what's going on. I don't know what I'm doing or who I am. I don't know what I want except...." The words tumbled out before I could make sense of them.

"Except what?" He cocked his head curiously.

"Except it has to include you."

"Oh." He looked at his feet. "Okay, you're right. Let's get you back. Can't have you out here for hours for nothing, can we? Plus, The Wise One thinks it might be best if you don't come back for a while," Spider said quietly as we walked.

My heart sank. Mum had mentioned this too. She said after the two incidents, it wouldn't be long before the others put two and two together and realised who I was.

I was a bit disappointed that our game of hide and seek around the town hadn't come to anything, but I supposed it was for the best. I wondered what would happen now with Spider. I wondered whether it was completely over now I had to stay away. They were right though, I knew it. Every time I came here, they would be looking for me. I wouldn't have put it past them to come into this territory just to get at Spider or me. It was only a matter of time before they realised who we were. If my dad was still part of a gang, the only dangerous gang around that matched the description and close enough for him to be seen in the area was that one. I was convinced the thugs after Mum and me that day were part of that gang too, along with Cole, Eldar, and Tray. I was better off out of that world. I also was sure the shooting was connected too, although apart from Mr E, Ivan, and Kym knowing the dead man and his son, and the police not yet saying anything about the other man in hospital, there was no evidence it was connected. Then there was that shifter Mum thought she saw in the window.

Once it was confirmed my dad was involved, we would have to move again. I wasn't sure which I was more worried about. My dad trying to find us or having to leave Spider.

As we walked back, we walked alongside each other, getting closer to each other to the point where we were almost leaning on each other. Static zipped between our fur as it softly brushed together as we swayed. He stopped and looked up. I had been enjoying the walk, completely involved in my own thoughts and the comfort of having him against me was so natural. I was quite happy in my own world; I hadn't noticed we had company.

"Lila," Spider said as a beautiful female appeared from an overhanging tree. She leapt down with such grace. I instantly disliked her because she had interrupted my walk. Her sleek white and ginger fur almost shone like gold in the moonlight.

"Spider." She purred, flicking him in the face with her tail. "And... friend of yours?"

Suppressing a growl, I forced myself not to look or sound defensive.

Spider hip bumped me. "Yeah, she's not from around here. Just been showing her around," he said brightly. A cool calmness flowed across my skin, until she brushed her slender body along his.

"Another one. Really." She purred. "Are the local girls not good enough for you?" She sat opposite me, licking her paw. I ground my teeth together, not daring to speak in case I ended up clawing her.

Spider laughed nervously but kept his head up. "You make me sound like that's all I do." He winked at her.

Excuse me? Escort the new girls round? All he does?

"Is it not?" she asked, mid-lick. "I'll leave you to it. Come find me when you realise she's not worth it. You always do."

With that, she leapt back up into the tree and disappeared into the leaves. Spider glanced at me. The fur on the back of my neck bristled, but I had to show it didn't bother me. Who cared if he had a different female every night? I hadn't given in yet, so he wasn't mine. He was theirs for the taking, so why did it feel so difficult? I forced a smile.

"Friend of yours?" I purred, mocking Lila's voice.

He shifted his weight. "Don't listen to her! She's just upset because I've never been interested in her."

I raised an eyebrow and hip bumped him back. "Yeah, I believe you." I mewed playfully. "Come and find me like always...." I said in the same tone she had used and carried on down the path, deliberately swinging my hips and swaying my tail.

I heard a low growl from the tree above. Ha, she couldn't get to me.

"No, seriously. I have dated a bit. Not a lot though. Sometimes Leroy, one of Cole's lackeys, would assign me to show the newbies round. That's what I had been doing the night you, er, well... that night." The way he rushed his words, I could tell he wasn't comfortable talking about it, but I needed to.

"You still haven't told me why you were there that night. Why you were right there, watching." I heard him swallow.

"Well, The Leader and I thought we could get to know a couple of them. Try to figure out why they keep bothering us, who they're looking for or targeting, if anyone at all. My job was to fact find. I guess I just got caught up in it all as I wasn't thinking very clearly." I nodded and heard his sigh of relief. I wasn't angry. I didn't even need an explanation as deep down I knew he wasn't on their side and it must have been something along the lines of what he said.

"And the females?" I added.

"They groom them, in advance. Especially if they think they'll be ready to mate when the initiation takes place. I didn't realise the females were a prize before that. It was just showing them around with a view of them joining. I thought they were testing me."

The idea of grooming females to be used as prizes sickened me. There must be more to this than him just spying. I looked at him and knew when he wouldn't meet my eyes. Yep, I was right. He was trying to cover something up.

"So, you were involved in the grooming." Even without knowing about the initiation, I wasn't comfortable with this.

"Occasionally," he said eventually, but didn't offer any explanation.

"On that occasion?" I pushed.

He still wouldn't meet my eyes. He nodded. "Yes. On that occasion. I had rounded up a few, a group which included a house pet and another one. She wasn't too fussed about following me though. I'm sure she knew where she was going. If she'd run, I'd have let her, despite having Leroy there. I felt bad for them, but I didn't really have much to do with them. I met them and another male, new to shifting and groomed into it by either Eldar or Cole."

I thought of how terrified the house pets had been in the kennel, and how knowing and calming Nita and the tortoiseshell had been. Where were they now? The other shifters wouldn't have got away as easily as I had, and I guessed it was rounding them up that stalled them from coming straight after me.

"I didn't know the initiation was on Friday until I was actually there that night working," Spider said. "All I knew was that my orders were to take the male across first, then lead the females there. I took them then went out to find more, and it was only when I arrived with the other bloke that I saw how many had arrived since I had dropped off the girls." His voice shook. "I wanted to leave, but they told me to stay. You don't argue with them once they're there. It's a trust thing. They would have expected me to enter the next one."

"So, how did you get past Eldar and Cole?" I asked, thinking about the hostility they had shown each other from across territory boundaries.

"Well, I approached the fat one. Leroy works for him. My friend said he was the easier one to get on with."

"Tray?"

"Yeah, that's the guy. Anyway, I said I was fed up with things over here and needed some action. We thought if I could get in with them, I might be able to find out who shot Martin and Sam, and who they were really after."

"Martin and Sam?" I asked, surprised. "I didn't realise this was about them."

"Why would you? Anyway, they knew us. We failed to protect them as obviously they were targeted. They got Martin in both forms, but only injured Sam. He'll recover, but he won't be the same. Sam couldn't shift, but he was great with knowing people. I was meant to get in and find out anything I could. I did run into Eldar once with Tray, and he laughed so hard. Promised he was looking forward to getting me in the ring when I was ready. I hate that guy. I hated you for going with him," he said with a snarl that made me take a step back. "I got involved to find out how they operate. It was pretty easy at first. When they asked how I knew Sam, I had to pretend I'd had drugs from him in the past. They seemed pretty interested in that and kept me around, I assume to keep an eye on me. After a week or so though, they started to ask me a lot more about life on our side. I let up a few bits, nothing that would mean anything though, and probably stuff they knew anyway. I didn't get any further than that. Eldar knew I'd be there on Friday, and that you... I guess now I understand why he didn't cause a fuss knowing I was spying. He knew you'd be there too and that it'd get to me. What if I hadn't reacted? Or if I had left early? That's pretty fucked up."

"You think?" I said sarcastically.

The fact Eldar had been grooming me, and that I had fallen for it, made my body itch. I needed to change the subject.

"So, why are there so many shifters around here? I mean, why here of all places?" I asked.

"Well, the gang recruits them, like I said. Leroy goes out and finds them and brings them back here. Some hear about us along the way and come looking. As a human, their boss has many bodyguards. He feels untouchable. In this world, he's done the same. He has so many shifters in his pockets, threatening them with their identities, death, their families. Most of the females are hooked on drugs or have something they need to hide so they will do anything for him. Our group seems to take on a few stragglers or those not suited to the gang. There aren't many of us, but we are powerful as humans, magic-wise. The Wise One and the Leader of our group are both gifted with magic, and they know how to protect the people the gang want to hurt. They hide them or move them on. Their boss only seems to find out when it's too late." He laughed.

"So why doesn't he just kill your leader as a human like Martin?" I asked, walking slower.

"He has to know him. As a human, if he knew who he was, he could walk up and shoot him, or send one of his lackeys in to do it for him. In the spirit world, he could turn him to dust, or in the shifter world, he could rip his throat out, but he has no idea who he is. He'd have to get him on both sides to make sure he couldn't come back. There are people who can do that. I've seen it, which is why our leader is so well hidden, even from us. Only a few know him, and even less know who he is as a human. Nowadays, he spends most of his time human; it hides him more. Our boss feels if he keeps his human routine, he won't be singled out."

He seemed quite proud of his leader. An idea of who it could be flickered across my mind. I pictured him there behind a newspaper, hiding from the world. An old badger hiding in a library. Now it was my turn to feel like the penny had dropped too late and it should have been obvious from the start. I tutted at myself.

"When you say they have to know him... that shooting recently? Your dad's friend? Do you think they....?"

"Exactly that," he said, sounding shocked I brought it up. "I think they thought they'd found him but got it wrong. I'm guessing their boss thought Martin might be The Leader, especially with Sam being quite well connected. I think that's what Sam needed to tell me the night he was attacked, only I didn't make it in time."

"I see. So as long as the leader is safe, there is a way to one day push him back?"

"I think so. Although, there are a lot of them, and they're growing. Leroy is travelling farther and farther, bringing them here, and their initiations are getting more brutal. I don't know why they need all that power, but it isn't for anything good. I think if we can figure out who their leader is and get to him remotely, using magic, maybe we can take him down, but then there will be another to take his place. We'd have to take the whole lot down. I'm glad I'm out of it and back to marking territories. It was scary in there."

"You seemed comfortable enough." I mewed and he stopped.

"No, not comfortable. Good at acting," Spider said. "I'm not safe in the territory either. They could still come in and find me because they know I rescued you. Eldar must have known I couldn't bear to see you there. I did wonder why he kept telling me I was going to love my surprise. If he came into the town, he might be able to trace my scent and who I am as a human. Then, if he knew who I am in both forms and killed me, I think that would weaken us all. We can't keep humans out in the way we keep out shifters, so he could enter the town in human form and find somewhere to shift before looking. We would find him, but if there was no one near where he shifted, it might take us hours before we even realised he was there. We can't touch them in human form, so the scent lines are literally just a warning. There aren't enough of us to patrol, and even less of us to patrol in pairs. Sometimes if we know there is a threat we go in small groups, but this leaves other boundaries completely open. I think they know and test this regularly. We need to mix it up. They have the numbers but don't know enough about our magic to risk it. We're only safe because they're playing cautiously at the moment. We need to be clever. If they knew who I am as a human, if they saw me enter and leave a safehouse and guessed correctly, they wouldn't have to wait for me here. They could get to me anytime. I'd have to move."

"Like my mum. And me." I sighed. There was an ache I couldn't describe, nor did I know where it came from, but looking at Spider, I was assured we shared this feeling. Who knew cats had so many expressions? I had come to be quite good at reading them in my short time there.

"Maybe we could leave together," he suggested with

a grin.

"I thought you hated me," I teased.

"I do." He laughed. "I really, really hate you."

CHAPTER 31

Ena

On the way back to the safehouse, we passed a couple of shifters Spider knew; an owl who watched from a rowan tree at the end of the road, and a small bat who circled the house. He stopped to pass on a report that he'd seen nothing. Spider seemed more relaxed after hearing that. We had also passed Lila again, although this time she stayed on the opposite side of the road and moved away quickly when she saw us coming. Spider told me not to worry about her. She kept herself to herself unless she thought she could gain something. I wondered what she could gain from Spider, except Spider. I wasn't going to let her have any part of him. Two could play at the 'mine' game. I'd never really been one for possessiveness, but it was growing on me.

We entered the yard, and Spider paused to speak

with Gray. I leapt back into the kitchen window and sat on the worktop on the other side, watching him. In my mind, I begged him to follow. I wanted to spend some more time with him alone, to talk to him. He looked up and saw me watching him. He said, "One minute," to Gray, who winked.

"What's up?" he asked from outside. I didn't answer. I leapt down from the worktop and made my way to the door with my tail in the air.

I heard him follow, and excitement whipped through me. Now I needed to shift. I'd never shifted in front of anyone before, except my mum by accident.

All I heard as I headed for the bedroom was the padding of our paws. I slipped into the dark room and headed for the en-suite. Once inside, I sat on top of the toilet seat and shifted. I prayed I didn't make any strange sounds. Once done, I listened. I could hear him breathing loudly in the bedroom and suddenly wanted to stay in the bathroom until he'd gone.

"Ena?" he asked softly. By the subtle change in his voice, I knew he had shifted. As a cat, his voice was slightly higher pitched and sounded younger. I imagined mine must have too. I splashed cold water onto my face and dabbed it with some toilet paper, rose, then left the en-suite. He was sitting on the edge of the bed, wearing blue denim jeans and a tight black t-shirt with the Foo Fighters logo on the back. He had grown a bit of stubble over the last week or, so and his black floppy hair was a mess. He looked beautiful, and I was very aware I was still dressed for work and probably sweaty. I sat down on the bed next to him, completely ignoring my phone and my bag.

"Ivan." His heart rate picked up as I said his name.

"I wanted to protect you," he said, with his hand covering his face. I leaned my head against his shoulder and breathed him in. His weight shifted, and his strong arm pulled me into him.

"I know. I did want to come and make sure you were safe," I replied shakily.

"I know. I'm sorry I treated you badly. I'm not great with real people." He pulled my chin up with his hand. His skin rough, I liked it. He kissed me very gently on the chin, then on the nose, and finally on my lips. I collapsed into my emotions, kissing him back with everything I had. This was so much more powerful than our first kiss. This was more than I'd ever wanted. I thrust my hands through his hair and pulled him down on the bed next to me.

–

My phone rang, and I frowned. Where was I? There was a ray of sunlight coming through the curtains, and my feet were cold. Why were my feet cold? I realised they were out of the duvet. My back and sides were blissfully hot though, and what was that...? An arm was wrapped around me from behind. I was lying in bed naked with Ivan fast asleep behind me. My phone buzzed again. I pulled myself out from under his arm and scrabbled about on the floor, looking for my phone. When I found it, Mum had just hung up for the twelfth time. I also had two missed calls from Maisy and sixteen texts. Oh, shit. I grabbed my top and looked around for my pants.

Ivan opened his eyes and made an amused noise before he realised I was getting dressed.

"Damn," he said as I pulled on my trousers.

"Yes, damn. I'm in big trouble."

He smirked and took my hand to pull me back into bed. He kissed me, and I let him, but I had to leave.

"I'm sorry," I said, pulling the door open. "I'll call you."

I left him in bed and hurried home. I didn't care that I was in the same clothes as the night before or that I hadn't brushed my hair; I needed to get back in for Bea.

I couldn't even pull the *I fell asleep on Maisy's sofa* line because Mum had called Maisy. Maisy had tried to call me, and eventually had to tell Mum I was out with a man. I was a grown woman. Of course I could go out with a man if I wanted to, so why did I feel so ashamed?

Mum said I was feeling guilty because I had lied, and because I hadn't given a thought to Bea, which was true.

What was it with me and guilt these days? It had begun to manifest in so many parts of my life. That morning that I didn't leave Bea's side except to take a shower after Mum said I smelled like a dirty stop out. My mind wandered between guilt and happiness when I thought back to the night before.

It was only after I had been home for a few hours that she sat opposite me at the kitchen table and told me what had happened while I was gone. Apparently, while I was out, Mum was in the lounge with Bea, and one of her candles on the mantle above the fireplace flickered on without being lit. Mum blew it out but it relit. This was one of the spells set up to warn Mum of anyone trying to enter our protected property without permission. We knew it didn't work with delivery men or the postman. It had to be someone with impure intent to activate the candle, which stayed lit for some time while Mum had sat in the lounge, listening. She had heard scrambling noises outside but nothing more. She hadn't looked out of the window in case whoever was there saw her, so she kept in the corner of the room by the basket where she'd put Bea down to sleep, waiting for me to come home.

After an hour or so, the candle had gone out, so she relaxed, and that was when she started to call me to let me know to be careful coming home and that she would try and set up a spell to banish anyone unwanted from the front and back of the house. When she couldn't get hold of me, she had panicked and would have gone out looking for me had Maisy not admitted I was out with a man. Although, she couldn't tell Mum who the man was, so obviously, Mum was very unsettled thinking I wasn't coming home. Of course, with someone snooping around and me suddenly being with a man I'd never mentioned before, she put two and two together and came up with six.

Mum had called the police around three a.m., but they said I was a grown woman, probably on a date, and if I still hadn't made contact by the morning, they would come round and take more details.

The candle had flickered on again around four a.m. but then went off and stayed off. Mum spent the rest of the night setting up a banishing spell, which explained the black candle in the lounge window when I arrived home, and the smell of incense and oil. Mum was furious with me, but I could also see the relief. I tried to imagine what I would have been like if Bea hadn't come home, that hollow emptiness was hard to shake off. Especially with what happened on Friday night when I almost hadn't got away. How was she to know it hadn't happened again? How would she know they hadn't grabbed me on my way home from work and taken my phone? I promised her I wouldn't stay out again without telling her and insisted it was truly an accident that I fell asleep. She seemed to believe me, but I did have to tell her who I was out with. Once I had told her, she softened a little, but still wasn't happy about it and went straight to call Mally. It was then I realised I didn't have Ivan's number to call him. Radio silence from me it would be then.

I hoped Ivan wouldn't get it in the neck from his mum too.

-

Ivan

I was in trouble. Deep trouble.

That morning after she left, I stayed in the safehouse for a while longer, tidying up. I thought about what had happened whilst I cleaned the bathroom and made the bed before sitting for a while with my head in my hands. Not because I was upset. I was elated. I had just spent the night with a beautiful woman, a woman who had taken me by surprise and given me something I didn't know I needed. She'd crept up on me and I'd hated her for it, but now I wasn't sure how to move forward.

I hadn't noticed myself changing much day-to-day, but I had, and it had started when she came into my life. When I'd found out she and Night Flower were the same person, betrayal was at the forefront. Ecstatic and devastated at the same time. How long had she known who I was? I had been working with her the whole time, making her life hell, trying to push her away because I didn't like feeling different. My innate pull toward her seemed like I was cheating on a shifter who wasn't even with me, and yet was the biggest part of me. She had known the whole time who I was and said nothing. At first, embarrassed and burning with shame, like she'd been laughing at me behind my back, but then that kiss. That wasn't the action of someone who was making a joke of me. Even if she was trying to fake it, there was no way the energy we shared wasn't real. I became ten times lighter in that moment. My cheeks heated as I recalled how I'd been so rough with her, but my soul had been melting to a point where there was nothing but space. Pure bliss. Until the realisation of what I was doing came crashing down and I pushed her away. Still, she had come back, accepted me, decided I was worth it.

Was I worth it?

I gripped my hair in my fists and gritted my teeth. The night before had been incredible. My heart raced just thinking about her body under mine. Her soft fingers on my skin.

I was convinced our souls were connected, but whenever I was near her, I could feel an incredible energy hidden away behind a screen of self-doubt. She had no idea what our world was about and no way to realise her potential. I could help her, but I knew it would be met with refusal from our parents. They would think it was for the best.

When I'd arrived home that morning, I was met with hostility. I'd come in on an incredible high, ready for breakfast and a shower, but my heart sank when I saw the stony face of my mother and father sitting at the dining table, waiting for me. It wasn't like my parents to be hostile, however that night, whilst Ena and I were spending the hours together in the safehouse, our boundaries had been breached. Whoever it was had somehow managed to pick up her scent. The scent led them directly to her door. It must have been Eldar. He knew her scent well, and the road connecting to where she lived was on their territory, so it was only a matter of time before they found her. Not only that, but her mother had been calling. Which meant that my mother now had much higher expectations of how I should have behaved. It wasn't my fault someone had taken advantage of a clear crossing, but still, I should have expected it after what had happened at the initiation, or at least asked for extra cover. I just hadn't thought. I'd let them down.

They had known where I was. Gray had told them when they had asked. He had also told them who I was with. It wasn't that they were unhappy I was with Ena, but for some reason, they still expected me to be out there. They expected me to have been alert and awake, but still no one had come for me. Surely I was allowed some time off, for God's sake. I told them as much. I had worked all day until I quit my job and worked most of the night, every night. Weekends were the same. I was out at least once a day. I might not have ever wanted a break before, but now all I wanted to do was grab E and drive until we met the sea, to stay there away from everyone. She'd have to come back for her baby though. I sighed, thinking about how complicated things were getting. Mum had been right about her being single, but I had been right about her being a mother. We hadn't discussed it. There wasn't anything to discuss as far as I was concerned. If she was a mother, she was a mother. It was just another thing to love about her.

I didn't want to argue with my parents, so I promised I'd be more careful and do as they asked whilst out. I had to make it my priority to find out who had been on our territory and why. Still, they had to respect the fact that I needed some time to explore what could be. They didn't exactly agree, but they liked Ena, and they had to love me regardless, so they relented.

After a quick shower and some toast, I put on my playlist as loud as I could bear it, trying to blur out my thoughts, but still I found myself thinking about her. The way she walked, the way she tucked her hair behind her ears. Things I hadn't realised I'd noticed. All that time I thought I needed to get rid of her, but now she wasn't there, the dull ache settled like dust on glass. Coating my once steady yet loathed routine I called a life, with a blanket of fear mingled with hope. I'd have to see her again. The pull of Night Flower and Ena tightened like a coiled spring in my chest, a pressure that needed to be released. I had to go into work first to clear out my office, but I couldn't wait to see her again.

–

Ena

A couple of days later, I was in the kitchen with a bagel, Mum was upstairs, and Bea was sitting in her high chair, splatting her hands in her porridge, when Ivan called. I didn't recognise the number, so my finger hovered over the green answer button before I answered.

"Hello?"

Bea took that moment to scream at me for her water beaker. I cooed at her and passed her the beaker. She plastered it with porridge from her sticky hands. I heard a warm chuckle on the other end of the phone.

"Say hi for me," Ivan said.

I couldn't help but smile. "How did you get my number?" I asked. Remembering I hadn't even bothered to try and find out his, I blushed.

"I went into the warehouse for some of my stuff this morning. I grabbed your CV out of my desk drawer at the same time. They can keep everyone else's." The sneaky git. "Hope that's okay."

"Yeah, that's fine," I replied in a voice that didn't

sound like me. I pulled faces to Bea whilst I waited for him to say something else.

"Good. Good."

I couldn't think of anything else to say, but Mum came into the kitchen and broke the silence. I mumbled, "Just a sec," and put my hand over the speaker part of the phone.

"Sorry," Mum whispered. "Is it Maisy? I'll be quick. I just wanted to grab my favourite granddaughter. She can come for a wander with me, can't she? I want to go to Aldi."

I nodded and grabbed a wet wipe to wipe the porridge off her hands. I put the phone down face down on the table for a moment, in case Mum glanced at the screen and decided to make a fuss. I picked Bea up from the highchair, and after giving her a quick squeeze, I handed her to Mum, and she left the room with Bea waving to me with her chubby fingers over Mum's shoulder.

"Sorry about that. Mum's just taking Bea out for a bit," I said a little breathlessly when I picked the phone back up.

"They out for a while?" he asked casually.

"Er, I'm not sure. They're going to Aldi." I shrugged, even though I knew he couldn't see me.

"Fancy coming over for a bit?"

"Could do," I said. "Not sure what your mum would

say though. I'm probably a bad influence."

"She's not home today. She's gone out for shop supplies. Dad isn't here either."

"Library?" I asked with a laugh.

"Where else?" I could hear the smile in his voice. It sounded like it was easier for him talking on the phone. Despite the pauses, he sounded more like Spider. He didn't have that on edge, distracted tone he used at work.

"Okay, I'll come over now. Mum's taken the car though, so I'll have to walk."

"I could come get you?"

"No, it's fine." I was anxious about being alone in a car with him, which was odd, because I was offering to meet him alone in his house. Even though we had spent the night together, I was still nervous as this would be our first planned meet up. I wasn't sure what to expect. "I won't be long. See you shortly." A car journey, however short, would have built up too much strange tension, so walking was a great way for me to calm my nerves.

"Okay, bye," he said and hung up.

Although I had been up a while, I was still in my PJs. I ran upstairs to change, scribbled a quick note to Mum saying I had popped over to Mally's to speak with Ivan about something and that I would text when I was leaving but wouldn't be long. Part of me wanted to say I had gone to the library to make my life easier. I knew she'd probably have a few things to say about me running straight to Ivan's the second she left the house, but I didn't really care. Once it was done, it was done, and she'd have to accept it.

An hour later, I was sitting in his kitchen. He'd let me in and offered me a seat. It was a bit awkward and surreal. I wasn't really sure how to act around him as this was probably the only time we had met in person that we hadn't been forced together somehow. Meeting him after having some sort of forward planning didn't seem normal. With some hesitation which lead me to believe he was as nervous as I, he let me in, pulled out a chair, he sat on the opposite end of the table. He leaned back and grinned at me. An attempt in hiding his insecurities from me by leaving himself exposed. I saw through it.

"Okay, so I'm here," I began, leaning my chin on my hands, elbows on the table.

"So you are," he said, taking a deep breath in. His eyes wandered to the hem of my low-cut top.

I don't remember how we got to his bedroom. I don't remember leaving the kitchen. I don't remember the stairs. I don't remember the door to his room. I do remember that we ran, sort of, and that there was a lot of giggling, mostly from me.

–

"What happens now our worlds have crossed?" I asked, running my hands through his hair.

We lay together side by side on the bed, his chest moving up and down barely covered by the blanket, his skin shining with sweat. He had his eyes closed and a smile on his lips. I lay fully under the duvet but was completely aware of the fact I was still naked and would have to leave soon. We didn't have much time together at all.

"Well," he began, flipping onto his side to face me, his warm breath on my face. I closed my eyes, breathing it in. "For a start, we know who we are in both worlds." He trailed his finger up my arm until his hand was in my hair, and he pulled me in for a kiss. He tasted a bit like toothpaste. I bet he'd brushed them just before I was due to arrive.

"I can't believe I didn't notice your name. I mean, I knew it, but I didn't make any sort of connection. I can't believe it took me weeks to see it." He let me go, and I pulled him back, needing to be closer. I buried my face in the gap between his neck and shoulder.

"Shame you're not as observant as you thought you were, huh?" I said softly, kissing his jaw just under his ear. He didn't smell like coffee today, just aftershave and peppermints. Maybe all the coffee was a work thing.

"If anyone wanted to hurt us though, if they knew who we were in both worlds, it would be easy. If they didn't, they couldn't kill us, just weaken us. They'd need to get to both forms of our souls."

"Mmmm hmmm," I murmured, barely listening.

"And now if someone got to one of us, they could try to get us to give the other one up." He shifted his head to the side, shuffling my head back onto the pillow. I felt his eyes burning into me, so I opened mine.

"That's not going to happen though, right?" I breathed, wanting to kiss him again. Every part of me ached for him. I ran my hand down his chest, feeling the muscles on his abdomen and finally resting on his hip bone. I traced a circle there with my finger, wondering how much time we had, but I knew it was almost time for me to head back home. I couldn't leave Bea for long. She was my priority, no matter where this was headed. He sighed as he guessed my thoughts.

"I'd die before telling them who you are." He pressed his lips to mine a final time before grinning widely and pulling off my blanket.

I squealed and swatted at him. "Damn, it's cold," I shrieked, trying to grab it back.

"Shh, Mum will hear you." He laughed.

We had heard a door shut downstairs and assumed Mally had come home from shopping. We had been lying in bed quietly for a while before, so I wasn't worried she'd walk in or have heard anything, but there was still the chance she'd come up the stairs. We dressed quickly, and he went ahead into the hall to check the coast was clear. It was, so we quickly went downstairs to the kitchen, hoping she'd be in the shop. I leant back against the door and shot him a look saying I didn't want to go. He sighed again.

"You need to go," he said, reaching past me to unlock and open the door. I almost fell out backwards.

"You dick," I scolded as I lost my balance.. He laughed out loud. A genuine, free, happy laugh. It was a completely different sound and one I never expected to hear from Ivan. I clumsily made my way over to the gate, cursing him under my breath. He was sexy, but so damn childish.

He waited in the doorway as I checked the street. It was clear. I pulled out my phone to text Mum to say I was on my way home. I jogged there, and when I was back, I sent Ivan a text to let him know I had arrived. It read: *Home now. Next time, we bonfire that damned brown suit.*

CHAPTER 32

Ena

"So, details!" Maisy said.

I had barely knocked on the door when she pulled it open, grinning from ear to ear. She must have seen me drive by to park.

"Okay, okay. Let me get in first."

It had been a while since I had been there. More regret. I'd not even let my best friend in on anything that was going on.

I made myself comfortable on her sofa whilst Maisy went into her kitchen. I laughed out loud when she returned with two huge bowls of popcorn.

"Gotta have popcorn for this." She laughed, almost throwing my bowl at me and perching herself on the arm of another chair. "It's gonna be entertaining, I can tell."

"Oh, for goodness' sake, Mais!" I laughed, throwing

a piece of popcorn at her. It bounced off her forehead.

"So, where have you been, you little hussy, and what the hell happened? Your mum was so mad with you!" Maisy stuffed her mouth full.

I winced. "Yeah, she was pissed! I dunno. I just got carried away and we fell asleep." Carried away didn't cover it.

"That's it? No way! You're not getting off that easily."

Well, there was no way I could tell her about the whole being a cat thing, even though I wanted to. I thought that might have been a bit much for her on that occasion. Secret boyfriend was what she was expecting.

"Well, you know I said I didn't know where things were going with Ivan?" I began. She nodded, still munching popcorn and staring at me with wide eyes like a child. I couldn't help but smile back.

"It's so complicated. I don't know where to begin. He was a right shit at work. We had a big fight and I stormed out. He ended up quitting anyway, but I don't think that was to do with me. Then, after one shift, I was really pissed off with him because Kym, another girl at work, asked him out...." I'd forgotten all about Kym, but saying her name, I realised that it had bothered me and hadn't gone away.

"Shut up! What a cow! Did she know you had a thing?" Maisy asked. "So, he was seeing you then went off with her?"

I nodded. "I don't think anything happened. It was after that shooting. They both knew the guy involved so they went off to talk about it, only he hasn't mentioned it or her since. He just left it as it was. Anyway, so after that, he asked me out for a drink because he knew how mad I was at him. Mad was an understatement, I'm telling you."

"Rightly so!" Maisy chirped up. "Who the hell does that?"

"I know! Anyway... we went out, and I guess we lost track of time because before I knew it, Mum was freaking out and it was morning!"

Maisy raised an eyebrow and threw a piece of popcorn back at me. "You liar! As if that's what happened."

"I'm not giving you details of *that*." I laughed. "But yeah, there was more to it."

"So, you went to his place? Doesn't he live with his mother?" She snorted.

"He has a flat," I lied. "So we went back there. It wasn't planned, but we just walked around a bit and ended up there. I went in to wait for a taxi home, and well..."

She looked thoughtful. "Have you seen him since? Are you together now?"

"I'm not sure. I think so. We have, um, done it again

since. Slept together, I mean."

"When?"

"Yesterday." The heat in my cheeks must have been visible.

"Shut up!" Maisy shouted, dropping her bowl of popcorn on the floor.

I stayed at Maisy's for a few hours, talking about Ivan. She wanted more details. The physical description kind, although not too many, just his abs and his skinny jeans, that sort of thing. She told me all about her boring family dinner and insisted I come with her on the next one because all her mum and aunt did was mither her about getting a nice boyfriend and settling down. She had said she didn't meet anyone in the library, which caused them to insist she think about her future and moving jobs. I couldn't see her leaving the library any time soon. She was in love with that place. So in love, I could see her there as a ghost one day, throwing books at the staff who took over.

CHAPTER 33

Ena

On my way home, I decided to pop into Tesco for a few bits. I walked down the baby food aisle, completely in a world of my own. For a moment, I was completely unaware of anything around me until a hand landed on my shoulder, making me jump. I turned to see a young man, probably about the same age as me, though he had had a rough time by the looks of him. His head was shaved, and he had a scar that ran along one side of his face, and another fresh cut beside his nose. His blue eyes appraised me before he put up a finger to his mouth to shush me.

"I've just brought a message," he said in a low tone, looking both ways down the aisle before looking back at me. "We know who you are. We know where you live." He moved the finger from my face as a lady with a trolley turned down the aisle toward us. As a cover up he said, "Ah, okay, so you recommend this one?" He grabbed something from the shelf, but I couldn't tell you what it was if I tried.

The lady paid no interest in us and went about her shopping a few feet away. I blinked at him.

"What do you mean?" I asked calmly.

He glanced at the lady with the trolley. "I mean, we know. We need to talk to you. But not like this." He waved his hand up and down as if to gesture *not like a human.*

"Tonight. Usual time. By the park," he said, turning and hurrying away. I could have called out. I could have raised an alarm, but I didn't. I just stood rooted to the spot with a box of crackers in my hand.

"You okay, love?" the lady asked, making me jump again.

I sighed. "Yes, sorry. Just in a world of my own," I said as brightly as I could manage, feeling tears prickle in the corners of my eyes.

"I'm like that all the time." She laughed. "Grab yourself some chocolate on the way out. See you."

I sat in the car, calming my mind before driving home. I didn't want to meditate in the car, but I needed something so I could drive home without crashing. I stared at myself in the rear-view mirror. How could they know who I was? I didn't know who they were. They must have been watching me to know I was in Tesco, and to approach me in a supermarket too. They must have done that to protect themselves as well as me. Was it random, or had they followed me from Maisy's? Or to Maisy's? It was sickening.

Adjusting the mirror and reversing out, I didn't notice I was still being watched at first. The car behind me pulled out of a space just after I had driven past, and I thought nothing of it as they turned right like me. It was only after they had been right behind me for the last three turns that I realised. Feeling uneasy after the incident in Tesco, I thought I'd drive around a bit. I was only one turn away from the street which led to my house, and there was no way I wanted to lead anyone there in case they didn't know for sure. Instead of turning left at the next junction, I turned right and started to head back towards the town via the park. The car behind followed. I started to look at their number plate to see if I could remember the number, but it was difficult whilst trying to watch the road and keep calm about being followed. Where was I supposed to go? I couldn't go home, nor to Maisy's, even though they might have already seen me there that morning. I couldn't go to Ivan's, even though I desperately wanted to pick up my bag and dial his number. The police station seemed like a good idea. It was on the far edge of town, as if I was going to drive toward the city, so it would give me a good few minutes to make sure they were definitely following me. I managed to keep my speed steady and focused on the traffic. One set of lights passed, and then the second. I couldn't quite see who was in the car behind me, but they had hair and a beard. The glare from the sun on the car hid his facial features, but it wasn't the man from inside Tesco. Shit. How many were there?

As I neared the police station, the car seemed to slow. They must have realised where I was headed and decided to back off. I turned left to pull into the station car park and watched as the car drove on past the turning. They didn't stop.

I turned off the engine but didn't dare open the doors. I just sat there, listening to the quiet, but when that became unbearable, I clicked play on the CD player. I don't know how long I had been sitting there with tears rolling down my cheeks, but I had been noticed by a PCSO, and she was headed in my direction. I wound my window down.

At the police station, I called my mum and told her not to worry, even though I knew it was impossible not to worry about something like this. I also told the police I had been followed in Tesco but didn't tell them everything that was said, only that he had told me they knew who I was and that I didn't know what he had meant by that. I couldn't give them much of a description of the man in the car and described the car as best I could.

The lady PSCO who had come to me whilst I was crying in my car offered me a lift home, which, of course, I accepted. Another officer drove my car home shortly after. Neither were followed, not by cars or humans anyway, but I was not convinced there weren't others out there.

As soon as the police had gone, Mum was straight on the phone to Mr E. Bea and I watched CBeebies until my own phone rang. It was Ivan.

He said he'd overheard his dad on the phone to Mum and was worried. That warm, fuzzy feeling, so welcome as he confirmed he cared about me.

"Do you need me to come over?" he asked. I watched Bea on her playmat and considered saying yes.

"It's probably not the best idea. I'd love you to, but I should probably stay in with Mum right now. She worries, you know." I didn't have to see him nodding to know he was.

"She would be. I'm worried. Dad's worried too. I wish we knew who it was who spoke to you. Must be one of the new guys." He was quiet for a minute. "I'll have to go out tonight and see if I can find anything out. You, on the other hand... I don't want you coming out."

"Since when did you get to tell me...."

"This isn't a joke, Ena." His tone changed. "Whoever it is who knows you, do you really want them getting hold of you and taking you back to Eldar and Cole? What if I can't get to you in time this time?"

"Okay, okay," I agreed. "I won't come out. I just don't like the idea of you being out there too. They know you betrayed them and helped me to escape. They must be after you too."

More radio silence. *Teletubbies* came on, and Bea clapped her hands. I clapped mine too until she turned away from me to watch. I absent-mindedly built a tower from Duplo whilst thinking of what to say next.

"I'm sorry, by the way," he began. "For being so mean at work. I just get so angry sometimes and take it out on the first person I see. Obviously, I couldn't shout at John, but I was frustrated with things happening in the spirit plane, angry about work, just so... I dunno, I felt like I wasn't even there. Like it didn't matter how I spoke to people because I didn't belong there anyway. I was trapped in a deep fog. Then you came along, and I wanted to be nice. I just found myself getting really defensive."

The conversation had gone off on a tangent I wasn't expecting. I wasn't sure exactly what to say, so I took a moment to sort through my thoughts. He must have been thinking about this a lot. He coughed at the other end of the phone for my attention.

"That's okay," I said. "Well, it's not okay, but I get it. People are hard sometimes, especially if you don't feel like you're in the right place. You were really mean though, and it did upset me."

"I wanted to upset you. I wanted you to quit, and I wanted you to scream at me. I thought the only place I belonged was on the other side and not here. I wanted to stay there. Every time I was forced into this world, I was trapped. I hated it, and every time someone spoke to me, I got so cross with myself and with them. I don't know what happened. Somehow, I started to change my mindset. I started to feel like I did matter, that it was wrong to be so rude, but part of me couldn't stop myself. I started to think about you. I couldn't get you out of my head, but then what I had with, well... it took me a while to get my head around the fact that you were the same person. I wanted to hurt you. I blamed you for making me want you. I just didn't admit it to myself."

"So...?" I urged when he paused.

"So, I'm admitting it now. I hope you can forgive me."

"I can." *Just like that.*

It was the truth. Somehow, we had just moved on. He had hurt me, but the thought that we wouldn't have a chance to see how this worked out hurt more than what he had already said and done. I could let it go.

Mum came down the stairs and made me jump as she flung the door open.

"I'm going to have to go now. You free sometime tomorrow?" I asked hopefully.

"Sure. Come over to the shop, or I could meet you somewhere? Let me check things out tonight first. I really don't like the idea of you being followed."

"Maybe you should follow me. Then you can direct all your pent-up anger onto whoever you catch along the way. If they saw your face the way it is half the time in the warehouse, I'm sure they'd back off." I laughed, but he didn't.

"Thanks. Thought you forgave me?"

"I did, you idiot. Still hate you though." I giggled. Bea heard the sound and came over to climb on my knee and grab the phone.

"Me too. Call you tomorrow."

Mum and I spent the whole evening pricing up flats on Rightmove. There were a few in the next town that were only twenty minutes from here, but far enough for now to throw anyone off. Mum would still need her job. I was about to mention I had thought about quitting my job too but thought better of it after seeing some of the prices they wanted for the houses per calendar month. The cheaper ones were nearer the city, and neither of us really wanted to be closer to it. The other option was to move out of the area completely, but Mr E said it might be better not to. He and Mally could still help us if we weren't too far away. Mum was sceptical but agreed.

CHAPTER 34

Ena

The next morning was Monday, and I knew I had work that evening but still had the whole day off. My sinuses pricked as though I was coming down with a cold. I shoved on my slippers and picked Bea up from her cot. She had been shuffling around, babbling to herself for a good ten minutes, so I thought she was ready to get up and head downstairs. I grabbed my phone on the way out of my room.

Ivan hadn't rung yet, but he was probably still asleep. I didn't know what time he was usually out until, and I hadn't thought to ask. I sat Bea on the rug in the lounge with some of her toys and nipped into the kitchen to put the kettle on. There was already a mug out with half-drunk camomile, so I knew Mum must have been up. She was probably getting dressed.

I warmed some milk for Bea's porridge and poured my tea, leaving the bag in. I grabbed a bowl and poured some cereal and milk ready.

Whilst I ate, I kept checking my phone, waiting for a call or a text. He'd only had my number for a few days, so I didn't know why I was suddenly so clingy and expectant. I found myself frowning at it, running through various reasons he might not have called, but kept coming back to the idea that he was asleep.

You're being possessive, E. Give the guy a break.

Still, I had this feeling something was off. He seemed the kind of person who didn't really do the phone thing, so I tried to think about something else until Mum came back in to finish her tea.

"Ena, you're up." I knew by the way she wouldn't meet my eyes that something had happened. My insides squirmed knowingly.

"Mum, what is it?" I asked. "I'm here, you know."

She gave me half a smile. "It's not something to worry about for a minute. I'm just waiting for a phone call then I'll have a chat with you about it."

A chat with me? About what? If she wouldn't tell me now, it must be something big. Maybe she had seen another figure outside. More weirdos trying to get in. My phone buzzed, and my heart skipped a beat when I saw *Ivan* flash up on the screen.

Don't go to work.

Odd message. I replied quickly asking why, then put my phone back down on the table. Mum watched me but still didn't look me in the eye. I strapped Bea into her highchair when my phone buzzed again. My pulse raced and I scooped the phone up so quickly I almost knocked my cereal on the floor, but it was just Maisy. I didn't even read the text, just slammed the phone back down and occupied myself by helping Bea with her breakfast. I gave her a few spoons of porridge then handed her the spoon. She chewed it a little then just used her fingers. I sliced up some banana and added them to her bowl.

Mum's phone rang. "Be right back." She hurried from the room. Something was going on. Something to do with me, and judging by the text message, perhaps work too. I couldn't concentrate on eating, so I fumbled around, helping Bea and trying not to get nervous, even though I could feel anxiety pushing its way to the surface. I forced it back down as best I could. Maybe I should do some yoga or something. Something Bea might enjoy watching too. I stretched, and my back and shoulders tingled like I'd been working out. I hoped I wasn't coming down with the flu.

I cleaned my daughter up and hugged her whilst I looked for a children's yoga video on YouTube. I found a Harry Potter one, and the girl hosting seemed fun enough to keep Bea's attention for a few minutes while I had a stretch. It did help me feel better, especially as Bea crawled around my feet, and whenever I had to lie down to pose, she climbed on me, her knees poking me in the stomach and her feet in my face. I laughed and tickled her. The little monkey giggled and did it again. It became a new game.

I would have forgotten about Mum being cryptic and heading off with her phone had it not been for this odd feeling, like I wasn't quite myself. Bea and I had finished the yoga video by the time she came back down.

"Mum, can you watch her a sec while I go grab her some clothes?" I asked, jumping up. I was looking for a distraction to stop me calling Ivan, but Mum put her hand up.

"Whilst she's quiet, come and sit at the table for a second."

I followed her into the kitchen. "What's this about, Mum?" I asked, the anxious feeling bubbling inside me again.

"I'll put the kettle on."

"No, tell me first." I put my hand on her arm. "Please."

Mum nodded and sat down at the table next to me. "That was Mally on the phone. I'm afraid something happened last night." She gave my hand a squeeze. "Ivan was shadowing a couple of the other shifters who were out scent marking. He had some of the others do his run so he could watch from a distance to see if anyone caused any trouble around the park area where they had said to meet you. They didn't find anyone or anything."

"That's good, right?"

She shook her head. "It was until then. He and the others headed back towards the far end of the territory up by the junction out of town, but Ivan came back alone, wanting to speak with someone. I forget who they said he was meant to be meeting, but when he got there, he was jumped."

The feelings I had been bottling up all morning, from first waking and feeling that something wasn't quite right, to it building into a tight ball in my chest, seemed to have nowhere else to go. It forced its way out, causing me to hyperventilate. I gripped the side of the table and sucked in long, ragged breaths. My body shook as it all flooded out. It was a minute before my breathing and heart rate began to settle down. Mum knew not to jump up and make it a huge issue. She knew I needed to let it out. If she'd tried to comfort me, I'd have pushed her away. My mind created the illusion that the kitchen was shrinking, becoming dark.

Mum put her hands on top of mine to help calm me. Grounding me. I nodded so she knew I was ready to hear more. "He can't remember how many there were, but maybe three. He smelled them before he could see them. He got away, but he's pretty shaken up. He couldn't run to any of the safehouses so he hid in someone's garden by the police station until first light." Mum was struggling to speak, and I was struggling to listen. I looked through the doorway at Bea innocently bashing two blocks together, completely clueless to our conversation and how Mummy felt her world was falling apart. I choked back a sob.

"They must have been waiting for him. He couldn't smell them until it was too late," Mum said flatly, finally getting control of her voice. My hands were shaking. I stuck them in my armpits to steady them, opening my mouth and closing it like a fish as I couldn't find the right thing to ask.

"Is he...? Can I...?" was all that came out.

"He's been pretty badly injured, darling. Devan thinks it might be best not to visit today, but don't go to work either just in case they're still out there."

I stared blankly at her. She rarely used Mr Ealing's first name. I rubbed my face with my hands and realised my cheeks were wet. Tears were streaming from my eyes, and I hadn't even registered.

"Where is he now?" I asked, my voice sounding strangled.

"He's at home. Mally has used several healing spells, and she's had to make him go to sleep for a while too. He'll be okay, but he needs to sleep now."

I was going to be sick. At least he was at home and he had someone to look after him. I picked up my phone and only saw the text I hadn't read from Maisy. He must have sent his before Mally made him sleep. I shuffled uneasily in my chair.

"I think I need a shower," I said after a few minutes.

"I'll be with Bea." Mum headed into the lounge. As she did, she gave her a huge smile, and Bea held out her arms for grandma cuddles. I slipped by and up the stairs to the bathroom, shut the door, and collapsed onto the floor. I didn't cry, but I lay there for a long time.

I called in sick to work. John didn't sound pleased, but he didn't say anything other than to feel better soon, and he'd see if Kym could stay an extra hour to help out. I thanked him and said I was hoping to be in the next day. I already knew I had no intention of going in on Tuesday either.

I messaged Maisy back, telling her I wasn't feeling well. I kept my phone nearby in case Ivan rang, but he didn't. Mum exhausted every house rental page there was on the internet before making a list of six to go and view. She made the appropriate calls and arrangements. She too had called in sick, which I knew was a big thing for her, especially with it not being far into term.

I heard nothing all day, and it was gone midnight when I crawled into bed, but I couldn't sleep. I lay there with my eyes open in the dark, thinking about everything that had brought me to this point. Only a couple of months ago, it'd been just me and Bea, our occasional visits to Maisy, our library visits, and not being incredibly close to Mum. In such a short time, I had found a job, found a friend who I really cared about, found an extended family who seemed to love and trust me, and the whole shifting thing. I had been attacked and abused, but also, I had found something incredible with Ivan and Spider, and while I still had no clue what was going on or where it was headed, at least something existed. I had hated him and then had feelings for him. I had been rude to people and then found out new and remarkable things about them and myself. Even though I was so confused about all of it, I had found my way through and had hope it would get better. How could it not? Somehow, I had to find a way to make it work. For Bea, for Mum, for Ivan and Maisy, for Mally and Mr Ealing, and also for me.

I was deep in thought when my phone started to ring. With Bea being fast asleep, I reached over to hang up on whoever it was but then saw it was Ivan. My heart leapt into my mouth, and I couldn't get a word out other than a squeak of, "Hey."

"Hey there." He sounded tired, but that was to be expected.

"Are you okay?" I urged, sitting up and wondering where my slippers were. I didn't want to hang up, but I didn't want to wake Bea either. "One sec," I said, slipping out of my room and down the stairs to the kitchen.

"You there?" he asked as I darted through the doors.

"I am. Sorry, I had to change rooms. What

happened?" I thought I might burst into tears.

"I'm okay. They got me really good though. Nothing I can't handle." He chuckled. "Almost had to go to the hospital, but Mum got it all under control. I think I have a few cracked ribs. My chest is killing me."

I bit my lip. "Who jumped you?"

"I don't know. I didn't recognise any of them. I was on my way to meet a friend for some details. He said he knew who followed you. One of my shifter friends put me on to him and he'd agreed to meet as long as I promised I wouldn't tell anyone he'd blabbed. I don't know what happened to him as I ran into Lila on the way. He must have got spooked and ran, but when I arrived, they got me from behind or above. I had no chance. I only just got away." He sounded weak, and like he was really disappointed in himself. "I can't imagine what it might have been like if you had come out. We found nothing by the park, but then those three... they didn't even ask me for any information, they just laid straight into me. I swear they'd have killed me."

I gasped out loud and he stopped. "Thank God they didn't. I don't know what I'd have done."

"You'd have been fine. Probably better off anyway."

"Don't," I hissed. "You're stuck with me now. You're not getting out of this that easily."

"You mean by almost getting killed? I don't call that easy."

"You know I didn't mean *that*. Oh, God. I'm so glad you're okay, even though you're not. When can I see you? I need to see you." My words ran into each other. I became aware how tightly I was holding onto the kitchen table and loosened my grip.

"Not sure. I need to heal a bit. Trust me, my face isn't pretty, not that it was anyway, but at least you could see both of my eyes."

I sucked my breath in through my teeth. "Do you really think they'd have killed you?"

Of all the questions going through my head, why did I have to ask that one?

"I do," he replied. "They tried. I am very lucky."

"How did you get away?"

"Not sure. I had one on my back, one had a hold of my tail, and the other one of my front legs. The two who had a hold of me were pulling. I was already passing out at that point. One of them slipped, and when he let go to regain his grip, I managed to flip the one off my back. I think he thought I was already gone because he seemed surprised. I don't know how I managed to run. All I could see were spots in my eyes. I couldn't hear anything. I managed to get through a couple of hedges and under a fence. They could have caught me easily, but they didn't. I think they just gave up. Maybe they got bored, I don't know. I passed out. When I came to, I could barely move. Gray found me and alerted my dad, who came and got me in the car. I was still in cat form." He groaned in pain. "I think they thought I was going to die anyway." His voice trailed off.

"You sound exhausted."

"You're surprised?" He started to laugh, then it became a cough. "I need sleep. Stay on the line?"

"Sure," I agreed, heading back up the stairs.

"Where are you?" He yawned.

"Back in bed now. I'll get settled and put the phone by my ear."

"Okay. Night night," he said sleepily. I pulled up my duvet and lay the phone on my pillow. I could just about hear him breathing in the quietness of my room.

"Night," I replied yawning myself. That night, I dreamt I was falling. Just falling. I seemed to fall forever.

CHAPTER 35

Ena

Everything was rippling out of control. From the smallest step into that world, everything changed for all of us. My troubled sleep brought me into the morning with a headache. Bea was shouting something that sounded like "Ma" at me from her cot. A quick glance at my phone and I knew the battery had gone, so I plugged it in to charge and lifted Bea out for a cuddle, cooing back to her, "Ma, ma, ma. You clever baby." I couldn't let her see how much this was affecting me. She had no idea. She grounded me when nothing else could. I really needed that right then.

Tuesday was slow. Not much happened. Ivan spent most of the day asleep, so I didn't hear from him apart from a couple of quick texts. He needed to rest, but at least I knew he was getting better. I was still worried, but not that he might die on me. Mum had gone out to look at a couple of flats and to the corner shop. She said she wasn't followed, not that she knew of, but thought it best for me to carry something extra around with me like an amulet or a pendant. I couldn't think why it would do me any good, but if it would make Mum happy, then I'd do it. I hadn't planned on leaving the house and the emotional burden of calling in sick to work again knowing they needed me was more than I needed. I really couldn't face the warehouse.

I'd taken to carrying around the piece of amethyst Mum had given me. While holding Bea, I was okay, but she was getting fed up with my sudden clinginess. I needed to feel like I had an anchor. I was floating away in my thoughts, and as if sensing this, Mum handed me a piece of smoky quartz.

John called me on Wednesday, asking if I was feeling better because he really needed someone to push out the orders. He was struggling to organise things on the website without Ivan, and one of the temps had also quit. Kym and Ben were doing their best, but they needed an extra pair of hands to finish the orders for that evening. I agreed, and though Mum wasn't happy with the idea, she agreed to drop me off and pick me up afterwards. I wished Ivan could have picked me up, but he still couldn't really walk, let alone drive. I hadn't told him I was going back into work because I didn't want him to worry.

Mum was a bit flustered for most of the day. She was impatient because of the amount of time it took to go through searches and deposits for rental houses or apartments. She had complained most of the day and was deciding between two now. Both had pros and cons, and even though she told me all about them, I wasn't paying much attention. Mr E said if we stuck to our routine, they might think they'd got the wrong people and move on.

The thought of packing all my stuff up sickened me. It was such a big job, and it wasn't fair that we even had to consider it. Still, I needed Bea safe, and she wouldn't really notice now at ten months old. As long as we were settled, and I didn't have to move her around once she'd started school. I hated being moved during school, and it was on my list of things I never wanted to put her through. One move was okay, but more than one was too much for me on the back of how many times I had moved.

That evening, Mum dropped me off. It was raining quite heavily, so I hoped that might help if there was anyone looking for us. The visibility was poor, so we had that on our side. I was glad I took my hoody with me because the warehouse was freezing that evening. The huge space between the aisles seemed like walking down the fridge aisles in a supermarket.

Kym was pleased to see me. She came over and gave

me a squeeze and asked where I had been. She didn't seem to believe I had been ill and coughed something into her hand that sounded like *pulled a sicky* which made me spit out my coffee. John had totally believed me though, commenting on how pale I still looked.

Together, we flew through the orders. Kym was due to leave at nine but agreed to stay the extra hour so we could catch up on the missed orders.

A little later, I was trying to keep up with Kym and her constant talk of men. I tried to pay attention, but my mind kept drifting off elsewhere.

"Darren wasn't that great a kisser... but he did have the Ferrari, which is a huge bonus, don't you think? Ena?"

She snapped me back from my thoughts. "A Ferrari? Really?" I asked, trying to make it seem like I had been listening.

"Yeah, it's purple, honestly, you should see the inside of it. All leather, and the sound system is amazing! I was with him until around ten then I went to meet Kris."

"Kris?" I frowned. How many were there?

"Yes. Kris. Keep up, Ena! Honestly, you're in the clouds this evening. Any reason why?" The way she looked at me startled me for a moment. It was a knowing look, like she thought there was more too my being off poorly. I shook my head a little too quickly.

"No, just tired. Pulled a sicky, remember? So, go on.

How many men was it again?"

She grinned at me. "Three! In one night! Can you believe it? I think I'll keep Kris and Darren. Don't think I'll keep the other one on though I just wanted to see what he was like in bed."

"Not great then?" I wasn't really bothered either way, but I needed to keep talking as a distraction from my thoughts of Ivan.

"Nothing spectacular, but he does have a hotel in town, so is quite well off, plus he sells weed," she added as if it was completely normal for someone to do that. "Can't get it from Sam anymore, can I." She shrugged.

"Sam? Ivan's friend? Isn't he still in hospital?"

"He's out now but, I couldn't exactly rock up there, could I? *Hi, I sort of know you. We met in a club. Can I have some stuff please?*" She laughed.

"You did go to the hospital, didn't you!" I teased, giving her an elbow to her side.

"How did you know? Couldn't get past his wife!"

How the heck did she keep up with all these men? I was having a hard enough time with one.

"You and Mr Grumpy Arse from the office got it together yet?"

She took me by surprise asking because, so far, all she'd done was talk about herself.

"Er, what makes you say that?" I stuttered, wishing my face hadn't flushed scarlet and betrayed me.

"It's obvious you're into him. Anyone could see that. I told him so just before he quit. I asked him out for a drink, and he was about ready to accept until you walked past, then he changed his mind. It was like he completely forgot what we were talking about."

She seemed a little put out by this rejection. I didn't feel sorry for her though. Especially after the evening she had just described to me. I, on the other hand, was elated. Especially after how she spoke about guys, I had felt personally hurt thinking he might have become another one of her hook-ups.

"He changed his mind?" I asked curiously. I hadn't asked him about it, and after him being beaten up, I didn't think it was really a good time to bring it up. I could ask Kym though. She was happy to chat about anything and seemed to enjoy that the focus was now on me and our former arsehole supervisor.

"Yeah. I was on my way out and I saw him standing in the corridor, looking at his phone. He was still there after I'd been to the loo, so I asked him what he was doing."

"Just like that? Did he not have a go at you?" I picked up the remaining orders but didn't look at them.

"No. He just said he was texting a friend who was in hospital. I asked if he meant Sam. I saw him opening up the betting shop the other day, you know. Didn't speak to me though, the ignorant git. His wife probably wasn't impressed. Anyway, I said I needed a drink and he said he could do with one too. We were set to go until you walked past, and he went all tense again." She pouted before giving me a wink.

"So, if he wanted to go with you, what changed?" I asked. I didn't believe it was me who stopped him from going, but it was nice to be told that. "He told me he was going to meet you on Friday when I saw him."

"Probably trying to get a reaction from you."

"Well, he got one." I laughed, thinking about how I shouted at him. "I had a right go at him."

"No way." Kym pushed her hair over her shoulder. "Wish I'd been there."

We finished our orders at just gone ten. Security came down to check if I needed anyone to escort me home, but I refused them. Kym was wondering why, so I told her I was followed in town in the car and in the supermarket.

"Wow, you have had a busy week." She grabbed her bag and coat. Her blue and pink hair flicked over her shoulder as she spun round.

"I've enjoyed chatting to you tonight, Ena. We should catch up properly."

"I'd like that."

Now I knew nothing had happened between her and Ivan, My heart was a little lighter. She'd never given me any reason to dislike her, it was all in my head or implied by Ivan. The bloody fool knew how to infuriate me.

"Okay. Bernard's Coffee. Saturday. Eleven-thirty. See you then," Kym stated as if I had no choice on any of the details.

"Of course. See you tomorrow. We can chat more then."

"I'm not in tomorrow," she sang as she ran out into the car park with her flimsy raincoat over her head toward her waiting taxi.

I glanced around for Mum but couldn't see her yet. I checked my phone and she had sent a text and was on her way. I stepped back inside the doorway to wait. The double doors into the corridor were closed behind me, and I stood in a little porch type entrance. It was still raining, but not as much as it had been four hours ago. I watched the water washing across the car park like a river; I was surprised it hadn't flooded. To the right of the building was where the car park was exposed to the main road and the little side road that joined the car park to it. To my left was another brick wall, but halfway along, it stopped and continued with one of those temporary metal fences, the type that are usually cable tied together. It must have been about six foot tall and separated the scrubby area at the end of the car park to what I thought must have been a building site at some point. I'd never taken much notice of it, but that evening, the rain bounced off the railings and rattled in the wind, the end one scraping on the wall. I was staring at where I thought I could hear the scraping noise coming from when I heard another.

"Ena Bedford," said a voice somewhere to my left.

I strained my eyes to see, but in the rain and the poor light, I couldn't really see anything. Deciding it might just have been in my head, I shuffled back slightly and ignored it, putting my hand in my pocket for my phone, ready to call the police if I needed to.

"Ena. It's okay, I'm a friend." I scanned the wall for the security cameras by the door, wondering if they were still live.

"If you're a friend, show yourself," I said with a slightly trembling voice. My phone was now in my hand. I dialled 999 but hovered my thumb over the call button. I scanned the car park for Mum's car lights.

I didn't expect to see anyone, but a small figure appeared not far ahead of me. It hopped along the ground toward me. In the dark, it looked a bit like a minion from *Despicable Me*, but as it got closer, I saw it was a large owl.

"Oh," I said, staring at it. It wasn't at all what I expected.

"Oh indeed," said the owl with a frown. "Can I stand under there with you? It's bloody awful out here."

I nodded and stepped to the side. I didn't need to

make room as there was plenty, but I wanted to seem polite. I wondered if The Wise One could have sent her. It was possible.

The owl's voice was female. Her feathers were dark brown, and her talons were huge. She ruffled her feathers to shake off the rain. If you had told me a couple of months before that I'd be standing in the dark talking to an owl, I'd have marked you as completely insane. I rolled my eyes at the thought.

"Horrible night, isn't it?" she said with a shiver. I agreed it was, half hoping security would come through the doors to stand with me, and half hoping they wouldn't because they'd catch me taking to an owl.

"My name's Marple. I know your father."

I swallowed hard, ready to press call. "You know my... who?" I began to ask, but she cut me off.

"Your father wishes to speak with you. It's very difficult here. Too dangerous. He has asked me to ask you to shift. He needs to you to meet him. You can choose when, but you must come to the traffic lights by the junction out of town after dark. He said usual time. You must speak with the cat you find there."

"Can you tell me why it's so important? Why can't he phone me? What if I don't want to see him?" I growled, frustrated.

"Don't know. It's not my problem," Maple said shortly and hopped back off into the dark car park. I didn't see if she flew or if she shifted, but I was so grateful Mum arrived at that very moment. I pretty much fell into the car and pulled the door closed so quickly I caught my shoelaces in it.

Mum kept me downstairs with her for most of that night. She made me promise to go and have some lessons with Mally to try and learn a little about how to protect myself. She showed me a few basic spells, but I couldn't remember much about them. I was too distracted that they now knew where I worked. I knew I had to quit my job, which was a shame because I did like seeing the extra pennies adding up in the bank on the run up to Bea's first birthday and Christmas. Also, with Mum having to get a rental property on top of this one. Luckily though, she paid the mortgage off on this one years ago, so she didn't have any outgoings on this house other than bills. She said if we got settled, she could always rent this house out, although that would be a bit like knowingly projecting ill wishes onto whoever moved in as they might be targeted by mistake. We agreed that if we did move, we would leave our house unoccupied for a while and only pop back to check on it and pick up the post. Mum said she didn't want to register everything for another place and change all her addresses with details because then anyone could find us from those details.

She was off to the estate agents' first thing to finalise

a few bits on the property she'd chosen on the internet, so I stayed in with Bea. I opened the back door because the house stank of burnt sage, it was a consuming and choking stench. Mum had been going all out on the protection; I just wished it wasn't so smelly. I stood in the kitchen, waiting for the kettle to boil and flicking through the post, wondering exactly how many pieces of post would pile up over a few days of us not being there, and that if anyone cottoned on to the fact we came back every few days, it wouldn't be hard for them to wait for us when we came to get it.

One of the letters was for me. It was handwritten, which was strange because who would be sending me post that wasn't a bill? I opened it and read it. It was very formal for a handwritten letter.

Ena,

I am not sure that you understand the importance that we meet so I thought I would send this in advance of your decision. I trust you were given the relevant information.

It has been a long time, and I am sure you have many questions.

I would hate to have to influence you in other ways.

I look forward to our meeting.

Yours, _____ (fill in the blank yourself)

(Dad, Father, Pop, Sperm Donor – whatever name

you wish to choose will be fine)

I noted the lack of an actual given name, just a series of meaningless titles. Well, meaningless to me, anyway. Clearly, he didn't want to be personal about all of this, otherwise he'd have signed with a name, not some shitty line and sarcastic statement. I wondered if Bea's real father would be like this if he ever found out about her one day. I balled my fists together and pursed my lips as my heart began to race.

Mum was out, so my first instinct was to close and lock the back door, peering out of the window at the garden boundaries, looking for anything different, then I curled up on the sofa. The blinds were already closed in the lounge, so I couldn't see out and no one could see in, but I felt violated. He knew we were here. He'd known all along.

Bea was playing on the rug with some of her toys, putting her blocks in to their box and taking them out again. I watched her for a minute until I grounded. There was something soothing about watching a child play. Her peaceful, playful mood calmed me.

I called Ivan, and he answered on the first ring. I read the letter to him. He suggested they'd be watching the house but didn't think they'd do anything If I left. He thought they'd give me a chance to make the decision to go and see my dad. I made it clear I had no intention of going, which seemed to soothe him. His injuries were still causing him pain, but he could get up and move around the house a little now, so it should be okay for me to visit. Whilst we waited for Mum to get home, we continued to chat. Small talk at first, mostly about what he'd been binge watching on Netflix waiting for the meds to kick in, and how his Mum had been insistent on him covering himself with some sort of herby-scented ointment she'd made. He admitted it did help him to feel better, but it stank. I told him how our house smelled like burnt sage, and he laughed and welcomed me to the world of witches. Why couldn't we be witches with less burning of things?

"I have a theory about who attacked me," he said.

"The gang?" I asked.

"Well, yes, but I think they must have been watching me as birds. Something I wouldn't have been able to see if they were high above me. Something I wouldn't have been able to smell if they were far enough away. They must have been birds, then changed into something else. That must have been when I noticed them."

This had crossed my mind too. I told him of the owl I had met at work. He cursed me for going back in, but I didn't feel like arguing, so I smoothed it over instead.

"I'm quitting though," I said. "Tonight."

"You can't go back in tonight," he hissed. From his tone, I half expected him to appear and keep me prisoner.

"I don't think they'll do anything tonight. They'll

give me chance to read the letter and make a decision about meeting them. I think you're right about that part. By usual time, I think they mean after work because that's when I usually shift. They'll let me leave work, but I know they'll be watching me. I'll be safe in the warehouse though. I think if I don't turn up for work, they'll assume I won't be going out anywhere and might risk coming to the house. If I'm at work, they might think I'm considering it. Just one last night. John was really stuck last night with orders and Kym isn't in tonight either. It's just me and Ben."

He sighed. "Okay, fine, but I'll have to send someone to watch the building. Don't expect me to be happy about it." I could tell he was in a bad mood with me.

"I don't," I said calmly. "Shall I still come over?" I wanted to go over, even if he was grumpy, but judging his mood swings was still quite new to me.

"Yes, still come over. I just don't want you going out at night on your own." He sounded frustrated.

"Aww, see do you care."

He grunted.

"Oh, I hear Mum. I'd best go." I bounded off the sofa to get the door. "See you soon."

CHAPTER 36

Ivan

As soon as she hung up, I called Tiz, hoping he was in human form. The thought of Ena coming over was pushed to the back of my mind temporarily, and the thought of protecting her whilst she was at work was now at the forefront. I gave him a quick rundown of what had gone on.

"Sure thing. I'll sort something out. If they are watching from nearby, it's a security breach. I might need some others out with me if we come across anyone. Am I okay to call some of the others?"

"Yeah. Do whatever you need to do, just get them out. I want everyone out. I want to know everyone who is out tonight, them and us. Tell them I'll pay them if you need to." I grabbed a fistful of hair and pulled it in frustration, aware I was repeating myself, but I didn't know how else to make it sound important. I wasn't used to this helplessness. This was all I could do to watch her if she insisted on going in.

"I don't think it'll come to that," Tiz replied. "You sure she's worth it?"

I growled at him and could almost see him rolling his eyes. "Yes. She is." I cleared my throat. I was getting tired again. I'd need to sleep again before she arrived.

"Then we'll do whatever you need. You've looked out for us enough times." He laughed.

"Thanks, mate. Honestly, I'm lucky to have you."

I was. I could count on Tiz when I needed him.

"Naff off with the soppiness," he said flatly. "Mental her dad's on that side of the fence though. Does it not all seem a bit coincidental to you? They ramp up the violence, she shows up, then they get worse? I can't help feeling she might be here to spy on us all."

"I can vouch for her. If you're not comfortable doing what I need you to do...." I could hear my voice changing tone and steadied myself. I'd go out myself if I had to.

"No. It'll be done, boss. If you say so, it's so."

Feeling a little better that Tiz was sorting this out for me, but also irritated he'd dared question it. I dropped my phone on the side and let my mind wander. My body was exhausted, and my chest ached from talking with cracked and bruised ribs. I was covered in marks in varying colours so bold that it almost looked like make-up from a movie. When I coughed again, I spat out blood. Great, just when I thought I was healing. I gripped my chest tightly, trying to ease some of the pressure, but it was no good. I'd have to take some more painkillers. I hated taking them, but I wasn't going to lie in bed for the next week while Ena was being followed, unless it was me doing the following.

-

Ena

I made Mum, Bea, and me some lunch whilst Mum told me about the apartment we were going to be moving to for a while. It didn't have a garden, but we didn't really use ours anyway, and Mum could grow her herbs in the kitchen or utility. From the sounds of it, it wasn't too bad. It was a large, two-bedroom place in a converted police building that had recently been renovated. It hadn't been a police station in years. The developers had completely gutted the building and turned it into four brand new homes. Ours was on the ground floor, which was ideal with the pushchair, not that I really wanted to go anywhere, but Bea would need fresh air. The apartment was on the far side of town in an area that used to be a very small village, but over time, it had merged with the town as buildings were built in the space between. There was even a new housing estate being built there on what was once a green belt. The school Mum worked at was in walking distance, which would be a bonus for her in the evenings, especially now it was getting later in the year.

I promised I'd start packing my things that evening but told Mum we had been invited over to Mally's. I played it in a way that made it sound like I needed to discuss my learning about witchcraft and how to protect myself, but really, I just wanted to go and check on Ivan. I was sure she knew it was really the latter, but she didn't say anything except to ask me if I still had the books I had checked out from the library a few weeks ago. I took them along, even though taking books on witchcraft to a house full of witches seemed a bit embarrassing.

When we arrived, I set Bea up in the lounge on her playmat with Mum and Mr E as Mally wanted me to join her in the shop. I was nervous but went anyway. She was quite cheerful, despite someone trying to kill her son. She always seemed to have a smile for me, which made me feel insanely guilty that I didn't really want to admit this stuff intrigued me. My head told me if I admitted there might be something in this whole witch thing, I might suddenly be seen as mad. My heart disagreed. When I thought about it, anyone who I did see regularly would either believe in this anyway or wouldn't care. Maisy would think it was really cool. The word *witch* seemed like something from a fantasy film, not a real life every day thing, and yet there we were talking about it.

She went through a few of the basics with me, making circles of salt and telling me the basic beliefs, which were surprising. I'd never thought the basic principles were something so simple that I had been believing all along anyway. To love and respect the natural world around you, trust there is more out there for our soul or spirit, and that it will remain until we have learned all we can, be it in this life or the next. The way she spoke of our souls was soothing. I already knew part of me could shift, and I could protect my soul in that way, but I also believed after this life I would remain. Mally insisted that any soul mates or close relationships I had in this world would be carried on, and a soul will recognise another, even though in consciousness we might not. A soul will know its soul mate, but they are not always drawn together. It will search without us knowing until it has found it.

"So, do you think Ivan and..." I began, suddenly stopping and wishing I hadn't said that out loud.

"Sometimes they say love at first sight is the souls reconnecting, but you have to accept it on a conscious level, and that depends on you as a person. You may choose to give in, you may not. Souls do not always reconnect fully in each life. Sometimes you will carry on searching, not knowing you had once found it. You can still have a full and happy life. I think when it happens, it isn't always clear. It is often confusing. Familiar, yet distant. You feel you can't trust it, but you have already opened yourself up to it. I think we were about to lose Ivan to the shifter world. In this one, he was so hard to get along with. He struggled and was rude and hurtful because of it, but then when your souls reconnected, on some level, he knew. At first, he wouldn't give in to it because on a conscious level he didn't know what was going on, but his soul knew yours. If you hadn't been who you are, you might have left and never seen him again. He would have carried on and lived his life, and so would you, but everything changed the day you met, whether you want to believe it or not."

I nodded. I didn't have to say anything more about it. We both already knew the answer to my partly asked question. I thought about how he'd tried to be nice to me at the gym and wondered if that was part of his subconscious calling to me. It might be true that he had suddenly realised something within him had, in fact, found something it needed. I had changed too. I had barely known him, and yet I was drawn to him. I had been drawn to Eldar too, but that was different. What I had with Spider was on a different level to the lusting and craving attention I felt for Eldar. It was nauseating thinking of how I had been around him and understood why Spider had been so angry.

She told me we were to harm no one, at least not intentionally, and certainly not with spells or trying to influence something to happen to them. She said this was how many witches ended up being in such a bad place. Most were peaceful and worked with the world around them, only influencing the positive or using energies for healing and protection, but that could only go so far. This, she said, was why they lived among people who believed other things, and no one thought any different. We didn't talk about being a witch because, in most cases, it simply wasn't relevant. No one asked, so we didn't say. Part of her oath and the oaths taken by many others said we also couldn't involve someone else in a spell or do a spell for them without their permission unless it was a very specific circumstance. If there was any doubt they would agree it was for the best then you simply didn't do the spell. Some witches believed spells could be used for darker means, or even greed. Wishing you had enough money for something positive was one thing, but greed and taking more than you needed also fell into the harmful category.

I didn't do much in the shop except listen to her. Her voice seemed strained, and she needed to sip water to be able to keep talking. Even though she was tired, I sensed she wanted to tell me as much as she could, so I let her. I looked at her aged skin and hair and wondered how she looked so much older than she was. She wasn't that much older than Mum, but looked at least twenty years more. As for Mr Ealing, he must have been in his fifties or early sixties, but he looked like he was later seventies and moved around just the same. I mentioned this about Mr E, and she said he had a very old soul and sometimes the magic he'd had to use had drained him. The more it drained him, the older he looked. It took a little more of his life every time, but his soul had been around for a very long time anyway, so he always aged that little bit quicker. She said she believed he didn't have much longer to go in this life but was certain he'd have one last round in him. I wasn't entirely sure what she meant and thought it best not to ask. I wondered if Ivan might be the same.

"Does that make you feel sad?" I asked, knowing if I found out Ivan would age quicker because of the magic he used, I'd be devastated. "Knowing he might pass on soon, drained from protecting others?"

Mally smiled and took my hand. "It does and it doesn't. If that is what is meant to be then it will be. He has healed and he has loved. He has protected but also fought for what he believes is right. I cannot stop him from being who he is, and yes, when he is gone, I will miss him, but I cannot stop him. We will find each other again."

I nodded. She had some strength in her. I admired that.

We started with something basic for me to work on. It was basically imagining I was in a bubble. I had to imagine that me and my energies were safe inside, and whilst I could see through, nothing could get inside to me. I had to project my positivity onto the outside of my bubble and concentrate on keeping everything else out. She also told me to choose an item of clothing. In the past, witches used cloaks which were adorned with protective spells and energies so, as they walked, the cloak on their back would help keep their business in and everyone else's out. If you used certain spells, people might not even notice you pass as your cloak would cover you from their eyes. It was believed that no one could harm you if you were wearing your protective cloak. Nowadays though, someone walking about in a cloak would look odd, especially in the middle of summer, so modern witches often chose an item of clothing that could cover their heads, shoulders, and back. Something they could hide themselves inside and pass through the crowds unnoticed. Mally suggested that the younger generation favoured a hoody. This seemed sensible. I could quite easily hide myself in a hoody. She was about to take me through a couple of the spells needed to make this work when Mr Ealing popped his head around the door.

"Ivan's awake. He was asking how long you'd be."

I glanced at Mally. Time had flown and I hadn't even noticed. I must have been genuinely interested, and I realised I was mentally exhausted.

"Go, my child," she said, her eyes warm. "We can

continue later."

The stairs creaked. I hadn't noticed the last time I had been there, but then I had flown up them without thinking of anything but getting Ivan stripped off as quickly as possible. Now, I stepped up them slowly and anxiously. I could hear Bea babbling away downstairs. She'd been happy enough playing in the lounge and wasn't really fussed about me just passing through. I could hear the distant chatter between the grown-ups, but I was also very aware of my heart drumming in my chest and the blood rushing through my ears. I ran my hand over the banister, using it as a way to keep me from turning around and walking straight back downstairs.

I paused for a second outside Ivan's bedroom door, listening. I took a deep breath and ran my hands through my hair a few times to flatten it, pulled up my black jeggings, and adjusted my top. It was more to do with being self-conscious and nervous about him being so injured rather than looking nice. I had no idea what he was going to look like behind the door. I thought about knocking, but instead, I leaned against the door, opening it a little. The curtains and windows were open, so the room was light and airy, which was refreshing as the corridor was suddenly stifling.

"Ena?" he asked croakily. He coughed and said my name again more clearly.

"It's me," I said brightly, stepping into the room.

His bed was in the corner, diagonally opposite the door, he lay on top of the covers, propped up on his elbow with the TV remote in one hand and the other in his hair. My heart skipped a beat. I wished I'd brought some water with me because my mouth was suddenly so dry that I didn't dare speak.

It was hard not to notice his black eye. It must have been huge at the time, but now it was a gross shade of purple, and the whites of his eyes were bloodshot. His nose was crooked, like it had been broken and reset slightly off. It was swollen, as was part of his lip.

He smiled when he caught me looking at his lips and groaned. "Come here." He dropped the remote and reached out his hand for mine. Of course, I went to take it. I floated onto the edge of the bed and brushed my hand across his cheek. I kissed his lips softly, avoiding the swollen part.

He closed his eyes and sighed. "I've missed you and your stress." He chuckled, and I pouted.

"How rude. Luckily, I brought my stress with me." I traced my finger along his jaw. "Oh, God. What did they do? You look like you've been hit by a truck."

"It's not as bad now." Ivan sat more upright. I could see it hurt him and then remembered he said some of his ribs were cracked.

I laid my palm on his chest and spread out my

fingers.

"Does it still hurt?"

"Sometimes. It hurts more when I lie down, which is a shame because, now you're here..."

"Enough of that, thank you," I said playfully. "Everyone's downstairs."

"So they are. Ah, well. I guess we'll just have to talk then." He put his arm around my shoulder, and I leaned into him, trying to avoid leaning on his ribs but finding that impossible. I grabbed a spare pillow and stuck it between us.

Instead of talking, however, we kissed.

He cupped my breast through my t-shirt as if it were the most normal thing in the world to do. I leaned against his warm body, breathing in his smell. I was sure there were things I could attempt without him having to move so much, but I didn't want to break the comfortableness of us just sitting there.

"Hmm, no coffee?" I observed out loud.

He made a noise of amusement, but the sound that followed told me that laughing hurt his chest. "No. Mum won't bring me any. You could though. Seriously, I have withdrawals."

"Nah, I'm a bit afraid of your mum." I smiled. "She'll curse me."

"She won't curse you for coffee. Leading me astray though... well, she might for that."

"I haven't led you anywhere, you've led yourself! Up and down the garden path and all around the houses!" I snapped, sounding offended. I wasn't, but his face was a picture until he realised I was joking. We looked at each other for a moment and I was about to lean in to kiss him, but he turned his head away and shuffled back on the bed.

His lips pursed together, and I wondered what he was thinking. I squeezed his hand to let him know I was listening.

"I can't believe Eldar's boundary is so close to your house. It makes it difficult to protect properly. We can't detect them on their side," he said finally, looking at our hands held together on the edge of the bed. I gave him another squeeze. Dreamy moment obviously over.

"I know. At least we're moving now though," I said. "Maybe they'll lose interest."

Ivan shook his head. "They won't. Not after that night. They won't let us get away with that. I wouldn't be surprised if it was them who had this done to me. I don't trust the fact that neither Cole nor Eldar have been seen since anywhere near that boundary. It's their area to patrol and mark, so where are they?"

I'd tried not to think about them since that night, but they crept up on me every now and then. I had trusted them too easily, and why? I wasn't great with people, and for some reason, allowed myself to be sucked in by their friendliness and their power. I wondered if it had been some sort of spell, but they didn't seem to know any magic other than shifting. It had all been me. My fault and mine alone. I had gone to talk to them. I had been over friendly. I had allowed that to happen, and even when I knew I had been safe on Spider's family's side of the lines and the unease in the back of my mind had warned me, I had never admitted it to myself fully. That night with Eldar in the park, when we cuddled, it was just something that happened without me really thinking about it. How must that have looked to someone who was trying to keep me safe? Mally's teachings from the afternoon crept into my thoughts.

"I'm sorry," I said quietly, turning away and pulling my hand back to rest on my knees. Ivan moved with me.

"You didn't know." He wrapped his arm around my chest, leaning me back into him.

"You tried to tell me. I didn't listen."

"You had to learn for yourself. We had only met a few times. You didn't know if you could trust me, and knowing how mean I was at work, I wouldn't trust me either."

"No, it was my fault." I sniffed. "I let it happen. I didn't listen. I had only known them for five minutes too, and I went willingly whilst you stood and watched."

He sighed and looked thoughtful again. He was gorgeous when he frowned, even with a black eye. How easily I shifted and melted. I was so easy to read, and so easy to let my guard down at the slightest bit of attention.

"Pull out that drawer." He pointed at his computer desk. I reached over and slid out the drawer. It was clearly a junk drawer. I grinned as he shrugged. "That box on the side, pass it to me."

I pulled out a plastic takeaway tub full of odds and ends. He took off the lid, a battery, and I saw some string, a USB charging cable, a couple of conkers, and goodness knows what else. I grinned at the normality of it. Everyone has a junk drawer with random crap in a box. The sort of things you don't know why you kept but can't part with just in case you need them. He fumbled around in the box for a moment before pulling out an old-looking thin chain with a small object on the end. He took my hand and held my palm flat then dropped the item onto it. When he moved his hands, I saw it was a necklace. On the end was a small and slightly battered pentacle. A star within a circle. It fit nicely in my hand.

"It's silver," he said, blushing. I pretended not to notice, but it was hard not to squirm a little at the flush in his cheeks. "It's just very old and could do with a good clean. I'll get Mum to cleanse it first though."

"It's pretty." In its own way, it was. I could see a couple of small dents in the circle. He was right, it did need a good clean, but it was a pretty pendant.

"Will you take it?" I could tell by his tone and the look in his eyes he was expecting me to say yes, so I did.

"I will," I said. "I'll wear it after it's had a cleanse." There was no way I was wearing it straight from the junk tub. Goodness knows what else was in there.

"Probably best." He chuckled, replacing the lid on the box and throwing it back into the drawer. I pushed it closed.

I heard footsteps on the stairs. It was Mum.

"Ena, come and have some tea. You've not got long until work," She hovered outside on the landing.

"Okay," I shouted back. "She's worried we're up to something," I whispered to Ivan.

"As much as I'd love to prove her right, I think I'd best hold off until I'm a little less breakable." He grinned.

I grabbed his t-shirt and pulled him towards me, pausing to breathe in before kissing him, and when I did, all my fears and frustrations fell away like dandelion seeds in the wind. I didn't know where they went but let them fall where they may.

CHAPTER 37

Ena

We ate at Mally's that afternoon. They decided to have dinner early because I had to head off, and even Ivan managed to hobble down the stairs to take part. He got a good scolding from his mum for his trouble. I was then taken to work in a taxi just before six. I wished I'd brought a few things with me now as I hadn't really expected to stay at their house for so long. I had planned on getting ready for work from home, but the clothes I wore were fine, and I had a black hoody in Bea's changing bag.

Work dragged. It was only Ben and me that evening, and knowing I planned to quit made it drag more. There looked like there were far too many orders for us to tackle on our own, and two hours into our shift, John appeared, looking stressed, telling us Kym had handed in her notice. Great. That was exactly what I wanted to hear. I didn't want to let John down, but I had to keep myself safe.

Ben helped me with the ladders a couple of times, but other than that, I didn't see much of him as we hurried around with our order forms, picking and packing. I had my headphones in. Alkaline Trio helped keep some sort of pace going for me. It didn't stop me from constantly checking the time though. Ben must have noticed because every time he saw me at the end of an aisle or by the printer, he became a live version of the speaking clock, which was both infuriating and funny at the same time.

We picked up the pace and were doing quite well. It seemed a lot of the orders were small, so we only had to find one or two items each time and package them up. The time wasted came from waiting for labels to print. I bobbed about the warehouse, completely distracted by my orders and the music in my ears. I almost didn't notice the huge rat sitting on the shelf at my eye level. It was only because I dropped a packet of envelopes that I noticed at all. When I stood up, there it was in my face. My mind didn't register *shifter*, it only registered rat.

I jumped back, shocked, and dropped my envelopes for a second time. I was cursing myself loudly over my music when Ben rounded the corner.

"What's with you?" he asked with an amused look on his face.

I pulled out my headphones. "There was a damn rat on the shelf. Flipping thing gave me a heart attack," I said in the same tone I had been cursing in. I pointed at the shelf, but the rat had gone.

"A rat? That's gross." Ben held out his hand to take the envelopes from me. I think he thought I was more shook up than I actually was. Yes, it had given me a fright, but I wasn't afraid of rats.

We made for the packing station. I was getting the vibe Ben thought of himself as a sort of big brother to me. It soothed me a little, although I had no idea where the thought came from.

"I wonder if John knows there are rats in here. It's probably all the rain we've had. I bet it's from that scrubby bit looking for somewhere dry," Ben said, looking toward the empty office.

"I'll report it later," I said, still a bit flustered. "Thanks, Ben."

Ben nodded and patted me on the back as you might a child. "Not many now." He looked at the few orders that were left.

"We make a pretty good team. I thought we'd be here all night," I offered brightly, making conversation.

His dark eyes lit up. "Don't tell John that, he might let me go. I'm still a temp, and if he decides two people can make it work, who do you think he'll be letting go first?"

He was right. There was a fine line between looking like a good, efficient team and looking like a team that could survive a man down.

"But if Kym's quit, that does just leave the two of us. You're fine," I said, playfully punching him on the shoulder.

"Good point." Ben grinned, seeming a little happier in his job safety. "He's still got his day staff though. He could move hours around."

"No one wants to work in the evening. It's just a bonus, I think, so he can offer quicker delivery to people who order later in the day. He probably won't lose much by dropping both of us," I said, but then quickly added. "I don't think he will though."

I was going to quit the job too, although now I felt awful about leaving Ben alone in the warehouse, especially now the office down there was empty too. If Ben was alone, maybe John would stop the evening shift altogether and shut the whole place at six. It must have cost him a fortune in the winter to heat the place. He couldn't have been making that much money with us being in.

I'd forgotten about the rat because I was now thinking about how I was going to tell John I was also leaving, and about whether I should give Ben a heads up or play the chicken card and say nothing. Knowing me, I'd just say a cheery goodbye and then not turn up tomorrow, and pray I didn't bump into him again. He was a nice lad, but I didn't owe him anything. I was sure he wouldn't think twice about me if he were to quit.

I was walking around an aisle just along from where I had first saw the rat when a feeling like I was being watched snaked over my skin. This made me look around more often and turn off my music. I left my headphones in my ears for some reason, possibly comfort. I needed the music to calm and distract me, but there was something in that feeling, an instinct that warned me to be alert. I wished the orders were finished so I could leave and head back to Mally's. Even though the music was off, the lyrics still played in my head.

I looked down at my order. I was on the right aisle, I just needed the right bay. This time, the customer wanted rolls of brown paper and two large boxes of staples. I counted as I walked, very aware I was counting out loud and my voice seemed loud in the huge, silent space of the warehouse. A space which was suddenly huge and empty. I wondered where Ben was.

There was something behind me, I could feel it. I knew it was there before turning around. It was as if my cat senses were becoming fluid. I didn't have to think about them, but as a human, I was always second guessing. I suppose if I let myself go to them, maybe there wouldn't be much of me left. Or could I still be me, but extra?

I took a deep breath and turned around. When I did, the rat was sitting on the floor right behind me. It looked up at me. There was no way this was a regular rat. Rats didn't follow you around, did they?

"Shift," it said in a voice I could hardly hear. "Then we can talk."

I shook my head. "I don't talk to rats," I said, not knowing what to say but wanting to sound brave.

"That's a shame." The rat walked toward me. I took two steps back before he stopped and sighed. "Fine. I'll go higher." He leapt up onto the first shelf and scrabbled up the cardboard boxes to the next shelf. He was about shoulder height now and easier to hear. I lowered my head slightly in curiosity.

"Did my dad send you?" I asked the rat, glancing around for Ben. If he appeared around the corner and saw me talking to a rat, it'd look very strange.

The rat shrugged. "I don't know who sent me. Just that I was sent."

"Okay. So why were you sent?" I asked, still looking around.

"I'm here to tell you you need to cut contact with them. We will take the territory, and when we do, we will not discriminate. We will take everybody. You need to shift. You need to meet with us and negotiate your move to us."

I listened carefully but didn't speak for a minute.

When I did, my voice was shaky, and my body shivered with adrenaline.

"Who is *we*?" I asked, ready to drop my orders and run back to Mally's.

"You know who we are," the rat said. "I was told you were given instructions of where to go."

I nodded. "I have no intention of going anywhere with any of you. I certainly won't be shifting." The rat rubbed his face with his paws before jumping back down to the floor.

"Look, kid, you seem nice. Trust me, this is off record. I don't make a habit of going round scaring young ladies, honestly. Do what you need to do, but don't underestimate them. They will get to you if you ignore this, and they will send more of us to watch you. They won't give you the time to hide."

I sighed and decided to try something else very quickly before he left. "Thank you. That's very sincere of you. When they told you I'd be here, what did they look like, and what did they tell you of me? It'll help me decide. That way I won't take long."

I saw the tiny face crease as the rat frowned. I thought he wasn't going to answer. Maybe I hadn't put enough pleading in my voice. I dropped to a crouch and forgot all about looking out for Ben.

"Please?" I whispered. "I don't want to be afraid." The rat blinked and nodded.

"He was a cat." He paused, suddenly seeming less sure of himself. "Really fat, and he laughed a lot." *Tray.* "He just gave me the message. Said you'd be here. He said if I needed to, I should mention your daughter, but, honestly, I don't want to be doing that. You're a kid yourself."

I opened my mouth to speak, but nothing came out. I just crouched there, wide-eyed. Of course they knew about Bea. How could they not? I shivered again, as though the temperature had plummeted.

"I'm going now," he said. "Take care of yourself, and if I were you, I'd do what they asked." I raised my hand to say goodbye, but he was already scuttling off back underneath the shelving units.

I stood up and frowned.

"What on Earth are you doing?" Ben's booming voice from the end of the aisle behind me made me jump. He laughed. "You're jumpy tonight."

I forced a laugh and tried to calm my shaking hands by sticking them in my armpits. "It's that damn rat," I said, tutting. "I keep thinking I can hear it. I'll be glad when I can get home."

"What are you like." Ben laughed, putting a strong arm around my shoulders. "Come on. There's not many left. Let's do them together."

That sounded perfect.

Mum was in the lounge with Mally when I returned. I chose not to tell her about the incident in the warehouse yet. I was tired and really didn't want any more learning things or long chats that night. I just wanted to feed Bea and head to bed, after checking in with Ivan first, of course. He wasn't in the lounge, so I assumed he'd gone back up to bed. The thought of my pyjamas and snuggling into my duvet was all I wanted to think about.

Bea was fast asleep in Mum's arms. I smiled at her and watched her face.

"She fell asleep not long after you left," Mum said as I picked Bea up for a cuddle. She didn't wake as I took her, so I thought maybe she didn't need feeding. I chose not to wake her but curled up in the corner of the sofa.

"Have you held her the whole time?" I asked, running my fingers through Bea's wispy hair.

Mum tutted. "No, I haven't, but I'm her grandma. So what if I held her the whole night?" I smiled at her warmly. "I agreed we should stop over, if that's okay with you."

I nodded sleepily. The warm house in contrast with the chill from outside and the surge of adrenaline and panic from earlier had drained me. I shivered again, but it wasn't from feeling cold. It was more the sudden wave of exhaustion.

"Where will we sleep?" I asked, trying to hide a yawn.

"In the spare room," Mum said, looking at me curiously. "Unless you had other ideas."

My cheeks heated. "Muuum!" I picked up a cushion and threw it at her. Seriously, that was the second time she had assumed all I wanted to do was jump into bed with my boyfriend. Well, I guess I did, but that wasn't the point. Still, if that's what they thought we were doing anyway, why disappoint them...?

"Okay, okay." She laughed. "I was young once too. If you did decide to, er, camp out on the *floor* in another room, I wouldn't mind. Just don't advertise it to his mother." The tone of amusement in her voice was too much.

I looked at the floor. "Urgh, you're so gross."

"Mally has a travel cot in the spare room for Bea, so you don't need to worry."

"That's great. I'll thank Mally when I see her. Where is she?" I asked.

"She's in the shop. She won't be long though. I'll head to bed when she comes back in."

I nodded. "Can I go up and check on the invalid?"

"See, I was right." Mum smirked. She got another cushion thrown at her for her trouble.

I practically flew up the stairs before remembering Mr E might be asleep in the next room along, so I knocked once on Ivan's door then went straight inside. He was lying on the bed without a blanket but had changed into what I assumed were his PJs. Loose cotton shorts and a light t-shirt. They were baggy and worn.

He made a snorting sound in his sleep. I giggled, and he stirred. He opened one eye, but the black eye stayed shut until he rubbed it.

"Ah, sorry. I tried to wait for you, but zed land was calling," he mumbled.

I reached out to take his hand. "What land?" I asked, unable to hide my huge grin. He batted my hand away in annoyance. "Who says zed land?" I tried to grab his hand back.

"People."

"Which people?"

"People like me." He shoved his hands under his bum so I couldn't grab them. I pouted. "So, work?" He half yawned, raising an eyebrow.

"Hmmm. Probably not the best thing to begin with."

He sat up and held out his arms, inviting me to come and sit with him on the bed. Comfortable knowing I could go over and sit with him and not worry about what he thought of me, I told him everything, and he waited quietly and said nothing. When I was finished, he took my chin in his hand and kissed the end of my nose.

"I need to get back out there," he said.

That was the last thing I wanted. It was bad enough they had beaten him up the first time, but now he felt he had to be out there to protect me.

"You need to rest." I reminded him, yawning. "So do I."

"Now you've quit, we can rest together all we like." I pulled a face. I hadn't technically quit yet. "Sit with me a while?" He pulled me onto his knees. He winced a little, but he said nothing, so neither did I.

"I will," I promised. "But first I should make sure Bea is settled."

"Of course. Go be with Bea." He yawned, releasing me. "If I'm asleep when you come back, don't wake me." He chuckled.

I went back downstairs, and just in time, as Mally was walking with Mum to the spare room. It was on the ground floor and through a door next to the stairs.

Once Bea was asleep in the travel cot and I had tucked her up in a blanket, I grabbed a Bourbon biscuit from the packet Mally had brought in for me. I had needed a snack after work. I was grateful. With it not being my house, I didn't want to ask. There was a double bed next to the travel cot. Mum was going to take the side nearest the wall, so I took the door side, but first I told her I was going to go to the upstairs bathroom and say goodnight to Ivan, insisting I was only saying goodnight.

In the bathroom, I brushed my teeth with my finger as I hadn't got my toothbrush. Mally had given me a nightgown to borrow, but I thought I might ask Ivan if I could borrow a pair of his PJ shorts instead and sleep in my top. That was if he was still awake when I returned. He was.

"I just spoke to Dad," he began. "He said he'll catch up with Tiz in the morning and see what he knows about the shifter in the warehouse." I should have been expecting to go straight back into this.

"Thank you."

"I asked him about going back out there. We don't have the numbers to watch everywhere. I need to get out and see if I can convince anyone to join us," Ivan said, without looking directly at me. "He said I need to wait until at least after the weekend."

"I should hope so." I frowned. "It's only been days. You have cracked ribs and... things." The words came out too quickly. He gave me a half smile. "I got you into this. You can't expect me to be happy to hear you're going straight back out. You've been in two fights recently because of me. What if they kill you in the next one? I can ignore Dad. He might give up if he thinks we've moved on." My train of thought had shifted, and I had lost track of my point.

"You're not the only one in the town who needs protection. That's really selfish, you know?" he said sharply.

I inhaled quickly. "I didn't expect to be, the way you were rounding up the females." I did not mean to say that, and I hadn't even been thinking it. It came from nowhere. I bit my lip, willing myself to shut the hell up.

"That's below the belt. At least I wasn't rubbing myself all over them."

Not sure I believed that.

"I thought we were past all that?" I shot at him. Obviously, I wasn't, otherwise I wouldn't have commented on the females. Logically, I knew I wasn't the only one who needed protecting. There must have been more than shifters there all expecting to be hidden from the gang for whatever reason. I blamed the shock of seeing the rat, the tiredness, and the confusion about my dad. I shouldn't have taken it out on Ivan.

"Are we?" Ivan said in a tone I didn't like. "Maybe I was wrong about you. I thought you understood." I got the impression he regretted saying that because he face-palmed himself.

"Yeah, I get it. I'm just a stupid girl who got in the way." I could feel the tears in my eyes, and he sighed.

"We don't need to do this," he said in a different tone. He spoke slowly and carefully. "I need to get back out there and see what's happening, and you need to trust my reasons. I don't want to get angry with you, E, but you're making it very difficult not to. Yes, it was easier before you came along, but we were still defending ourselves against them advancing. This was the only place we could keep those who escaped safe before they could move away and start again. Your dad complicated things, but that's not your fault. You were meant to be a shifter, and you are what you are, no matter how you think about it. It was all just so badly timed. There is so much more going on than you know about, and if you're going to stay, you need to learn that."

I swallowed and nodded. "I'm not trying to be selfish. I just get so caught up in everything."

"It's hard not to. You've been through a lot in a short amount of time. I do care about you, I really do, but I have others depending on me, and I can't give up on them either."

I did understand, it just took a while for my brain to catch up with my heart. I was being irrational, but I had had a really emotional evening. All I wanted was a hug and a mug of tea, neither of which I was getting. Mum would have given me both had we been at home.

I suddenly missed the process and routine of something as simple as making tea. I was expecting nothing from Ivan as, so far, even after any softness he had displayed, he was still Ivan. Ivan who had been stuffy at work. Someone who was usually emotionally shut off and had the empathy of a toilet brush. I had just decided to leave when he gave me the biggest hug he'd ever given me. I didn't hug him back though. I just leaned into him with eyes that felt as though someone had been rubbing them with straw. We said nothing, but there was nothing we needed to say.

We fell asleep. I don't remember how. I had a dream. I did remember that.

I stood on the edge of a cliff, looking out to the sea, the wind streaking through my hair, which was whipping around my face. I could smell the saltiness of the ocean, and in the clear sky, see thousands of stars. The bright, full moon reflecting off the sea and the rocks below made the waves look as though they were dancing. I stood alone on the cliff, but as I looked below onto the beach, I could see a woman, slim and dark-haired, in what looked like a long, flowing gown of silk, tight at the waist but so long that it trailed behind her. She ran barefoot along the beach, leaving the waves to wash away her footprints as they lapped the shore. I blinked and was suddenly down on the beach with the urge to follow. As I ran, four paws thudded against the wet sand. I bounded with ease after her, and when she stopped and turned, I realised that she was me. She didn't look at me, but beyond, at someone else coming down the beach. In the moonlight, his hair looked grey. He wore a white shirt, open at the front, and tight black jeans with ripped knees. He too was barefoot. The footprints that were left behind were not of a man, but perfectly formed paw prints which didn't wash away with the sea. Instead, they filled up like little pools, each one reflecting the light from the sky.

He was breathtakingly beautiful. My heart ached,

and I reached for him. As I did, I was in my own body, the form of me who met him in the other plane had gone. He took my hand, and in it he placed a tiny silver pentacle. It was about the size of a five pence piece and burned my hand like it was freshly moulded. I looked up, hoping to see his face, his eyes, but in that moment, he was swept away with the wind, leaving nothing but sand. I woke up, my pillow wet from tears I must have cried in my sleep. My heart was heavy as I realised he must have loved me as much as I was beginning to realise I loved him.

As I lay there in the dark listening to him breathing, A new heartache for leaving Bea moved in. I got up slowly and quietly, covering Ivan with the duvet before I left. I stood in the doorway and looked at him. He hadn't woken when I slipped out of bed. He hadn't even moved when I'd covered him with the duvet. I watched him sleep for a moment, wondering where the hell we were headed. How could he be such a different person in one form and then another the next? How quickly he'd snapped back to being both people in one. Maybe this was the real Ivan, and the shifting had split his personality to the two extremes. One horrible but occasionally trying, and the other bouncy and free but occasionally moody and brooding. On their own both specific character types, but together it was really hard to read or understand sometimes. I closed the door behind me and padded down the stairs to the room at the bottom where I could hear Mum inside breathing deeply in her sleep. Bea didn't stir, so I only took a moment to check her for fear of waking her, then I took off my bra and socks and climbed into bed in my clothes. On the wall I was facing, I could see a sliver of moonlight from between the blinds. I thought of my dream, then remembered the necklace Ivan had given me earlier in the day. I put my hand into my jeggings pocket and found it. Smiling, I put it around my neck, ignoring the fact that it was filthy, and went back to sleep.

My second dream was nothing like the first. It was dark, but something told me it was day time. A small shaft of light was shining over my eyes, making it hard to see. There was something else there with me, the cold, dead body of something I couldn't make out. I looked down at it, unable to see clearly. I could see and smell the blood over a layer of cigarettes and the sharpness of vodka. I wasn't afraid, and part of me told me I had done this. Triumph set the tone, yet was shadowed by grief. As I drifted off, listening to the wind outside with a song soothing my mind, I reassured myself it was just my anxiety playing tricks on me.

CHAPTER 38

Mr Ealing

"Tiz, a word?" He'd known I was there. I could sense that much, but I also knew he had hoped I would let him carry on home without stopping him. Even though his sigh was subtle, I still picked up on it. It annoyed me, the lack of respect, but I was too old to be bothering about things like that. Was I really too old? In my bones, my fur, when I took a step, the relentless march of aging plagued me. Everything in me screamed that I should give in and move on now, but in this life, I wasn't really old at all. I had more to give and would stubbornly stick around, no matter what my soul told me.

"Sir?" he said, turning. His body was about to sag, but he straightened up. He was tired but didn't want to show it.

"I heard there was a breach this evening."

"A breach, sir?" I knew he had found something by the way his eyes narrowed slightly. He would have told me about it later had I not been there. I didn't need to nod. He knew I knew something, so he resumed his relaxed stance. "Sorry, Leader. I am exhausted this evening.

"Do not apologise for being tired, Tiz. I appreciate everything you do, and I know how much time you're spending running around at the moment. Try to relax and tell me what you know. That's all I ask." "It must be important for you to come back out, sir." Tiz cocked his head.

I let out a light laugh. "Ena came home from work. There had been an intruder there. Luckily, this one seemed like he didn't want to be there, so he left after giving her a message. I'm just interested in how he got in and how he got past everyone."

"We caught a scent, but it wasn't until after she'd left for the evening. Actually, we caught two. One was a bird, an owl I think, and we only caught it because it was wet, and he had been on the ground. We followed the first scent to the car park. We then picked up Ena's and the other."

"Ah, yes. There was an owl. Now, the rat?"

"There was a slight rat scent, but there was also something else I couldn't recognise. It had taken another form, but it wasn't a predator scent. Possibly a mouse or a squirrel. Something very close to a rat. It must have got in whilst we were in other areas of the warehouse. There were only three of us at one point, and if they were watching, they'd have seen Thomas leave to cover the park boundary. They'd have seen Beany head down to the offices at the back, and while Matt and I were on one side, they could have easily got in. It was raining so hard at one point we couldn't smell a thing, sir. They knew what they were doing sending in something small in the rain." I could tell by how he spoke that he was embarrassed and angry about it getting through, but there was also a tone of something else. I guessed he was wondering why it was so important.

"Thank you, Tiz. It's been a horrendous night so far, and I'm grateful for you all being out here at all getting soaked. This particular rat was sent by her father. Did you manage to pick up where it was heading?"

"We followed the scent towards the farms by Ena's, but we must have been ten minutes behind it because as we neared, the scent disappeared. Probably covered by the rain."

"Indeed. Well, you go home and rest. How many are still out?"

"Seven, I think. Thomas will be out for a couple of hours more, then he's due to watch one of the safehouses, but because I pulled him out tonight, Shed's going to cover that one. Sid's covering for me, and then Paws will be out covering for Beany."

"Paws? She's one of the new ones, right?" I asked.

So many names. I had my inner few, but there were some newer ones I hadn't yet had the pleasure of meeting. I would have to ask The Wise One to give me a run through of who everyone was.

"She is. She's got potential, sir. She's fast and has a flair for enchantments but is still very new. She was pulled from the city with her younger brother. We still haven't found her parents, and to be honest, I don't think they made it. I've housed her with Millie and her daughter. Remember, Vic was one of the ones shot..." His voice trailed off. The muscles in his jaw flexed.

"Go home and sleep. I'll stay out a while." I padded toward him and put my paw on his shoulder. "Thank you again, Tiz. Spider is lucky to have you at his side. Oh, and stop calling me sir."

"Thanks, Leader. Uh, sorry. One more thing. Night Flower? Will she be trouble? I'd protect her with my life for Spider, but any ideas on how this will pan out? It would seem everyone and his dog knows who she is now in both forms."

"I may have made a mistake bringing her into our world, but she did have the effect on Spider that I wanted. She keeps him grounded. However, I fear that when pushed too far, we won't be able to rein her in. She has her father's spirit."

Tiz was right to be nervous. I was nervous about the whole thing myself, and I wasn't about to admit it to Ivan or Mally. There was something amiss about the situation we had found ourselves in, the advancing gang from the city, Ena and her father. Something I hadn't yet put my finger on.

I skirted around by the warehouses myself. The rain had stopped, but the ground was still wet. Petrichor and petrol fumes from the road were the most dominant smells, but there were more subtle scents if you knew what to look for. It came very easily to me. My body might have been slower and shabbier than it used to be, but my mind was still very much awake. I walked around the car park, avoiding the areas where it was a little flooded from the rain. It would drain, but it wasn't worth getting my paws wet. There was a huge metal fence separating the car park from some barren building land. Scanning the car park, I couldn't see a good way across without getting soaked, so I decided to leave that area well alone.

I followed the fence to where it became a wall on the far side of the warehouse, then passed the main entrance around to the left and to the other side of the building. I smelled nothing unusual and exactly what Tiz had mentioned. Rat, bird, and I think it was squirrel. He'd possibly used a squirrel form to get in under the warehouse roof as I couldn't see any holes or gaps where he might have gotten in on my level, and I couldn't smell any evidence of another shifter, but that didn't mean he didn't have help. I could smell the markings of our cats and stoat, so that meant Skeet came by at some point. As confused and unsettled as they were, at least our group was trying to do as we'd asked.

All was quiet, apart from the occasional rumble of traffic passing on the main road. I paused on a flagstone to stretch before checking the other side of the building. There was nothing unusual there either. It was probably coming up for four a.m. I wondered when the next patrol would be coming through.

Feeling a couple of drops of rain, I decided to continue, stretching my legs before arching my back. I hoped it wouldn't rain as I was hoping to make a quick journey home in bird form. My bird forms were clumsy, and I wasn't the best flier, even worse in the rain. I chuckled to myself as I padded along.

I hadn't got far when I heard voices. Quiet at first, but they got louder as I approached. I was back along the main road now, streetlamps making the road glitter and puddles shine. They reflected in my eyes as my pupils widened to take in more light. Even though the road was lit, it was still less bright than the security lights I had walked past before on the edge of the warehouse car park. Intrigued by the voices, I decided to make my way towards them, drawn in by something in my subconscious. The moisture felt static in the air, like I was walking through a cloud. I could almost see the droplets suspended there, smell them as I walked through them and they clung to my face. I breathed in and made sure I was hidden by my enchantments before approaching.

"He was jumped! You already know why." I heard Tiz's tired voice. He sounded angry. I wondered who could have been talking to him this whole time. He had been on his way home. I got a waft of her scent on the air; Lila.

"I didn't know it was bad enough to keep him from being out. I thought they just roughed him up a little." She purred, and Tiz growled.

"Lila, stop following me and let me go home, okay? Spider isn't out. You've mithered me enough. I'm tired and I don't want to get cross with you, but I will."

Good for you.

I nodded from my hiding place behind the wall. I was watching the two talk like some stalker, but I was curious why his voice was raised and why he hadn't gone straight home. I was about to step round into the light and tell Tiz to walk away when my fur bristled. Another presence was making its way towards me. I had noticed it too late, distracted by the two shifters ahead of me. My body turned rigid, and my paws prepared to run. I stiffened my back legs, twisting my ears to listen and breathing in deeply through my mouth to try and taste the air. The footsteps didn't stop. Whoever it was was confident I wouldn't run, and they knew I was there. They must have known me well to be able to see me. I relaxed a little and forced myself to turn. Relief poured through me.

"Old man." The shifter behind me laughed. "Hiding round corners now?" A large orange and grey cat head bumped me in the hip and the tension left my body, leaving only the physical aches I wished would numb.

"They surprised me. I wasn't expecting them on my route back." I forced a deep breath out to clear my head. A friend of mine in his cat form, Oz, searched my face before nodding.

"They get in the way these youngsters. As it happens, I was looking for Lila. She was going to drop by, but when she didn't, I got worried about her." Oz peered round the corner to where Lila sat in the light from one of the lamps, licking one of her paws. I could imagine Tiz rolling his eyes as he turned to leave.

"Where is his Flower this evening?" she asked, and he groaned.

Just walk on, Tiz. Ignore her.

"I don't know, and I don't really care." He stepped away.

"Huh, funny that. Why does she need all this attention if you don't care?" she said as if she was talking to herself but loud enough for us all to hear. "Where's my protection? After all, surely if there are rogue males hanging around trying to get to you guys, we should all be as well watched as she is."

"You all are, Lila. What's your point? She hasn't got any more protection than you have." Tiz growled, tiredness getting the better of him.

"I mean, I personally don't need someone traipsing after me, watching my back, but the way Spider mopes after her puts a target on her back, don't you think? If anyone saw that they'd think she was more special than she is."

"Everyone is special here, Lila. Even you, but you are doing my head in right now, so I'm going home."

"Curious, isn't it? She shows up and suddenly everything gets worse. Are you not worried that she's the one causing all of this? What if she's one of them? Whenever she shifts, someone dies." She purred, leaping to her feet and gliding to his side. She rubbed herself along his body and thrust her head underneath his chin. He groaned, and this time not in annoyance. It was clear he had stopped listening to anything she was saying.

Whatever Lila wanted, she was going to get it. She circled him, nudging and nipping his fur, letting her tail wrap itself over his back as he stood still, fighting the arousal. She knew what she was doing, but what she wanted to know so badly escaped me. It seemed more than being jealous, but with Lila, it was possible that was all it was.

"Unless you're coming home with me, I suggest you stop that," Tiz said through gritted teeth. I hadn't seen him move a muscle, but I could tell from the smell of him he was desperate to respond to her. Oz elbowed me in the side, his face a picture of amusement.

"I'll come home with you. You know I will. I know you have needs, my darling." Lila purred, licking his ear. He closed his eyes momentarily. "We can talk later."

As they walked off down the street, probably quicker than they normally would have, I wondered what she was thinking, other than the obvious. She was using him, but why?

"Kids, eh?" Oz said.

I snorted. "Bloody right. What the hell was that about?"

"Well, at least I know where she is, the hussy. I can head back now. I'm getting too old for this shifting lark, Leader. Every time I change, I wonder if I still have the same number of muscles or joints. I lose feeling in at least one every time."

"I understand that, old friend. I'm the same. Let me walk you back."

We turned back the way he had come and made our way through the town towards the café where he lived. He loved that café; he was so proud of it. It was his whole world.

"Why the fuss over Lila, anyway? She can handle herself better than most of us," I said, knowing they had a family connection somewhere but not really knowing the full story.

"Ah, she's a good kid really. She offered to help keep an eye on the place, you know? With everyone getting picked off left, right, and centre, I was feeling a little uneasy." I tensed, and he added, "Not your fault, but she said she'd stop by on her rounds for a quick coffee. I feel bad for her. She doesn't have many friends, not after Spider ditched her so quickly. So, I waited up for her and she didn't show. It's not some dirty old man thing, if that's what you were thinking."

My head snapped up. "That was the furthest thing from my mind," I said, although I wasn't sure I even believed myself with the way she behaved. Even older men craved company. I shrugged it off. "You do know she and Spider were never a thing, don't you? And what really brings you out here? Where did you think she was?" I asked, hoping to get a little more to the story.

He paused. "Ah, you got me. Sam called me before, around midnight."

"Sam? Is he out of hospital now?" This surprised me as I thought Ivan would have told me.

"Yeah, but he's still not right, poor kid. He reckons the guy who shot him was in the town earlier in the day.

He said it was definitely him."

"Why did he go to you and not to me?" I asked, deflated. Surely as the leader I was the first one they should come to. I swallowed hard and pretended it hadn't bothered me.

"I dunno. I guess I was just the first to answer my phone. He didn't ring me until late, so I've no idea why he didn't call before then. Stress? I expect he tried Spider first."

"Shh, not here. Not everyone knows we have a family connection, and I'd like to keep it that way," I hissed. The ones who knew he was my son would surely go after him. They probably already knew. I needed to be more careful.

Oz continued as if I hadn't spoken. "Sam said he saw him and was worried. I said I'd keep an eye out and pass it on when I saw Lila, who I was expecting shortly after, but she didn't turn up. I waited and then decided to head out in case someone had got her on her way to the café."

"So, you think the man who killed Sam's dad is out tonight? Somewhere in the town? I'm not sure we could find him if he's in human form. Not without Sam."

"We could ask that police dog who knows your s... I mean, Spider. He was there on the night. He might remember his scent."

It was an idea, but I didn't really want Spider out until he had recovered a little more, especially if the killer was out. If they were looking for specific shifters, maybe he'd be targeted again. Yes, he needed to come out soon for the good of the group, but that night, I needed to be selfish and keep him out of it.

"I'll look into it," I said.

Oz made a grunting noise. I knew he wasn't happy with my answer, but I needed time to think it all through.

We had walked back to the end of the road near the café where Oz lived without even thinking about our route. We talked the whole way, and our bodies moved in the direction naturally without us even checking we were on the right path. Certain routes were just innate at that point.

We were saying our goodbyes when a gunshot sounded in the quiet of the night. Then a second later, another. Then silence. For a moment, we stood rooted to the spot, fur on end and backs arched, not daring to move a muscle. Someone screamed, and a couple of people opened their windows to look outside. It was really late, so most would have been fast asleep. Oz and I shared a worried look. We must have stood there for a couple of minutes, not knowing whether to return home or follow the sounds of the shots.

We saw the flashing lights of an ambulance pass. No sirens, but the lights blinking madly cast reflections onto the wet road as it went.

"We should leave now," Oz said quietly. I could feel

the fear seeping from his fur and leaned against him in comfort.

"Go inside quickly. I will call you later in the morning. If you see Lila, let me know she's safe. I'm sure she's still with Tiz, but please check up on her." I patted him on the back with my paw. I wobbled slightly, forgetting my weary body. Oz eyed me with a look of worry, more about my wobble I was sure than for Lila.

"I will, friend. I'll let you know anything I hear." He crossed the road and nudged open a wooden gate a few doors down from his café and disappeared inside. Part of me wanted to follow the sounds I could hear a few streets away, the sounds of loud conversations and of vehicles, dogs even. I listened to the sounds as they carried through the quiet air between us. I had to go home. My soul tugged me in the opposite direction, an innate desire to be home with Mally and the others.

I moved as fast as I could without actually running, wanting to be able to still hear things around me without the noise of the blood pumping through my ears or the wind rushing past. My mind raced at a hundred miles an hour. Another shooting? Could it be the same man? I wondered who he was targeting. Who could I call to double check? I would have to send Gray out. I knew he'd be at the safehouse. I hoped it wasn't any of ours whilst out on patrols. I wondered if Oz was really out looking for Lila. It seemed unlikely, but then so did Lila flirting with

Tiz and persuading him to take her home. I always knew she was into Spider but thought she'd let it go by now. I wondered what all that was about when I remembered her strange questioning as she flirted. She had wanted to know where Spider was, yet I remembered telling her about him being jumped myself. Things didn't add up, but maybe it was all just a huge coincidence. I'd have to try and keep an eye on her, but first, home to have a cup of tea and a chat with Mally if she was awake.

CHAPTER 38

Ena

We didn't stay at Mally's for long in the morning. Ivan joined us for a while in the lounge, but Mr E had to help him change that morning as he was struggling with his clothes. From the looks of him, the whole thing had exhausted him as he couldn't sit upright and instead leaned against the wall, holding his chest tightly. I had worried when he managed to get from the door to the sofa with Mr E under his arm holding him steady that Bea wouldn't like him or be scared of him with his bruises, or if she might feel a little jealousy when I went to sit next to him. However, it was quite the opposite. My little chubby baby went straight to him with her toy bear and held her arms up to him to be picked up. I lifted her up onto the sofa with us and she pretty much threw the bear at him, giggling. He pretended to be hurt but then laughed and passed the bear back. Cue a game which repeated itself for the next fifteen minutes until Bea got bored and was distracted by Mum grabbing our things to go. Ivan's phone rang, and he spent the following twenty minutes talking to Tiz. I huffed quietly, watching his facial expressions change from concern, to surprise then he turned away. I pouted, wishing he'd hang up.

He seemed surprised by something he had been told and let out a small laugh. Mr E looked up sharply and narrowed his eyes, I wondered if something had happened that Ivan wasn't supposed to know about. Mr Ealing looked tired, his skin a shade of grey I hadn't seen on him before. He must have sensed me watching him because just as I was wondering what magic he might be really good at, he turned to face me and grinned at me as we locked eyes. I looked away and flushed, hoping it wasn't mind reading.

It was time to get back, and I wanted a minute to say goodbye to Ivan on my own. Mum picked up Bea and said she'd wait in the car whilst I tapped my watch impatiently with raised eyebrows. Ivan waved his hand at me and shot me a half smile. I shook my head and began to tap my foot. He laughed. The sound of him laughing made my heart feel like it was full of lava.

"Sorry, mate. I'll call you straight back," Ivan said, looking from me to Mum, and then hung up his phone. Mally and Mr E stood together and left the room at the same time, mumbling something about helping Mum to the car. Mum gave me a wink as she left the room. I put my hands over my face, my ears burning.

"Parents." Ivan laughed with one arm around me and the other clinging to his sore chest. "Remind me to move out after all this has blown over."

I gave him a half smile and put my hand over his. "So you can sit on the phone and ignore me some more?" I joked, pretend punching him in the arm. "I hope you feel better soon."

"I already am." He looked down at me. He lifted my chin, and we shared a very slow kiss. For a minute, I completely forgot we were in his parents' front room. All I wanted to do was pull him down onto the sofa with me as our kiss intensified and I tingled all over. A kiss would have to do for now. I thought of how Mally had said souls were connected. In that moment, I was one hundred percent convinced ours were so bound together you'd find it hard to tell them apart.

-

Ivan

As much as I loved Ena's company, I was exhausted. My ribs and chest ached, my legs were going to give way, and my arms hung like lead. That was without the tingling feeling in my cheekbones and eyebrow. Yet, when she kissed my bruised lips, the stinging pain merged into warmth, and I seemed to forget about how much it hurt. We could be anywhere, just us, and everything around us was a blur. If I'd died right there and then, I might not have even noticed.

As we broke apart, I looked down at her face, her dark eyes hooded by her long eyelashes, looking up at me with nervousness that matched mine. Like we had both just realised we had something special, something neither of us expected. I could have stood there forever, staring into her eyes. As she walked away, the aches returned, as though I was only whole when she was there by my side. I watched her leave the room, her dark hair bouncing as she went. I licked my bottom lip. The bruise stung, I liked it.

Just getting down the stairs had taken it out of me, but I didn't want to give in and have Dad help me back up to my room yet, so I shuffled into the shop, thinking I'd call Tiz back from there. He had begun to tell me something important. Important and very worrying. Someone had been shot last night, one of our own. He'd only just found out and rang me straight away. It had taken everything in me to keep a straight face and tone of voice so I didn't worry my family too soon. Tiz was sketchy on the details and it bothered had me that he had suddenly changed the subject before telling me who, which until I heard Lila's voice had seemed strange.

Hearing her saying goodbye in the background had made me laugh out loud. She shared our coven so names would come out soon enough, but he mustn't have wanted to have that conversation with her there and then. Just like I had kept it from Ena. It wasn't something I'd wanted to get into as she was leaving.

Mum hadn't yet opened the shop, so as I went in, I flicked on the lights and lit a couple of the candles behind the counter, more from habit than anything. I checked the oil burner on the shelf then fumbled through the top drawer, looking for a glass vial of myrrh.

After refilling the burner and lighting the candle underneath, I moved over to the small bowl of sand in a cupboard by the shop door. I dropped two cones of incense onto the sand and lit them, one sandalwood, and the other white sage. Mum's head appeared around the doorway to the house.

"Unlock the door. I'll be through momentarily."

I grunted in reply and undid the deadbolt then unlocked the door to the shop. I swung the closed sign to the open side in the window, absent-mindedly thinking that I didn't know what the time was. I needed coffee. Lots of coffee. My mind raced through the names of those who had been out last night. I needed to know who had been involved.

I'd just hobbled back across the shop and grabbed the counter in time for my legs to give way. I only just made it onto a stool, falling sideways and grabbing the counter to steady myself, when the door to the shop opened and someone hurried inside.

Straightening up, I realised I knew the man. He was around my age, with short, spiky blonde hair and a tattoo of a rose on his neck. He wore a blue bandana over part of his head, and a denim jacket. Huge, bright red Dr Marten lace ups went half way up his short legs.

"Baz, I wasn't expecting you." I said, surprised to see him. It had been months. He rarely came to this part of town, and only if he needed something from us. I hoped he hadn't seen me stumble.

"Ives." He stuck out his hand and took mine, shaking it roughly before letting it go. "Your old man around?" He was on edge, his eyes bloodshot and his skin cold. An icy chill flooded through my veins. This was linked with the attack Tiz had begun to tell me about on the phone, before he was distracted, before I had to hang up.

"Yeah, somewhere. Hang on. Dad!" I called loud enough I knew Mum would at least hear me and send him through. I stared at him, concerned. "Tell me what happened?" I asked in a tone that sounded like a command.

He looked behind himself at the door and his brows knitted together. "You not heard? I thought Tiz rang you."

"Yeah, he did, but I don't know all the details. I said

I'd ring him back. Start from the beginning!"

"It's all gone to shit. Casey was shot last night. Fucking shot. Tommy too." The colour drained from his face, and he wrung his hands. Shit, not Casey. Poor Casey was only free a matter of weeks. We'd persuaded her to leave the city after meeting her boyfriend, Tommy, one night on the boundary. We had caught him scent marking after some of that city gang had been teasing us by crossing over. He was terrified, nothing like the others. Nothing like Eldar and Cole. He told us he was there only to get his girlfriend out. His girlfriend lived in a place that sent ladies to be the company of well-paying men. One night, he managed to sneak her out of a window at the house where she was working. They both shifted and managed to get away to us. We had promised them protection, and now we had failed. I felt like I had been punched in the gut. Again.

"And Ryan?" Ryan was Baz's teenage brother. My mouth was dry. The taste of blood surprised me, and I realised I had subconsciously bitten my lip. I pulled the phone from my pocket and flicked through my texts in case I had missed something since our call earlier.

"Ryan and I were there. We were asleep when we heard the shots. Man, they were so loud it went right through me. I thought the roof was falling in or something. Ry ran down the stairs and knocked one of the men over. They fought and he got out of the door. I got the other and..." He looked at his shoes, his drawn and pale face pinking slightly and his nostrils flaring. I put my hand on his to ground us both. The smell of the incense was suddenly choking.

"I killed him, Ives. One minute he was alive, and we were fighting. I got the gun off him, but seeing Casey on the floor... She'd shifted, but it hadn't helped her. The blood, the darkness. I hit him. Hard. I hit him again. I fucking killed him." Tears welled in his eyes, and he covered his face with his hands.

I banged my fist down onto the counter, angry eyes drawn to the incense by the door which had now burned itself down to the bottom of the cone. The smoky curl flowing to the ceiling dragged my hopes of this gang ever leaving us with it.

Dad came in through the door slowly, as though he was expecting exactly what was going on. "Did you see them?" His question direct, ignoring the emotional effect it was obviously having on Baz.

I ground my teeth together. How dare he be so unfeeling?

"No. The one who ran had a balaclava on, and the other too. I was going to pull it off when the police arrived. Ry and I shifted and got away through the door. We watched them bring the bodies outside. Tommy and Case were on the pavement, just thrown there like the animal carcasses they looked like. The bastard who shot them was taken away on a stretcher. I could smell he was dead though. A man came by, talking to one of the policemen whilst another picked up Case and Tommy by the legs and walked off. Just walked off as though nothing had happened. We didn't see where they went. We tried, Leader. We tried." Baz sank down to his knees, and his shoulders shook with sobs. I'd never seen him like this. My heart broke for him, for Casey and Tommy, and for Ryan.

"You did your best, son," Dad said to him, clearing his throat. "I'll take you through to the kitchen. Mally will call Ryan for you." Baz nodded and pulled himself to his feet. He looked me in the eyes before following Dad from the room. I let out a breath I hadn't noticed I was holding.

A few minutes later, Dad returned and pulled up a stool next to mine. I stared at the door, avoiding his glare. I struggled to force the anger down where I couldn't reach it, helplessly pulling comforting thoughts up towards me to stop me from drowning. It wasn't working. My nails dug into my palms, drawing blood.

"The rat, the shootings. It's not safe, Ivan. She needs to stop shifting and go somewhere safe," he said softly.

I should have known he'd make this about her. It was his bloody fault she had come into our world in the first place. Neither had said, but I put two and two together. The library. The guide. It wasn't something she would have gone looking for on her own.

This was about all of us now. She had nothing to do with getting Casey out. They would have come over and tried to kill us regardless of her unless he thought something else was going on and he wasn't telling me. We had to keep Ena and our protecting those we helped escape from the gang separate. I pointed that out to him, and he said nothing.

"I'm not sure stopping shifting will help if they know her in both forms and where she lives. Move her, yes, but she needs to learn to control her shifting better. She needs more training. We can give her that, surely." My desire to protect her blazed in my chest.

"Fine. We'll try, once only, but if it doesn't work, you must convince her to stop and to leave. I know I thought it was a good time to bring her into this world, but I was wrong. I thought it might help you, help all of us, but I think it made matters worse. They have realised who she is. They have realised she is the daughter of one of their powerful shifters, and now he knows about it, there is nothing that will stop him from coming in to get her. Casey was unfortunate. We did everything we could to help her escape, but now we need to tighten things up. We don't have time for training to go wrong. Think of Bea. If something goes wrong, Rachel will have to move again with a baby and go through all of this again when one day she might learn she can shift too."

I nodded and still refused to look at him. I waited

for his next demand, knowing it was coming.

"She needs to quit work."

"Don't you think I've told her that?"

"Tell her again," he barked.

"This isn't the 1920s. I can't just rock up and say, 'oh by the way, quit your job.' I have told her, but it's up to her now. She told me last night was her last, and I believe her."

"Ivan, I'm sorry, but that isn't good enough now. If she's anything like her father, she's going to wake up and realise she has more going on than she knows about. There's no way she doesn't have other gifts as well as being a witch like her mother. We need to make sure she sticks on the right side of things."

"Are you suggesting she'll betray us?" I growled, forcing myself to face him. I wanted anger. I wanted him to look at me with the same power I was looking at him, but again, he showed no emotion. It was hopeless. I was never going to get what I needed from him.

"I'm suggesting it's a possibility. Her father was one of my best friends. At first I thought he'd never…"

"Fuck that. There's no way. No way in hell." I banged my fist on the counter for the second time and ground my teeth together so hard I might have cracked one. Still, he sat. I couldn't read him at all.

"I have money. I could take her away," I said, knowing full well I couldn't. I was trapped there like a canary in a cage.

"And Bea too?" He raised his eyebrow, eyes twinkling as the flames from the candles flickered.

"Of course." Where Ena went, Bea went too.

"And what about us? The shootings? The people you've worked so hard to get out? We lost two today. Two who were almost ready to be moved and hidden away forever. Their paperwork was almost ready. We have to keep going, protecting those we have promised to protect. I can't do it without you, and we are going to lose, son. Sooner if you leave. I agree, we'll train her, but if you get the slightest feeling she's going to bolt, take things into her own hands, or meet her father, you need to be prepared to do something about it. None of this was a coincidence. I wonder if Lila knew something about it when she..."

"Lila? She spent the night with Tiz last night. She couldn't have seen anything" The fog in my head whirled so fast I thought I might be sick. I heard Dad strike a match.

"Ah, he managed to tell you that, did he? Funny he should tell you that when two people had died..."

"He told me someone was shot. He was going through how he'd found out and who he'd sent out to deal with it when I heard her in the background. He might have told me who it was after she'd left, had I not cut him off to say goodbye to Ena." She must have been home by now. I wondered whether to give her a call. Still Dad was right, Tiz could have opened with *Casey was shot*, rather than *someone was shot*. It didn't make sense. Why would he care if Lila had heard their names?

"They know we had Casey here, Ivan. They knew exactly where to look. They have managed to get messages under our noses to Ena at work. They're showing us that they're still in charge. We don't have the numbers. We don't have a way to push them back. If she thinks she's helping by going over there, we might as well kill ourselves," he said in a softer tone. The kind of tone you'd use when a child's rabbit has died.

I could feel sweat dripping down my back, and I grabbed a fist full of hair. "I don't know what I need to do," I admitted, frustrated, furious, and afraid. I needed to be angry, to hit something. I needed to release it all.

Mum's voice cut my thoughts short. Her instant soothing powers cut through the tension, melting us both.

"Dev, Rachel's on the phone. It's an emergency."

Dad pushed himself to his feet.

"Head upstairs and rest," he said, dismissing me like a child. "Lock the shop first."

Lock the bloody shop? Was he serious? What was the emergency? I followed him from the shop and grabbed him roughly by the shoulder.

"Is it Ena?" I asked. "The emergency?"

"I'll deal with it, son. You need some sleep."

"If it's to do with Ena, how the hell do you expect me to sleep?" I growled hobbling back to lock the shop door. He shrugged and made his way to the kitchen to where Mally was waiting with the phone. I followed as quickly as I could, but when I got into the lounge he had already shut the kitchen door behind him. I cursed loudly and flopped onto the sofa.

A calming wave swept through me, like a cool breeze across my skin. I prickled with goosebumps, knowing it was Mum's magic. I couldn't help but let my anger melt away with each breath out.

"They're fine, darling," she said, softly with a hand on my shoulder. I closed my eyes, allowing the magic to wash away my red haze so I could think more clearly.

"I fear something very wrong happened last night. From what Rachel told me on the telephone, I am getting a little worried. As for your father, he is just as scared as you are, but the coven will be looking to him for answers he does not have. He isn't sure he'll be able to do enough to protect us. Don't look so forlorn. Ena is perfectly fine."

"Perfectly fine," I repeated. "Something very wrong did happen last night. Perhaps there is a lot more to it?"

By then, everyone would know what happened to Tommy and his girlfriend, unless Tiz was the one sharing the news. He had seemed guarded on the phone. I still needed to call him back. Mum nodded and came to sit down beside me, holding a black candle in one hand and a small bag of salt in the other.

"Tell me all about it."

As I told her what had happened, she listened and didn't say a word. She shed a lone tear, which she wiped away as quickly as it appeared, and with a sigh, hugged me tightly.

"No matter what happens, we are in this together. Our souls and destinies are entwined, shifted or not."

End

Ena's Playlist

Blink 182 – Apple Shampoo.

The Used – Yesterday's feelings.

Foo Fighters album.

Foo Fighters – Walking after You

The Used – I'm a fake

Linkin Park – Somewhere I belong

Rival Schools – Used for Glue

Muse – Supermassive Black Hole

Pink – My Attic

Norah Jones – Seven Years

System of a Down – Toxicity

Spider's Playlist

Placebo

Alkaline Trio – Settle for Satin

A Perfect Circle – Thinking of You

Taking back Sunday = Cute without the E

The Coral – Skeleton Key

Hoobastank – The Reason

Linkin Park - Crawling

Alanis Morrissette – Head Over Feet

The Red Jumpsuit apparatus – Face Down

My Chemical romance – I'm not OK (I promise)

Adam Jensen – I'm a Sucker for a Liar in a Red

Dress

Keane – Somewhere only we know

George Ezra

Better off Dead – New Found Glory

Goldfinger - Here in your bedroom

Shelly Poole - Lose Yourself

Foo Fighters – Lonely as You

Jimmy Eat World - Pain

The Offspring – You're Gonna Go Far Kid

Alkaline Trio – Blue Carolina

Bullet for my Valentine – Tears don't fall

Story of the Year – Until the day I die

Drowning Pool – Tear Away

My Chemical Romance – Famous last words.

The Used – Light with the Sharpened Edge

The Used – Yesterdays Feelings

My Chemical Romance – Famous last words

Linkin Park – One More Light

THANK YOU...

There are so many people I'd like to thank!! The first on my list being you guys, those of you who have taken the time to read Ena and Ivan's story and hopefully you'd like to see how it's going to end! Don't worry I won't keep you waiting for very long. If not, and you want to make up your own ending that's fantastic, I love coming up with new endings to stories, exploring everything that could have been! Keep being imaginative and thank you for reading this far. Thank you.

I want to thank my family who have supported my endless ramblings and hours at my laptop. For the time's I have dragged them to the woods, giving them no place to hide from my lectures on trees and where to look for moss, I thank them. Those times mean as much to me as the love and patience I have been given whilst writing my stories. I love you all very much!

I thank my friends, especially those who have

helped me along in my journey, giving me feedback, beta reading my work and being there for me when I've wanted to give up! You know who you are and I will love you forever too! Thank you.

I want to thank my Body Shop at Home family, without you guys I would never have stuck to working from home to make the extra pennies I needed for editing and covers. You have changed my life!

To H.A.Robinson, you are an inspiration. Thank you for your help and encouragement, listening to my silly questions and helping me to go for it! Go read her work she really is astounding! (Remember the tissues though, she will have you balling your eyes out).

To Eleanor at Shower of Schmidt for my gorgeous covers! To Kyra Lennon for my editing and to Irish Ink Publishing for my formatting.

Just thank you :D. Since I was small, I have dreamed of sitting surrounded by green and being able to share my stories! Because of all of you, I can.

Printed in Great Britain
by Amazon

24746339R00284